Published by Sophene 2019

Scandinavian Tales was first published in 2019 by Sophene Pty Ltd.

These tales were originally edited and translated to English by
Jennie Hall, Clara Stroebe, and Frederick H. Martens.

www.sophenebooks.com

ISBN-13: 978-1-925937-19-0

SCANDINAVIAN
TALES

COLLECTION OF CLASSIC
SCANDINAVIAN FOLK TALES

CONTENTS

WHAT THE SAGAS WERE

Iceland is a little country far north in the cold sea. Men found it and went there to live more than a thousand years ago. During the warm season they used to fish and make fish-oil and hunt sea-birds and gather feathers and tend their sheep and make hay. But the winters were long and dark and cold. Men and women and children stayed in the house and carded and spun and wove and knit. A whole family sat for hours around the fire in the middle of the room. That fire gave the only light. Shadows flitted in the dark corners. Smoke curled along the high beams in the ceiling. The children sat on the dirt floor close by the fire. The grown people were on a long narrow bench that they had pulled up to the light and warmth. Everybody's hands were busy with wool. The work left their minds free to think and their lips to talk. What was there to talk about? The summer's fishing, the killing of a fox, a voyage to Norway. But the people grew tired of this little gossip. Fathers looked at their children and thought:

"They are not learning much. What will make them brave and wise? What will teach them to love their country and old Norway? Will not the stories of battles, of brave deeds, of mighty men, do this?"

So, as the family worked in the red firelight, the father told of the kings of Norway, of long voyages to strange lands, of good fights. And in farmhouses all through Iceland these old tales were told over and over until everybody knew them and loved them. Some men could sing and play the harp. This made the stories all the more interesting. People called such men "skalds," and they called their songs "sagas."

Every midsummer there was a great meeting. Men from

all over Iceland came to it and made laws. During the day there were rest times, when no business was going on. Then some skald would take his harp and walk to a large stone or a knoll and stand on it and begin a song of some brave deed of an old Norse hero. At the first sound of the harp and the voice, men came running from all directions, crying out:

"The skald! The skald! A saga!"

They stood about for hours and listened. They shouted applause. When the skald was tired, some other man would come up from the crowd and sing or tell a story. As the skald stepped down from his high position, some rich man would rush up to him and say:

"Come and spend next winter at my house. Our ears are thirsty for song."

So the best skalds traveled much and visited many people. Their songs made them welcome everywhere. They were always honored with good seats at a feast. They were given many rich gifts. Even the King of Norway would sometimes send across the water to Iceland, saying to some famous skald:

"Come and visit me. You shall not go away empty-handed. Men say that the sweetest songs are in Iceland. I wish to hear them."

These tales were not written. Few men wrote or read in those days. Skalds learned songs from hearing them sung. At last people began to write more easily. Then they said:

"These stories are very precious. We must write them down to save them from being forgotten."

After that many men in Iceland spent their winters in writing books. They wrote on sheepskin; vellum, we call it. Many of these old vellum books have been saved for hundreds of years, and are now in museums in Norway. Some leaves are lost, some are torn, all are yellow and crumpled. But they are precious. They tell us all that we know about that olden time. There are the very words that the men of Iceland wrote so long ago—stories of kings and of battles and of ship-sailing. Some of those old stories I have told in this book.

THE BABY

King Halfdan lived in Norway long ago. One morning his queen said to him:

"I had a strange dream last night. I thought that I stood in the grass before my bower. I pulled a thorn from my dress. As I held it in my fingers, it grew into a tall tree. The trunk was thick and red as blood, but the lower limbs were fair and green, and the highest ones were white. I thought that the branches of this great tree spread so far that they covered all Norway and even more."

"A strange dream," said King Halfdan. "Dreams are the messengers of the gods. I wonder what they would tell us," and he stroked his beard in thought.

Some time after that a serving-woman came into the feast hall where King Halfdan was. She carried a little white bundle in her arms.

"My lord," she said, "a little son is just born to you."

"Ha!" cried the king, and he jumped up from the high seat and hastened forward until he stood before the woman.

"Show him to me!" he shouted, and there was joy in his voice.

The serving-woman put down her bundle on the ground and turned back the cloth. There was a little naked baby. The king looked at it carefully.

"It is a goodly youngster," he said, and smiled. "Bring Ivar and Thorstein."

They were captains of the king's soldiers. Soon they came.

"Stand as witnesses," Halfdan said.

Then he lifted the baby in his arms, while the old serving-woman brought a silver bowl of water. The king dipped his hand into it and sprinkled the baby, saying:

"I own this baby for my son. He shall be called Harald. My naming gift to him is ten pounds of gold."

Then the woman carried the baby back to the queen's room.

"My lord owns him for his son," she said. "And no wonder! He is perfect in every limb."

The queen looked at him and smiled and remembered her dream and thought:

"That great tree! Can it be this little baby of mine?"

THE TOOTH THRALL

When Harald was seven months old he cut his first tooth. Then his father said:

"All the young of my herds, lambs and calves and colts, that have been born since this baby was born I this day give to him. I also give to him this thrall, Olaf. These are my tooth-gifts to my son."

The boy grew fast, for as soon as he could walk about he was out of doors most of the time. He ran in the woods and climbed the hills and waded in the creek. He was much with his tooth thrall, for the king had said to Olaf:

"Be ever at his call."

Now this Olaf was full of stories, and Harald liked to hear them.

"Come out to Aegir's Rock, Olaf, and tell me stories," he said almost every day.

So they started off across the hills. The man wore a long, loose coat of white wool, belted at the waist with a strap. He had on coarse shoes and leather leggings. Around his neck was an iron collar welded together so that it could not come off. On it were strange marks, called runes, that said:

"Olaf, thrall of Halfdan."

But Harald's clothes were gay. A cape of gray velvet hung from his shoulders. It was fastened over his breast with great gold buckles. When it waved in the wind, a scarlet lining flashed out, and the bottom of a little scarlet jacket showed. His feet and legs were covered with gray woolen tights. Gold lacings wound around his legs from his shoes to his knees. A band of gold held down his long, yellow hair.

It was a wild country that these two were walking over.

They were climbing steep, rough hills. Some of them seemed made all of rock, with a little earth lying in spots. Great rocks hung out from them, with trees growing in their cracks. Some big pieces had broken off and rolled down the hill.

"Thor broke them," Olaf said. "He rides through the sky and hurls his hammer at clouds and at mountains. That makes the thunder and the lightning and cracks the hills. His hammer never misses its aim, and it always comes back to his hand and is eager to go again."

When they reached the top of the hill they looked back. Far below was a soft, green valley. In front of it the sea came up into the land and made a fiord. On each side of the fiord high walls of rock stood up and made the water black with shadow. All around the valley were high hills with dark pines on them. Far off were the mountains. In the valley were Halfdan's houses around their square yard.

"How little our houses look down there!" Harald said. "But I can almost—yes, I can see the red dragon on the roof of the feast hall. Do you remember when I climbed up and sat on his head, Olaf?"

He laughed and kicked his heels and ran on.

At last they came to Aegir's Rock and walked up on its flat top. Harald went to the edge and looked over. A ragged wall of rock reached down, and two hundred feet below was the black water of the fiord. Olaf watched him for a while, then he said:

"No whitening of your cheek, Harald? Good! A boy that can face the fall of Aegir's Rock will not be afraid to face the war flash when he is a man."

"Ho, I am not afraid of the war flash now," cried Harald.

He threw back his cape and drew a little dagger from his

belt.

"See!" he cried; "does this not flash like a sword? And I am not afraid. But after all, this is a baby thing! When I am eight years old I will have a sword, a sharp tooth of war."

He swung his dagger as though it were a long sword. Then he ran and sat on a rock by Olaf.

"Why is this Aegir's Rock?" he asked.

"You know that Asgard is up in the sky," Olaf said. "It is a wonderful city where the golden houses of the gods are in the golden grove. A high wall runs all around it. In the house of Odin, the All-father, there is a great feast hall larger than the whole earth. Its name is Valhalla. It has five hundred doors. The rafters are spears. The roof is thatched with shields. Armor lies on the benches. In the high seat sits Odin, a golden helmet on his head, a spear in his hand. Two wolves lie at his feet. At his right hand and his left sit all the gods and goddesses, and around the hall sit thousands and thousands of men, all the brave ones that have ever died.

"Now it is good to be in Valhalla; for there is mead there better than men can brew, and it never runs out. And there are skalds that sing wonderful songs that men never heard. And before the doors of Valhalla is a great meadow where the warriors fight every day and get glorious and sweet wounds and give many. And all night they feast, and their wounds heal. But none may go to Valhalla except warriors that have died bravely in battle. Men who die from sickness go with women and children and cowards to Niflheim. There Hela, who is queen, always sneers at them, and a terrible cold takes hold of their bones, and they sit down and freeze.

"Years ago Aegir was a great warrior. Aegir the Big-handed, they called him. In many a battle his sword had sung, and he had sent many warriors to Valhalla. Many swords had bit into his flesh and left marks there, but never a one had struck him to death. So his hair grew white and his arms thin. There was peace in that country then, and Aegir sorrowed, saying:

"'I am old. Battles are still. Must I die in bed like a woman? Shall I not see Valhalla?'

"Now thus did Odin say long ago:

"'If a man is old and is come near death and cannot die in fight, let him find death in some brave way and he shall feast with me in Valhalla.'

"So one day Aegir came to this rock.

"'A deed to win Valhalla!' he cried.

"Then he drew his sword and flashed it over his head and held his shield high above him, and leaped out into the air and died in the water of the fiord."

"Ho!" cried Harald, jumping to his feet. "I think that Odin stood up before his high seat and welcomed that man gladly when he walked through the door of Valhalla."

"So the songs say," replied Olaf, "for skalds still sing of that deed all over Norway."

OLAF'S FARM

At another time Harald asked:

"What is your country, Olaf? Have you always been a thrall?"

The thrall's eyes flashed.

"When you are a man," he said, "and go a-viking to Denmark, ask men whether they ever heard of Olaf the Crafty. There, far off, is my country, across the water. My father was Gudbrand the Big. Two hundred warriors feasted in his hall and followed him to battle. Ten sons sat at meat with him, and I was the youngest. One day he said:

"'You are all grown to be men. There is not elbow-room here for so many chiefs. The eldest of you shall have my farm when I die. The rest of you, off a-viking!'

"He had three ships. These he gave to three of my brothers. But I stayed that spring and built me a boat. I made her for only twenty oars because I thought few men would follow me; for I was young, fifteen years old. I made her in the likeness of a dragon. At the prow I carved the head with open mouth and forked tongue thrust out. I painted the eyes red for anger.

"'There, stand so!' I said, 'and glare and hiss at my foes.'

"In the stern I curved the tail up almost as high as the head. There I put the pilot's seat and a strong tiller for the rudder. On the breast and sides I carved the dragon's scales. Then I painted it all black and on the tip of every scale I put gold. I called her 'Waverunner.' There she sat on the rollers, as fair a ship as I ever saw.

"The night that it was finished I went to my father's feast. After the meats were eaten and the mead-horns came round,

I stood up from my bench and raised my drinking-horn high and spoke with a great voice:

"'This is my vow: I will sail to Norway and I will harry the coast and fill my boat with riches. Then I will get me a farm and will winter in that land. Now who will follow me?'

"'He is but a boy,' the men said. 'He has opened his mouth wider than he can do.'

"But others jumped to their feet with their mead-horns in their hands. Thirty men, one after another, raised their horns and said:

"'I will follow this lad, and I will not turn back so long as he and I live!'

"On the next morning we got into my dragon and started. I sat high in the pilot's seat. As our boat flashed down the rollers into the water I made this song and sang it:

> *'The dragon runs.*
> *Where will she steer?*
> *Where swords will sing,*
> *Where spears will bite,*
> *Where I shall laugh.'*

"So we harried the coast of Norway. We ate at many men's tables uninvited. Many men we found overburdened with gold. Then I said:

"'My dragon's belly is never full,' and on board went the gold.

"Oh! it is better to live on the sea and let other men raise your crops and cook your meals. A house smells of smoke, a ship smells of frolic. From a house you see a sooty roof, from a ship you see Valhalla.

"Up and down the water we went to get much wealth and much frolic. After a while my men said:

"'What of the farm, Olaf?'

"'Not yet,' I answered. 'Viking is better for summer. When the ice comes, and our dragon cannot play, then we will get our farm and sit down.'

"At last the winter came, and I said to my men:

"'Now for the farm. I have my eye on one up the coast a way in King Halfdan's country.'

"So we set off for it. We landed late at night and pulled our boat up on shore and walked quietly to the house. It was rather a wealthy farm, for there were stables and a storehouse and a smithy at the sides of the house. There was but one door to the house. We went to it, and I struck it with my spear.

"'Hello! Ho! Hello!' I shouted, and my men made a great din.

"At last some one from inside said:

"'Who calls?'

"'I call,' I answered. 'Open! or you will think it Thor who calls,' and I struck my shield against the door so that it made a great clanging.

"The door opened only a little, but I pushed it wide and leaped into the room. It was so dark that I could see nothing but a few sparks on the hearth. I stood with my back to the wall; for I wanted no sword reaching out of the dark for me.

"'Now start up the fire,' I said.

"'Come, come!' I called, when no one obeyed. 'A fire! This is cold welcome for your guests.'

"My men laughed.

"'Yes, a stingy host! He acts as though he had not expected us.'

"But now the farmer was blowing on the coals and putting on fresh wood. Soon it blazed up, and we could see about us. We were in a little feast hall, with its fire down the middle of it. There were benches for twenty men along each side. The farmer crouched by the fire, afraid to move. On a bench in a far corner were a dozen people huddled together.

"'Ho, thralls!' I called to them. 'Bring in the table. We are hungry.'

"Off they ran through a door at the back of the hall. My men came in and lay down by the fire and warmed themselves, but I set two of them as guards at the door.

"'Well, friend farmer,' laughed one, 'why such a long face? Do you not think we shall be merry company?'

"'We came only to cheer you,' said another. 'What man wants to spend the winter with no guests?'

"'Ah!' another then cried out, sitting up. 'Here comes something that will be a welcome guest to my stomach.'

"The thralls were bringing in a great pot of meat. They set up a crane over the fire and hung the pot upon it, and we sat and watched it boil while we joked. At last the supper began. The farmer sat gloomily on the bench and would not eat, and you cannot wonder; for he saw us putting potfuls of his good beef and basket-loads of bread into our big mouths. When the tables were taken out and the mead-horns came round, I stood up and raised my horn and said to the farmer:

"'You would not eat with us. You cannot say no to half of my ale. I drink this to your health.'

"Then I drank half of the horn-full and sent the rest across the fire to the farmer. He took it and smiled, saying:

"'Since it is to my health, I will drink it. I thought that all this night's work would be my death.'

"'Oh, do not fear that!' I laughed, 'for a dead man sets no tables.'

"So we drank and all grew merrier. At last I stood up and said:

"'I like this little taste of your hospitality, friend farmer. I have decided to accept more of it.'

"My men roared with laughter.

"'Come,' they cried, 'thank him for that, farmer. Did you ever have such a lordly guest before?'

"I went on:

"'Now there is no fun in having guests unless they keep you company and make you merry. So I will give out this law: that my men shall never leave you alone. Hakon there shall be your constant companion, friend farmer. He shall not leave you day or night, whether you are working or playing or sleeping. Leif and Grim shall be the same kind of friends to your two sons.'

"I named nine others and said:

"'And these shall follow your thralls in the same way. Now, am I not careful to make your time go merrily?'

"So I set guards over every one in that house. Not once all that winter did they stir out of sight of some of us. So no tales got out to the neighbors. Besides, it was a lonely place, and by good luck no one came that way. Oh! that was fat and easy living.

"Well, after we had been there for a long time, Hakon came in to the feast one night and said:

"'I heard a cuckoo today!'

"'It is the call to go a-viking,' I said.

"All my men put their hands to their mouths and shouted. Their eyes danced. Big Thorleif stood up and stretched himself.

"'I am stiff with long sitting,' he said. 'I itch for a fight.'

"I turned to the farmer.

"'This is our last feast with you,' I said.

"'Well,' he laughed, 'this has been the busiest winter I ever spent, and the merriest. May good luck go with you!'

"'By the beard of Odin!' I cried; 'you have taken our joke like a man.'

"My men pounded the table with their fists.

"'By the hammer of Thor!' shouted Grim. 'Here is no stingy coward. He is a man fit to carry my drinking-horn, the horn of a sea-rover and a sword-swinger. Here, friend, take it,' and he thrust it into the farmer's hand. 'May you drink heart's-ease from it for many years. And with it I leave you a name, Sif the Friendly. I shall hope to drink with you some-time in Valhalla.'

"Then all my men poured around that farmer and clapped him on the shoulder and piled things upon him, saying:

"'Here is a ring for Sif the Friendly.'

"'And here is a bracelet.'

"'A sword would not be ashamed to hang at your side.'

"I took five great bracelets of gold from our treasure chest and gave them to him.

"The old man's eyes opened wide at all these things, and at the same time he laughed.

"'May Odin send me such guests every winter!' he said.

"Early next morning we shook hands with our host and boarded the 'Waverunner' and sailed off.

"'Where shall we go?' my men asked.

"'Let the gods decide,' I said, and tossed up my spear.

"When it fell on the deck it pointed up-shore, so I steered

in that direction. That is the best way to decide, for the spear will always point somewhere, and one thing is as good as another. That time it pointed us into your father's ships. They closed in battle with us and killed my men and sunk my ship and dragged me off a prisoner. They were three against one, or they might have tasted something more bitter at our hands. They took me before King Halfdan.

"'Here,' they said, 'is a rascal who has been harrying our coasts. We sunk his ship and men, but him we brought to you.'

"'A robber viking?' said the king, and scowled at me.

"I threw back my head and laughed.

"'Yes. And with all your fingers it took you a year to catch me.'

"The king frowned more angrily.

"'Saucy, too?' he said. 'Well, thieves must die. Take him out, Thorkel, and let him taste your sword.'

"Your mother, the queen, was standing by. Now she put her hand on his arm and smiled and said:

"'He is only a lad. Let him live. And would he not be a good gift for our baby?'

"Your father thought a moment, then looked at your mother and smiled.

"'Soft heart!' he said gently to her; then to Thorkel, 'Well, let him go, Thorkel!'

"Then he turned to me again, frowning.

"'But, young sharp-tongue, now that we have caught you we will put you into a trap that you cannot get out of. Weld an iron collar on his neck.'

"So I lived and now am your tooth thrall. Well, it is the luck of war. But by the chair of Odin, I kept my vow!"

"Yes!" cried Harald, jumping to his feet. "And had a joke

into the bargain. Ah! Sometime I will make a brave vow like that."

OLAF'S FIGHT WITH HAVARD

At another time Harald said:

"Tell me of a fight, Olaf. I want to hear about the music of swords."

Olaf's eyes blazed.

"I will tell you of our fight with King Havard," he said.

"One dark night we had landed at a farm. We left our 'Waverunner' in the water with three men to guard her. The rest of us went into the house. The farmer met us at the door, but he died by Thorkel's sword. The others we shut into their beds. The door at each end of the hall we had barred on the inside so that nobody could surprise us. We were busy going through the cupboards and shouting at our good luck. But suddenly we heard a shout outside:

"'Thor and Havard!'

"Then there was a great beating at the doors.

"'He has two hundred fighters with him,' said Grim; 'for we saw his ships last night. Thirty against two hundred! We shall all drink in Valhalla to-night.'

"'Well,' I cried, 'Odin shall have no unwilling guest in me.'

"'Nor in me,' cried Hakon.

"'Nor in me,' shouted Thorkel.

"And that shout went all around, and we drew out our swords and caught up our shields.

"'Hot work is ahead of us,' said Hakon. 'Besides, we must leave none of this mead for Havard. Lend a hand, some one.'

"Then he and another pulled out a great tub that sat on the floor of the cupboard.

"'I drink to Valhalla to-night,' cried Thorkel the Thirsty, and he plunged his horn deep into the tub.

"When he brought it up, his sleeve was dripping and the sweet mead was running over from the horn.

"'Sloven!' cried Hakon, and he struck Thorkel with his fist and knocked him over into the cupboard.

"He fell against the wooden wall at the back, and a carved panel swung open behind him. He dropped down head first. In a minute he put his head out of the hole again. We all stood staring.

"'I think it is a secret passage,' he said.

"'We will try it,' I answered in a whisper. 'Throw dirt on the fire. It must be dark.'

"So we dug up dirt from the earth floor and smothered the fire. All this time there was a terrible shouting and hammering at the doors, but they were of heavy logs and stood.

"'I with four more will guard this door,' I said, pointing to the east end.

"Immediately four men stepped to my side.

"'And I will guard the other,' Hakon said, and four went with him.

"'The rest of you, down the hole!' I said. 'Close the door after you. If luck is with us we will meet at the ships. Now Thor and our good swords help us! Quick! The doors are giving way.'

"So we ten men stood at the doors and held back the king's soldiers. It was dark in the room, and the people out of doors could not tell how many were inside. Few were eager to be the first in.

"'Thirty swords are waiting in there to eat up the first man,' we heard some one say.

"We chuckled at that.

"But the king stood in the very doorway and fought. Our five swords held him back for a long time, but at last he pushed in, and his men poured after him. We ran back and hid behind some tubs in a dark corner. The king's men went groping about and calling, but they did not find us. The room was full of shouting and running and sword-clashing; for in the dark and the noise the men could not tell their own soldiers. More than one fell by his friend's sword. When it was less crowded about the doorway, I whispered:

"'Follow me in double line. We will make for the ships. Keep close together.'

"So that double line of men, with swords swinging from both sides, ran out through the dark. Swords struck out at us, and we struck back. Men ran after us shouting, but our legs were as good as theirs. But I and Hakon and one other were all that reached the ship. There we saw our 'Waverunner' with sail up and bow pointing to open sea. We swam out to her and climbed aboard. Then the men swung the sail to the wind, and we moved off. Even as we went, a spear whizzed through the air, and Hakon fell dead; for the king and all his men were running to the shore.

"'After them!' they were shouting.

"Then we heard the king call to the men in his boats lying out in the water:

"'Row to shore and take us in.'

"Thorkel was standing by my side. At that he laughed and said:

"'They do not answer. He left but a handful to guard his ships. They tasted our swords. And we went aboard and broke the oars and threw the sails into the water. It will be slow going for Havard to-night.'

"Then he turned to the shore and sang out loudly:

"'King Havard's ships are dead:

Olaf's dragon flies.

King Havard stamps the shore:

Olaf skims the waves.

King Havard shakes his fist.

Olaf turns and laughs.'

"That was the end of our meeting with King Havard."

FOES'-FEAR

Every day the boy Harald heard some such story of war or of the gods, until he could see Thor riding among the storm-clouds and throwing his hammer, until he knew that a brave man has many wounds, but never a one on his back. Many nights he dreamed that he himself walked into Valhalla, and that all the heroes stood up and shouted:

"Welcome! Harald Halfdanson!"

"Ah! the bite of the sword is sweeter than the kiss of your mother," he said to Olaf one day. "When shall I stand in the prow of a dragon and feast on the fight? I am hungry to see the world. Ivar the Far-goer tells me of the strange countries he has seen. Ah! we vikings are great folk. There is no water that has not licked our boats' sides. This cape of mine came in a viking boat from France. These cloak-pins came from a far country called Greece. In my father's house are golden cups from Rome, away on the southern sea. Every land pours rich things into our treasure-chest. Ivar has been to a strange country where it is all sand and is very hot. The people call their country Arabia. They have never heard of Thor or Odin. Ivar brought beautiful striped cloth from there, and wonderful, sweet-smelling waters. Oh! when shall the white horses of the sea lead me out to strange lands and glorious battles?"

But Harald did something besides listen to stories. Every morning he was up at sunrise and went with a thrall to feed the hunting dogs. Thorstein taught him to swim in the rough waters of the fiord. Often he went with the men a-hunting in the woods and learned to ride a horse and pull a bow and throw a lance. Ivar taught him to play the harp and to make up songs. He went much to the smithy, where the warriors mended their helmets and made their spears and swords of iron and bronze. At first he only watched the men or worked the bellows, but soon he could handle the tongs and hold the red-hot iron, and after a long time he learned to use the hammer and to shape metal. One day he made himself a spear-head. It was two feet long and sharp on both edges. While the iron was hot he beat into it some runes. When the men in the smithy saw the runes they opened their eyes wide and looked at the boy, for few Norsemen could read.

"What does it say?" they asked.

"It is the name of my spear-point, and it says, 'Foes'-fear,'" Harald said. "But now for a handle."

It was winter and the snow was very deep. So Harald put on his skees and started for a wood that was back from shore. Down the mountains he went, twenty, thirty feet at a slide, leaping over chasms a hundred feet across. In his scarlet cloak he looked like a flash of fire. The wind shot past him howling. His eyes danced at the fun.

"It is like flying," he thought and laughed. "I am an eagle. Now I soar," as he leaped over a frozen river.

He saw a slender ash growing on top of a high rock.

"That is the handle for 'Foes'-fear,'" he said.

The rock stood up like a ragged tower, but he did not stop because of the steep climb. He threw off his skees and thrust his hands and feet into holes of the rock and drew himself up. He tore his jacket and cut his leather leggings and scratched his face and bruised his hands, but at last he was on the top. Soon he had chopped down the tree and had cut a straight pole ten feet long and as big around as his arm. He went down, sliding and jumping and tearing himself on the sharp stones. With a last leap he landed near his skees. As he did so a lean wolf jumped and snapped at him, snarling. Harald shouted and swung his pole. The wolf dodged, but quickly jumped again and caught the boy's arm between his sharp teeth. Harald thought of the spear-point in his belt. In a wink he had it out and was striking with it. He drove it into the wolf's neck and threw him back on the snow, dead.

"You are the first to feel the tooth of 'Foes'-fear,'" he said, "but I think you will not be the last."

Then without thinking of his torn arm he put on his skees and went leaping home. He went straight to the smithy and smoothed his pole and drove it into the haft of the spear-point. He hammered out a gold band and put it around the joining place. He made nails with beautiful heads and drove them into the pole in different places.

"If it is heavy it will strike hard," he said.

Then he weighed the spear in his hand and found the balancing point and put another gold band there to mark it.

Thorstein came in while he was working.

"A good spear," he said.

Then he saw the torn sleeve and the red wound beneath.

"Hello!" he cried. "Your first wound?"

"Oh, it is only a wolf-scratch," Harald answered.

"By Thor!" cried Thorstein, "I see that you are ready for better wounds. You bear this like a warrior."

"I think it will not be my last," Harald said.

HARALD IS KING

Now when Harald was ten years old his father, King Halfdan, died. An old book that tells about Harald says that then "he was the biggest of all men, the strongest, and the fairest to look upon." That about a boy ten years old! But boys grew fast in those days for they were out of doors all the time, running, swimming, leaping on skees, and hunting in the forest. All that makes big, manly boys.

So now King Halfdan was dead and buried, and Harald was to be king. But first he must drink his father's funeral ale.

"Take down the gay tapestries that hang in the feast hall," he said to the thralls. "Put up black and gray ones. Strew the floor with pine branches. Brew twenty tubs of fresh ale and mead. Scour every dish until it shines."

Then Harald sent messengers all over that country to his kinsmen and friends.

"Bid them come in three months' time to drink my father's funeral ale," he said. "Tell them that no one shall go away empty-handed."

So in three months men came riding up at every hour. Some came in boats. But many had ridden far through mountains, swimming rivers; for there were few roads or bridges in Norway. On account of that hard ride no women came to the feast.

At nine o'clock in the night the feast began. The men came walking in at the west end of the hall. The great bonfires down the middle of the room were flashing light on everything. The clean smell of this wood-smoke and of the pine branches on the floor was pleasant to the guests. Down each side of the hall stretched long, backless benches, with room for three hundred men. In the middle of each side rose the high seat, a great carved chair on a platform. All along behind the benches were the black and gray draperies. Here hung the shields of the guests; for every man, when he was given his place, turned and hung his shield behind him and set his tall spear by it. So on each wall there was a long row of gay shields, red and green and yellow, and all shining with gold or bronze trimmings. And higher up there was another row of gleaming spear-points. Above the hall the rafters were carved and gaily painted, so that dragons seemed to be crawling across, or eagles seemed to be swooping down.

The guests walked in laughing and talking with their big voices so that the rafters rang. They made the hall look all the brighter with their clothes of scarlet and blue and green, with their flashing golden bracelets and head-bands and sword-scabbards, with their flying hair of red or yellow.

Across the east end of the hall was a bench. When the men were all in, the queen, Harald's mother, and the women who lived with her, walked in through the east door and sat upon this bench.

Then thralls came running in and set up the long tables before the benches. Other thralls ran in with large steaming kettles of meat. They put big pieces of this meat into platters of wood and set it before the men. They had a few dishes of silver. These they put before the guests at the middle of the tables; for the great people sat here near the high seats.

When the meat came, the talking stopped; for Norsemen ate only twice a day, and these men had had long rides and were hungry. Three or four persons ate from one platter and drank from the same big bowl of milk. They had no forks, so they ate from their fingers and threw the bones under the table among the pine branches. Sometimes they took knives from their belts to cut the meat.

When the guests sat back satisfied, Harald called to the thralls:

"Carry out the tables."

So they did and brought in two great tubs of mead and set one at each end of the hall. Then the queen stood up and called some of her women. They went to the mead tubs. They took the horns, when the thralls had filled them, and carried them to the men with some merry word. Perhaps one woman said as she handed a man his horn:

"This horn has no feet to be set down upon. You must drink it at one draught."

Perhaps another said:

"Mead loves a merry face."

The women were beautiful, moving about the hall. The queen wore a trailing dress of blue velvet with long flowing sleeves. She had a short apron of striped Arabian silk with gold fringe along the bottom. From her shoulders hung a long train of scarlet wool embroidered in gold. White linen covered her head. Her long yellow hair was pulled around at the sides and over her breast and was fastened under the belt of her apron. As she walked, her train made a pleasant rustle among the pine branches. She was tall and straight and strong. Some of her younger women wore no linen on their heads and had their white arms bare, with bracelets shining on them. They, too, were tall and strong.

All the time men were calling across the fire to one another asking news or telling jokes and laughing.

An old man, Harald's uncle, sat in the high seat on the north side. That was the place of honor. But the high seat on the south side was empty; for that was the king's seat. Harald sat on the steps before it.

The feast went merrily until long after midnight. Then the thralls took some of the guests to the guest house to sleep, and some to the beds around the sides of the feast hall. But some men lay down on the benches and drew their cloaks over themselves.

On the next night there was another feast. Still Harald sat on the step before the high seat. But when the tables were gone and the horns were going around, he stood up and raised high a horn of ale and said loudly:

"This horn of memory I drink in honor of my father, Halfdan, son of Gudrod, who sits now in Valhalla. And I vow that I will grind my father's foes under my heel."

Then he drank the ale and sat down in the king's high seat, while all the men stood up and raised their horns and shouted:

"King Harald!"

And some cried:

"That was a brave vow."

And Harald's uncle called out:

"A health to King Harald!"

And they all drank it.

Then a man stood up and said:

"Hear my song of King Halfdan!" for this man was a skald.

"Yes, the song!" shouted the men, and Harald nodded his head.

So the skald took down his great harp from the wall behind him and went and stood before Harald. The bottom of the harp rested on the floor, but the top reached as high as the skald's shoulders. The brass frame shone in the light. The strings were some of gold and some of silver. The man struck them with his hand and sang of King Halfdan, of his battles, of his strong arm and good sword, of his death, and of how men loved him.

When he had finished, King Harald took a bracelet from his arm and gave it to him, saying:

"Take this as thanks for your good song."

The guests stayed the next day and at night there was another feast. When the mead horns were going around, King Harald stood up and spoke:

"I said that no man should go away empty-handed from drinking my father's funeral ale."

He beckoned the thralls, and they brought in a great treasure-chest and set it down by the high seat. King Harald opened it and took out rich gifts—capes and sword-belts and beautiful cloth and bracelets and gold cloak-pins. These he sent about the hall and gave something to every man. The guests wondered at the richness of his gifts.

"This young king has an open hand," they said, "and deep treasure-chests."

After breakfast the next morning the guests went out and stood by their horses ready to go, but before they mounted, thralls brought a horn of mead to each man. That was called the stirrup-horn, because after they drank it the men put their feet to the stirrups and sprang upon their horses and started. King Harald and his people rode a little way with them.

All men said that that was the richest funeral feast that ever was held.

HARALD'S BATTLE

Now King Halfdan had many foes. When he was alive they were afraid to make war upon him, for he was a mighty warrior. But when Harald became king, they said:

"He is but a lad. We will fight with him and take his land."

So they began to make ready. King Harald heard of this and he laughed and said:

"Good! 'Foes'-fear' is thirsty, and my legs are stiff with much sitting."

He called three men to him. To one he gave an arrow, saying:

"Run and carry this arrow north. Give it into the hands of the master of the next farm, and say that all men are to meet here within two weeks from this day. They must come ready for war and mounted on horses. Say also that if a man does not obey this call, or if he receives this arrow and does not carry it on to his next neighbor, he shall be outlawed from this country, and his land shall be taken from him."

He gave arrows to the other two men and told them to run south and east with the same message.

So all through King Harald's country men were soon busy mending helmets and polishing swords and making shields. There was blazing of forges and clanging of anvils all through the land.

On the day set, the fields about King Harald's house were full of men and horses. After breakfast a horn blew. Every man snatched his weapons and jumped upon his horse. Men of the same neighborhood stood together, and their chief led them. They waited for the starting horn. This did not look like our army. There were no uniforms. Some men wore helmets, some did not. Some wore coats of mail, but others wore only their jackets and tights of bright-colored wool. But at each man's left side hung a great shield. Over his right shoulder went his sword-belt and held his long sword under his left hand. Above most men's heads shone the points of their tall spears. Some men carried axes in their belts. Some carried bows and arrows. Many had ram's horns hanging from their necks.

King Harald rode at the front of his army with his standard-bearer beside him. Chain-armor covered the king's body. A red cloak was thrown over his shoulders. On his head was a gold helmet with a dragon standing up from it. He carried a round shield on his left arm. The king had made that shield himself. It was of brass. The rivets were of silver, with strangely shaped heads. On the back of Harald's horse was a red cloth trimmed with the fur of ermine.

King Harald looked up at his standard and laughed aloud.

"Oh, War-lover," he cried, "you and I ride out on a gay journey."

A horn blew again and the army started. The men shouted as they went, and blew their ram's horns.

"Now we shall taste something better than even King Harald's ale," shouted one.

Another rose in his stirrups and sniffed the air.

"Ah! I smell a battle," he cried. "It is sweeter than those strange waters of Arabia."

So the army went merrily through the land. They carried no tents, they had no provision wagons.

"The sky is a good enough tent for a soldier," said the Norsemen. "Why carry provisions when they lie in the farms beside you?"

After two days King Harald saw another army on the hills.

"Thorstein," he shouted, "up with the white shield and go tell King Haki to choose his battle-field. We will wait but an hour. I am eager for the frolic."

So Thorstein raised a white shield on his spear as a sign that he came on an errand of peace. He rode near King Haki, but he could not wait until he came close before he shouted out his message and then turned and rode back.

"Tell your boy king that we will not hang back," Haki called after Thorstein.

King Harald's men waited on the hillside and watched the other army across the valley. They saw King Haki point and saw twenty men ride off as he pointed. They stopped in a patch of hazel and hewed with their axes.

"They are getting the hazels," said Thorstein.

"Audun," said King Harald to a man near him, "stay close to my standard all day. You must see the best of the fight. I want to hear a song about it after it is over."

This Audun was the skald who sang at the drinking of King Halfdan's funeral ale.

King Haki's men rode down into the valley. They drove down stakes all about a great field. They tied the hazel twigs to the stakes in a string. But they left an open space toward King Harald's army and one toward King Haki's. Then a man raised a white shield and galloped toward King Harald.

"We are ready!" he shouted.

At the same time King Haki raised a red shield. King Harald's men put their shields before their mouths and shouted into them. It made a great roaring war-cry.

"Up with the war shield!" shouted King Harald. "Horns blow!"

There was a blowing of horns on both sides. The two armies galloped down into the field and ran together. The fight had begun.

All that day long swords were flashing, spears flying, men shouting, men falling from their horses, swords clashing against shields.

"Victory flashes from that dragon," Harald's men said, pointing to the king's helmet. "No one stands before it."

And, surely, before night came, King Haki fell dead under "Foes'-fear." When he fell, a great shout went up from his warriors, and they turned and fled. King Harald's men chased them far, but during the night came back to camp. Many brought swords and helmets and bracelets or silver-trimmed saddles and bridles with them.

"Here is what we got from the foe," they said.

The next morning King Harald spoke to his men:

"Let us go about and find our dead."

So they went over all the battle-field. They put every man on his shield and carried him and laid him on a hill-top. They hung his sword over his shoulder and laid his spear by his side. So they laid all the dead together there on the hill-top. Then King Harald said, looking about:

"This is a good place to lie. It looks far over the country. The sound of the sea reaches it. The wind sweeps here. It is a good grave for Norsemen and Vikings. But it is a long road and a rough road to Valhalla that these men must travel. Let the nearest kinsman of each man come and tie on his hell-shoes. Tie them fast, for they will need them much on that hard road."

So friends tied shoes on the dead men's feet. Then King Harald said:

"Now let us make the mound."

Every man set to work with what tools he had and heaped earth over the dead until a great mound stood up. They piled stones on the top. On one of these stones King Harald made runes telling how these men had died.

After that was done King Harald said:

"Now set up the pole, Thorstein. Let every man bring to that pole all that he took from the foe."

So they did, and there was a great hill of things around it. Harald divided it into piles.

"This pile we will give to Thor in thanks for the victory," he said. "This pile is mine because I am king. Here are the piles for the chiefs, and these things go to the other men of the army."

So every man went away from that battle richer than he was before, and Thor looked down from Valhalla upon his full temple and was pleased.

The next morning King Harald led his army back. But on the way he met other foes and had many battles and did not lose one. The kings either died in battle or ran away, and Harald had their lands.

"He has kept his vow," men said, "and ground his father's foes under his heel."

So King Harald sat in peace for a while.

GYDA'S SAUCY MESSAGE

Now Harald heard men talk of Gyda, the daughter of King Eric.

"She is very beautiful," they said, "but she is very proud, too. She can both read and make runes. No other woman in the world knows so much about herbs as she does. She can cure any sickness. And she is proud of all this!"

Now when King Harald heard that, he thought to himself:

"Fair and proud. I like them both. I will have her for my wife."

So he called his uncle, Guthorm, and said:

"Take rich gifts and go to Gyda's foster-father and tell him that I will marry Gyda."

So Guthorm and his men came to that house and they told the king's message to the foster-father. Gyda was standing near, weaving a rich cloak. She heard the speech. She came up and said, holding her head high and curling her lip:

"I will not waste myself on a king of so few people. Norway is a strange country. There is a little king here and a little king there—hundreds of them scattered about. Now in Denmark there is but one great king over the whole land. And it is so in Sweden. Is no one brave enough to make all of Norway his own?"

She laughed a scornful laugh and walked away. The men stood with open mouths and stared after her. Could it be that she had sent that saucy message to King Harald? They looked at her foster-father. He was chuckling in his beard and said nothing to them. They started out of the house in anger. When they were at the door, Gyda came up to them again and said:

"Give this message to your King Harald for me: I will not be his wife unless he puts all of Norway under him for my sake."

So Guthorm and his men rode homeward across the country. They did not talk. They were all thinking. At last one said:

"How shall we give this message to the king?"

"I have been thinking of that," Guthorm said; "his anger is no little thing."

It was late when they rode into the king's yard; for they had ridden slowly, trying to make some plan for softening the message, but they had thought of none.

"I see light through the wind's-eyes of the feast hall," one said.

"Yes, the king keeps feast," Guthorm said. "We must give our message before all his guests."

So they went in with very heavy hearts. There sat King Harald in the high seat. The benches on both sides were full of men. The tables had been taken out, and the mead-horns were going round.

"Oh, ho!" cried King Harald. "Our messengers! What news?"

Then Guthorm said:

"This Gyda is a bold and saucy girl, King Harald. My tongue refuses to give her message."

The king stamped his foot.

"Out with it!" he cried. "What does she say?"

"She says that she will not marry so little a king," Guthorm answered.

Harald jumped to his feet. His face flushed red. Guthorm stretched out his hand.

"They are not my words, O King; they are the words of a silly girl."

"Is there any more?" the king shouted. "Go on!"

"She said: 'There is one king in Denmark and one king in Sweden. Is there no man brave enough to make himself king of all Norway? Tell King Harald that I will not marry him unless he puts all of Norway under him for my sake.'"

The guests sat speechless, staring at Guthorm. All at once the king broke into a roar of laughter.

"By the hammer of Thor!" he cried, "that is a good message. I thank you, Gyda. Did you hear it, friends? King of all Norway! Why, we are all stupids. Why did we not think of that?"

Then he raised his horn high.

"Now hear my vow. I say that I will not cut my hair or comb it until I am king of all Norway. That I will be or I will die."

Then he drank off the horn of mead, and while he drank it, all the men in the hall stood up and waved their swords and shouted and shouted. That old hall in all its two hundred years of feasts had not heard such a noise before.

"Ah, Harald!" Guthorm cried, "surely Thor in Valhalla smiled when he heard that vow."

The men sat all night talking of that wonderful vow.

On the very next day King Harald sent out his war-arrows. Soon a great army was gathered. They marched through the country north and south and east and west, burning houses and fighting battles as they went. People fled before them, some to their own kings, some inland to the deep woods and hid there. But some went to King Harald and said:

"We will be your men."

"Then take the oath, and I will be friends with you," he said.

The men took off their swords and laid them down and came one by one and knelt before the king. They put their heads between his knees and said:

"From this day, Harald Halfdanson, I am your man. I will serve you in war. For my land I will pay you taxes. I will be faithful to you as my king."

Then Harald said:

"I am your king, and I will be faithful to you."

Many kings took that oath and thousands of common men. Of all the battles that Harald fought, he did not lose one.

Now for a long time the king's hair and beard had not been combed or cut. They stood out around his head in a great bushy mat of yellow. At a feast one day when the jokes were going round, Harald's uncle said:

"Harald, I will give you a new name. After this you shall be called Harald Shockhead. As my naming gift I give you this drinking-horn."

"It is a good name," laughed all the men.

After that all people called him Harald Shockhead.

During these wars, whenever King Harald got a country for his own, this is what he did. He said:

"All the marshland and the woodland where no people live is mine. For his farm every man shall pay me taxes."

Over every country he put some brave, wise man and called him Earl. He said to the earls:

"You shall collect the taxes and pay them to me. But some you shall keep for yourselves. You shall punish any man who steals or murders or does any wicked thing. When your people are in trouble they shall come to you, and you shall set the thing right. You must keep peace in the land. I will not have my people troubled with robber vikings."

The earls did all these things as best they could; for they were good strong men. The farmers were happy. They said:

"We can work on our farms with peace now. Before King Harald came, something was always wrong. The vikings would come and steal our gold and our grain and burn our houses, or the king would call us to war. Those little kings are always fighting. It is better under King Harald."

But the chiefs, who liked to fight and go a-viking, hated King Harald and his new ways. One of these chiefs was Solfi. He was a king's son. Harald had killed his father in battle. Solfi had been in that battle. At the end of it he fled away with two hundred men and got into ships.

"We will make that Shockhead smart," he said.

So they harried the coast of King Harald's country. They filled their ships with gold. They ate other men's meals. They burned farmhouses behind them. The people cried out to the earls for help. So the earls had out their ships all the time trying to catch Solfi, but he was too clever for them.

In the spring he went to a certain king, Audbiorn, and said to him:

"Now, there are two things that we can do. We can become this Shockhead Harald's thralls, we can kneel before him and put our heads between his knees. Or else we can fight. My father thought it better to die in battle than to be any man's thrall. How is it? Will you join with my cousin Arnvid and me against this young Shockhead?"

"Yes, I will do it," said the king.

THE SEA FIGHT

Many men felt as Solfi did. So when King Audbiorn and King Arnvid sent out their war arrows, a great host gathered. All men came by sea. Two hundred ships lay at anchor in the fiord, looking like strange swimming animals because of their high carved prows and bright paint. There were red and gold dragons with long necks and curved tails. Sea-horses reared out of the water. Green and gold snakes coiled up. Sea-hawks sat with spread wings ready to fly. And among all these curved necks stood up the tall, straight masts with the long yardarms swinging across them holding the looped-up sails.

When the starting horn blew, and their sails were let down, it was like the spreading of hundreds of curious flags. Some were striped black and yellow or blue and gold. Some were white with a black raven or a brown bear embroidered on them, or blue with a white sea-hawk, or black with a gold sun. Some were edged with fur. As the wind filled the gaudy sails, and the ships moved off, the men waved their hands to the women on shore and sang:

> *"To the sea! To the sea!*
> *The wind in our sail,*
> *The sea in our face,*
> *And the smell of the fight.*
> *After ship meets ship,*
> *In the quarrel of swords*
> *King Harald shall lie*
> *In the caves under sea*
> *And Norsemen shall laugh."*

In the prow stood men leaning forward and sniffing the salt air with joy. Some were talking of King Harald.

"Yesterday he had a hard fight," they said. "Today he will be lying still, dressing his wounds and mending his ships. We shall take him by surprise."

They sailed near the coast. Solfi in his "Sea-hawk" was ahead leading the way. Suddenly men saw his sail veer and his oars flash out. He had quickly turned his boat and was rowing back. He came close to King Arnvid and called:

"He is there, ahead. His boats are ready in line of battle. The fox has not been asleep."

King Arnvid blew his horn. Slowly his boats came into line with his "Sea-stag" in the middle. Again he blew his horn. Cables were thrown across from one prow to the next, and all the ships were tied together so that their sides touched. Then the men set their sails again and they went past a tongue of land into a broad fiord. There lay the long line of King Harald's ships with their fierce heads grinning and mocking at the newcomers. Back of those prows was what looked like a long wall with spots of green and red and blue and yellow and shining gold. It was the locked shields of the men in the bows, and over every shield looked fierce blue eyes. Higher up and farther back was another wall of shields; for on the half deck in the stern of every ship stood the captain with his shield-guard of a dozen men.

Arnvid's people had furled their sails and were taking down the masts, but the ships were still drifting on with the wind. The horn blew, and quickly every man sprang to his place in bow and stern. All were leaning forward with clenched teeth and widespread nostrils. They were clutching their naked swords in their hands. Their flashing eyes looked over their shields.

Soon King Arnvid's ships crashed into Harald's line, and immediately the men in the bows began to swing their swords at one another. The soldiers of the shield-guard on the high decks began to throw darts and stones and to shoot arrows into the ships opposite them.

So in every ship showers of stones and arrows were falling, and many men died under them or got broken arms or legs. Spears were hurled from deck to deck and many of them bit deep into men's bodies. In every bow men slashed with their swords at the foes in the opposite ship. Some jumped upon the gunwale to get nearer or hung from the prow-head. Some even leaped into the enemy's boat.

King Harald's ship lay prow to prow with King Arnvid's. The battle had been going on for an hour. King Harald was still in the stern on the deck. There was a dent in his helmet where a great stone had struck. There was a gash in his shoulder where a spear had cut. But he was still fighting and laughed as he worked.

"Wolf meets wolf today," he said. "But things are going badly in the prow," he cried. "Ivar fallen, Thorstein wounded, a dozen men lying in the bottom of the boat!"

He leaped down from the deck and ran along the gunwale, shouting as he went:

"Harald and victory!"

So he came to the bow and stood swinging his sword as fast as he breathed. Every time it hit a man of Arnvid's men. Harald's own warriors cheered, seeing him.

"Harald and victory!" they shouted, and went to work again with good heart.

Slowly King Arnvid's men fell back before Harald's biting sword. Then Harald's men threw a great hook into that boat and pulled it alongside and still pushed King Arnvid's people back.

"Come on! Follow me!" cried Harald.

Then he leaped into King Arnvid's boat, and his warriors followed him.

"He comes like a mad wolf," King Arnvid's men said, and they turned and ran back below the deck.

Then Arnvid himself leaped down and stood with his sword raised.

"Can this young Shockhead make cowards of you all?" he cried.

But Harald's sword struck him, and he fell dead. Then a big, bloody viking of King Arnvid leaped upon the edge of the ship and stood there. He held his drinking-horn and his sword high in his hands.

"Ran and not you, Shockhead, shall have them and me!" he cried, and leaped laughing into the water and was drowned.

Many other warriors chose the same death on that terrible day.

All along the line of boats men fought for hours. In some places the cables had been cut, and the boats had drifted apart. Ships lay scattered about two by two, fighting. May boats sank, many men died, some fled away in their ships, and at the end King Harald had won the battle. So he had King Arnvid's country and King Audbiorn's country. Many men took the oath and became his friends. All people were talking of his wonderful battles.

KING HARALD'S WEDDING

It had taken King Harald ten years to fight so many battles. And all that time he had not cut his hair or combed it. Now he was feasting one day at an earl's house. Many people were there.

"How is it, friends?" Harald said. "Have I kept my vow?"

His friends answered:

"You have kept your vow. There is no king but you in all Norway."

"Then I think I will cut my hair," the king laughed.

So he went and bathed and put on fresh clothes. Then the earl cut his hair and beard and combed them and put a gold band about his head. Then he looked at him and said:

"It is beautiful, smooth, and yellow."

And all people wondered at the beauty of the king's hair.

"I will give you a new name," the earl said. "You shall no longer be called Shockhead. You shall be called Harald Hairfair."

"It is a good name," everybody cried.

Then Harald said:

"But I have another thing to do now. Guthorm, you shall take the same message to Gyda that you gave ten years ago."

So Guthorm went and brought back this answer from Gyda:

"I will marry the king of all Norway."

So when the wedding time came, Harald rode across the country to the home of Gyda's father, Eric. Many men followed him. They were all richly dressed in velvet and gold.

For three nights they feasted at Eric's house. On the next night Gyda sat on the cross-bench with her women. A long veil of white linen covered her face and head and hung down to the ground. After the mead-horns had been brought in, Eric stood up from his high seat and went down and stood before King Harald.

"Will you marry Gyda now?" he asked.

Harald jumped to his feet and laughed.

"Yes," he said. "I have waited long enough."

Then he stepped down from his high seat and stood by Eric. They walked about the hall. Before them walked thralls carrying candles. Behind them walked many of King Harald's great earls. Three times they walked around the hall. The third time they stopped before the cross-bench. King Harald and Eric stepped upon the platform, where the cross-bench was.

Eric gave a holy hammer to Harald, and it was like the hammer of Thor. Harald put it upon Gyda's lap, saying:

"With this holy hammer of Thor's, I, Harald, King of Norway, take you, Gyda, for my wife."

Then he took a bunch of keys and tied it to Gyda's girdle, saying:

"This is the sign that you are mistress of my house."

After that, Eric called out loudly:

"Now, are Harald, King of Norway, and Gyda, daughter of Eric, man and wife."

Then thralls brought meat and drink in golden dishes. They were about to serve it to Gyda for the bride's feast, but Harald took the dish from them and said:

"No, I will serve my bride."

So he knelt and held the platter. When he did that his men shouted. Then they talked among themselves, saying:

"Surely Harald never knelt before. It is always other people who kneel to him."

When the bride had tasted the food and touched the mead-horn to her lips she stood up and walked from the hall. All her women followed her, but the men stayed and feasted long.

On the next morning at breakfast Gyda sat by Harald's side. Soon the king rose and said:

"Father-in-law, our horses stand ready in the yard. Work is waiting for me at home and on the sea. Lead out the bride."

So Eric took Gyda by the hand and led her out of the hall. Harald followed close. When they passed through the door Eric said:

"With this hand I lead my daughter out of my house and give her to you, Harald, son of Halfdan, to be your wife. May all the gods make you happy!"

Harald led his bride to the horse and lifted her up and set her behind his saddle and said:

"Now this Gyda is my wife."

Then they drank the stirrup-horn and rode off.

"Everything comes to King Harald," his men said; "wife and land and crown and victory in battle. He is a lucky man."

KING HARALD GOES
WEST-OVER-SEAS

Now many men hated King Harald. Many a man said:

"Why should he put himself up for king of all of us? He is no better than I am. Am I not a king's son as well as he? And are not many of us kings' sons? I will not kneel before him and promise to be his man. I will not pay him taxes. I will not have his earl sitting over me. The good old days have gone. This Norway has become a prison. I will go away and find some other place."

So hundreds of men sailed away. Some went to France and got land and lived there. Big Rolf-go-afoot and all his men sailed up the great French River and won a battle against the French king himself. There was no way to stop the flashing of his battle-axes but to give him what he wanted. So the king made Rolf a duke, gave him broad lands and gave him the king's own daughter for wife. Rolf called his country Normandy, for old Norway. He ruled it well and was a great lord, and his sons' sons after him were kings of England.

Other Norsemen went to Ireland and England and Scotland. They drew up their boats on the river banks. The people ran away before them and gathered into great armies that marched back to meet the vikings in battle. Sometimes the Norsemen lost, but oftener they won, so that they got land and lived in those countries. Their houses sat in these strange lands like warriors' camps, and the Norsemen went among their new neighbors with hanging swords and spears in hand, ever ready for fight.

There are many islands north of Scotland. They are called the Orkneys and the Shetlands. They have many good harbors for ships. They are little and rocky and bare of trees. Wild sea-birds scream around them. On some of them a man can stand in the middle and see the ocean all about him. Now the vikings sailed to these islands and were pleased.

"It is like being always in a boat," they said. "This shall be our home."

So it went until all the lands round about were covered with vikings. Norse carved and painted houses brightened the hillsides. Viking ships sailed all the seas and made harbor in every river. Norsemen's thralls plowed the soil and planted crops and herded cattle, and gold flowed into their masters' treasure-chests. Norse warriors walked up and down the land, and no man dared to say them nay.

These men did not forget Norway. In the summers they sailed back there and harried the coast. They took gold and grain and beautiful cloth back to their homes. In Norway they left burning houses and weeping women.

Every summer King Harald had out his ships and men and hunted these vikings. There are many little islands about Norway. They have crags and caves and deep woods. Here the vikings hid when they saw King Harald's ships coming. But Harald ran his boat into every creek and fiord and hunted in every cave and through all the woods and among the crags. He caught many men, but most of them got away and went home laughing at Harald. Then they came back the next summer and did the same deeds over again. At last King Harald said:

"There is but one thing to do. I must sail to these western islands and whip these robbers in their own homes."

So he went with a great number of ships. He found as brave men as he had brought from Norway. These vikings had brought their old courage to their new homes. King Harald's fine ships were scarred by viking stones and scorched by viking fire. The shields of Harald's warriors had dents from viking blows. Many of those men carried viking scars all their lives. And many of King Harald's warriors walked the long, hard road to Valhalla, and feasted there with some of these very vikings that had died in King Harald's battles. But after many hard fights on land and sea, after many men had died and many had fled away to other lands, King Harald won, and he made the men that were yet in the islands take the oath, and he left his earls to rule over them. Then he went back to Norway.

"He has done more than he vowed to do," people said. "He has not only whipped the vikings, but he has got a new kingdom west-over-seas."

Then they talked of that dream that his mother had.

"King Harald was that great tree," they said. "The trunk was red with the blood of his many battles, but higher up the limbs were fair and green like this good time of peace. The topmost branches were white because Harald will live to be an old man. Just as that tree spread out until all of Norway was in its shade, and even more lands, so Harald is king of all this country and of the western islands. The many branches of that tree are the many sons of Harald, who shall be earls and kings in Norway, and their sons after them, for hundreds of years."

HOMES IN ICELAND

Men had been feasting in Ingolf's house. But there was no laughing and no shouting of jokes. Ingolf sat in his high seat frowning and gloomy. His head hung on his breast. He was staring into the fire. Now he raised his head and looked about the hall.

"Comrades," he said, "what shall we do? Herstein and Holmstein died by our swords. Their kinsmen hunger to kill us. Besides, when Harald hears of our deed, there will not be a safe place in Norway for us. He will never let a man fight out an honest quarrel. Where shall we go?"

A man stood up from the bench.

"We have friends in the Shetlands," he said. "Let us find homes there."

Then Leif, in the high seat opposite Ingolf, stood up.

"No, not the Shetlands, my foster-brother. They are crowded already. Besides, Harald will not long keep his hands off them. Then they will be no better than Norway. England and Ireland and Scotland are old. My eyes ache for something new. What of that far island that Floki found? It is empty. We could choose our land from the whole country. There is good fishing. There are green valleys. And Butter Thorolf says that butter drops from every weed. There are mountains and deserts where we may find adventure. I say, let us steer for Iceland!"

When he stopped, many of the men shouted:

"Yes! Iceland!"

But an old man stood up.

"We have all laughed at that tale of Butter Thorolf's," he said. "But Floki himself said that the sea about the island is full of ice that pushes upon the land, that no ship can live in that water in the winter, that great mountains of ice cover the island. Did not all his cattle die there of hunger and cold, and did he not come back to Norway cursing Iceland?"

"Oh, Sighvat, you are old and fearful," called out Leif, and he laughed.

Then he stretched himself up and threw back his head.

"Are we afraid of ice? Have we not seen angry water before? I have been hungry, but I have never died of it. Surely if there are fish in the sea and grass in the valleys, we can live there. I should like to stand on a hill and look around on a wide land and think, 'This is all ours,' and out upon a rough sea and think, 'Far off there are our foes and they dare not come over to us.' Besides, we shall have no Shockhead Harald to lord it over us. We can come and go and feast and fight as we please. We shall be our own kings. And our ships will be always waiting to take us away, when we are weary of it. And we shall see things that other men have never seen. I am tired of the old things. Perhaps in after days men will make songs about 'those foster-brothers, Ingolf and Leif, who made a new country in a wonderful land, and whose sons and grandsons are mighty men in Iceland!'"

Ingolf leaped up from his chair.

"By the strong arm of Thor!" he cried, "I like the sound of it. Now I make my vow."

He raised his drinking-horn.

"I vow that I will find this Iceland and pass the winter there, and that if man can live upon it I will go back there and set up my home."

"And I vow that I will follow my foster-brother," cried Leif.

And many men vowed to go.

So on the next day they began to make ready a boat. They looked her over carefully and recalked every seam and freshly painted her and put into her their strongest oars and made her a new sail.

"This will be the longest voyage that she ever made," Ingolf said.

When the work was done, they put into her great stores, axes, hammers, fish-nets, cooking-kettles, kegs of ale, chests of hard bread, chests of smoked meat, brass kettles full of flour, skin bottles of water. They stowed these things away in the ends of the ship. When they were ready they put in four head of cattle.

"We shall need the milk and perhaps the meat," Ingolf said.

Many men wished to go, but Ingolf had said:

"There is little room to spare and little food and drink. I have planned for half a year. But perhaps we must be sailing longer than that. Our food may run short. We must not have extra mouths to feed. There are thirty oars in our boat. I will take only one man for every oar, and Leif and I will steer."

So they started off. Leif stood in the prow leaning forward and looking far ahead, and he sang:

> *"What does the swimming dragon smell?*
> *A stormy sea, an empty land,*
> *Hunger, darkness, giants, fire.*
> *Leif and his sword do laugh at that."*

They sailed for days and saw no land. Sometimes they passed ships and always made sure to sail close enough to hail them.

"Where are you going?" Ingolf would call.

"To Norway," would come back the answer.

"For trade or fight?" Leif would shout.

Then would ring out a great laugh from that boat and this answer:

"A shut mouth is a good friend."

So the two ships sailed on, and the men were glad to have heard a greeting and to have called one.

But at last there were the Shetlands.

"We will go in here and rest," Ingolf said.

When they rowed to shore a certain Shetland man stood there. He watched them land and looked them all over. Then he walked up to Ingolf and said:

"You look like brave men. Welcome to Shetland. You shall come to my house and rest your legs from ship-going and fill your stomachs. I hunger for news of Norway."

So they went to his house and stayed there for three days. And good it seemed to be near a fire and in a quiet bed and before a steaming platter. When they went to the shore to start off again, the Shetland man had his thralls carry a keg of ale and a great kettle of cooked meat and put them into the ship.

"Think of me when you eat this," he said.

Then the Norsemen put to sea again and sailed for a long time.

One day a terrible storm came up; the sky was black; the wind howled through the ship. Great waves leaped in the sea.

"Down with the sail and out with the oars!" Ingolf shouted.

So the men furled the sail and took down the mast and laid it along the bottom of the boat. As they worked, one man was washed overboard and drowned. The men sat down to row, but the tumbling waves tossed the boat about and poured over her and broke three of the oars. But still the men held on. They were wet to the skin and were cold, and their arms and legs ached with the hard work, and they were hungry from the long waiting, but not one face was white with fear.

"Ran, in her caves under sea, wants us for company tonight," Ingolf laughed.

So they tossed about all night, but in the morning the wind died down. Great waves still rolled, and for days the sea was rough, but they could put up the sail. Then one day Leif, as he sat in the pilot's seat, jumped to his feet and sang:

> *"To eyes grown tired with looking far,*
> *All at once appeared an island,*
> *A stretching-place for sea-legs,*
> *A quiet bed for backs grown stiff*
> *On rowing-bench on rolling sea.*
> *A place to build a red fire*
> *And thaw the blood that sea-winds froze."*

But when they came near they saw no place to land. The island was like a mountain of rock standing out of the water. The sides were steep and smooth. They sailed around it, but found no place to climb up.

"There are many other islands here," said Leif. "We will try another."

So he steered to another. It, too, was a steep rock, but one side sloped down to the water and was green with grass.

"Oh, I have not seen anything so good as that green grass since I looked into my mother's face," one man said.

There was a little harbor there. The men rowed in and quickly jumped out and put the rollers under the ship and pulled her upon shore. Then they threw themselves down on the grass and rolled and stretched their arms and shouted for joy. After that they built a fire and warmed themselves and cooked a meal and ate like wolves. They slept there that night.

In the morning before Ingolf's men started away they were standing high up on the hillside, looking about. They saw no houses on any of the islands, but they saw smoke rise from one hillside.

"Some other men, like us, weary of the sea and stopping to rest," said Ingolf.

They saw the island that they had sailed around the night before.

"There can surely be nothing but birds' nests on top of that," Sighvat said.

"Look!" cried another, pointing.

Men were standing on the flat top of that island. They were letting a boat down the steep side with ropes. When it struck the water, they made a rope fast to the rock and slid down it into the ship and sailed off.

"Some robber vikings from Scotland or Ireland," laughed Leif. "It is a good hiding place for treasure."

Soon Ingolf and his men got into their ship and were off. Old Sighvat grumbled.

"Is this land not new enough and empty enough and far enough? I am tired of sea, sea, sea, and nothing else."

"We started for Iceland," said Ingolf, "and I will not stop before I come there. I have a vow. Did you make none, Sighvat?"

Then they were on the water again for weeks with no

sight of land.

"Oh! I would give my right hand to see a dragon pawing the water off there and to fling a word to its men," Sighvat said.

"No hope of that," replied Ingolf. "Only three dragons before ours have ever swept this water, and men are not sailing this way for pleasure or riches."

So only the desolate sea stretched around them. Sometimes it was smooth and shining under the sun. Often it was torn by winds, and a gray sky hung over it, and the men were drenched with rain. Once they ran into a fog. For three days and nights they could not see sun or stars to steer by. They forgot which way was north. When after three days the fog lifted, they found that they had been going in the wrong direction, and they had to turn around and sail all that weary way over again. But at last one afternoon they saw a white cloud resting on the water far off. As they sailed toward it, it grew into long stretches of black, hilly shore with a blue ice mountain rising from it. The sun was going down behind that mountain, and long lines of pink and of shining green, and great purple shadows streaked the blue.

"It is Iceland!" shouted the men.

"It is like Asgard the Shining," Ingolf said.

But it was still far off. Men can see a long way there because the air is so clear. So Ingolf and his people sailed on for hours and at last came into a harbor. A little green valley sloped up from it. On one side was the bright ice mountain. Back of it were bare black and red hills. In that valley Ingolf and his men drew up their boat and camped. At supper that night one of the men said:

"I almost think I never felt a fire before or had warm food

in my mouth."

The men laughed.

"It is four months since we left Norway," Ingolf said. "Few men have ever been on the sea so long."

That night they put up the awning in the boat and slept under it.

After that some men went fishing every day in the row-boat that they had. And Ingolf took others, and they sailed along the shore, seeing what kind of a land this was. But winter began to come on. Then Ingolf said:

"Remember what Floki said of the ice and the rough sea in winter. Soon we cannot sail any longer. Let us choose a place to stay and build a hut there and cut hay for our cattle."

So they did. Their hut was a little mean thing of stones and turf. They kept the cattle and the hay in it. Sometimes they slept there, when it was very cold. But most of the time they ate and slept by a great bonfire out of doors where it was clean. Leif said:

"I like the cold air of the sea better than the bad-smelling air of a house, even though it is warm."

Now every day Ingolf and Leif and some of the men walked about the island. At night they all sat around the campfire and talked of what they had seen during the day.

"This is surely a wonderful land," Ingolf said once. "It is at the same time like Niflheim and like Asgard. Here is a spot green and soft, a sweet cradle for men. Next it is a mountain of ice where men would freeze to death. And next to that is a hill of rock that seems to have come out of some great fire. Yesterday I saw a cave on the seashore. The door of it was big enough for a giant. The waves broke at the doorstep. A terrible roaring came from the cave. I think it is the home of a giant.

I think that giants of fire and giants of frost made this island. I have seen great basins in the rocks filled with warm water. They looked like giants' bath-tubs. I have seen boiling water shoot up out of the ground. I have walked, and have felt and heard a great rumbling under me as though some giant were sleeping there and turning over in his sleep. One day I stood on a mountain and looked inland. There was a wide desert of sand and black and red rock with nothing growing on it. The fierce wind blew dirt into my eyes, and the cold of it froze the marrow in my bones. When I have seen these things I have cursed the country, and have said: 'The gods hate Iceland. I will not stay here.' But then I have walked through beautiful warm valleys where the winds did not come. I saw in my mind the flowers that we found last summer. I saw our cattle feeding on the sweet grass. I thought of the sea full of good fish. I saw my house built among green fields, and my wife sitting in her home, and my children playing among the flowers and making up tales about the bright ice mountains. I saw the wide, rough seas between me and Harald and our foes. Then I thought to myself, 'It is the sweetest home on earth.' As for me, I am coming here to live. What do you say, comrades?"

"Have I not vowed to follow you, foster-brother?" said Leif. "And indeed I never saw a land that I liked better. I don't believe in your giants. My sword is my god, and my ship is my temple, and I like this land to set them up in."

They sat about the fire long that night making plans.

"You shall go home and get our women and our things, Ingolf," said Leif. "I will off to Ireland and have a frolic. There will be little play of swords in this empty land, and I want to have one last game before I hang up my battle-knife. Besides, I will come to you with a ship full of gold and clothes and house-hangings such as we cannot get here, and they will cost me nothing but the swing of a sword."

As they talked, Ingolf looked up at the sky. The northern lights were quivering there. They were like great flames of yellow and green and red.

"See," he said, and pointed. "We are not so far that the gods will forget us. There is the flash of the armor of the Valkyrias. A battle is on somewhere, and Odin has sent his maidens to choose the heroes for Valhalla."

Leif only laughed and lay down to sleep.

So in the spring they all went back to Norway. Leif got ready the boat again and merrily sailed for Ireland.

"Here I go to get riches for our new land," he said.

Ingolf set his men to cutting down pines in the forest and some to building a new ship. He had his thralls plant large crops of grain and grind flour and make new kegs and chests of wood. He himself worked much at the forge, making all kinds of tools—spades, axes, hammers, hunting-knives, cooking kettles. The women were busy weaving and sewing new clothes. Ingolf sold his house and land and everything that he could not take with him.

After about two years Leif came back. He had ten thralls that he had got in Ireland. He took Ingolf aboard his ship and raised the covers of great chests. Gold helmets, silver-trimmed drinking-horns, embroidered robes, and swords flashed out.

"Did I not say that I would come back with a full ship?" he laughed.

At last all things were ready for starting.

"Today I will sacrifice to Thor and Odin," Ingolf said. "If the omens are good we will start to-morrow."

"Well, go, foster-brother," laughed Leif. "But I have better things to do. I will be putting the cattle into the ship and will have all ready."

So Ingolf and his men went into the forests a little way. There in a cleared space stood a large building. In front of this temple the men killed two horses for Odin. Ingolf caught some of the blood in a brass bowl. He raised it and looked up at the sky and said:

"All-wise and all-father Odin, and Thor who loves the thunder, I give these horses to you. Tell me whether it is your will that we go to Iceland."

As he said that, a raven flew over his head. Ingolf watched it.

"It is Odin's will that we go," he said. "He sent his raven to tell us. It is flying straight toward Iceland."

The men shouted with joy at that.

Now they hung some of the meat of the horses on a tree near the temple.

"For the ravens of Odin," they said.

Ingolf carried the bowl of blood into the temple. He went through the feast hall in front to a little room at the back. Here stood wooden statues of the gods in a semicircle. Before them was a stone altar. Ingolf took a little brush of twigs that lay on it and dipped it into the blood and sprinkled the statues.

"You shall taste of our sacrifice," he said. "Look kindly on us from your happy seats in Asgard."

Then they went into the feast hall. There thralls were boiling the horseflesh in pots over the fire. The tables were standing ready before the benches. Ingolf walked to the high seat. All the others took their places at the benches. When the horns came round, Ingolf made this vow:

"I vow that I will build my house wherever these pillars

lead me."

He put his hand upon a tall post that stood beside the high seat. There was one at each side. They were the front posts of the chair. But they stood up high, almost to the roof. They were wonderfully carved and painted with men and dragons. On the top of each one was a little statue of Thor with his hammer.

At the end of the feast Ingolf had his thralls dig these pillars up. He had a little bronze chest filled with the earth that was under the altar.

"I will take the pillars of my high seat to Iceland," he said, "and I will set up my altar there upon the soil of Norway, the soil that all my ancestors have trod, the soil that Thor loves."

So they carried the pillars and the chest of earth and the statues of the gods, and put them into Ingolf's boat.

"It is a well-packed ship," the men said. "There is no spot to spare."

Tools, and chests of food, and tubs of drink, and chests of clothes, and fishing nets were stowed in the bows of both boats. In the bottom were laid some long, heavy, hewn logs.

"The trees in Iceland are little," Ingolf said. "We must take the great beams for our homes with us."

Standing on these logs were a few cattle and sheep and horses and pigs. The rowers' benches were along the sides. In the stern of each boat was a little cabin. Here the women and children were to sleep. But the men would sleep on the timbers in the middle of the boat and perhaps they would put up the awning sometimes.

At last everyone was aboard. Men loosed the rope that held the boats. The ships flashed down the rollers into the water, and Ingolf and Leif were off for Iceland. As they sailed away everyone looked back at the shore of old Norway. There were tears in the women's eyes. Helga, Leif's wife, sang:

> *"There was I born. There was I wed.*
> *There are my father's bones.*
> *There are the hills and fields,*
> *The streams and rocks that I love.*
> *There are houses and temples,*
> *Women and warriors and feasts,*
> *Ships and songs and fights—*
> *A crowded, joyous land.*
> *I go to an empty land."*

There was the same long voyage with storm and fog. But at last the people saw again the white cloud and saw it growing into land and mountains. Then Ingolf took the pillars of his high seat and threw them overboard.

"Guide them to a good place, O Thor!" he cried.

The waves caught them up and rolled them about. Ingolf followed them with his ship. But soon a storm came up. The men had to take down the sails and masts, and they could do nothing with their oars. The two ships tossed about in the sea wherever the waves sent them. The pillars drifted away, and Ingolf could not see them.

"Remember your pillars, O Thor!" he cried.

Then he saw that Leif's ship was being driven far off.

"Ah, my foster-brother," he thought, "shall I not have you to cheer me in this empty land? O Thor, let him not go down to the caves of Ran! He is too good a man for that."

On the next day the storm was not so hard, and Ingolf put in at a good harbor. A high rocky point stuck out into the sea. A broad bay with islands in the mouth was at the side. Behind the rocky point was a level green place with ice-mountains shining far back.

After a day or two Ingolf said:

"I will go look for my pillars."

So he and a few men got into the rowboat and went along the shore and into all the fiords, but they could not find the pillars. After a week they came back, and Ingolf said:

"I will build a house here to live in while I look for the posts. This way is uncomfortable for the women."

So he did. Then he set out again to look for the pillars, but he had no better luck and came back.

"I must stay at home and see to the making of hay and the drying of fish," he said. "Winter is coming on, and we must not be caught with nothing to eat."

So he stayed and worked and sent two of his thralls to look for the holy posts. They came back every week or two and always had to say that they had not found them. Midwinter was coming on.

"Ah!" said Ingolf's wife one day, "do you remember the gay feast that we had at Yule-time? All our friends were there. The house rang with song and laughter. Our tables bent with good things to eat. Walls were hung with gay draperies. The floor was clean with sweet-smelling pine-branches. Now look at this mean house; its dirt floor, its bare stone walls, its littleness, its darkness! Look at our long faces. No one here could make a song if he tried. Oh! I am sick for dear old Norway."

"It is Thor's fault," Ingolf cried. "He will not let me find his posts."

He strode out of the house and stood scowling at the gray sea.

"Ah, foster-brother!" he said. "It was never so gloomy when you were by my side. Where are you now? Shall I never hear your merry laugh again? That spot in my palm burns, and my heart aches to see you. That arch of sod keeps rising before my eyes. Our vows keep ringing in my ears."

At last the long, gloomy winter passed and spring came.

"Cheer up, good wife," Ingolf said. "Better days are coming now."

But that same day the thralls came back from looking for the posts.

"We have bad news," they said. "As we walked along the shore looking for the pillars we saw a man lying on the shore. We went up to him. He was dead. It was Leif. Two well-built houses stood near. We went to them. We knew from the carving on the door-posts that they were Leif's. We went in. The rooms were empty. Along the shore and in the wood back of the house we found all of his men, dead. There was no living thing about."

Ingolf said no word, but his face was white, and his mouth was set. He went into the house and got his spears and his shield and said to his men:

"Follow me."

They put provisions into the boat and pushed off and sailed until they saw Leif's houses on the shore of the harbor. There they saw Leif and the men who were his friends, dead. Their swords and spears were gone. Ingolf walked through the houses calling on Helga and on the thralls, but no one answered. The storehouse was empty. The rich hangings were gone from the walls of the houses. There was nothing in the stables. The boat was gone.

Ingolf went out and stood on a high point of land that

jutted out into the water. Far along the coast he saw some little islands. He turned to his men and said:

"The thralls have done it. I think we shall find them on those islands."

Then he went back to Leif and stood looking at him.

"What a shame for so brave a man to fall by the hands of thralls! But I have found that such things always happen to men who do not sacrifice to the gods. Ah, Leif! I did not think when we made those vows of foster-brotherhood that this would ever happen. But do not fear. I remember my promise. I had thought that a man's blood is precious in this empty land, but my vow is more precious."

Now they laid all those men together and tied on their hell-shoes.

"I need my sword for your sake, foster-brother. I cannot give you that. But you shall have my spears and my drinking-horn," said Ingolf. "For surely Odin has chosen you for Valhalla, even though you did not sacrifice. You are too good a man to go to Niflheim. You would make times merry in Valhalla."

So Ingolf put his spears and his drinking-horn by Leif. Then the men raised a great mound over all the dead. After that they went aboard their boat and sailed for the islands that Ingolf had seen. It was evening when they reached them.

"I see smoke rising from that one," Ingolf said, pointing.

He steered for it. It was a steep rock like that one in the Faroes, but they found a harbor and landed and climbed the steep hill and came out on top. They saw the ten thralls sitting about a bonfire eating. Helga and the other women from Leif's house sat near, huddled together, white and frightened. One of the thralls gave a great laugh and shouted:

"This is better than pulling Leif's plow. To-morrow we will sail for Ireland with all his wealth."

"To-morrow you will be freezing in Niflheim," cried Ingolf, and he leaped among them swinging his sword, and all his men followed him, and they killed those thralls.

Then Ingolf turned to Helga. She threw herself into his arms and wept. But after a while she told him this story:

"When springtime came, Leif thought that he would sow wheat. He had but one ox. The others had died during the winter. So he set the thralls to help pull the plow. I saw their sour looks and was afraid, but Leif only laughed:

"'What else can thralls expect?' he said. 'Never fear them, good wife.'

"Now one day soon after that the thralls came running to the house calling out:

"'The ox is dead! The ox is dead!'

"Leif asked them about it. They said that a bear had come out of the woods and killed it, and that they had scared the beast away. They pointed out where it had gone. Then Leif called his men and said:

"'A hunt! I had not hoped for such great sport here. Ah, we will have a feast off that bear!'

"So they took their spears and went out into the woods. As soon as they were gone, the thralls came running into the house and took down all the swords and shields from the wall and ran out. In some way they met my lord and his men in the woods and killed them. Then they came back and took everything in the house and dragged us to the boat and sailed here."

"O my brother!" said Ingolf, "where is that song about 'those two foster-brothers, Ingolf and Leif, who made a new country in a wonderful land, and whose sons and grandsons are mighty men in Iceland'? But come home with me, Helga."

So they took the women and Leif's things and Leif's boat and sailed home. The next day after they came to Ingolf's house, Helga said:

"We have made your family larger, brother Ingolf. Will you not take Leif's two houses and live in them? He does not need them now. He would like you to have them."

"It would be pleasant to live there," Ingolf said. "I thank you."

So the next day they loaded everything aboard the two ships and sailed for Leif's house. There they stayed for a year. Ingolf still sent his thralls out to look for the pillars. He was careful always to have hay, so his cattle prospered. That spring he planted wheat, but it did not grow well.

"This is sickly stuff," Ingolf said. "It takes too much time and work. It is better to save the land for hay. Perhaps we can sometime go back to Norway for flour."

At last one day the thralls came home and said:

"We have found the pillars."

Ingolf jumped to his feet. He cried out:

"You have kept me waiting three years, Thor. But as soon as my house and temple are built, I will sacrifice to you three horses as a thank-offering."

"It is a long way off, master," the thralls said, "and we have found much better places in our walks about the island."

"Thor knows best," Ingolf answered. "I will settle where he leads me."

So that summer they loaded everything into the ships again and sailed west along the coast until they came to the place where the pillars were. The land there was low and green. On both sides were low hills. A little lake glistened back from shore. In the valley were hot springs, with steam rising from them.

"It looks like smoke," the men said. "It is very strange to see hot water and smoke come out of the ground."

In front of this green land was a good harbor with islands in it. Far over the sea toward the north shone a great ice-mountain.

"I like the place," Ingolf said. "I will make this land mine."

So he built fires at the mouth of the river near there, and stood by them and called out loudly:

"I have put my fire at the mouth of these rivers. All the land that they drain is mine, and no man shall claim it but me. I will call this place Reykjavik."

Then Ingolf built his feast hall. He himself carved the beams and the door-posts. Gaily painted dragons leaned out from the doors and stood up from the gables. Men and animals fought on the door-posts. For the doors he made at the forge great iron hinges. Their ends curved and spread all over the door. Near his feast hall he built a storehouse and a kitchen and a smithy and a stable and a bower for the women.

"We do not need a sleeping-house for guests," he said. "Who would be our guests?"

He roofed all his buildings with turf. It made them look like green mounds with gay carved and painted walls under them. He built also a temple, and on that was beautiful carving. In this he set up those statues that had been in his old temple. He put up, too, those pillars of his high seat that had been drifting about so long. Under them he laid the soil of Norway that he had brought in the little bronze chest.

"I have kept my vow, O Thor!" he cried.

Then he sacrificed three horses that he had promised to

Thor. After that was over, he said:

"Here is a good field for sport. Let us have some of the old games that we used to play at home. Who will wrestle with me?"

So they wrestled there and ran races and swam in the water. The women sat and looked on.

"Oh, this is good to see!" Helga cried. "We are as gay as we used to be in old Norway."

But it was not many weeks before Ingolf said:

"I wish that I might sometime see sails in that harbor. I wish that I might think, 'Around this point of land is another farm, and across the bay is another. I can go there when I am very lonely.' I wish that I might sometime be invited to a feast. I wish that I might sometimes hear the good, clanging music of weapons at play. It is a good land, but we have lived alone for four years. I am hungry for new faces and for tidings of Norway."

One night as he and his men sat about the long fire in the feast hall, a servant threw a great piece of wood upon the fire. It was streaked with faded paint and it showed bits of carving.

"See," said Ingolf, pointing to it, "see what is left of a good ship's prow! What lands have you seen, O dragon's head? What battles have you fought? What was your master's name? Where did the storm meet you? Perhaps he was coming to Iceland, comrades. Would it not have been pleasant to see his sail and to shake his hand and to welcome him to Iceland? But instead he is in Ran's caves, and only his broken prow has drifted here."

Now it was not many months after that when one of the men came running into the feast hall, shouting:

"A sail! a sail in the harbor!"

All those men gave a shout with no word in it, as though their hearts had leaped into their throats. They jumped up and ran to the shore and stood there with hungry eyes. When the men landed, those Icelanders clapped them on the shoulders, and tears ran down their faces. For a long time they could say nothing but "Welcome! Welcome!"

But after a while Ingolf led them to the feast hall and had a feast spread at once. While the thralls were at work, the men stood together and talked. Such a noise had never been in that hall before.

"We have already built our fires and claimed our land up the shore a way," the leader said. "Men in Norway talk much of Ingolf and Leif, and wonder what has happened to them."

Then Ingolf told them of all that had come to pass in Iceland; and then he asked of Norway.

"Ah! things are going from bad to worse," the newcomers said. "Harald grows mightier every day. A man dare not swing a sword now except for the king. We came here to get away from him. Many men are talking of Iceland. Soon the sea-road between here and Norway will be swarming with dragons."

And so it was. Ships also came from Ireland and from the Shetlands and the Orkneys.

"Harald has come west-over-seas," the men of these ships said, "and has laid his heavy hand upon the islands and put his earls over them. They are no place now for free men."

So by the time Ingolf was an old man, Iceland was no longer an empty land. Every valley was spotted with bright feast halls and temples. Horses and cattle pastured on the hillsides. Smoke curled up from kitchens and smithies. Gay ships sailed the waters, taking Iceland cloth and wool and Iceland fish and oil and the soft feathers of Iceland birds to Norway to sell, and bringing back wood and flour and grain.

When Ingolf died, his men drew up on the shore the boat in which he had come to Iceland. They painted it freshly and put new gold on it, so that it stood there a glittering dragon with head raised high, looking over the water. Old Sighvat lifted a huge stone and carried it to the ship's side. With all his strength he threw it into the bottom. The timbers cracked.

"If this ship moves from here," he said, "then I do not know how to moor a ship. It is Ingolf's grave."

Then men laid Ingolf upon his shield and carried him and placed him on the high deck in the stern near the pilot's seat where he had sat to steer to Iceland. They hung his sword over his shoulder. They laid his spear by his side. In his hand they put his mead-horn. Into the ship they set a great treasure-chest filled with beautiful clothes and bracelets and head-bands. Beside the treasure-chest they piled up many swords and spears and shields. They put gold-trimmed saddles and bridles upon three horses. Then they killed the horses and dragged them into the ship. They killed hunting-dogs and put them by the horses; for they said:

"All these things Ingolf will need in Valhalla. When he walks through the door of that feast hall, Odin must know that a rich and brave man comes. When he fights with those heroes during the day, he must have weapons worthy of him. He must have dogs for the hunt. When he feasts with those heroes at night he must wear rich clothes, so that those feasters shall know that he was a wealthy man and generous, and that his friends loved him."

Ingolf's son tied on his hell-shoes for the long journey.

"If these shoes come untied," he said, "I do not know how to fasten hell-shoes."

Then he went out of the ship and stood on the ground with his family. All the men of Iceland were there.

"This is a glorious sight," they said. "Surely no ship ever carried a richer load. Inside and out the boat blazes with gold and bronze, and, high over his riches, lies the great Ingolf, ready to take the tiller and guide to Valhalla, where all the heroes will rise up and shout him welcome."

Then the thralls heaped a mound of earth over the ship. This hill stood up against the sky and seemed to say: "Here lies a great man." Sighvat put a stone on the top, with runes on it telling whose grave it was. All this time a skald stood by and played on his harp and sang a song about that time when Ingolf came to Iceland. He called him the father of Iceland. People of that country still read an old story that the men of that long ago time wrote about Ingolf, and they love him because he was a brave man and "the first of men to come to Iceland."

ERIC THE RED

It was a spring day many years after Ingolf died. All the free-men in the west of Iceland had come to a meeting. Here they made laws and punished men for having done wrong. The meeting was over now. Men were walking about the plain and talking. Everybody seemed much excited. Voices were loud, arms were swinging.

"It was an unjust decision," some one cried. "Eric killed the men in fair fight. The judges outlawed him because they were afraid. His foe Thorgest has many rich and powerful men to back him."

"No, no!" said another. "Eric is a bloody man. I am glad he is out of Iceland."

Just then a big man with bushy red hair and beard stalked through the crowd. He looked straight ahead and scowled.

"There he goes," people said, and turned to look after him.

"His hands are as red as his beard," some said, and frowned.

But others looked at him and smiled, saying:

"He walks like Thor the Fearless."

"His story would make a fine song," one said. "As strong and as brave and as red as Thor! Always in a quarrel. A man of many places—Norway, the north of Iceland, the west of Iceland, those little islands off the shore of Iceland. Outlawed from all of them on account of his quarrels. Where will he go now, I wonder?"

This Eric strode down to the shore with his men follow-ing.

"He is in a black temper," they said. "We should best not

talk to him."

So they made ready the boat in silence. Eric got into the pilot's seat and they sailed off. Soon they pulled the ship up on their own shore. Eric strolled into his house and called for supper. When the drinking-horns had been filled and emptied, Eric pulled himself up and smiled and shouted out so that the great room was full of his big voice:

"There is no friend like mead. It always cheers a man's heart."

Then laughter and talking began in the hall because Eric's good temper had come back. After a while Eric said:

"Well, I must off somewhere. I have been driven about from place to place, like a seabird in a storm. And there is always a storm about me. It is my sword's fault. She is ever itching to break her peace-bands[14] and be out and at the play. She has shut Norway to me and now Iceland. Where will you go next, old comrade?" and he pulled out his sword and looked at it and smiled as the fire flashed on it.

"There are some of us who will follow you wherever you go, Eric," called a man from across the fire.

"Is it so?" Eric cried, leaping up. "Oh! then we shall have some merry times yet. Who will go with me?"

More than half the men in the hall jumped to their feet and waved their drinking-horns and shouted:

"I! I!"

Eric sat down in his chair and laughed.

"O you bloody birds of battle!" he cried. "Ever hungry for new frolic! Our swords are sisters in blood, and we are brothers in adventure. Do you know what is in my heart to do?"

He jumped to his feet, and his face glowed. Then he laughed as he looked at his men.

"I see the answer flashing from your eyes," he said, "that you will do it even if it is to go down to Niflheim and drag up Hela, the pale queen of the stiff dead."

His men pounded on the tables and shouted:

"Yes! Yes! Anywhere behind Eric!"

"But it is not to Niflheim," Eric laughed. "Did you ever hear that story that Gunnbiorn told? He was sailing for Iceland, but the fog came down, and then the wind caught him and blew him far off. While he drifted about he saw a strange land that rose up white and shining out of a blue sea. Huge ships of ice sailed out from it and met him. I mean to sail to that land."

A great shout went up that shook the rafters. Then the men sat and talked over plans. While they sat, a stranger came into the hall.

"I have no time to drink," he said. "I have a message from your friend Eyjolf. He says that Thorgest with all his men means to come here and catch you to-night. Eyjolf bids you come to him, and he will hide you until you are ready to start; for he loves you."

"Hunted like a wolf from corner to corner of the world!" Eric cried angrily. "Will they not even let me finish one feast?"

Then he laughed.

"But if I take my sport like a wolf, I must be hunted like one. So we shall sleep to-night in the woods about Eyjolf's house, comrades, instead of in these good beds. Well, we have done it before."

"And it is no bad place," cried some of the men.

"I always liked the stars better than a smoky house fire," said one.

"Can no bad fortune spoil your good nature?" laughed

Eric. "But now we are off. Let every man carry what he can."

So they quickly loaded themselves with clothes and gold and swords and spears and kettles of food. Eric led his wife Thorhild and his two young sons, Thorstein and Leif. All together they got into the boat and went to Eyjolf's farm. For a week or more they stayed in his woods, sometimes in a secret cave of his when they knew that Thorgest was about. And sometimes Eyjolf sent and said:

"Thorgest is off. Come to my house for a feast."

All this time they were making ready for the voyage, repairing the ship and filling it with stores. Word of what Eric meant to do got out, and men laughed and said:

"Is that not like Eric? What will he not do?"

Some men liked the sound of it, and they came to Eric and said:

"We will go with you to this strange land."

So all were ready and they pushed off with Eric's family aboard and those friends who had joined him. They took horses and cattle with them, and all kinds of tools and food.

"I do not well know where this land is," Eric said. "Gunnbiorn said only that he sailed east when he came home to Iceland. So I will steer straight west. We shall surely find something. I do not know, either, how long we must go."

So they sailed that strange ocean, never dreaming what might be ahead of them. They found no islands to rest on. They met heavy fogs.

One day as Eric sat in the pilot's seat, he said:

"I think that I see one of Gunnbiorn's ships of ice. Shall we sail up to her and see what kind of a craft she is?"

"Yes," shouted his men.

So they went on toward it.

"It sends out a cold breath," said one of the men.

They all wrapped their cloaks about them.

"It is a bigger boat than I ever saw before," said Eric. "The white mast stands as high as a hill."

"It must be giants that sail in it, frost giants," said another of the men.

But as they came nearer, Eric all at once laughed loudly and called out:

"By Thor, that Gunnbiorn was a foolish fellow. Why, look! It is only a piece of floating ice such as we sometimes see from Iceland. It is no ship, and there is no one on it."

His men laughed and one called to another and said:

"And you thought of frost giants!"

Then they sailed on for days and days. They met many of these icebergs. On one of them was a white bear.

"Yonder is a strange pilot," Eric laughed.

"I have seen bears come floating so to the north shore of Iceland," an old man said. "Perhaps they come from the land that we are going to find."

One day Eric said:

"I see afar off an iceberg larger than any one yet. Perhaps that is our white land."

But even as he said it he felt his boat swing under his hand as he held the tiller. He bore hard on the rudder, but he could not turn the ship.

"What is this?" he cried. "A strong river is running here. It is carrying our ship away from this land. I cannot make head against it. Out with the oars!"

So with oars and sail and rudder they fought against the current, but it took the boat along like a chip, and after a while they put up their oars and drifted.

"Luck has taken us into its own hands," Eric laughed. "But this is as good a way as another."

Sometimes they were near enough to see the land, then they were carried out into the sea and thought that they should never see any land again.

"Perhaps this river will carry us to a whirlpool and suck us under," the men said.

But at last Eric felt the current less strong under his hand.

"To the oars again!" he called.

So they fought with the current and sailed out of it and went on toward land. But when they reached the shore they found no place to go in. Steep black walls shot up from the sea. Nothing grew on them. When the men looked above the cliffs they saw a long line of white cutting the sky.

"It is a land of ice," they said.

They sailed on south, all the time looking for a place to go ashore.

"I am sick of this endless sea," Thorhild complained, "but this land is worse."

After a while they began to see small bays cut into the shore with little flat patches of green at their sides. They landed in these places and stretched and warmed themselves and ate.

"But these spots are only big enough for graves," the men said. "We can not live here."

So they went on again. All the time the weather was growing colder. Eric's people kept themselves wrapped in their cloaks and put scarfs around their heads.

"And it is still summer!" Thorhild said. "What will it be in winter?"

"We must find a place to build a house now before the winter comes on," said Eric. "We must not freeze here."

So they chose a little spot with hills about it to keep off the wind. They made a house out of stones; for there were many in that place. They lived there that winter. The sea for a long way out from shore froze so that it looked like white land. The men went out upon it to hunt white bear and seal. They ate the meat and wore the skins to keep them warm. The hardest thing was to get fuel for the fire. No trees grew there. The men found a little driftwood along the shore, but it was not enough. So they burned the bones and the fat of the animals they killed.

"It is a sickening smell," Thorhild said. "I have not been out of this mean house for weeks. I am tired of the darkness and the smoke and the cattle. And all the time I hear great noises, as though some giant were breaking this land into pieces."

"Ah, cheer up, good wife!" Eric laughed. "I smell better luck ahead."

Once Eric and his men climbed the cliffs and went back into the middle of the land. When they came home they had this to tell:

"It is a country of ice, shining white. Nothing grows on it but a few mosses. Far off it looks flat, but when you walk upon it, there are great holes and cracks. We could see nothing beyond. There seems to be only a fringe of land around the edge of an island of ice."

The winter nights were very long. Sometimes the sun showed for an hour, sometimes for only a few minutes, sometimes it did not show at all for a week. The men hunted by the bright shining of the moon or by the northern lights.

As it grew warmer the ice in the sea began to crack and move and melt and float away. Eric waited only until there was a clear passage in the water. Then he launched his boat, and they sailed southward again. At last they found a place that Eric liked.

"Here I will build my house," he said.

So they did and lived there that summer and pastured their cattle and cut hay for the winter and fished and hunted.

The next spring Eric said:

"The land stretches far north. I am hungry to know what is there."

Then they all got into the boat again and sailed north.

"We can leave no one here," Eric had said. "We cannot tell what might come between us. Perhaps giants or dragons or strange men might come out of this inland ice and kill our people. We must stay together."

Farther north they found only the same bare, frozen country. So after a while they sailed back to their home and lived there.

One spring after they had been in that land for four years, Eric said:

"My eyes are hungry for the sight of men and green fields again. My stomach is sick of seal and whale and bear. My throat is dry for mead. This is a bare and cold and hungry land. I will visit my friends in Iceland."

"And our swords are rusty with long resting," said his men. "Perhaps we can find play for them in Iceland."

"Now I have a plan," Eric suddenly said. "Would it not be pleasant to see other feast halls as we sail along the coast?"

"Oh! it would be a beautiful sight," his men said.

"Well," said Eric, "I am going to try to bring back some

neighbors from Iceland. Now we must have a name for our land. How does Greenland sound?"

His men laughed and said:

"It is a very white Greenland, but men will like the sound of it. It is better than Iceland."

So Eric and all his people sailed back and spent the winter with his friends.

"Ah! Eric, it is good to hear your laugh again," they said.

Eric was at many feasts and saw many men, and he talked much of his Greenland.

"The sea is full of whale and seals and great fish," he said. "The land has bear and reindeer. There are no men there. Come back with me and choose your land."

Many men said that they would do it. Some men went because they thought it would be a great frolic to go to a new country. Some went because they were poor in Iceland and thought:

"I can be no worse off in Greenland, and perhaps I shall grow rich there."

And some went because they loved Eric and wanted to be his neighbors.

So the next summer thirty-five ships full of men and women and goods followed Eric for Greenland. But they met heavy storms, and some ships were wrecked, and the men drowned. Other men grew heartsick at the terrible storm and the long voyage and no sight of land, and they turned back to Iceland. So of those thirty-five ships only fifteen got to Greenland.

"Only the bravest and the luckiest men come here," Eric said. "We shall have good neighbors."

Soon other houses were built along the fiords.

"It is pleasant to sail along the coast now," said Eric. "I see smoke rising from houses and ships standing on the shore and friendly hands waving."

LEIF AND HIS NEW LAND

Now Eric had lived in Greenland for fifteen years. His sons Thorstein and Leif had grown up to be big, strong men. One spring Leif said to his father:

"I have never seen Norway, our mother land. I long to go there and meet the great men and see the places that skalds sing about."

Eric answered:

"It is right that you should go. No man has really lived until he has seen Norway."

So he helped Leif fit out a boat and sent him off. Leif sailed for months. He passed Iceland and the Faroes and the Shetlands. He stopped at all of these places and feasted his mind on the new things. And everywhere men received him gladly; for he was handsome and wise. But at last he came near Norway. Then he stood up before the pilot's seat and sang loudly:

> *"My eyes can see her at last,*
> *The mother of mighty men,*
> *The field of famous fights.*
> *In the sky above I see*
> *Fair Asgard's shining roofs,*
> *The flying hair of Thor,*
> *The wings of Odin's birds,*
> *The road that heroes tread.*
> *I am here in the land of the gods,*
> *The land of mighty men."*

For a while he walked the land as though he were in a

dream. He looked at this and that and everything and loved them all because it was Norway.

"I will go to the king," he said.

He had never seen a king. There were no kings in Iceland or in Greenland. So he went to the city where the king had his fine house. The king's name was Olaf. He was a great-grandson of Harald Hairfair; for Harald had been dead a hundred years.

Now the king was going to hold a feast at night, and Leif put on his most beautiful clothes to go to it. He put on long tights of blue wool and a short jacket of blue velvet. He belted his jacket with a gold girdle. He had shoes of scarlet with golden clasps. He threw around himself a cape of scarlet velvet lined with seal fur. His long sword stuck out from under his cloak. On his head he put a knitted cap of bright colors. Then he walked to the king's feast hall and went through the door. It was a great hall, and it was full of richly-dressed men. The fires shone on so many golden head-bands and bracelets and so many glittering swords and spears on the wall, and there was so much noise of talking and laughing, that at first Leif did not know what to do. But at last he went and sat on the very end seat of the bench near him.

As the feast went on, King Olaf sat in his high seat and looked about the hall and noticed this one and that one and spoke across the fire to many. He was keen-eyed and soon saw Leif in his far seat.

"Yonder is some man of mark," he said to himself. "He is surely worth knowing. His face is not the face of a fool. He carries his head like a lord of men."

He sent a thrall and asked Leif to come to him. So Leif walked down the long hall and stood before the king.

"I am glad to have you for a guest," the king said. "What are your name and country?"

"I am Leif Ericsson, and I have come all the way from Greenland to see you and old Norway."

"From Greenland!" said the king. "It is not often that I see a Greenlander. Many come to Norway to trade, but they seldom come to the king's hall. I shall be glad to hear about your land. Come up and speak with me."

So Leif went up the steps of the high seat and sat down by the king and talked with him. When the feast was over the king said:

"You shall live at my court this winter, Leif Ericsson. You are a welcome guest."

So Leif stayed there that winter. When he started back in the spring, the king gave him two thralls as a parting gift.

"Let this gift show my love, Leif Ericsson," he said. "For your sake I shall not forget Greenland."

Leif sailed back again and had good luck until he was past Iceland. Then great winds came out of the north and tossed his ship about so that the men could do nothing. They were blown south for days and days. They did not know where they were. Then they saw land, and Leif said:

"Surely luck has brought us also to a new country. We will go in and see what kind of a place it is."

So he steered for it. As they came near, the men said:

"See the great trees and the soft, green shore. Surely this is a better country than Greenland or than Iceland either."

When they landed they threw themselves upon the ground.

"I never lay on a bed so soft as this grass," one said.

"Taller trees do not grow in Norway," said another.

"There is no stone here as in Norway, but only good black dirt," Leif said. "I never saw so fertile a land before."

The men were hungry and set about building a fire.

"There is no lack of fuel here," they said.

They stayed many days in this country and walked about to see what was there. A German, named Tyrker, was with Leif. He was a little man with a high forehead and a short nose. His eyes were big and rolling. He had lived with Eric for many years, and had taken care of Leif when he was a little boy. So Leif loved him.

Now one day they had been wandering about and all came back to camp at night except Tyrker. When Leif looked around on his comrades, he said:

"Where is Tyrker?"

No one knew. Then Leif was angry.

"Is a man of so little value in this empty land that you would lose one?" he said. "Why did you not keep together? Did you not see that he was gone? Why did you not set out to look for him? Who knows what terrible thing may have happened to him in these great forests?"

Then he turned and started out to hunt for him. His men followed, silent and ashamed. They had not gone far when they saw Tyrker running toward them. He was laughing and talking to himself. Leif ran to him and put his arms about him with gladness at seeing him.

"Why are you so late?" he asked. "Where have you been?"

But Tyrker, still smiling and nodding his head, answered in German. He pointed to the woods and laughed and rolled his eyes. Again Leif asked his question and put his hand on Tyrker's shoulder as though he would shake him. Then Tyrker answered in the language of Iceland:

"I have not been so very far, but I have found something wonderful."

"What is it?" cried the men.

"I have found grapes growing wild," answered Tyrker, and he laughed, and his eyes shone.

"It cannot be," Leif said.

Grapes do not grow in Greenland nor in Iceland nor even in Norway. So it seemed a wonderful thing to these Norsemen.

"Can I not tell grapes when I see them?" cried Tyrker. "Did I not grow up in Germany, where every hillside is covered with grapevines? Ah! it seems like my old home."

"It is wonderful," Leif said. "I have heard travelers tell of seeing grapes growing, but I myself never saw it. You shall take us to them early in the morning, Tyrker."

So in the morning they went back into the woods and saw the grapes. They ate of them.

"They are like food and drink," they cried.

That day Leif said:

"We spent most of the summer on the ocean. Winter will soon be coming on and the sea about Greenland will be frozen. We must start back. I mean to take some of the things of this land to show to our people at home. We will fill the rowboat with grapes and tow it behind us. The ship we will load with logs from these great trees. That will be a welcome shipload in Greenland, where we have neither trees nor vines. Now half of you shall gather grapes for the next few days, and the other half shall cut timber."

So they did, and after a week sailed off. The ship was full of lumber, and they towed the rowboat loaded with grapes. As they looked back at the shore, Leif said:

"I will call this country Wineland for the grapes that

grow there."

One of the men leaped upon the gunwale and leaned out, clinging to the sail, and sang:

> *"Wineland the good, Wineland the warm,*
> *Wineland the green, the great, the fat.*
> *Our dragon fed and crawls away*
> *With belly stuffed and lazy feet.*
> *How long her purple, trailing tail!*
> *She fed and grew to twice her size."*

Then all the men waved their hands to the shore and gave a great shout for that good land.

For all that voyage they had fair weather and sailed into Eric's harbor before the winter came. Eric saw the ship and ran down to the shore. He took Leif into his arms and said:

"Oh, my son, my old eyes ached to see you. I hunger to hear of all that you have seen and done."

"Luck has followed me all the way," said Leif. "See what I have brought home."

The Greenlanders looked.

"Lumber! lumber!" they cried. "Oh! it is better stuff than gold."

Then they saw the grapes and tasted them.

"Surely you must have plundered Asgard," they said, smacking their lips.

At the feast that night Eric said:

"Leif shall sit in the place of honor."

So Leif sat in the high seat opposite Eric. All men thought him a handsome and wise man. He told them of the storm and of Wineland.

"No man would ever need a cloak there. The soil is richer than the soil of Norway. Grain grows wild, and you yourselves saw the grapes that we got from there. The forests are without end. The sea is full of fish."

The Greenlanders listened with open mouths to all this. They turned and talked to Leif's ship-comrades who were scattered among them.

Leif noticed two strangers, an old man who sat at Eric's side and a young woman on the cross-bench. He turned to his brother Thorstein who sat next to him.

"Who are these strangers?" he asked.

"Thorbiorn and his daughter Gudrid," Thorstein answered. "They landed here this spring. I never saw our father more glad of anything than to see this Thorbiorn. They were friends before we left Iceland. When they saw each other again they could not talk enough of old times. In the spring Eric means to give him a farm up the fiord a way. It seems that this Thorbiorn comes of a good family that has been rich and great in Iceland for years. And Thorbiorn himself was rich when our father knew him, and was much honored by all men. But ill luck came, and he grew poor. This hurt his pride. 'I will not stay in Iceland and be a beggar,' he said to himself. 'I will not have men look at me and say, "He is not what his father was." I will go to my friend Eric the Red in Greenland.'

"Then he got ready a great feast and invited all his friends. It was such a feast as had not been in Iceland for years. Thorbiorn spent on it all the wealth that he had left. For he said to himself, 'I will not leave in shame. Men shall remember my last feast.' After that he set out and came to Greenland.

"Is not Gudrid beautiful? And she is wise. I mean to marry her, if her father will permit it."

Now Leif settled down in Greenland and became a great man there. He was so busy and he grew so rich that he did not think of going to Wineland again. But people could not forget his story. Many nights as men sat about the long fires they talked of that wonderful land and wished to see it.

WINELAND THE GOOD

On an autumn, a year or two after Leif came home, Eric and his men saw two large ships come to land not far down the shore from the house.

"They look like trading ships," Eric said. "Let us go down to see them."

"I will go, too," Gudrid said. "Perhaps they will have rich cloth and jewelry. It is long since I had my eyes on a new dress."

So they all went down and found two large trading ships lying in the water. A great many men were on the shore making a fire.

"Welcome to Greenland!" called Eric. "What are your names and your country?"

Then a fine, big man walked out from among the men and went up to Eric.

"I am Thorfinn," he said, "a trader. I sailed this summer from Iceland with forty men and a shipload of goods. On the sea I met this other ship from Iceland. The master is Biarni. Come and look at my goods."

So he rowed Eric and Gudrid out and they went aboard his boat. Thorfinn opened his chests and showed Eric gleaming swords and bracelets and axes and farm tools. But before Gudrid he spread beautiful cloth and gold embroidery and golden necklaces. As they looked, he told of doings in Iceland and asked of Greenland.

"We never see such things as these in this bare land," Gudrid said, as she smoothed a beautiful dress of purple velvet. "I envy the women of Iceland their fair clothes."

"There is no need of that," Thorfinn said, "for this dress

is yours and anything else from my chests that you like. Here is a necklace that I beg you to take. It did not have a fairer mistress in Greece where I got it."

"You are a very generous trader," Gudrid said.

Then Thorfinn gave Eric a great sword with a gold-studded scabbard. After a while he took them to Biarni's ship. He also gave them gifts. They all talked and laughed much while they were together.

"You are merry comrades," Eric said. "I ask you both and all your men to spend the winter at my house. You can put your goods into my storehouses."

"By my sword! a generous offer," said Thorfinn. "As for me, I am happy to come."

Biarni and all the rest said the same thing. Thorfinn walked to the house with Eric and Gudrid, while the other men sailed to the ship-sheds and pulled their boats under them.

Then Thorfinn saw to the unloading and storing of his goods.

"Is this Gudrid your daughter?" he asked of Eric one day.

"She is the widow of my son Thorstein," Eric said. "He died the same winter that they were married. Her father, too, died not long ago. So Gudrid lives with me."

Now all that winter until Yule-time Eric spread a good feast every night. There was laughter through his house all the time. Often at the feasts the men cast lots to see whether they might sit on the cross-bench with the women. Sometimes it was Thorfinn's luck to sit by Gudrid. Then they talked gaily and drank together.

At last Yule was coming near. Eric went about the house gloomy then. One day Thorfinn put his hand on Eric's shoulder and said:

"Something is troubling you, Eric. We have all noticed that you are not gay as you used to be. Tell me what is the matter."

"You have carried yourselves like noble men in my house," Eric answered. "I am proud to have you for guests. Now I am ashamed that you should not find a house worthy of you. I am ashamed that when you leave me you will have to say that you never spent a worse Yule than you did with Eric the Red in Greenland. For my cupboards are empty."

"Oh, that is easily mended," Thorfinn said. "No house could feed eighty men so long and not feel it. I never knew so generous a host before. But I have flour and grain and mead in my boat. You are welcome to all of it. You have only to open the doors of your own storehouses. It is a little gift."

So Eric used those things, and there was never a merrier Yule feast than in his house that winter.

When Yule was over, Thorfinn said to Eric:

"Gudrid is a beautiful and wise woman. I wish to have her for my wife."

"You seem to be a man worthy of her," Eric said.

So that winter Gudrid and Thorfinn were married and lived at Eric's house.

One day Thorfinn said to Eric:

"I have heard much of this wonderful Wineland since I have been here. It seems to me that it is worth while to go and see more of it."

"My son Thorstein and I tried it once," said Eric. "It was the year after Leif came back. We set out with a fair ship and with glad hearts, but we tossed about all summer on the sea and got nowhere. We were wet with storm, lean with hunger and illness, and heartsick at our bad luck."

"And yet," Thorfinn said, "another time we might have better weather. I have never seen so fair a land as this seems to be."

Then he went to Leif and talked long with him. Leif told him in what direction he had sailed to come home, and how the shores looked that he had passed.

"I think I could find my way," Thorfinn said. "My heart moves me to try this frolic."

He spoke to Gudrid about it.

"Oh, yes!" she cried. "Let us go. It is long since I felt a boat leaping under me. I am tired of sitting still. I want to feel the warm days and see the soft grass and the high trees and taste the grapes of this Wineland the Good."

Then he talked with his men and with Biarni.

"We are ready," they all said. "We are only waiting for a leader."

"Then let us go!" cried Thorfinn.

So in the spring they fitted up their two ships and put into them provisions and a few cattle. Some of Eric's men also got ready a boat, so that three ships set sail from Eric's harbor carrying one hundred and sixty men to Wineland. As they started, Gudrid stood on the deck and sang:

> *"I will feast my eyes on new things—*
> *On mighty trees and purple grapes,*
> *On beds of flowers and soft grass.*
> *I will sun myself in a warm land."*

They sailed on and past those shores that Leif had spoken of. Whenever they saw any interesting place they sailed in and looked about and rested there.

They had gone far south, past many fair shores with woods on them, when Gudrid said one day:

"This is a beautiful bay with a smooth, green field by it, and the great mountains far back. I should like to stay there for a little while."

So they sailed in and drew their ships up on shore. They put up the awnings in them.

"These shall be our houses," Thorfinn said.

They were strange-looking houses—shining dragons with gay backs lying on the yellow sand. Near them the Norsemen lighted fires and cooked their supper. That night they slept in the ships. In the morning Gudrid said:

"I long to see what is back of that mountain."

So they all climbed it. When they stood on the top they could see far over the country.

"There is a lake that we must see," Thorfinn said.

"I should like to sail around that bay," said Biarni, pointing.

"I am going to walk up that valley yonder," one of the men said.

And everyone saw some place where he would like to go. So for all that summer they camped in that spot and went about the country seeing new things. They hunted in the woods and caught rabbits and birds and sometimes bears and deer. Every day some men rowed out to sea and fished. There was an island in the bay where thousands of birds had their nests. The men gathered eggs here.

"We have more to eat than we had in Greenland or Iceland," Thorfinn said, "and need not work at all. It is all play."

Near the end of summer Thorfinn spoke to his comrades.

"Have we not seen everything here? Let us go to a new

place. We have not yet found grapes."

Thorfinn and Biarni and all their men sailed south again. But some of Eric's men went off in their boat another way. Years afterward the Greenlanders heard that they were shipwrecked and made slaves in Ireland.

After Thorfinn and Biarni had sailed for many days they landed on a low, green place. There were hills around it. A little lake was there.

"What is growing on those hillsides?" Thorfinn said, shading his eyes with his hand.

He and some others ran up there. The people on shore heard them shout. Soon they came running back with their hands full of something.

"Grapes! Grapes!" they were shouting.

All those people sat down and ate the grapes and then went to the hillside and picked more.

"Now we are indeed in Wineland," they said. "It is as wonderful as Leif's stories. Surely we must stay here for a long time."

The very next day they went into the woods and began to cut out lumber. The huts that they built were little things. They had no windows, and in the doorways the men hung their cloaks instead of doors.

"We can be out in the air so much in this warm country," said Gudrid, "that we do not need fine houses."

The huts were scattered all about, some on the side of the lake, some at the shore of the harbor, some on the hillside. Gudrid had said:

"I want to live by the lake where I can look into the green woods and hear sweet bird-noises."

So Thorfinn built his hut there.

As they sat about the campfire one night, Biarni said:

"It is strange that so good a land should be empty. I suppose that these are the first houses that were ever built in Wineland. It is wonderful to think that we are alone here in this great land."

All that winter no snow fell. The cattle pastured on the grass.

"To think of the cold, frozen winters in Greenland!" Gudrid said. "Oh! this is the sun's own land."

In the beginning of that winter a little son was born to Gudrid and Thorfinn.

"A health to the first Winelander!" the men shouted and drank down their wine; for they had made some from Wineland grapes.

"Will he be the father of a great country, as Ingolf was?" Biarni mused.

Gudrid looked at her baby and smiled.

"You will be as sunny as this good land, I hope," she said.

They named him Snorri. He grew fast and soon crept along the yellow sand, and toddled among the grapevines, and climbed into the boats and learned to talk. The men called him the "Wineland king."

"I never knew a baby before," one of the men said.

"No," said another. "Swords are jealous. But when they are in their scabbards, we can do other things, even play with babies."

"I wonder whether I have forgotten how to swing my sword in this quiet land," another man said.

One spring morning when the men got up and went out from their huts to the fires to cook they saw a great many canoes in the harbor. Men were in them paddling toward shore.

"What is this?" cried the Norsemen to one another. "Where did they come from? Are they foes? Who ever saw such boats before? The men's faces are brown."

"Let every man have his sword ready," cried Thorfinn. "But do not draw until I command. Let us go to meet them."

So they went and stood on the shore. Soon the men from the canoes landed and stood looking at the Norsemen. The strangers' skin was brown. Their faces were broad. Their hair was black. Their bodies were short. They wore leather clothes. One man among them seemed to be chief. He spread out his open hands to the Norsemen.

"He is showing us that he has no weapons," Biarni said. "He comes in peace."

Then Thorfinn showed his empty hands and asked:

"What do you want?"

The stranger said something, but the Norsemen could not understand. It was some new language. Then the chief pointed to one of the huts and walked toward it. He and his men walked all around it and felt of the timber and went into it and looked at all the things there—spades and cloaks and drinking-horns. As they looked they talked together. They went to all the other huts and looked at everything there. One of them found a red cloak. He spread it out and showed it to the others. They all stood about it and looked at it and felt of it and talked fast.

"They seem to like my cloak," Biarni said.

One of the strangers went down to their canoes and soon came back with an armload of furs—fox-skins, otter-skins, beaver-skins. The chief took some and held them out to Thorfinn and hugged the cloak to him.

"He wants to trade," Thorfinn said. "Will you do it, Biarni?"

"Yes," Biarni answered, and took the furs.

"If they want red stuff, I have a whole roll of red cloth that I will trade," one of the other men said.

He went and got it. When the strangers saw it they quickly held out more furs and seemed eager to trade. So Thorfinn cut the cloth into pieces and sold every scrap. When the strangers got it they tied it about their heads and seemed much pleased.

While this trading was going on and everybody was good-natured, a bull of Thorfinn's ran out of the woods bellowing and came towards the crowd. When the strangers heard it and saw it they threw down whatever was in their hands and ran to their canoes and paddled off as fast as they could.

The Norsemen laughed.

"We have lost our customers," Biarni said.

"Did they never see a bull before?" laughed one of the men.

Now after three weeks the Norsemen saw canoes in the bay again. This time it was black with them, there were so many. The people in them were all making a horrible shout.

"It is a war-cry," Thorfinn said, and he raised a red shield. "They are surely twenty to our one, but we must fight. Stand in close line and give them a taste of your swords."

Even as he spoke a great shower of stones fell upon them. Some of the Norsemen were hit on the head and knocked down. Biarni got a broken arm. Still the storm came fast. The strangers had landed and were running toward the Norsemen. They threw their stones with sling-shots, and they yelled all the time.

"Oh, this is no kind of fighting for brave men!" Thorfinn

cried angrily.

The Norsemen's swords swung fast, and many of the strangers died under them, but still others came on, throwing stones and swinging stone axes. The horrible yelling and the strange things that the savages did frightened the Norsemen.

"These are not men," some one cried.

Then those Norsemen who had never been afraid of anything turned and ran. But when they came to the top of a rough hill Thorfinn cried:

"What are we doing? Shall we die here in this empty land with no one to bury us? We are leaving our women."

Then one of the women ran out of the hut where they were hiding.

"Give me a sword!" she cried. "I can drive them back. Are Norsemen not better than these savages?"

Then those warriors stopped, ashamed, and stood up before the wild men and fought so fiercely that the strangers turned and fled down to their canoes and paddled away.

"Oh, I am glad they are gone!" Thorfinn said. "It was an ugly fight."

"Thor would not have loved that battle," one said.

"It was no battle," another replied. "It was like fighting against an army of poisonous flies."

The Norsemen were all worn and bleeding and sore. They went to their huts and dressed their wounds, and the women helped them. At supper that night they talked about the fight for a long time.

"I will not stay here," Gudrid said. "Perhaps these wild men have gone away to get more people and will come back and kill us. Oh! they are ugly."

"Perhaps brown faces are looking at us now from behind

the trees in the woods back there," said Biarni.

It was the wish of all to go home. So after a few days they sailed back to Greenland with good weather all the way. The people at Eric's house were very glad to see them.

"We were afraid you had died," they said.

"And I thought once that we should never leave Wineland alive," Thorfinn answered.

Then they told all the story.

"I wonder why I had no such bad luck," Leif said. "But you have a better shipload than I got."

He was looking at the bundles of furs and the kegs of wine.

"Yes," said Thorfinn, "we have come back richer than when we left. But I will never go again for all the skins in the woods."

The next summer Thorfinn took Gudrid and Snorri and all his people and sailed back to Iceland, his home. There he lived until he died. People looked at him in wonder.

"That is the man who went to Wineland and fought with wild men," they said. "Snorri is his son. He is the first and last Winelander, for no one will ever go there again. It will be an empty and forgotten land."

And so it was for a long time. Some wise men wrote down the story of those voyages and of that land, and people read the tale and liked it, but no one remembered where the place was. It all seemed like a fairy tale. Long afterwards, however, men began to read those stories with wide-open eyes and to wonder. They guessed and talked together, and studied this and that land, and read the story over and over. At last they have learned that Wineland was in America, on the eastern shore of the United States, and they have called Snorri the first American, and have put up statues of Leif Ericsson, the first comer to America.

THE ISLE OF UDRÖST

Once upon a time there lived at Vaerö, not far from Röst, a poor fisherman, named Isaac. He had nothing but a boat and a couple of goats, which his wife fed as well as she could with fish leavings, and with the grass she was able to gather on the surrounding hills; but his whole hut was full of hungry children. Yet he was always satisfied with what God sent him. The only thing that worried him was his inability to live at peace with his neighbor. The latter was a rich man, thought himself entitled to far more than such a beggarly fellow as Isaac, and wanted to get him out of the way, in order to take for himself the anchorage before Isaac's hut.

One day Isaac had put out a few miles to sea to fish, when suddenly a dark fog fell, and in a flash such a tremendous storm broke, that he had to throw all his fish overboard in order to lighten ship and save his life. Even then it was very hard to keep the boat afloat; but he steered a careful course between and across the mountainous waves, which seemed ready to swallow him from moment to moment. After he had kept on for five or six hours in this manner, he thought that he ought to touch land somewhere. But time went by, and the storm and fog grew worse and worse. Then he began to realize that either he was steering out to sea, or that the wind had veered, and at last he made sure the latter was the case; for he sailed on and on without a sight of land. Suddenly he heard a hideous cry from the stern of the boat, and felt certain that it was the *drang*, who was singing his death-song. Then he prayed God to guard his wife and children, for he thought his last hour had come. As he sat there and prayed, he made out something black; but when his boat drew nearer, he noticed that it was only three cormorants, sitting on a piece of drift-wood and—swish! he had passed them. Thus he sailed for a long time, and grew so hungry, so thirsty and so weary that he did not know what to do; for the most part he sat with the rudder in his hand and slept. But all of a sudden the boat ran up on a beach and stopped. Then Isaac opened his eyes. The sun broke through the fog, and shone on a beautiful land. Its hills and mountains were green to their very tops, fields and meadows lay among their slopes, and he seemed to breathe a fragrance of flowers and grass sweeter than any he had ever known before.

"God be praised, now I am safe, for this is Udröst!" said Isaac to himself. Directly ahead of him lay a field of barley, with ears so large and heavy that he had never seen their like, and through the barley-field a narrow path led to a green turf-roofed cottage of clay, that rose above the field, and on the roof of the cottage grazed a white goat with gilded horns, and an udder as large as that of the largest cow. Before the door sat a little man clad in blue, puffing away at a little pipe. He had a beard so long and so large that it hung far down upon his breast.

"Welcome to Udröst, Isaac!" said the man.

"Good day to you, father," said Isaac, "and do you know me?"

"It might be that I do," said the man. "I suppose you want to stay here overnight?"

"That would suit me very well, father," was Isaac's reply.

"The trouble is with my sons, for they cannot bear the smell of a Christian," answered the man. "Did you meet them?"

"No, I only met three cormorants, who were sitting on a piece of drift-wood and croaking," was Isaac's reply.

"Well, those were my sons," said the man, and emptied his pipe, "and now come into the house, for I think you must be hungry and thirsty."

"I'll take that liberty, father," said Isaac.

When the man opened the door, everything within was so beautiful that Isaac could not get over his admiration. He had never seen anything like it. The table was covered with the finest dishes, bowls of cream, and salmon and game, and liver dumplings with syrup, and cheese as well, and there were whole piles of doughnuts, and there was mead, and everything else that is good. Isaac ate and drank bravely, and yet his plate was never empty; and no matter how much he drank, his glass was always full. The man neither ate much nor said much; but suddenly they heard a noise and clamor before the house, and the man went out. After a time he returned with his three sons, and Isaac trembled inwardly when they came through the door; but their father must have quieted them, for they were very friendly and amiable, and told Isaac he must use his guest-right, and sit down and drink with them; for Isaac had risen to leave the table, saying he had satisfied his hunger. But he gave in to them, and they drank mead together, and became good friends. And they said that Isaac must go fishing with them, so that he would have something to take with him when he went home.

The first time they put out a great storm was raging. One of the sons sat at the rudder, the second at the bow, and the third in the middle; and Isaac had to work with the bailing-can until he dripped perspiration. They sailed as though they were mad. They never reefed a sail, and when the boat was full of water, they danced on the crests of the waves, and slid down them so that the water in the stern spurted up like a fountain.

After a time the storm subsided, and they began to fish. And the sea was so full of fish that they could not even put out an anchor, since mountains of fish were piled up beneath them. The sons of Udröst drew up one fish after another. Isaac knew his business; but he had taken along his own fishing-tackle, and as soon as a fish bit he let go again, and at last he had caught not a single one. When the boat was filled, they sailed home again to Udröst, and the sons cleaned the fish, and laid them on the stands. Meanwhile Isaac had complained to their father of his poor luck. The man promised that he should do better next time, and gave him a couple of hooks; and the next time they went out to fish, Isaac caught just as many as the others, and when they reached home, he was given three stands of fish as his share.

At length Isaac began to get homesick, and when he was about to leave, the man made him a present of a new fishing-boat, full of meal, and tackle and other useful things. Isaac thanked him repeatedly, and the man invited him to come back when the season opened again, since he himself was going to take a cargo to Bergen, in the second *stevne*, and Isaac could go along and sell his fish there himself. Isaac was more than willing, and asked him what course he should set when he again wanted to reach Udröst. "All you need do is to follow the cormorant when he heads for the open sea, then you will be on the right course," said the man. "Good luck on your way!"

But when Isaac got underway, and looked around, there was no Udröst in sight; far and wide, all around him, he saw no more than the ocean.

When the time came, Isaac sailed to join the man of Udröst's fishing-craft. But such a craft he had never seen before. It was two hails long, so that when the steersman, who was on look-out in the stern, wanted to call out something to the rower, the latter could not hear him. So they had stationed another man in the middle of the ship, close by the mast, who had to relay the steersman's call to the rower, and even he had to shout as loudly as he could in order to make himself heard.

Isaac's share was laid down in the forepart of the boat; and he himself took down the fish from the stands; yet he could not understand how it was that the stands were continually filled with fresh fish, no matter how many he took away, and when he sailed away they were still as full as ever. When he reached Bergen, he sold his fish, and got so much money for them that he was able to buy a new schooner, completely fitted out, and with a cargo to boot, as the man of Udröst had advised him. Late in the evening, when he was about to sail for home, the man came aboard and told him never to forget those who survived his neighbor, for his neighbor himself had died; and then he wished Isaac all possible success and good fortune for his schooner, in advance. "All is well, and all stands firm that towers in the air," said he, and what he meant was that there was one aboard whom none could see, but who would support the mast on his back, if need be.

Since that time fortune was Isaac's friend. And well he knew why this was so, and never forgot to prepare something good for whoever held the winter watch, when the schooner was drawn up on land in the fall. And every Christmas night there was the glow and shimmer of light, the sound of fiddles and music, of laughter and merriment, and of dancing on the deserted schooner.

THE NEIGHBOR
UNDERGROUND

Once upon a time there was a peasant who lived in Tele-marken, and had a big farm; yet he had nothing but bad luck with his cattle, and at last lost his house and holding. He had scarcely anything left, and with the little he had, he bought a bit of land that lay off to one side, far away from the city, in the wildwood and the wilderness. One day, as he was passing through his farm-yard, he met a man.

"Good-day, neighbor!" said the man.

"Good-day," said the peasant, "I thought I was all alone here. Are you a neighbor of mine?"

"You can see my homestead over yonder," said the man. "It is not far from your own." And there lay a farm-holding such as he had never before seen, handsome and prosperous, and in fine condition. Then he knew very well that this must be one of the underground people; yet he had no fear, but invited his neighbor in to drink a glass with him, and the neighbor seemed to enjoy it.

"Listen," said the neighbor, "there is one thing you must do for me as a favor."

"First let me know what it is," said the peasant.

"You must shift your cow-stable, because it is in my way," was the answer he gave the peasant.

"No, I'll not do that," said the peasant. "I put it up only this summer, and the winter is coming on. What am I to do with my cattle then?"

"Well, do as you choose; but if you do not tear it down, you will live to regret it," said his neighbor. And with that he went his way.

The peasant was surprised at this, and did not know what to do. It seemed quite foolish to him to start in to tear down his stable when the long winter night was approaching, and besides, he could not count on help.

One day as he was standing in his stable, he sank through the ground. Down below, in the place to which he had come, everything was unspeakably handsome. There was nothing which was not of gold or of silver. Then the man who had called himself his neighbor came along, and bade him sit down. After a time food was brought in on a silver platter, and mead in a silver jug, and the neighbor invited him to draw up to the table and eat. The peasant did not dare refuse, and sat down at the table; but just as he was about to dip his spoon into the dish, something fell down into his food from above, so that he lost his appetite. "Yes, yes," said the man, "now you can see why we don't like your stable. We can never eat in peace, for as soon as we sit down to a meal, dirt and straw fall down, and no matter how hungry we may be, we lose our appetites and cannot eat. But if you will do me the favor to set up your stable elsewhere, you shall never go short of pasture nor good crops, no matter how old you may grow to be. But if you won't, you shall know naught but lean years all your life long."

When the peasant heard that, he went right to work pulling down his stable, to put it up again in another place. Yet he could not have worked alone, for at night, when all slept, the building of the new stable went forward just as it did by day, and well he knew his neighbor was helping him.

Nor did he regret it later, for he had enough of feed and corn, and his cattle waxed fat. Once there was a year of scarcity, and feed was so short that he was thinking of selling or slaughtering half his herd. But one morning, when the milkmaid went into the stable, the dog was gone, and with him all the cows and the calves. She began to cry and told the peasant. But he thought to himself, that it was probably his neighbor's doings, who had taken the cattle to pasture. And sure enough, so it was; for toward spring, when the woods grew green, he saw the dog come along, barking and leaping, by the edge of the forest, and after him followed all the cows and calves, and the whole herd was so fat it was a pleasure to look at it.

THE SECRET CHURCH

Once the schoolmaster of Etnedal was staying in the mountains to fish. He was very fond of reading, and so he always carried one book or another along with him, with which he could lie down, and which he read on holidays, or when the weather forced him to stay in the little fishing-hut. One Sunday morning, as he was lying there reading, it seemed as though he could hear church bells; sometimes they sounded faintly, as though from a great distance; at other times the sound was clear, as though carried by the wind. He listened long and with surprise; and did not trust his ears—for he knew that it was impossible to hear the bells of the parish church so far out among the hills—yet suddenly they sounded quite clearly on his ear. So he laid aside his book, stood up and went out. The sun was shining, the weather was fine, and one group of churchgoers after another passed him in their Sunday clothes, their hymnbooks in their hands. A little further on in the forest, where he had never before seen anything but trees and brush, stood an old wooden church. After a time the priest came by, and he was so old and decrepit that his wife and daughter led him. And when they came to the spot where the schoolmaster was standing, they stopped and invited him to come to church and hear mass. The schoolmaster thought for a moment; but since it occurred to him that it might be amusing to see how these people worshiped God, he said he would go along, if he did not thereby suffer harm. No, no harm should come to him, said they, but rather a blessing. In the church all went forward in a quiet and orderly manner, there were neither dogs nor crying children to disturb the service, and the singing was good—but he could not make out the words. When the priest had been led to the pulpit he delivered what seemed to the listening schoolmaster a really fine and edifying sermon—but one, it appeared to him, of quite a peculiar trend of thought, which he was not always able to follow. Nor did the "Our Father in heaven ..." sound just right, and the "Deliver us from evil ..." he did not hear at all. Nor was the name of Jesus uttered; and at the close no blessing was spoken.

When mass had been said, the schoolmaster was invited to the parsonage. He gave the same answer he had already returned, that he would be glad to go if he suffered no harm thereby. And as before, they assured him he would not lose; but rather gain thereby. So he went with them to the parsonage, just such an attractive and well-built parsonage like most in the neighborhood. It had a garden with flowers and apple-trees, with a neat lattice fence around it. They invited him to dinner, and the dinner was well cooked and carefully prepared. As before, he said that he would gladly accept their invitation, if he came to no harm thereby, and was given the same reply. So he ate with them, and said later that he had noticed no difference between this food and the Christian dinner he had received when, once or twice, he had been asked to dinner by the priest of the village church. When he had drunk his coffee, the wife and daughter drew him aside into another room, and the wife complained that her husband had grown so old and decrepit that he could not keep up much longer. Then she began to say that the schoolmaster was such a strong and able man, and finally, that she and her daughter would like to have him for priest, and whether he would not stay and succeed the old father. The schoolmaster objected that he was no scholar. But they insisted that he had more learning than was needed in their case, for they never had any visits from the bishop, nor did the dean ever hold a chapter, for of all such things they knew nothing. When the schoolmaster heard that, he said that even though he had the necessary scholarship, he doubted very much that he had the right vocation, and since this was a most important matter for him and for them, it would be unwise to act too hurriedly, so he would ask for a year to think it over. When he had said that, he found himself standing by a pond in the wood, and could see neither church nor parsonage. So he thought the matter was at an end. But a year later, just as the term he had set was up, he was working on a house, for during the school vacation he busied himself either with fishing or carpentering. He was just straddling a wall when he saw the pastor's daughter, the one whom he had seen in the mountains, coming straight toward him. She asked him if he had thought over the matter. "Yes," said he, "I have thought it over, but I cannot; since I cannot answer for it before God and my own conscience." That very moment the pastor's daughter from underground vanished; but immediately after he cut himself in the knee with the ax in such wise that he remained a cripple for life.

THE COMRADE

Once upon a time there was a peasant boy, who dreamed that he would get a princess, from far, far away, and that she was as white as milk, and as red as blood, and so rich that her riches had no end. When he woke, it seemed to him as though she were still standing before him, and she was so beautiful and winning that he could not go on living without her. So he sold all that he had, and went forth to look for her. He wandered far, and at last, in the winter-time, came into a land where the roads all ran in straight lines, and made no turns. After he had wandered straight ahead for full three months, he came to a city. And there a great block of ice lay before the church door, and in the middle of it was a corpse, and the whole congregation spat at it as the people passed by. This surprised the youth, and when the pastor came out of the church, he asked him what it meant. "He was a great evil-doer," replied the pastor, "who has been executed because of his misdeeds, and has been exposed here in shame and derision." "But what did he do?" asked the youth.

"During his mortal life he was a wine-dealer," answered the pastor, "and he watered the wine he sold."

This did not strike the youth as being such a terrible crime. "Even if he had to pay for it with his life," said he, "one might now grant him a Christian burial, and let him rest in peace." But the pastor said that this could not be done at all; for people would be needed to break him out of the ice; and money would be needed to buy a grave for him from the church; and the gravedigger would want to be paid for his trouble; and the sexton for tolling the bells; and the cantor for singing; and the pastor himself for the funeral sermon.

"Do you think there is any one who would pay all that money for such an arrant sinner's sake?" inquired the pastor.

"Yes," said the youth. If he could manage to have him buried, he would be willing to pay for the wake out of his own slender purse.

At first the pastor would hear nothing of it; but when the youth returned with two men, and asked him in their presence whether he refused the dead man Christian burial, he ventured no further objections.

So they released the wine-dealer from his block of ice, and laid him in consecrated ground. The bells tolled, and there was singing, and the pastor threw earth on the coffin, and they had a wake at which tears and laughter alternated. But when the youth had paid for the wake, he had but a few shillings left in his pocket. Then he once more set out on his way; but had not gone far before a man came up behind him, and asked him whether he did not find it tiresome to wander along all alone.

"No," said the youth, he always had something to think about. The man asked whether he did not need a servant.

"No," said the youth, "I am used to serving myself, so I have no need of a servant; and no matter how much I might wish for one, I still would have to do without, since I have no money for his keep and pay."

"Yet you need a servant, as I know better than you do," said the man, "and you need one upon whom you can rely in life and death. But if you do not want me for a servant, then let me be your comrade. I promise that you will not lose thereby, and I will not cost you a shilling. I travel at my own expense, nor need you be put to trouble as regards my food and clothing."

Under these circumstances the youth was glad to have him for a comrade, and they resumed their journey, the man as a rule going in advance and pointing out the way.

After they had wandered long through various lands, over hills and over heaths, they suddenly stood before a wall of rock. The comrade knocked, and begged to be let in. Then the rock opened before them, and after they had gone quite a way into the interior of the hill, a witch came to meet them and offered them a chair. "Be so good as to sit down, for you must be weary!" said she.

"Sit down yourself!" answered the man. Then she had to sit down and remain seated, for the chair had power to hold fast all that approached it. In the meantime they wandered about in the hill, and the comrade kept looking around until he saw a sword that hung above the door. This he wanted to have, and he promised the witch that he would release her from her chair if she would let him have the sword.

"No," she cried, "ask what you will. You can have anything else, but not that, for that is my Three-Sisters Sword!" (There were three sisters to whom the sword belonged in common.) "Then you may sit where you are till the world's end!" said the man. And when she heard that she promised to let him have the sword, if he would release her.

So he took the sword, and went away with it; but he left her sitting there, after all. When they had wandered far, over stony wastes and desolate heaths, they again came to a wall of rock. There the comrade again knocked, and begged to be let in. Just as before, the rock opened, and when they had gone far into the hill, a witch came to meet them with a chair and bade them be seated, "for you must be tired," said she.

"Sit down yourself!" said the comrade. And what had

happened to her sister happened to her, she had to seat herself, and could not get up again. In the meantime the youth and his comrade went about in the hill, and the latter opened all the closets and drawers, until he found what he had been searching for, a ball of golden twine. This he wished to have, and promised he would release her from the chair if she would give it to him. She told him he might have all she possessed; but that she could not give him the ball, since it was her Three-Sisters Ball. But when she heard that she would have to sit in the chair till the Day of Judgment, she changed her mind. Then the comrade took the ball, and in spite of it left her sitting where she was. Then they wandered for many a day through wood and heath, until they came to a wall of rock. All happened as it had twice before, the comrade knocked, the hill opened, and inside a witch came to meet them with a chair, and bade them sit down. The two had gone through many rooms before the comrade spied an old hat hanging on a hook behind the door. The hat he must have, but the old witch would not part with it, since it was her Three-Sisters Hat, and if she gave it away she would be thoroughly unhappy. But when she heard that she would have to sit there until the Day of Judgment if she did not give up the hat, she at last agreed to do so. The comrade took the hat, and then told her to keep on sitting where she sat, like her sisters.

At length they came to a river. There the comrade took the ball of golden twine and flung it against the hill on the other side of the river with such force that it bounded back. And when it had flown back and forth several times, there stood a bridge, and when they had reached the other side, the comrade told the youth to wind up the golden twine again as swiftly as possible, "for if we do not take it away quickly, the three witches will cross and tear us to pieces." The youth wound as quickly as he could, and just as he was at the last thread, the witches rushed up, hissing, flung themselves into the water so that the foam splashed high, and snatched at the end of the thread. But they could not grasp it, and drowned in the river.

After they had again wandered on for a few days, the comrade said: "Now we will soon reach the castle in which she lives, the princess of whom you dreamed, and when we reach it, you must go to the castle and tell the king what you dreamed, and your journey's aim." When they got there, the youth did as he was told, and was very well received. He was given a room for himself, and one for his servant, and when it was time to eat, he was invited to the king's own table. When he saw the princess, he recognized her at once as the vision of his dream. He told her, too, why he was there, and she replied that she liked him quite well, and would gladly take him, but first he must undergo three tests. When they had eaten, she gave him a pair of gold shears and said: "The first test is that you take these shears and keep them, and give them back to me to-morrow noon. That is not a very severe test," she said, and smiled, "but, if you cannot stand it, you must die, as the law demands, and you will be in the same case as the suitors whose bones you may see lying without the castle gate."

"That is no great feat," thought the youth to himself. But the princess was so merry and active, and so full of fun and nonsense, that he thought neither of the shears nor of himself, and while they were laughing and joking, she secretly robbed him of the shears without his noticing it. When he came to his room in the evening, and told what had occurred, and what the princess had said to him, and about the shears which she had given him to guard, his comrade asked: "And have you still the shears?"

The youth looked through all his pockets; but his shears were not there, and he was more than unhappy when he realized that he had lost them.

"Well, well, never mind. I will see whether I can get them back for you," said his comrade, and went down into the stable. There stood an enormous goat which belonged to the princess, and could fly through the air more swiftly than he could walk on level ground. The comrade took the Three-Sisters Sword, gave him a blow between the horns, and asked: "At what time does the princess ride to meet her lover to-night?" The goat bleated, and said he did not dare tell; but when the comrade had given him another thump, he did say that the princess would come at eleven o'clock sharp. Then the comrade put on the Three-Sisters Hat, which made him invisible, and waited for the princess. When she came, she anointed the goat with a salve she carried in a great horn, and cried out: "Up, up! over gable and roof, over land and sea, over hill and dale, to my dearest, who waits for me in the hill!"

As the goat flew upward, the comrade swung himself up in back, and then they were off like the wind through the clouds: it was not a long journey. Suddenly they stood before a wall of rock, she knocked, and then they took their way into the interior of the hill, to the troll who was her dearest. "And now a new suitor has come who wants to win me, sweetheart," said she. "He is young and handsome, but I will have none but you," she went on, and made a great time over the troll. "I have set him a test, and here are the shears that he was to keep and guard. You shall keep them now!" Then both of them laughed as though the youth had already lost his head. "Yes, I will keep them, and take good care of them, and a kiss from you shall pledge the truth, when crows are cawing around the youth!" said the troll; and he laid the shears in an iron chest with three locks. But at the moment he was dropping the shears into the chest, the comrade caught them up. None could see him, for he was wearing the Three-Sisters Hat. So the troll carefully locked the empty chest, and put the key into a hollow double-tooth, where he kept other magic things. "The suitor could hardly find it there," said he.

After midnight the princess set out for home. The comrade swung himself up in back again, and the trip home did not take long.

The following noon the youth was invited to dine at the king's table. But this time the princess kept her nose in the air, and was so haughty and snappish that she hardly condescended to glance in the youth's direction. But after they had eaten, she looked very solemn, and asked in the sweetest manner: "You probably still have the shears I gave you to take care of yesterday?"

"Yes, here they are," said the youth; and he flung them on the table so that they rang. The princess could not have been more frightened had he thrown the shears in her face. But she tried to make the best of a bad bargain, and said in a sweet voice: "Since you have taken such good care of the shears, you will not find it hard to keep my ball of gold twine for me. I should like to have it back by to-morrow noon; but if you cannot give it to me then, you must die, according to the law." The youth thought it would not be so very hard, and put the ball of gold twine in his pocket. Yet the princess once more began to toy and joke with him, so that he thought neither of himself nor of the ball of gold twine, and while they were in the midst of their merry play she stole the golden ball from him, and then dismissed him.

When he came up into his room, and told what she had said and done, his comrade asked: "And have you still the ball of gold twine?"

"Yes, indeed," said the youth, and thrust his hand into the pocket in which he had placed it. But there was no ball in it, and he fell into such despair that he did not know what to do.

"Do not worry," said his comrade. "I will see whether I cannot get it back for you." He took his sword and his hat, and went to a smith and had him weld twelve extra pounds of iron to his sword. Then, when he entered the stable, he gave the goat such a blow between the horns with it that he staggered, and asked: "At what time does the princess ride to her dearest to-night?"

"At twelve o'clock sharp," said the goat.

The comrade once more put on his Three-Sisters Hat, and waited until the princess came with the horn of ointment and anointed the goat. Then she repeated what she had already said: "Up, up! over gable and tower, over land and sea, over hill and dale, to my dearest who waits for me in the hill!" And when the goat arose, the comrade swung himself up in back, and off they were like lightning through the air. Soon they had reached the troll-hill, and when she had knocked thrice they passed through the interior of the hill till they met the troll who was her dearest.

"What manner of care did you take of the golden shears I gave you yesterday, my friend?" asked the princess. "The suitor had them, and he gave them back to me."

That was quite impossible, said the troll, for he had locked them up in a chest with three locks, and had thrust the key into his hollow tooth. But when they had unlocked the chest and looked, there were no shears there. Then the princess told him that she had now given him her ball of golden twine.

"Here it is," said she. "I took it away from him again without his having noticed it; but what are we to do if he is a master of such arts?"

The troll could not think of anything to suggest; but after they had reflected a while they hit on the idea of lighting a great fire, and burning the ball of gold twine, for then the suitor could surely not regain it. Yet when she threw it into the flames, the comrade leaped forward and caught it, without being seen, for he was wearing the Three-Sisters Hat. After the princess had stayed a little while she returned home, and again the comrade sat up behind, and the trip home was swiftly and safely made. When the youth was asked to the king's table, the comrade gave him the ball. The princess was still more sharp and disdainful in her remarks than before, and after they had eaten she pinched her lips, and said: "Would it not be possible for me to get my ball of gold twine again, which I gave you yesterday?"

"Yes," said the youth, "you can have it; there it is!" and he flung it on the table with such a thud that the king leaped up in the air with fright.

The princess grew as pale as a corpse; but she made the best of a bad bargain, and said that he had done well. Now there was only one more little test for him to undergo. "If you can bring me what I am thinking about by to-morrow noon, then you may have me and keep me."

The youth felt as though he had been condemned to death; for it seemed altogether impossible for him to know of what the princess was thinking, and still more impossible to bring her the thing in question. And when he came to his room his comrade could scarcely quiet him. He said he would take the matter in hand, as he had done on the other occasions, and at last the youth grew calmer, and lay down to sleep. In the meantime the comrade went to the smith, and had him weld an additional twenty-four pounds of iron on his sword. When this had been done, he went to the stable, and gave the goat such a smashing blow between the horns that he flew to the other side of the wall.

"At what time does the princess ride to her dearest tonight?" said he.

"At one o'clock sharp," bleated the goat.

When the time came, the comrade was standing in the stable, wearing his Three-Sisters Hat, and after the princess had anointed the goat and spoken her formula, off they went through the air as before, with the comrade sitting in back. But this time he was anything but gentle, and kept giving the princess a cuff here, and a cuff there, until she had received a terrible drubbing. When she reached the wall of rock, she knocked three times, the hill opened, and they flew through it to her dearest.

She complained bitterly to him, and said she would never have thought it possible that the weather could affect one so; it had seemed to her as though some one were flying along with them, beating her and the goat, and her whole body must be covered with black and blue spots, so badly had she been thrashed. And then she told how the suitor had again had the ball of twine. How he had managed to get it, neither she nor the troll could guess.

"But do you know the thought that came to me?" said

she. Of course the troll did not.

"Well," said she, "I have told him he is to bring me the thing I am thinking of by to-morrow noon, and that thing is your head. Do you think, dear friend, that he will be able to bring it to me?" and she made a great time over the troll.

"I do not think he can," said the troll, who felt quite sure of himself, and laughed and chortled with pleasure in the most malicious way. For he and the princess were firmly convinced that the youth would be more apt to lose his own head, and be left to the ravens, than that he would be able to bring the princess the head of the troll.

Toward morning the princess wanted to fly home again, but she did not venture to ride alone; the troll must accompany her. He was quite ready to do so, took his goat from the stable—he had one just like that of the princess—and anointed him between the horns. When the troll had mounted, the comrade swung up in back of him, and off they were through the air in the direction of the king's castle. But on the way the comrade beat away lustily at the troll and his goat, and gave him thump after thump, and blow after blow with his sword, until they were flying lower and lower, and at last nearly fell into the sea across which their journey led them. When the troll noticed how stormy the weather was, he accompanied the princess to the castle, and waited outside to make sure that she really came home safely. But the moment when the door closed on the princess, the comrade hewed off his head, and went up with it to the youth's room.

"Here is the thing of which the princess was thinking," said he. Then everything was in apple-pie order, and when the youth was invited to the king's table and they had eaten, the princess grew as merry as a lark. "Have you, perhaps, the thing of which I was thinking?" "To be sure," said the youth, and he drew forth the head from beneath his coat, and flung it on the table so that the table and all that was on it fell over. The princess looked as though she had come from the grave; yet she could not deny that this was the thing of which she had thought, and now she had to take the youth, as she had promised. So the wedding was celebrated, and there was great joy throughout the kingdom.

But the comrade took the youth aside, and said that on their wedding-night he might close his eyes and pretend to sleep, but that, if he loved his life, and followed his advice, he would not sleep a wink until the princess was freed from her troll-skin. He must whip it off with nine new switches of birch-wood, and strip it off with three milk-baths beside; first he must scrub it off in a tub of year-old whey, then he must rub it off in a tub of sour milk, and finally, he must sponge it off in a tub of sweet milk. He had laid the birch switches beneath the bed, and had stood the tubs of milk in the corner; all was prepared. The youth promised to follow his advice, and do as he had told him. When night came, and he lay in his bed, the princess raised herself on her elbows, to see if he were really asleep, and she tickled him under the nose; but he was sleeping quite soundly. Then she pulled his hair and his beard. But it seemed to her that he slept like a log. Then she drew a great butcher's knife out from beneath her pillow, and wanted to cut off his head. But the youth leaped up, struck the knife from her hand, seized her by the hair, whipped her with the switches, and did not stop until not one was left. Thereupon he threw her into the tub of whey, and then he saw what sort of creature she really was, for her whole body was coal-black. But when he had scrubbed her in the whey, and rubbed her in the sour milk, and sponged her in the sweet milk, the troll-skin had altogether disappeared, and she was lovelier than she had ever been before.

On the following day the comrade said that now they must get on their way. The youth was ready to set forth, and the princess, too, for her dower had long since been made ready. During the night the comrade had brought all the gold and silver, and all the valuables which the troll had left in the hill to the castle, and when they wanted to start in the morning, the castle court-yard was so full they could scarcely get through. The dower supplied by the troll was worth more than the king's whole country, and they did not know how they were to take it home. But the comrade found a way out of the difficulty. The troll had also left six goats who could fly through the air. These he loaded so heavily with gold and silver that they had to walk on the ground, and were not strong enough to rise into the air; and what the goats could not carry, had to be left at the castle. Thus they traveled for a long time, but at last the goats grew so weary and wretched that they could go no further. The youth and the princess did not know what to do; but when the comrade saw that they could not move from the spot, he took the whole treasure on his back, topped it with the goats, and carried it all until they were no more than half a mile from the youth's home. Then the comrade said: "Now I must part from you, for I can stay with you no longer." But the youth would not hear of parting, and would not let him go at any price.

So he went along another half mile, but further than that he could not go, and when the youth pressed him, and insisted that he come home with him, and stay there; or that he at least celebrate their home-coming, he merely said no, he could not do so. Then the youth asked him what he wished in the way of payment for his company and aid. "If I am to wish for something, then I would like to have half of all that you may gain in the course of the next five years," said his comrade. And this was promised him.

Now when the comrade had gone, the youth hid all his treasure, and went straight home. And there they celebrated a home-coming feast that was talked about in seven kingdoms; and when that was over they spent the whole winter going back and forth with the goats, and his father's twelve horses, bringing all the gold and silver home.

After five years the comrade came again and asked for his share. Then the man divided all his possessions into two equal parts.

"Yet there is one thing you have not divided," said the comrade.

"What could that be?" asked the man. "I thought I had divided everything."

"You have been blessed with a child," said the comrade, "and that you must also divide into two equal parts."

Yes, such was really the case. Then he took up his sword, but when he raised it and was about to divide the child, his comrade seized the point of the sword so that he could not strike.

"Are you not happy, since you need not strike?" said he.

"Yes, indeed, I never was happier," said the man.

"That is how happy I was when you delivered me out of the block of ice," said the comrade. "Keep all you have: I need nothing, for I am a disembodied spirit." And he told him he was the wine-dealer who had lain in the block of ice before the church door, spat upon by all; and that he had become his comrade, and had aided him, because the youth had sacrificed all he had in order that he might have peace, and a burial in consecrated ground. He had been permitted to accompany him for the space of a year, and the time had run out when he had first parted with him. Now he had once more been allowed to visit him; yet on this occasion he would have to part for all time, for the bells of heaven were calling him.

ASPENCLOG

Aspenclog's mother was an aspen-tree. He slew the man who had chopped her down. Then he went to the king and asked whether he could give him work. He wanted no other pay than the right to give the king three good thumps on the back when there was no more work for him to do. The king agreed to this condition, for he thought he would always have enough work for him to do. Then he sent him to the forest to gather wood. But Aspenclog piled up such a tremendous load that two horses could not pull the wagon. So he took two polar bears, harnessed them to the wagon, drove it home, and left the bears in the stable, where they ate up all the king's cattle.

Then he was told to keep a mill grinding which the evil one often brought to a stop. No sooner had Aspenclog commenced to grind than, sure enough, the mill stopped. Aspenclog took a candle and made a search. No doubt of it, the evil one had wedged his leg between the mill-stones. No sooner had Aspenclog seen the leg, than he chopped it off with his club. Then the evil one came hobbling up on one leg, and begged fearfully and tearfully for the leg he had lost. No, he could not have it, said the youth, unless he gave him a bushel of money for it. But when the evil one had to pay Aspenclog the money, he thought to cheat him, and said that they would wager bushel against bushel, as to which of them could throw the highest. They argued a while about which was to throw first. At last Aspenclog had to begin. Now the evil one had a ball with which they were to throw. Aspenclog stood a long time looking at the moon. "Why do you do that?" asked the evil one. "Well, I would like to see whether I cannot throw the ball into the moon," said Aspenclog. "Do you see those black spots? Those are the balls I have already thrown up into the moon." Then the evil one was afraid of losing his ball, and he did not dare to let Aspenclog throw.

So they wagered bushel against bushel as to which one of them could blow the highest note. "You may blow first," said Aspenclog. "No, you!" Finally it was decided that Aspenclog should blow first. Then he went to a hill, took an enormous fir-tree and wound it around his horn like a reed. "Why do you do that?" asked the evil one. "Well, if I don't, the horn will burst when I blow it," was Aspenclog's answer. Now the evil one began to get frightened, and Aspenclog came home with half a ton of money.

But soon the king had no corn left to grind. And war broke out in the land. "Now he will have work enough to last him a lifetime," thought the king. And he told Aspenclog to go out against the enemy. Aspenclog was quite ready to do so; but wanted to have plenty of provisions to take with him. Then he set forth, and when he saw the enemy he sat down to eat. The enemy shot at him as hard as they could, but their bullets did not touch him. When Aspenclog had satisfied his hunger, he stood up, tore out an enormous oak by the roots, and lay about him with it. Before very long he had hewn down all of the enemy. Then he went back home to the king.

"Have you any more work for me?" he asked. "No, now I have no work left," said the king. "Then I will give you three good thumps on the back," said Aspenclog. The king begged permission to bolster himself up with pillows. "Yes, take as many as you want," said Aspenclog. Then he thumped, and at his first thump the king burst into pieces.

THE TROLL WEDDING

One summer, a long, long time ago, the folk of Melbustad went up to the hill pastures with their herd. But they had been there only a short time when the cattle began to grow so restless that it was impossible to keep them in order. A number of different maidens tried to manage them, but without avail; until one came who was betrothed, and whose betrothal had but recently been celebrated. Then the cattle suddenly quieted down, and were easy to handle. So the maiden remained alone in the hills with no other company than a dog. And one afternoon as she sat in the hut, it seemed to her that her sweetheart came, sat down beside her, and began to talk about their getting married at once. But she sat still and made no reply, for she noticed a strangeness about him. By and by, more and more people came in, and they began to cover the table with silverware, and bring on dishes, and the bridesmaids brought the bridal crown, and the ornaments, and a handsome bridal gown, and they dressed her, and put the crown on her head, as was the custom in those days, and they put rings on her hands.

And it seemed to her as though she knew all the people who were there; they were the women of the village, and the girls of her own age. But the dog was well aware that there was something uncanny about it all. He made his way down to Melbustad in flying leaps, and howled and barked in the most lamentable manner, and gave the people no rest until they followed him. The young fellow who was to marry the girl took his gun, and climbed the hills; and when he drew near, there stood a number of horses around the hut, saddled and bridled. He crept up to the hut, looked through a loop-hole in the wall, and saw a whole company sitting together inside. It was quite evident that they were trolls, the people from underground, and therefore he discharged his gun over the roof. At that moment the doors flew open, and a number of balls of gray yarn, one larger than the other, came shooting out about his legs. When he went in, there sat the maiden in her bridal finery, and nothing was missing but the ring on her little finger, then all would have been complete.

"In heaven's name, what has happened here?" he asked, as he looked around. All the silverware was still on the table, but all the tasty dishes had turned to moss and toadstools, and frogs and toads and the like.

"What does it all mean?" said he. "You are sitting here in all your glory, just like a bride?"

"How can you ask me?" answered the maiden. "You have been sitting here yourself, and talking about our wedding the whole afternoon!"

"No, I have just come," said he. "It must have been some one else who had taken my shape!"

Then she gradually came to her senses; but not until long afterward was she altogether herself, and she told how she had firmly believed that her sweetheart himself, and all their friends and relatives had been there. He took her straight back to the village with him, and so that they need fear no such deviltry in the future, they celebrated their wedding while she was still clad in the bridal outfit of the underground folk. The crown and all the ornaments were hung up in Melbustad and it is said that they hang there to this very day.

THE HAT OF THE *HULDRES*

Once upon a time there was a big wedding at a certain farmstead, and a certain cottager was on his way to the wedding-feast. As he chanced to cross a field, he found a milk-strainer, such as are usually made of cows' tails, and looking just like an old brown rag. He picked it up, for he thought it could be washed, and then he would give it to his wife for a dish-rag. But when he came to the house where they were celebrating the wedding, it seemed as though no one saw him. The bride and groom nodded to the rest of the guests, they spoke to them and poured for them; but he got neither greeting nor drink. Then the chief cook came and asked the other folk to sit down to the table; but he was not asked, nor did he get anything to eat. For he did not care to sit down of his own accord when no one had asked him. At last he grew angry and thought: "I might as well go home, for not a soul pays a bit of attention to me here." When he reached home, he said: "Good evening, here I am back again."

"For heaven's sake, are you back again?" asked his wife.

"Yes, there was no one there who paid any attention to me, or even so much as looked at me," said the man, "and when people show me so little consideration, it seems as though I have nothing to look for there."

"But where are you? I can hear you, but I cannot see you!" cried his wife.

The man was invisible, for what he had found was a *huldre* hat.

"What are you talking about? Can't you see me? Have you lost your wits?" asked the man. "There is an old hair strainer for you. I found it outside on the ground," said he, and he threw it on the bench. And then his wife saw him; but at the same moment the hat of the *huldres* disappeared, for he should only have loaned it, not given it away. Now the man saw how everything had come about, and went back to the wedding-feast. And this time he was received in right friendly fashion, and was asked to drink, and to seat himself at the table.

THE CHILD OF MARY

Far, far from here, in a great forest, there once lived a poor couple. Heaven blessed them with a charming little daughter; but they were so poor they did not know how they were going to get her christened. So her father had to go forth to see whether he could not find a god-father to pay for the child's christening. All day long he went from one to another; but no one wanted to be the god-father. Toward evening, as he was going home, he met a very lovely lady, who wore the most splendid clothes, and seemed most kind and friendly, and she offered to see that the child was christened, if she might be allowed to keep it afterward. The man replied that first he must ask his wife. But when he reached home and asked her she gave him a flat "no." The following day the man set out again; but no one wanted to be the god-father if he had to pay for the christening himself, and no matter how hard the man begged, it was all of no avail. When he went home that evening, he again met the lovely lady, who looked so gentle, and she made him the same offer as before. The man again told his wife what had happened to him, and added that if he could not find a god-father for his child the following day, they would probably have to let the lady take her, since she seemed to be so kind and friendly. The man then went out for the third time, and found no god-father that day. And so, when he once more met the friendly lady in the evening, he promised to let her have the child, if she would see that it was baptized. The following morning the lady came to the man's hut, and with her two other men. She then took the child and went to church with it, and it was baptized. Then she took it with her, and the little girl remained with her for several years, and her foster-mother was always good and kind to her.

Now when the girl had grown old enough to make distinctions, and had acquired some sense, it chanced that her foster-mother once wished to take a journey. "You may go into any room you wish," she said to the girl, "only you are not to go into these three rooms," and then she set out on her journey. But the girl could not resist opening the door to the one room a little way—and swish! out flew a star. When her foster-mother came home, she was much grieved to find that the star had flown out, and was so annoyed with her foster-child that she threatened to send her away. But the girl pleaded and cried, until at last she was allowed to remain.

After a time the foster-mother wanted to take another journey, and she forbade the girl, above all, to go into the two rooms which, as yet, she had not entered. And the girl promised her that this time she would obey her. But when she had been alone for some time, and had had all sorts of thoughts as to what there might be in the second room, she could no longer resist opening the second door a little way—and swish! out flew the moon. When the foster-mother returned, and saw the moon had slipped out, she again grieved greatly, and told the girl she could keep her no longer, and that now she must go. But when the girl again began to cry bitterly, and pleaded with such grace that it was impossible to deny her, she was once more allowed to remain.

After this the foster-mother wished to take another journey, and she told the girl, who was now more than half-grown, that she must take her request not to go, or even so much as peep into the third room, seriously to heart. But when the foster-mother had been away for some time, and the girl was all alone and bored, she could at last resist no longer. "O," thought she, "how pleasant it would be to take a peep into that third room!" It is true, that at first she thought she would not do it, because of her foster-mother; yet when the thought returned to her, she could not hold back, after all; but decided that she should and must by all means take a peep. So she opened the door the least little bit—and swish! out flew the sun. When the foster-mother then returned, and saw that the sun had flown out, she grieved greatly, and told the girl that now she could positively stay with her no longer. The foster-daughter cried and pleaded even more touchingly than before; but all to no avail. "No, I must now punish you," said the foster-mother. "But you shall have your choice of either becoming the most beautiful of all maidens, without the power of speech, or the most homely, yet able to talk. But you must leave this place." The girl said: "Then I would rather be the most beautiful of maidens without the power of speech"—and such she became, but from that time on she was dumb.

Now when the girl had left her foster-mother, and had wandered for a time, she came to a large, large wood, and no matter how far she went she could not reach its end. When evening came, she climbed into a high tree that stood over a spring, and sat down in its branches to sleep. Not far from it stood a king's castle, and early the next morning a serving-maid came from it, to get water from the spring for the prince's tea. And when the serving-maid saw the lovely face in the spring, she thought it was her own. At once she threw down her pail and ran back home holding her head high, and saying: "If I am as beautiful as all that, I am too good to carry water in a pail!" Then another was sent to fetch water, but the same thing happened with her; she, too, came back and said she was far too handsome and too good to go to the spring and fetch water for the prince. Then the prince went himself, for he wanted to see what it all meant. And when he came to the spring, he also saw the picture, and at once looked up into the tree. And so he saw the lovely maiden who was seated among its branches. He coaxed her down, took her back home with him, and nothing would do but that she must be his bride, because she was so beautiful. But his mother, who was still living, objected: "She cannot speak," said she, "and, maybe, she belongs to the troll-folk." But the prince would not be satisfied until he had won her. When, after a time, heaven bestowed a child upon the queen, the prince set a strong guard about her. But suddenly they all fell asleep, and her foster-mother came, cut the child's little finger, rubbed some of the blood over the mouth and hands of the queen, and said: "Now you shall grieve just as I did when you let the star slip out!" And with that she disappeared with the child. When those whom the prince had set to keep guard opened their eyes again, they thought that the queen had devoured her child, and the old queen wanted to have her burned; but the prince loved her so very tenderly, that after much pleading he succeeded in having her saved from punishment, though only with the greatest difficulty.

When heaven gave her a second child, a guard of twice as many men as had first stood watch was again set about her; yet everything happened as before, only that this time the foster-mother said to her: "Now you shall grieve as I did when you let the moon slip out!" The queen wept and pleaded—for when the foster-mother was there she could speak—but without avail. Now the old queen insisted that she be burned. But the prince once more succeeded in begging her free. When heaven gave her a third child, a three-fold guard was set about her. The foster-mother came while the guard slept, took the child, cut its little finger, and rubbed some of the blood on the queen's mouth. "Now," said she, "you shall grieve just as I did when you let the sun slip out!" And now the prince could in no way save her, she was to be and should be burned. But at the very moment when they were leading her to the stake, the foster-mother appeared with all three children; the two older ones she led by the hand, the youngest she carried on her arm. She stepped up to the young queen and said: "Here are your children, for now I give them back to you. I am the Virgin Mary, and the grief that you have felt is the same grief that I felt aforetimes, when you had let the star, the moon and the sun slip out. Now you have been punished for that which you did, and from now on the power of speech is restored to you!"

The happiness which then filled the prince and princess may be imagined, but cannot be described. They lived happily together ever after, and from that time forward even the prince's mother was very fond of the young queen.

STORM MAGIC

The cabin-boy had been traveling around all summer long with his captain; but when they began to prepare to set sail in the fall, he grew restless and did not want to go along. The captain liked him, for though he was no more than a boy, he was quite at home on deck, was a big, tall lad, and did not mind lending a hand when need arose; then, too, he did as much work as an able seaman, and was so full of fun that he kept the whole crew in good humor. And so the captain did not like to lose him. But the youth said out and out that he was not minded to take to the blue pond in the fall; though he was willing to stay on board till the ship was loaded and ready to sail. One Sunday, while the crew was ashore, and the captain had gone to a farm-holding near the forest, in order to bargain for small timber and log wood—presumably on his own account—for a deck load, the youth had been left to guard the ship. But you must know that he was a Sunday child, and had found a four-leaf clover; and that was the reason he had the second sight. He could see those who are invisible, but they could not see him.

And as he was sitting there in the forward cabin, he heard voices within the ship. He peered through a crack, and there were three coal-black crows sitting inside the deck-beams, and they were talking about their husbands. All three were tired of them, and were planning their death. One could see at once that they were witches, who had assumed another form.

"But is it certain that there is no one here who can overhear us?" said one of the crows. And by the way she spoke the cabin-boy knew her for the captain's wife.

"No, you can see there's not," said the others, the wives

of the first and second quartermasters. "There is not a soul aboard."

"Well, then I do not mind saying that I know of a good way to get rid of them," said the captain's wife once more, and hopped closer to the two others. "We will turn ourselves into breakers, wash them into the sea, and sink the ship with every man on board."

That pleased the others, and they sat there a long time discussing the day and the fairway. "But is it certain that no one can overhear us?" once more asked the captain's wife.

"You know that such is the case," said the two others.

"Well, there is a counter-spell for what we wish to do, and if it is used, it will go hard with us, for it will cost us nothing less than our lives!"

"What is the counter-spell, sister," asked the wife of the one quartermaster.

"Is it certain that no one is listening to us? It seemed to me as though some one were smoking in the forward cabin."

"But you know we looked in every corner. They just forgot to let the fire go out in the caboose, and that is why there's smoke," said the quartermaster's wife, "so tell away."

"If they buy three cords of birch-wood," said the witch,-- "but it must be full measure, and they must not bargain for it— and throw the first cord into the water, billet by billet, when the first breaker strikes, and the second cord, billet by billet, when the second breaker strikes, and the third cord, billet by billet, when the third breaker strikes, then it is all up with us!"

"Yes, that's true, sister, then it is all up with us! Then it is all up with us!" said the wives of the quartermasters; "but there is no one who knows it," they cried, and laughed loudly, and with that they flew out of the hatchway, screaming and croaking like ravens.

When it came time to sail, the cabin-boy would not go along for anything in the world; and all the captain's coaxing, and all his promises were useless, nothing would tempt him to go. At last they asked him whether he were afraid, because fall was at hand, and said he would rather hide behind the stove, hanging to mother's apron strings. No, said the youth, he was not afraid, and they could not say that they had ever seen him show a sign of so land-lubberly a thing as fear; and he was willing to prove it to them, for now he was going along with them, but he made it a condition that three cords of birch-wood were to be bought, full measure, and that on a certain day he was to have command, just as though he himself were the captain. The captain asked what sort of nonsense this might be, and whether he had ever heard of a cabin-boy's being entrusted with the command of a ship. But the boy answered that was all one to him; if they did not care to buy the three cords of birch-wood, and obey him, as though he were captain, for the space of a single day—the captain and crew should know which day it was to be in advance—then he would set foot on the ship no more, and far less would he ever dirty his hands with pitch and tar on her again. The whole thing seemed strange to the captain, yet he finally gave in, because he wanted to have the boy along with him and, no doubt, he also thought that he would come to his senses again when they were once under way. The quartermaster was of the same opinion. "Just let him command all he likes, and if things go wrong with him, we'll help him out," said he. So the birch-wood was bought, full-measure and without haggling, and they set sail.

When the day came on which the cabin-boy was to take command, the weather was fair and quiet; but he drummed up the whole ship's crew, and with the exception of a tiny bit of canvas, had all sails reefed. The captain and crew laughed at him, and said: "That shows the sort of a captain we have now. Don't you want us to reef that last bit of sail this very minute?" "Not yet," answered the cabin-boy, "but before long."

Suddenly a squall struck them, struck them so heavily that they thought they would capsize, and had they not reefed the sails they would undoubtedly have foundered when the first breaker roared down upon the ship.

The boy ordered them to throw the first cord of birch-wood overboard, billet by billet, one at a time and never two, and he did not let them touch the other two cords. Now they obeyed him to the letter, and did not laugh; but cast out the birch-wood billet by billet. When the last billet fell they heard a groaning, as though some one were wrestling with death, and then the squall had passed.

"Heaven be praised!" said the crew—and the captain added: "I am going to let the company know that you saved ship and cargo."

"That's all very well, but we are not through yet," said the boy, "there is worse to come," and he told them to reef every last rag, as well as what had been left of the topsails. The second squall hit them with even greater force than the first, and was so vicious and violent that the whole crew was frightened. While it was at its worst, the boy told them to throw overboard the second cord; and they threw it over billet by billet, and took care not to take any from the third cord. When the last billet fell, they again heard a deep groan, and then all was still. "Now there will be one more squall, and that will be the worst," said the boy, and sent every one to his station. There was not a hawser loose on the whole ship.

The last squall hit them with far more force than either of the preceding ones, the ship laid over on her side so that they thought she would not right herself again, and the breaker swept over the deck.

But the boy told them to throw the last cord of wood overboard, billet by billet, and no two billets at once. And when the last billet of wood fell, they heard a deep groaning, as though some one were dying hard, and when all was quiet once more, the whole sea was the color of blood, as far as eye could reach.

When they reached land, the captain and the quartermasters spoke of writing to their wives. "That is something you might just as well let be," said the cabin-boy, "seeing that you no longer have any wives."

"What silly talk is this, young know-it-all! We have no wives?" said the captain. "Or do you happen to have done away with them?" asked the quartermasters.

"No, all of us together did away with them," answered the boy, and told them what he had heard and seen that Sunday afternoon when he was on watch on the ship; while the crew was ashore, and the captain was buying his deckload of wood.

And when they sailed home they learned that their wives had disappeared the day of the storm, and that since that time no one had seen or heard anything more of them.

THE FOUR-SHILLING PIECE

Once upon a time there was a poor woman, who lived in a wretched hut far away from the village. She had but little to bite and less to burn, so she sent her little boy to the forest to gather wood. He skipped and leaped, and leaped and skipped, in order to keep warm, for it was a cold, gray autumn day, and whenever he had gathered a root or a branch to add to his bundle, he had to slap his arms against his shoulders, for the cold made his hands as red as the whortleberry bushes over which he walked. When he had filled his barrow, and was wandering homeward, he crossed a field of stubble. There he saw lying a jagged white stone. "O, you poor old stone, how white and pale you are! You must be freezing terribly!" said the boy; took off his jacket, and laid it over the stone. And when he came back home with his wood, his mother asked him how it was that he was going around in the autumn cold in his shirt-sleeves. He told her that he had seen a jagged old stone, quite white and pale with the frost, and that he had given it his jacket. "You fool," said the woman, "do you think a stone can freeze? And even if it had chattered with frost, still, charity begins at home. Your clothes cost enough as it is, even when you don't hang them on the stones out in the field!"—and with that she drove the boy out again to fetch his jacket. When he came to the stone, the stone had turned around, and had raised itself from the ground on one side. "Yes, and I'm sure it is because you have the jacket, poor fellow!" said the boy. But when he looked more closely, there was a chest full of bright silver coins under the stone. "That must be stolen money," thought the boy, "for no one lays money honestly earned under stones in the wood." And he took the chest, and carried it down to the pond nearby, and threw in the whole pile of money. But a four-shilling piece was left swimming on the top of the water. "Well, this one is honest, for whatever is honest will float," said the boy. And he took the four-shilling piece and the jacket home with him. He told his mother what had happened to him, that the stone had turned around, and that he had found a chest full of silver coins, and had thrown it into the pond because it was stolen money. "But a four-shilling piece floated, and that I took along, because it was honest," said the boy. "You are a fool," said the woman—for she was as angry as could be—"if nothing were honest save what floats on the water, there would be but little honesty left in the world. And if the money had been stolen ten times over, still you had found it, and charity begins at home. If you had kept the money, we might have passed the rest of our lives in peace and comfort. But you are a dunderhead and will stay a dunderhead, and I won't be tormented and burdened with you any longer. Now you must get out and earn your own living."

So the boy had to go out into the wide world, and wandered about far and near looking for service. But wherever he went people found him too small or too weak, and said that they could make no use of him. At last he came to a merchant. There they kept him to work in the kitchen, and he had to fetch wood and water for the cook. When he had been there for some time, the merchant decided to journey to far countries, and asked all his servants what he should buy and bring back home for them. After all had told him what they wanted, came the turn of the little fellow who carried wood and water for the kitchen. He handed him his four-shilling piece. "Well, and what am I to buy for it?" asked the merchant. "It will not be a large purchase." "Buy whatever it will bring, it is honest money, that I know," said the boy. His master promised to do so, and sailed away.

Now when the merchant had discharged his cargo in foreign parts and had reloaded, and had bought what his servants had desired, he went back to his ship, and was about to shove off. Not until then did he remember that the scullion had given him a four-shilling piece, with which to buy him something. "Must I go up to the city again because of this four-shilling piece? One only has one's troubles when one bothers with such truck," thought the merchant. Then along came a woman with a bag on her back. "What have you in your bag, granny?" asked the merchant. "O, it is only a cat! I can feed her no longer, and so I want to throw her into the sea in order to get rid of her," said the old woman. "The boy told me to buy whatever I could get for the four-shilling piece," said the merchant to himself, and asked the woman whether he could have her cat for four shillings. The woman agreed without delay, and the bargain was closed.

Now when the merchant had sailed on for a while, a terrible storm broke loose, a thunderstorm without an equal, and he drifted and drifted, and did not know where or whither. At last he came to a land where he had never yet been, and went up into the city.

In the tavern which he entered the table was set, and at every place lay a switch, one for each guest. This seemed strange to the merchant, for he could not understand what was to be done with all the switches. Yet he sat down and thought: "I will watch carefully, and see just what the rest do with them, and then I can imitate them." Yes, and when the food came on the table, then he knew why the switches were there: the place was alive with thousands of mice, and all who were sitting at the table had to work and fight and beat about them with their switches, and nothing could be heard but the slapping of the switches, one worse than the other. Sometimes people hit each other in the face, and then they had to take time to say, "Excuse me!"

"Eating is hard work in this country," said the merchant. "How is it the folk here have no cats?" "Cats?" said the people: they did not know what they were. Then the merchant had the cat that he had bought for the scullion brought, and when the cat went over the table, the mice had to hurry into their holes, and not in the memory of man had the people been able to eat in such comfort. Then they begged and implored the merchant to sell them his cat. At last he said he would let them have her; but he wanted a hundred dollars for her, and this they paid, and thanked him kindly into the bargain.

Then the merchant sailed on, but no sooner had he reached the high seas than he saw the cat sitting at the top of the main-mast. And immediately after another storm and tempest arose, far worse than the first one, and he drifted and drifted, till he came to a land where he had never yet been. Again the merchant went to a tavern, and here, too, the table was covered with switches; but they were much larger and longer than at the place where he had first been. And they were much needed; for there were a good many more mice, and they were twice the size of those he had first seen.

Here he again sold his cat, and this time he received two hundred dollars for her, and that without any haggling. But when he had sailed off and was out at sea a way, there sat the cat up in the mast. And the storm at once began again, and finally he was again driven to a land in which he had never been. Again he turned in at a tavern, and there the table was also covered with switches; but every switch was a yard and a half long, and as thick as a small broom, and the people told him that they knew of nothing more disagreeable than to sit down to eat, for there were great, ugly rats by the thousand. Only with toil and trouble could one manage to shove a bite of something into one's mouth once in a while, so hard was it to defend oneself against the rats. Then the cat was again brought from the ship, and now the people could eat in peace. They begged and pleaded that the merchant sell them his cat; and for a long time he refused; but at last he promised that they should have her for three hundred dollars. And they paid him, and thanked him, and blessed him into the bargain.

Now when the merchant was out at sea again, he considered how much the boy had gained with the four-shilling piece he had given him. "Well, he shall have some of the money," said the merchant to himself, "but not all of it. For he has to thank me for the cat, which I bought for him, and charity begins at home."

But while the merchant was thinking these thoughts, such a storm and tempest arose that all thought the ship would sink. Then the merchant realized that there was nothing left for him to do but to promise that the boy should have all the money. No sooner had he made his vow, than the weather turned fair, and he had a favoring wind for his journey home. And when he landed, he gave the youth the six hundred dollars and his daughter to boot. For now the scullion was as rich as the merchant himself and richer, and thereafter he lived in splendor and happiness. And he took in his mother and treated her kindly. "For I do not believe that charity begins at home," said the youth.

THE MAGIC APPLES

Once upon a time there was a lad who was better off than all the others. He was never short of money, for he had a purse which was never empty. He never was short of food, for he had a table-cloth on which, as soon as he spread it, he found all he wanted to eat and drink. And, besides, he had a magic wishing cap. When he put it on he could wish himself wherever he wanted, and there he would be that very moment.

There was only one thing that he lacked: he had no wife, and he was gradually coming into the years when it would be necessary for him to make haste.

As he was walking sadly along one fine day, it occurred to him to wish himself where he would find the most beautiful princess in the world. No sooner had he thought of it than he was there. And it was a land which he had never yet seen, and a city in which he had never yet been. And the king had a daughter, so handsome that he had never yet beheld her like, and he wanted to have her on the spot. But she would have nothing to do with him, and was very haughty.

Finally he despaired altogether, and was so beside himself that he could no longer be where she was not. So he took his magic cap and wished himself into the castle. He wanted to say good-by, so he said. And she laid her hand in his. "I wish we were far beyond the end of the world!" said the youth, and there they were. But the king's daughter wept, and begged to be allowed to go home again. He could have all the gold and silver in the castle in return. "I have money enough for myself," said the youth, and he shook his purse so that money just rolled about. He could sit down at the royal table and eat the finest food, and drink the finest wines, said she. "I have enough to eat and drink myself," said the youth. "See, you can sit down at the table," said he, and at once he spread his table-cloth. And there stood a table covered with the best one might wish; and the king himself ate no better.

After they had eaten, the king's daughter said: "O, do look at the handsome apples up there on the tree! If you were really kind, you would fetch me down a couple of them!" The youth was not lazy, and climbed up. But he had forgotten his table-cloth and his purse, and these she took. And while he was shaking down the apples his cap fell off. She at once put it on and wished herself back in her own room, and there she was that minute.

"You might have known it," said the youth to himself, and hurried down the tree. He began to cry and did not know what to do. And as he was sitting there, he sampled the apples which he had thrown down. No sooner had he tried one than he had a strange feeling in his head, and when he looked more closely, he had a pair of horns. "Well, now it can do me no more harm," said he, and calmly went on eating the apples. But suddenly the horns had disappeared, and he was as before. "Good enough!" said the youth. And with that he put the apples in his pocket, and set out to search for the king's daughter.

He went from city to city, and sailed from country to country; but it was a long journey, and lasted a year and a day, and even longer.

But one day he got there after all. It was a Sunday, and he found out that the king's daughter was at church. Then he sat himself down with his apples before the church door, and pretended to be a peddler. "Apples of Damascus! Apples of Damascus!" he cried. And sure enough, the king's daughter came, and told her maidens to go and see what desirable things the peddler from abroad might have to offer. Yes, he had apples of Damascus. "What do the apples give one?" asked the maiden. "Wisdom and beauty!" said the peddler, and the maiden bought.

When the king's daughter had eaten of the apples, she had a pair of horns. And then there was such a wailing in the castle that it was pitiful to hear. And the castle was hung with black, and in the whole kingdom proclamation was made from all pulpits that whoever could help the king's daughter should get her, and half the kingdom besides. Then Tom, Dick and Harry, and the best physicians in the country came along. But none of them could help the princess.

But one day a foreign doctor from afar came to court. He was not from their country, he said, and had made the journey purposely just to try his luck here. But he must see the king's daughter alone, said he, and permission was granted him.

The king's daughter recognized him, and grew red and pale in turn. "If I help you now, will you marry me?" asked the youth. Yes, indeed she would. Then he gave her one of the magic apples, and her horns were only half as large as before. "But I cannot do more until I have my cap, and my table-cloth, and my purse back again," said he. So she went and brought him the things. Then he gave her still another magic apple, and now the horns were no more than tiny hornlets. "But now I cannot go on until you have sworn that you will be true to me," said he. And she swore that she would. And after she had eaten the third apple, her forehead was quite smooth again, and she was even more beautiful than in days gone by.

Then there was great joy in the castle. They prepared for the wedding with baking and brewing, and invited people from East and West to come to it. And they ate and drank, and were merry and of good cheer, and if they have not stopped, they are merry and of good cheer to this very day!

SELF DID IT

Once upon a time there was a mill, in which it was impossible to grind flour, because such strange things kept happening there. But there was a poor woman who was in urgent need of a little meal one evening, and she asked whether they would not allow her to grind a little flour during the night. "For heaven's sake," said the mill-owner, "that is quite impossible! There are ghosts enough in the mill as it is." But the woman said that she must grind a little; for she did not have a pinch of flour in the house with which to make mush, and there was nothing for her children to eat. So at last he allowed her to go to the mill at night and grind some flour. When she came, she lit a fire under a big tar-barrel that was standing there; got the mill going, sat down by the fire, and began to knit. After a time a girl came in and nodded to her. "Good evening!" said she to the woman. "Good evening!" said the woman; kept her seat, and went on knitting. But then the girl who had come in began to pull apart the fire on the hearth. The woman built it up again.

"What is your name?" asked the girl from underground.

"Self is my name," said the woman.

That seemed a curious name to the girl, and she once more began to pull the fire apart. Then the woman grew angry and began to scold, and built it all up again. Thus they went on for a good while; but at last, while they were in the midst of their pulling apart and building up of the fire, the woman upset the tar-barrel on the girl from underground. Then the latter screamed and ran away, crying:

"Father, father! Self burned me!"

"Nonsense, if self did it, then self must suffer for it!"

came the answer from below the hill.

THE MASTER GIRL

Once upon a time there was a king who had several sons; I do not just know how many there were, but the youngest was not content at home, and insisted on going out into the world to seek his fortune. And in the end the king had to give him permission to do so. After he had wandered for a few days, he came to a giant's castle, and took service with the giant. In the morning the giant wanted to go off to herd his goats, and when he started he told the king's son he was to clean the stable in the meantime. "And when you are through with that, you need do nothing more for today, for you might as well know that you have come to a kind master," said he. "But you must do what you are told to do conscientiously and, besides, you must not go into any of the rooms that lie behind the one in which you slept last night, else your life will pay the forfeit."

"He surely is a kind master," said the king's son to himself, walked up and down the room, and whistled and sang; for, thought he, there would be plenty of time to clean the stable. "But it would be nice to take a look at the other room, there surely must be something in it that he is alarmed about, since I am not so much as to take a look," thought he, and went into the first room. There hung a kettle, and it was boiling, but the king's son could find no fire beneath it. "What can there be in it?" thought he, and dipped in a lock of his hair, and at once the hair grew just like copper. "That's a fine soup, and whoever tastes it will burn his mouth," said the youth, and went into the next room. There hung another kettle that bubbled and boiled; but there was no fire beneath it, either. "I must try this one, too," said the king's son, and again he dipped in a lock of his hair and it grew just like silver. "We have no such expensive soup at home," said the king's son, "but the main thing is, how does it taste?" and with that he went into the third room. And there hung still another kettle, a-boiling just like those in the two other rooms, and the king's son wanted to try this one, too. He dipped in a lock of his hair, and it came out like pure gold, and fairly shimmered.

Then the king's son said: "Better and better! But if he cooks gold here, I wonder what he cooks inside, there?" And he wanted to see, so he went into the fourth room. Here there was no kettle to be seen; but a maiden sat on a bench who must have been a king's daughter; yet whatever she might be, the king's son had never seen any one so beautiful in all his days. "Now in heaven's name, what are you doing here?" asked the maiden. "I hired myself out here yesterday," said the king's son. "May God be your aid, for it is a fine service you have chosen!" said she. "O, the master is very friendly," said the king's son. "He has given me no hard work to do today. When I have cleaned out the stable, I need do nothing more." "Yes, but how are you going to manage it?" she went on. "If you do as the others have done, then for every shovelful you pitch out, ten fresh shovelfuls will fly in. But I'll tell you how to go about it. You must turn around the shovel, and work with the handle, then everything will fly out by itself."

This he would do, said the king's son; and he sat there with her all day long, for they had soon agreed that they would marry, he and the king's daughter, and in this way his first day in the giant's service did not weary him at all. When evening came on, she told him that now he must clean out the stable before the giant came, and when he got there he thought he would try out her advice, and began to use the shovel as he had seen his father's grooms use it. And sure enough, he had to stop quickly, for after he had worked a little while, he hardly had room in which to stand. Then he did as the king's daughter had told him, turned the shovel around and used the handle. And in a wink the stable was as clean as though it had been scrubbed. When he had finished he went to the room that the giant had assigned him, and walked up and down, whistling and singing. Then the giant came home with his goats. "Have you cleaned out the stable?" he asked. "Yes, indeed, master, it is spick and span," said the king's son. "I'll have to see that," said the giant, and went into the stable; but it was just as the king's son had said. "You surely have been talking to the Master Girl, for you could not have done that alone," said the giant. "Master Girl? What is a Master Girl?" said the king's son, and pretended to be very stupid. "I'd like to see her, too." "You will see her in plenty of time," said the giant.

The next morning the giant went off again with his goats. And he told the king's son he was to fetch his horse from the pasture, and when he had done this, he might rest: "For you have come to a kind master," said he. "But if you enter one of the rooms which I forbade you entering yesterday, I will tear off your head," he said, and went away with his herd. "Indeed, you are a kind master," said the king's son, "but in spite of it I'd like to have another little talk with the Master Girl, for she is just as much mine as yours," and with that he went in to her. She asked him what work he had to do that day. "O, it is not so bad today," said the king's son. "I am only to fetch his horse from the pasture." "And how are you going to manage that?" asked the Master Girl. "Surely it is no great feat to fetch a horse from pasture," said the king's son, "and I have ridden swift horses before." "Yet it is not an easy matter to ride this horse home," said the Master Girl, "but I will tell you how to set about it: When you see the horse, he will come running up, breathing fire and flame, just as though he were a burning pine-torch. Then you must take the bit that is hanging here on the door, and throw it into his mouth, for then he will grow so tame that you can do what you will with him." He would take good note of it, said the king's son, and he sat there with the Master Girl the whole day long, and they chatted and talked about this and that, but mainly about how delightful it would be, and what a pleasant time they could have, if they could only marry and get away from the giant. And the king's son would have forgotten the pasture and the horse altogether, had not the Master Girl reminded him of them toward evening. He took the bit that hung in the corner, hurried out to the pasture, and the horse at once ran up, breathing fire and flame; but he seized the moment when he came running up to him with his jaws wide open, and threw the bit into his mouth. Then he stood still, as gentle as a young lamb, and he had no trouble bringing him to the stable. Then he went to his room again, and began to whistle and sing. In the evening the giant came home with his goats. "Did you fetch the horse?" he asked. "Yes, master," said the king's son. "It would make a fine saddle-horse, but I just took it straight to the stable." "I'll have to see that," said the giant, and went into the stable. But there stood the horse, just as the king's son had said. "You surely must have spoken to my Master Girl, for you could not have done that alone," said the giant. "Yesterday the master chattered about the Master Girl, and today he is talking about her again. I wish master would show me the creature, for I surely would like to see her," said the king's son, and pretended to be very simple and stupid. "You will get to see her in plenty of time," said the giant.

On the third morning the giant went off again with his goats. "Today you must go to the devil, and fetch me his tribute," said he to the king's son. "When you have done that, you may rest for the remainder of the time, for you have come to a kind master, and you might as well know it," and with that he went off. "You may be a kind master," said the king's son; "yet you hand over some pretty mean jobs to me in spite of it, but I think I'll look after your Master Girl a bit. You claim that she belongs to you, but perhaps, in spite of it, she may tell me what to do," and with that he went in to her. And when the Master Girl asked him what the giant had given him to do that day, he told her he must go to the devil and fetch a tribute. "But how will you go about it?" asked the Master Girl. "You will have to tell me that," said the king's son, "for I have never been to the devil's place, and even though I knew the way there, I still would not know how much to ask for." "I will tell you what you must do," said the Master Girl. "You must go to the rock behind the pasture, and take the club that is lying there, and strike the rock with it. Then one will come out whose eyes flash fire, and you must tell him your business. And if he asks how much you want, you must tell him as much as you can carry." He would take good note of it, said the king's son, and he sat there with the Master Girl all day long until evening, and he might be sitting there yet, if the Master Girl had not reminded him that he must still go to the devil about the tribute before the giant came home. So he set out, and did exactly as the Master Girl had told him: he went to the rock, took the club and beat against it. Then one came out from whose eyes and nose the sparks flew. "What do you want?" he asked. "The giant has sent me to fetch his tribute," said the king's son. "How much do you want?" the other again inquired. "I never ask for more than I can carry," was the reply of the king's son. "It is lucky for you that you did not ask for a whole ton at once," said the one on the hill. "But come in with me, and wait a while." This the king's son did, and saw a great deal of gold and silver lying in the hill like dead rock in an ore-pile. Then as much as he could carry was packed up, and with it he went his way. When the giant came home in the evening with his goats, the king's son was running about the room, whistling and singing as on the two preceding evenings. "Did you go to the devil for the tribute?" asked the giant. "Yes, indeed, master," said the king's son. "Where did you put it?" asked the giant again. "I stood the sack of gold outside on the bench," was the reply. "I must see that at once," said the giant, and went over to the bench. But the sack was really standing there, and it was so full that the gold and silver rolled right out when the giant loosened the string. "You surely must have spoken to my Master Girl," said the giant. "If that is the case I will tear your head off." "With your Master Girl?" said the king's son. "Yesterday master talked about that Master Girl, and today he is talking about her again, and the day before yesterday he talked about her, too! I only wish that I might get the chance to see her sometime!" said he. "Well, just wait until to-morrow," said the giant, "and then I will lead you to her myself," he said. "A thousand thanks, master," said the king's son, "but I think you are only joking!" The following day the giant took him to the Master Girl.

"Now you must slaughter him, and cook him in the big kettle, you know which one I mean. And when the soup is ready, you can call me," said the giant, and he lay down on the bench to sleep, and at once began to snore so that the hills shook. Then the Master Girl took a knife, and cut the youth's little finger, and let three drops of blood fall on the bench. Then she took all the old rags, and old shoes and other rubbish she could find, and threw them all into the kettle. And then she took a chest of gold-dust, and a lick-stone, and a bottle of water that hung over the door, and a golden apple, and two golden hens, and left the giant's castle together with the king's son as quickly as possible. After a time they came to the sea, and they sailed across; though where they got the ship I do not exactly know.

Now when the giant had been sleeping quite a while, he began to stretch himself on his bench. "Is dinner ready yet?" he asked. "Just begun!" said the first drop of blood on the bench. Then the giant turned around, went to sleep again, and went on sleeping for quite some time. Then he again turned around a little. "Is dinner not ready yet?" he said, but did not open his eyes—nor had he done so the first time—for he was still half asleep. "It is half ready!" called out the second drop of blood, and then the giant thought it was the Master Girl. He turned around on the bench and took another nap. After he had slept a couple of hours longer, he once more began to move about and stretch: "Is dinner still not ready?" said he. "Ready!" answered the third drop of blood. The giant sat up and rubbed his eyes. But he could not see who had called him, and so he called out to the Master Girl. But no one answered him. "O, I suppose she has gone out for a little," thought the giant, and he dipped his spoon in the kettle to try the dinner; but there was nothing but leather soles and rags and like rubbish cooked together, and he did not know whether it were mush or porridge. When he noticed this he began to see a light, and realize how matters had come to pass, and he grew so angry that he hardly knew what to do, and made after the king's son and the Master Girl in flying haste. In a short time he came to the sea, and could not cross. "But I know how to help myself," said he. "I will fetch my sea-sucker." So the sea-sucker came, and lay down and took two or three swallows, and thus lowered the water so that the giant could see the king's son and the Master Girl out on the ship. "Now you must throw the lick-stone overboard," said the Master Girl, and the king's son did so. It turned into a tremendous large rock square across the sea, and the giant could not get over, and the sea-sucker could drink up no more of the sea. "I know quite well what I must do," said the giant. "I must now fetch my hill-borer." So the hill-borer came, and bored a hole through the rock, so the sea-sucker could get through and keep on sucking. But no sooner were they thus far than the Master Girl told the king's son to pour a drop or so of the bottle overboard, and the sea grew so full that they had landed before the sea-sucker could so much as take a single swallow.

Now they wanted to go home to the father of the king's son; but he would not hear of the Master Girl's going afoot, since he did not think this fitting for either of them. "Wait here a little while, until I fetch the seven horses that stand in my father's stable," said the king's son. "It is not far, and I will soon be back; for I will not have my bride come marching home afoot." "No, do not do so, for when you get home to the castle you will forget me, I know that positively," said the Master Girl. "How could I forget you?" said the king's son. "We have passed through so many hardships together, and we love each other so dearly," said he. He wanted to fetch the coach and seven horses at all costs, and she was to wait by the seashore. So at last the Master Girl had to give in.

"But when you get there, you must not take time to greet a single person. You must at once go to the stable, harness the horses, and drive back as swiftly as you can. They will all come to meet you, but you must act as though you did not see them, and must not take a single bite to eat. If you do not do that, you will make both of us unhappy," said she. And he promised to do as she had said.

But when he got home to the castle, one of his brothers was just getting married, and the bride and all the guests were already there. They all crowded around him and asked him this, and asked him that, and wanted to lead him in. But he acted as though he saw none of them, led out the horses, and began to put them to the coach. And since they could by no manner of means induce him to come into the castle, they came out with food and drink, and offered him the best of all that had been prepared for the wedding feast.

But the king's son would taste nothing, and only made haste in order to get away. Yet, finally, the bride's sister rolled an apple over to him across the court-yard: "And if you will touch nothing else, then at least you might take a bite of the apple, for you must be hungry and thirsty after your long journey," said she, and he took the apple and bit into it. But no sooner did he have the bit of apple in his mouth than he had forgotten the Master Girl, and that he was to fetch her. "I think I must be going mad! What am I doing with the horses and the coach?" he said, and he led back the horses into the stable, and went back to the castle, and wanted to marry the bride's sister, the one who had thrown him the apple.

In the meantime the Master Girl sat by the seashore, and waited and waited; but no king's son came. Then she went on, and after she had gone a while, she came to a little hut that lay all by itself in the forest, near the king's castle. She went in and asked whether she might not stay there. Now the little hut belonged to an old woman, and she was an arrant and evil witch; at first she did not want to take in the Master Girl at all; but at last she agreed to do so for love of money. But the whole hut was as dark and dirty as a pig-sty; therefore the Master Girl said she would clean up a bit, so that things would look as they did in other, decent people's houses. The old woman would have none of it, and was very disagreeable and angry; but the Master Girl paid no attention to her. She took the chest of gold dust, and threw a handful into the fire, so that a ray of gold shone over the whole hut, and it was gilded outside and in. But when the gold flamed up, the old woman was so terribly frightened that she ran out as though the evil one were after her, and from pure rage she forgot to duck at the threshold, and ran her head against the door-post. And that was the end of her.

The following morning the bailiff came by. He was much surprised to see the little golden hut, glittering and sparkling there in the forest, and was still more surprised at the girl within the hut. He fell in love with her at once, and asked her whether she would not become the bailiff's lady. "Yes, but have you plenty of money?" said the Master Girl. Yes, he had quite a little, said the bailiff. Then he went home to fetch his money, and came back again at evening dragging along an enormous sack of it, which he stood on a bench before the door. The Master Girl said that, seeing he had so much money, she would accept him. And then she asked him to rake the fire, which she said she had forgotten to do. But as soon as he had the poker in his hand, the Master Girl cried: "May God grant that you hold the poker, and the poker hold you, and that sparks and ashes fly around you until morning!" And there the bailiff stood the whole night through, and sparks and ashes flew about him, nor were the sparks the less hot for all his complaining and begging. And when morning came, and he could let go the poker, he did not stay long; but ran off as though the evil one were at his heels. And those who saw him stared and laughed, for he ran like a madman, and looked as though he had been thrashed and tanned. And all would have liked to have known where he had come from, but he said not a word, for he was ashamed.

On the following day the clerk passed by the Master Girl's little house. He saw it glistening and shining in the woods, and went in to find out who lived there. When he saw the beautiful girl he fell even more deeply in love with her than the bailiff had, and lost no time in suing for her hand. The Master Girl asked him, as she had asked the bailiff, whether he had plenty of money. Money he had to spare, answered the clerk, and ran right home to fetch it. By evening he was back again with a great sack—it must have been as much again as the bailiff had brought—and stood it on the bench. And so she promised to take him. Then she asked him to shut the house-door, which she said she had forgotten to do. But when he had the door-knob in his hand, she cried: "May God grant that you hold the door-knob and that the door-knob hold you, and that you move back and forth with it all night long until morning!" And the clerk had to dance the whole night through, such a waltz as he had never tripped before, and he had no wish to repeat the experience. Sometimes he was ahead, and sometimes the door was, and so they went back and forth all night, from wall to post and post to wall, and he was nearly bruised to death. First he cursed, then he wailed and pleaded; but the door paid no attention to him, and flung open and shut until it dawned. When it at last released him, he hurried away as quickly as though he had stolen something, forgot his sackful of money, and his wish to marry, and was glad that the door did not come threshing along after him. All grinned and stared at the clerk, for he ran like a madman, and looked worse than if a ram had been butting him all night long.

On the third day the magistrate came by, and also saw the little golden house in the forest. And he, too, went in to see who lived in it. And when he saw the Master Girl, he fell so deeply in love with her that he sued for her hand as soon as he bade her good-day. But she told him just what she had told the others, that if he had plenty of money she would take him. He had money enough, said the magistrate, and he went straight home to fetch it. When he came back in the evening, he had a much bigger sack of money with him than the clerk had had, and he stood it on the bench. Then the Master Girl said she would take him. But first she asked him to go fetch the calf, which she had forgotten to bring to the stable. And when he had the calf by the tail she cried: "May God grant that you hold the calf's tail, and the calf's tail hold you, and that you fly about the world together until morning!" And with that the race began, over stick and stone, over hill and dale, and the more the magistrate cursed and yelled, the more madly the calf ran away. When it dawned there was hardly a whole bone in the magistrate's body, and he was so happy to be able to let go the calf's tail that he forgot his bag of money, and the whole occurrence. It is true that he went home more slowly than the bailiff and the clerk; but the slower he went the more time the people had to stare and grin at him, so ragged and badly beaten did he appear after his dance with the calf.

On the following day there was to be a wedding at the castle, and not only was the older prince to marry, but the one who had stayed with the giant as well, and he was to get the other bride's sister.

But when they entered the coach and were about to drive to church, one of the axles broke. They took another, and then a third, but all of them broke, no matter what kind of wood they used. It took a great deal of time, and they did not move from the spot, and got all out of sorts. Then the bailiff said, for he had also been invited to the wedding at the castle, that a maiden lived out in the forest, and "if they could only get the loan of her poker, it would be sure to hold." So they sent to the little house in the forest, and asked most politely whether the maiden would not loan them the poker of which the bailiff had spoken. And they got it, too, and then they had an axle that would not break.

But when they wanted to drive on, the bottom of the coach broke. They made a new bottom as well as they were able, but no matter how they put it together, nor what kind of wood they used, it kept on breaking again as soon as they had left the court-yard. And they were worse off than they had been with the axle. Then the clerk said—for if the bailiff was one of the company, you may be sure they had not forgotten to invite the clerk—"Out in the forest lives a maiden, and if you will get the loan of her house-door, I am sure it would not break." So they sent to the little house in the forest, and asked most politely whether the maiden would not loan them the golden house-door, of which the clerk had told them. And they got it, too, and were about to drive on, when suddenly the horses could not draw the coach. There were six, so they put to eight, and then ten and twelve, but though they put as many as they liked to the coach and helped along with the whip, still the coach would not budge. The day was already far advanced, and they simply had to get to church, and actually began to despair. But then the magistrate said that out in the golden house in the forest lived a maiden, "and if one could only get the loan of her calf, it would be sure to pull the coach, and though it were as heavy as a bowlder." They did not think it quite the thing to drive to church with a calf; but still there was nothing to do but to send to the maiden, and to ask her most politely, with a kind greeting from the king, if she would loan them the calf of which the magistrate had spoken. Nor did the Master Girl refuse them this time. And then, when they had put the calf to the coach, it moved from the spot quickly enough. It flew over stick and stone, hill and dale, so that the people inside could hardly catch their breath. First it was on the ground, and next it was in the air, and when they reached the church, it spun around it like a top, and they had the greatest difficulty in getting out and into the church. And going home they went still faster, and were nearly out of their wits by the time they reached the castle.

When they sat down to the table the king's son—the same who had been at the giant's—said it would be no more than right to invite the maiden, too, who had lent them the poker, and the door and the calf: "for if we had not had these things, we should not have moved from the spot." This seemed right to the king, so he sent five of his most distinguished courtiers to the little golden house. They were to carry the king's kindest greetings, and ask that the maiden come up to the castle and take dinner with them. "A kind greeting to the king, and if he is too good to come to me, then I am too good to go to him," said the Master Girl. So the king had to go to her himself, and then she went along with him at once, and the king saw very well that she was more than she appeared to be, and gave her a place at the head of the table, next to the young bridegroom. After they had been at dinner for a while, the Master Girl produced the rooster and the hen and the golden apple—they were the three things she had taken along from the giant's castle—and placed them on the table before her. At once the rooster and the hen began to fight for the golden apple. "Why, just see how the two fight for the golden apple!" said the king's son. "Yes, that is how we had to fight the time we wanted to get out of the rock!" said the Master Girl. And then the king's son recognized her, and was very happy. The witch who had rolled the apple over to him was duly punished, and then the wedding really began, and the bailiff, and the clerk and the magistrate held out to the very end, for all that their wings had been so thoroughly singed.

ANENT THE GIANT WHO DID NOT HAVE HIS HEART ABOUT HIM

Once upon a time there was a king who had seven sons, and he was so fond of them that he never could bear to have them all away from him at once, and one of them always had to stay with him. When they had grown up, six of them were to go forth and look for wives; but the youngest the king wanted to keep at home, and the others were to bring along a bride for him. The king gave the six the handsomest clothes that had ever been seen, clothes that glittered from afar, and each received a horse that had cost many hundred dollars, and so they set forth. And after they had been at the courts of many kings, and had seen many princesses, they at last came to a king who had six daughters. Such beautiful princesses they had not as yet met with, and so each of them paid court to one of them, and when each had won his sweetheart, they rode back home again. But they were so deeply in love with their brides that they altogether forgot they were also to bring back a princess for their young brother who had stayed at home.

Now when they had already covered a good bit of the homeward road, they passed close to a steep cliff-side where the giants dwelt. And a giant came out, looked at them, and turned them all to stone, princes and princesses. The king waited and waited for his six sons; but though he waited and yearned, they did not come. Then he grew very sad, and said that he would never really be happy again. "If I did not have you," he told his youngest, "I would not keep on living, so sad am I at having lost your brothers." "But I had already been thinking of asking your permission to set out and find my brothers again," said the youngest. "No, that I will not allow under any circumstances," answered the father, "otherwise you will be lost to me into the bargain." But the youth's mind was set on going, and he pleaded so long that finally the king had to let him have his way. Now the king had only a wretched old nag for him, since the six other princes and their suite had been given all the good horses; but that did not worry the youngest. He mounted the shabby old nag, and "Farewell, father!" he said to the king. "I will surely return, and perhaps I will bring my six brothers back with me." And with that he rode off.

Now when he had ridden a while he met a raven, who was lying in the road beating his wings, and unable to move from the spot because he was so starved. "O, dear friend, if you will give me a bite to eat, then I'll help you in your hour of direst need!" cried the raven. "I have not much food, nor are you likely to be able to help me much," said the king's son, "but still I can give you a little, for it is easy to see you need it." And with that he gave the raven some of the provisions he had with him. And when he had ridden a while longer, he came to a brook, and there lay a great salmon who had gotten on dry land, and was threshing about, and could not get back into the water. "O, dear friend, help me back into the water," said the salmon to the king's son, "and I will help you, too, in your hour of greatest need!" "The help you will be able to give me will probably not amount to much," said the prince, "but it would be a pity if you had to lie there and pine away." And with that he pushed the fish back into the water. Then he rode on a long, long way, and met a wolf; and the wolf was so starved that he lay in the middle of the road, and writhed with hunger. "Dear friend, let me eat your horse," said the wolf.

"My hunger is so great that my very inwards rattle, because I have had nothing to eat for the past two years!" "No," said the prince, "I cannot do that: first I met a raven, and had to give him my provisions; then I met a salmon and had to help him back into the water; and now you want my horse. That will not do, for what shall I ride on then?" "Well, my dear friend, you must help me," was the wolf's reply. "You can ride on me. I will help you in turn in your hour of greatest need." "The help you might give me would probably not amount to much; but I will let you eat the horse, since you are in such sorry case," returned the prince. And when the wolf had eaten the horse, the prince took the bit and put it in the wolf's mouth, and fastened the saddle on his back, and his meal had made the wolf so strong that he trotted off with the king's son as fast as he could. He had never ridden so swiftly before. "When we have gone a little further I will show you the place where the giants live," said the wolf; and in a short time they were there. "Well, this is where the giants live," said the wolf. "There you see your six brothers, whom the giant turned into stone, and yonder are their six brides; and up there is the door through which you must pass." "No, I would not dare do that," said the king's son. "He would murder me." "O no," was the wolf's reply, "when you go in you will find a princess, and she will tell you how to set about getting rid of the giant. You need only do as she says." And the prince went in, though he was afraid. When he entered the house the giant was not there; but in one of the rooms sat a princess, just as the wolf had said, and such a beautiful maiden the youth had never seen. "Now may God help you, how did you get in here?" cried the princess, when she saw him. "It is certain death for you. No one can kill the giant who lives here, for he hasn't his heart about him."

"Well, since I do happen to be here, I will at least make the attempt," said the prince. "And I want to try to deliver my brothers, who stand outside, turned to stone, and I would like to save you as well." "Well, if you insist upon it, we must see what we can do," replied the princess. "Now you must crawl under the bed here, and must listen carefully when I talk to the giant. But you must not make a sound." The prince slipped under the bed, and no sooner was he there than the giant came home. "Hu, it smells like the flesh of a Christian here!" he cried. "Yes," said the princess, "a jackdaw flew by with a human bone, and let it fall down the chimney. I threw it out again at once, but the odor does not disappear so quickly." Then the giant said no more about it. Toward evening he went to bed, but after he had lain there a while, the princess, who sat looking out of the window, said: "There is something I would have asked you about long ago, if only I had dared." "And what may that be?" inquired the giant. "I would like to know where you keep your heart, since you do not have it about you?" said the princess. "O, that is something you need not ask about; at any rate, it lies under the threshold of the door," was the giant's reply. "Aha," thought the prince under the bed, "that is where we will find it!"

The next morning the giant got up very early, and went into the forest, and no sooner had he gone than the prince and the king's daughter set about looking for the heart under the threshold of the door. Yet no matter how much they dug and searched—they found nothing. "This time he has fooled us," said the princess. "We'll have to try again." And she picked the loveliest flowers she could find and strewed them over the threshold—which they had put to rights again—and when the time drew near for the giant's return, the king's son crept under the bed once more. When he was beneath it, the giant came. "Hu hu, I smell human flesh!" he cried. "Yes," said the princess. "A jackdaw flew by with a human bone in her beak, and she let it fall down the chimney. I threw it out at once, but I suppose one can still smell it." Then the giant held his tongue, and said no more about it. After a time he asked who had strewn the flowers over the threshold. "O, I did that," said the princess. "What does it mean?" the giant then asked. "O, I am so fond of you that I had to do it, because I know that is where your heart lies." "Yes, of course," said the giant, "but it does not happen to lie there at all."

When he had gone to bed, the princess sat looking out of the window, and again asked the giant where he kept his heart, for she was so fond of him, said she, that she wanted to know above all things. "O, it is in the wardrobe there by the wall," said the giant. "Aha," thought the king's son under the bed, "that is where we will find it!"

The next morning the giant got up early, and went into the forest, and no sooner had he gone than the prince and the king's daughter set about looking for his heart in the wardrobe. Yet no matter how much they looked, they did not find it. "Well, well," said the princess, "we will have to try once more." Then she adorned the wardrobe with flowers and wreaths, and toward evening the king's youngest son again crawled under the bed. Then the giant came: "Hu hu, it smells of human flesh here!" he cried. "Yes," said the princess. "A jackdaw just this moment flew by with a human bone in her beak, and she let it fall down the chimney. I threw it out again at once, but it may be that you can still smell it." When the giant heard this, he had nothing further to say about it. But not long afterward he noticed that the wardrobe was adorned with flowers and wreaths, and asked who had done it. "I," said the princess. "What do you mean by such tomfoolery?" asked the giant. "O, I am so fond of you that I had to do it, since I know that is where your heart lies," was the reply of the princess. "Are you really so stupid as to believe that?" cried the giant. "Yes, surely, I must believe it," said the princess, "when you tell me so." "How silly you are," said the giant, "you could never reach the place where I keep my heart." "But still I would like to know where it is," answered the princess. Then the giant could no longer resist, and at last had to tell her the truth. "Far, far away, in a lake there lies an island," said he, "and on the island stands a church, and in the church there is a well, and in the well floats a duck, and in the duck there is an egg, and in the egg—is my heart!"

The next morning, before dawn, the giant went to the forest again. "Well, now I must get under way," said the prince, "and it is a way I wish I could find." So he said farewell to the princess for the time being, and when he stepped out of the door, the wolf was standing there waiting for him. He told him what had happened at the giant's, and said that now he would go to the well in the church, if only he knew the way. The wolf told him to climb on his back. He would manage to find the way, said he. And then they were off as though they had wings, over rock and wood, over hill and dale. After they had been underway for many, many days, they at last reached the lake. Then the king's son did not know how they were to get across. But the wolf told him not to worry, and swam across with the prince to the island. Then they came to the church. But the church-key hung high up in the tower, and at first the king's son did not at all know how they were to get it down. "You must call the raven," said the wolf, and that is what the king's son did. And the raven came at once, and flew right down with the key, and now the prince could enter the church. Then, when he came to the well, there was the duck, sure enough, swimming about as the giant had said. He stood by the well and called the duck, and at last he lured her near him, and seized her. But at the moment he grasped her and lifted her out of the water, she let the egg fall into the well, and now the prince again did not know how he was to get hold of it. "Well, you must call the salmon," said the wolf. That is what the king's son did, and the salmon came at once, and brought up the egg from the bottom of the well. Then the wolf told him to squeeze the egg a little. And when the prince squeezed, the giant cried out. "Squeeze it again!" said the wolf, and when the prince did so, the giant cried out far more dolefully, and fearfully and tearfully begged for his life. He would do all the king's son asked him to, said he, if only he would not squeeze his heart in two. "Tell him to give back their original form to your six brothers, whom he turned to stone, and to their brides, as well; and that then you will spare his life," said the wolf, and the prince did so. The troll at once agreed, and changed the six brothers into princes, and their brides into kings' daughters. "Now squash the egg!" cried the wolf. Then the prince squeezed the egg in two, and the giant burst into pieces.

When the king's youngest son had put an end to the giant in this way, he rode back on his wolf to the giant's home; and there stood his six brothers as much alive as ever they had been, together with, their brides. Then the prince went into the hill to get his own bride, and they all rode home together. And great was the joy of the old king when his seven sons all returned, each with his bride. "But the bride of my youngest is the most beautiful, after all, and he shall sit with her at the head of the table!" said the king. And then they had a feast that lasted for weeks, and if they have not stopped, they are feasting to this very day.

THE THREE PRINCESSES IN WHITELAND

Once upon a time there was a fisherman, who lived near the king's castle, and caught fish for the king's table. One day when he had gone fishing, he could not catch a thing. Try as he might, no matter how he baited or flung, not the tiniest fish would bite; but when this had gone on for a while, a head rose from the water and said: "If you will give me the first new thing that has come into your house, you shall catch fish a-plenty!" Then the man agreed quickly, for he could think of no new thing that might have come into the house. So he caught fish all day long, and as many as he could wish for, as may well be imagined. But when he got home, he found that heaven had sent him a little son, the first new thing to come into the house since he had made his promise. And when he told his wife about it, she began to weep and wail, and pray to God because of the vow her husband had made. And the woman's grief was reported at the castle, and when it came to the king's ears, and he learned the reason, he promised to take the boy and see if he could not save him. And so the king took him and brought him up as though he were his own son, until he was grown. Then one day the boy asked whether he might not go out fishing with his father, he wanted to so very much, said he. The king would not hear of it; but at last he was given permission, so he went to his father, and everything went well all day long, until they came home in the evening. Then the son found he had forgotten his handkerchief, and went down to the boat to get it. But no sooner was he in the boat than it moved off with a rush, and no matter how hard the youth worked against it with the oars, it was all in vain.

The boat drove on and on, all night long, and at last he came to a white strand, far, far away. He stepped ashore, and after he had gone a while he met an old man with a great, white beard. "What is this country called?" asked the youth. "Whiteland," was the man's answer, and he asked the youth where he came from, and what he wanted, and the latter told him. "If you keep right on along the shore," said the man, "you will come to three princesses, buried in the earth so that only their heads show. Then the first will call you—and she is the oldest—and beg you very hard to come to her and help her; and the next will do the same; but you must go to neither of them; walk quickly past them, and act as though you neither saw nor heard them. But go up to the third, and do what she asks of you, for then you will make your fortune."

When the youth came to the first princess, she called out to him, and begged him most earnestly to come to her; but he went on as though he had not seen her. And he passed the next one in the same manner; but went over to the third. "If you will do what I tell you to, you shall have whichever one of us you want," said she. Yes, he would do what she wanted. So she told him that three trolls had wished them into the earth where they were; but that formerly they had dwelt in the castle he saw on the edge of the forest.

"Now you must go to the castle, and let the trolls whip you one night through for each one of us," said she, "and if you can hold out, you will have delivered us." "Yes," said the youth, he could manage that. "When you go in," added the princess, "you will find two lions standing by the door; but if you pass directly between them, they will do you no harm. Go on into a dark little room and lie down, and then the troll will come and beat you; but after that you must take the bottle that hangs on the wall, and anoint yourself where he has beaten you, and you will be whole again. And take the sword that hangs beside the bottle, and kill the troll with it." He did as the princess had told him, passed between the lions as though he did not see them, and right into the little room, where he lay down. The first night a troll with three heads and three whips came, and beat the youth badly; but he held out, and when the troll had finished, he took the bottle and anointed himself, grasped the sword and killed the troll. When he came out in the morning the princesses were out of the ground up to their waists. The next night it was the same; but the troll who came this time had six heads and six whips, and beat him worse than the first one. But when he came out in the morning, the princesses were out of the ground up to their ankles. The third night came a troll who had nine heads and nine whips, and he beat and whipped the youth so severely that at last he fainted. Then the troll took him and flung him against the wall, and as he did so the bottle fell down, and its whole contents poured over the youth, and he was at once sound and whole again. Then he did not delay, but grasped the sword, killed the troll, and when he came out in the morning, the princesses were entirely out of the ground. So he chose the youngest of them to be his queen, and lived long with her in peace and happiness.

But at last he was minded to travel home, and see how his parents fared. This did not suit his queen; but since he wanted to go so badly, and finally was on the point of departure, she said to him: "One thing you must promise me, that you will only do what your father tells you to do, but not what your mother tells you to do." And this he promised. Then she gave him a ring which had the power of granting two wishes to the one who wore it. So he wished himself home, and his parents could not get over their surprise at seeing how fine and handsome he had become.

When he had been home a few days, his mother wanted him to go up to the castle and show the king what a man he had grown to be. His father said: "No, he had better not do that, for we will have to do without him in the meantime." But there was no help for it, the mother begged and pleaded until he went. When he got there he was more splendidly dressed and fitted out than the other king. This did not suit the latter, and he said: "You can see what my queen looks like, but I cannot see yours; and I do not believe yours is as beautiful as mine." "God grant she were standing here, then you would see soon enough!" said the young king, and there she stood that very minute. But she was very sad, and said to him: "Why did you not follow my advice and listen to your father? Now I must go straight home, and you have used up both of your wishes." With that she bound a ring with her name on it in his hair, and wished herself home.

Then the young king grew very sad, and went about day in, day out, with no other thought than getting back to his queen. "I must try and see whether I cannot find out where Whiteland is," thought he, and wandered forth into the wide world. After he had gone a while he came to a hill; and there he met one who was the lord of all the beasts of the forest—for they came when he blew his horn—and him the king asked where Whiteland was. "That I do not know," said he, "but I will ask my beasts." Then he called them up with his horn, and asked whether any of them knew where Whiteland might be; but none of them knew anything about it.

Then the man gave him a pair of snowshoes. "If you stand in them," said he, "you will come to my brother, who lives a hundred miles further on. He is the lord of the birds of the air. Ask him. When you have found him, turn the snowshoes around so that they point this way, and they will come back home of their own accord." When the king got there, he turned the snowshoes around, as the lord of the beasts had told him, and they ran home again. He asked about Whiteland, and the man called up all the birds with his horn, and asked whether any of them knew where Whiteland might be. But none of them knew. Long after the rest an old eagle came along; and he had been out for some ten years, but did not know either.

"Well," said the man, "I will lend you a pair of snowshoes. When you stand in them you will come to my brother, who lives a hundred miles further on. He is the lord of all the fishes in the sea. Ask him. But do not forget to turn the snowshoes around again." The king thanked him, stepped into the snowshoes, and when he came to the one who was lord of all the fishes in the sea, he turned them around, and they ran back like the others. There he once more asked about Whiteland.

The man called up his fishes with his horn, but none of them knew anything about it. At last there came an old, old carp, whom he had called with his horn only at the cost of much trouble. When he asked him, he said: "Yes, I know it well, for I was cook there for fully ten years. To-morrow I have to go back again, because our queen, whose king has not come home again, is going to marry some one else." "If such be the case," said the man, "I'll give you a bit of advice. Out there by the wall three brothers have been standing for the last hundred years, fighting with each other about a hat, a cloak and a pair of boots. Any one who has these three things can make himself invisible, and wish himself away as far as ever he will. You might say that you would test their possessions, and then decide their quarrel for them." Then the king thanked him, and did as he said. "Why do you stand there fighting till the end of time?" said he to the brothers. "Let me test your possessions if I am to decide your quarrel." That suited them; but when he had hat, cloak and boots, he told them: "I will give you my decision the next time we meet!" and with that he wished himself far away. While he was flying through the air he happened to meet the North Wind. "And where are you going?" asked the North Wind. "To Whiteland," said the king, and then he told him what had happened to him. "Well," said the North Wind, "you are traveling a little quicker than I am; for I must sweep and blow out every corner. But when you come to your journey's end, stand on the steps beside the door, and then I'll come roaring up as though I were going to tear down the whole castle. And when the prince who is to have the queen comes and looks out to see what it all means, I'll just take him along with me."

The king did as the North Wind told him. He stationed himself on the steps; and when the North Wind came roaring and rushing up, and laid hold of the castle walls till they fairly shook, the prince came out to see what it was all about. But that very moment the king seized him by the collar, and threw him out, and the North Wind took him and carried him off. When he had borne him away, the king went into the castle. At first the queen did not recognize him, for he had grown thin and pale because he had wandered so long in his great distress; but when he showed her the ring, she grew glad at heart, and then they had a wedding which was such a wedding that the news of it spread far and wide.

TROUBLE AND CARE

Far, far from here there once lived a king, who had three beautiful daughters. But he had no sons, and therefore he grew so fond of the three princesses that he granted their every wish. But in time the enemy invaded the country, and the king had to go to war. When he set out, the oldest princess begged him to buy her a ring that would prevent her dying as long as she wore it. The second princess asked him for a wreath that would make her happy whenever she looked at it, no matter how sad and troubled her heart might be. "Buy me trouble and care!" said the youngest. And the king promised everything.

When he had driven the enemy out of his own land, and out of the neighboring land as well, and was about to set out for home, he remembered what he had promised the three princesses. The ring and the wreath were easy enough to obtain; but trouble and care were to be had neither in one place nor in another, for all the people were so happy that the enemy had been driven out, that there was no sorrow nor care to be found in the entire kingdom. And since he could not buy it, it was not to be had at all, and he had to travel home without it, loathe as he was to do so.

When he was not far from the castle, his way took him through a thick forest. And there sat a squirrel in a tree by the road. "Buy me! buy me! My name is trouble and care!" it said. Thought the king to himself, It is better to have a squirrel than two empty hands, so he brought it along for his youngest daughter. And she was quite as well pleased with her present as her two sisters were with the ring and the wreath. The squirrel played about in her room, sometimes it balanced itself on the bed-posts, at others it would sit on the top of the wardrobe, and it always had a great deal to chatter about.

But as soon as it grew dark, it turned into a man. And he told her how an evil and malicious giantess dwelt in the golden forest, who had turned him into a squirrel because he would not marry her. During the night she had no power over him; but every morning at daybreak he had to slip back into his squirrel form.

And in the course of time the princess actually wanted to marry Trouble and Care; but when they were betrothed, he begged her earnestly, and as best he knew how, never to light a light at night, and try to look at him, "for then both of us would be unhappy," said he. No, said she, she would be quite sure not to do so.

And every evening, when the princess had lain down and blown out the light, she would hear a man go into Trouble and Care's room; but when morning dawned, the squirrel sat on her bed-post and greeted her, and chattered and babbled about all sorts of things.

Once, when she thought Trouble and Care had gone to sleep, she could not help herself; but stood up quietly, lit a light and crept softly into his room and to his bed, and when the ray of light fell on him, she saw that he was far, far hand-somer than the most handsome prince. He was so surpass-ingly handsome that she bent over him in order to see more clearly, and finally she could not help herself, but had to kiss him. And then, three drops of wax from the candle fell on his chest, and he awoke.

"But how could you have done this!" he cried, and was quite unhappy. "Had you only waited three days longer, I should have been free!" said he. "But now I must return to the evil giantess and marry her, and all is over between us."

"Can I not follow you there?" asked the princess. "No, that is something you could not do in all your days, for if you rest or even so much as bend your knees to sit down, you will go back during the night as far as you came forward during the day," said he; leaped to the door, and disappeared.

Then the princess wept and wailed, and waited for him to return; but she heard and saw nothing more of him. After a few days she grew so restless and wretched that she could no longer remain at home, and implored her maid to go along with her to search for the golden forest. The girl finally allowed herself to be moved; but she would not agree to set out until she had gotten together a yard of drilling, a yard of ticking, and a yard of fine linen; and she got them at once, as you may imagine, for there was no shortage of such things in the castle.

So they set out and wandered far, and ever farther, until their feet ached, and their spirits fell. Toward evening they came into the middle of a thick, dark forest; and climbed up into a high tree. The princess was so tired that the maid had to hold her in her arms while she slept a little. But during the night the ground about the tree grew alive with wolves, in the most sinister fashion, and they howled and cried, so that the princess did not venture to close her eyes another moment. But when daylight appeared in the skies, it seemed as though the wolves had suddenly all been blown away.

The following day they wandered far and ever farther, until their feet ached more, and their spirits sank lower. Toward evening they again came to the middle of a thick, dark forest. And they once more climbed into a high, high tree; but the princess was so tired that the maid had to hold her in her arms while she slept a little. When it grew darker, a most alarming number of bears flocked together under the tree, and began to dance and turn in a circle, with alarming speed, and all at once they tried to climb the tree. So the princess and her maid had to stand up in the tree-top the whole night through, and could not close an eye; but when day came, it seemed as though the bears sank into the earth in a single moment.

The third day they wandered far and ever farther, and then a bit more. Toward evening they again came to a thick, dark forest. There they again climbed into a high, high tree; but no sooner were they up in the tree than the ground beneath the tree and the whole forest were alive with lions, and they all roared and howled together in such a gruesome way that the echoes came back from rock and woodland. Suddenly they began to dance and whirl around in such a terrible fashion that the earth trembled, and in between they would clutch the tree again, and try to shake and loosen it, as though they would pull it out root and branch. The princess and her maid had to stand up in the very tree-top, and though they were so tired they could have fallen down from time to time, neither of them dared think of sleeping. But the moment day dawned, the lions all suddenly disappeared from the face of the earth, where they were, walking and standing.

Then they stumbled along, this way and that, the whole day long, until their feet ached harder than hard, and their spirits sank lower than low. They lost path and direction, and though they hunted north and south and east and west, they could not find the way out of the great, dark forest.

At last the princess grew tired and sad beyond all measure, and wanted to sit down every moment, in order to rest a little; but the maid held her and dragged her forward, and never let her bend her knees for a moment to sit down, because then they would have gone back just as far as they had come that day; for you must know that the giantess in the golden forest had so arranged matters.

In the evening they came to an enormous, horrible rock. "I will knock here," said the maid, and tapped and knocked. "O no," said the princess, "please don't knock here, you can see how ugly everything is here!" "Who is knocking there at my door?" cried the giantess in the rock, in a loud, harsh manner, opened the door, and stuck her nose—it was all of a yard long—out through the crack.

"The youngest princess and her maid, they want to get to a prince in the golden forest, whose name is Trouble and Care," was the maid's reply.

"O, faugh!" cried the giantess, "that is so far to the north that one can neither sail nor row there. But what do you want of Trouble and Care? Is this, perhaps, the princess who wanted to marry him?" asked the giantess. Yes, this was the princess. "Well, she will never get him as long as she lives," said the giantess, "for now he must marry the great giantess in the golden forest. You might just as well go back home now as later," said she. No, they would not turn back for anything, and the maid asked whether it would not be possible for her to take them in for the darkest part of the night. "I can take you in easily enough," said the giantess, "but when my husband comes home he will tear off your heads, and eat you up!" But there was no help for it, they could not go on in the middle of the night. Then the maid pulled out the yard of ticking, and gave it to the giantess for linen. "It can't be true! It can't be true!" cried she. "Here I have been married all of a hundred years, and have never yet had any ticking!" And she was so pleased that she invited the wanderers in, received them kindly, and took the best care of them. After a while, when they had strengthened themselves with food and drink, the giantess said to them: "Yes, he is a ferocious fellow, is my husband, and I will have to hide you in the anteroom. Perhaps he will not find you then." And she prepared a bed for them, as soft and comfortable as a bed can be; but they did not care to lie down in it, nor sit in it; no, they could not even close their eyes, for they had to watch to see that their knees did not bend. So they stood the whole night through, and took turns holding each other up, for by now the maid was so weary and wretched that she was ready to give in.

Toward midnight it began to thunder and rumble in a terrible manner. This was the troll coming home; and no sooner had he thrust his first head in at the door than he cried out loudly and harshly: "Faugh! faugh! I smell Christian bodies!" and he rushed about in so wild and furious a manner that the sparks flew. "Yes," said the giantess, "a bird flew past with a bone from a Christian, and he let it drop down the chimney. I threw it out again as quickly as I could, but perhaps one can smell it still," said the giantess, and soothed him again. And he was satisfied with her explanation. But the next morning the giantess told him that the youngest princess and her maid had come in search of a prince named Trouble and Care, in the golden forest. "O faugh! that is so far to the north that one can neither sail nor row there!" the troll at once cried. "It is the princess who wanted to marry him, I know, but she will never get him as long as she lives, for he has to marry the great giantess in three days' time. But the maidens shall not get away from me! Where are they, where are they?" he cried, and sniffed and snuffed about in every corner. "O no, you must not touch them," said the giantess. "They have given me a yard of ticking, and here I have been married now for more than a hundred years, and have never owned any ticking. Therefore you must lend them your seven-mile waistcoat to the nearest neighbor," said the giantess, and pleaded for the girls. And the troll was willing when he heard how kind they had been to his wife.

When they had eaten and were ready to travel, he put his seven-mile waistcoat on them: "And now you must repeat: 'Forward over willow bush and pine-tree, over hill and dale, to the nearest neighbor,'" said he. "And when you get there you must say: 'You are to be hung up this evening where you were put on this morning!'" The maidens did as he said, and were carried for miles, over hill and dale. In the evening, at dusk, they again came to a great, ugly rock. There they pulled off the seven-mile waistcoat and said: "You are to be hung up this evening where you were put on this morning," and then the waistcoat ran home by itself.

"I will knock here," said the maid, and knocked and thumped on the rock. "O no," said the princess, "please do not knock here. You can see how sinister everything is here!" "Who is thumping at my door?" cried the giantess inside the rock, more loudly and harshly than the first one, and she opened the door and thrust her nose, that was all of two yards long, right through the crack. "Here stand the youngest princess and her maid, and they are looking for a prince named Trouble and Care, who lives in the golden forest," answered the maid. And then this giantess also said it was so far north that one could neither sail nor row there, and wanted them to turn back by all means. "You might just as well turn back now as later," said she. But this the maidens did not want to do at all, and the maid asked whether she would not, perhaps, take them in for the night, and if it were only the darkest part of the night. "Yes, I can take you in easily enough," said the giantess, "but when my husband comes home to-night, he will tear off your heads and eat you up!" Then the maid pulled out a yard of drilling, and gave it to the giantess for linen. "It can't be true! It can't be true! here I have been married now for over two hundred years, and I have never yet had any drilling in the house," cried the giantess, and she was so pleased that she invited them in, and received them kindly, and saw that they wanted for nothing. After a while, when they had strengthened themselves with food and drink, the giantess said: "Yes, he is a ferocious fellow, is my husband, and he eats up every Christian who comes here, root and branch. I'll have to put you in the anteroom, perhaps he will not find you there," and she prepared a bed for the maidens. But they did not dare either to lie down nor sit on it, not for a single moment, for they had to watch to see that they did not bend their knees. So they stood there the whole night through, and took turns holding each other up, while each snatched a little sleep.

Toward midnight it began to rumble and thunder in such a terrible manner that they could feel the earth tremble beneath them. Then the troll came rushing in. "Faugh! faugh! I smell Christian bodies!" he cried out loudly and harshly, and thrashed about in such a furious way that the sparks flew from him as from a fire. "Yes," said the giantess, "a bird flew by, and let a bone from a Christian fall through the chimney. I threw it out again as quickly as I could, but it may well be the case that the smell still lingers," said she, and quieted her husband. And he was satisfied with her explanation. But when he got up in the morning, she told him that the youngest princess and her maid had come in search of a prince named Trouble and Care, in the golden forest. When the troll heard that, he also said that it was so far north that one could neither sail nor row there. "That is the princess who wanted to marry him. Yes, I know; but she will never get him as long as she lives, for he must marry the great giantess herself in two days' time," said the troll. "And where are they, these maidens? They shall not escape from me with their lives!" he shouted, and sniffed and snuffed about everywhere. "O no, you must not harm them!" said the giantess, and told him that they had given her a yard of drilling for linen. "Therefore you must lend them your seven-mile waistcoat to the nearest neighbor," said she. And he was willing at once, when he heard how kind they had been to his giantess. When they had eaten in the morning, he put his seven-mile waistcoat on them. "When you reach your goal, you need only say: 'Where you were put on this morning, there you are to hang again to-night!' and then the seven-mile waistcoat will travel home by itself," said the troll. Then they were carried for miles, over hill and dale, on and on. In the evening, at dusk, they again came to a great, ugly rock.

"I will knock here!" said the maid, and knocked and thumped on the rock. "O no," said the princess, "please do not knock here, you can see how sinister everything looks here!" "Who is thumping at my door?" the giantess cried inside the rock, in a ruder and harsher manner than the other two giantesses, and she opened the door just far enough so that she could thrust her nose, which was all of three yards long, through the crack. "Here stand the youngest princess and her maid, in search of a prince named Trouble and Care, who lives in the golden forest," was the maid's reply. "O faugh!" cried the giantess, "that is so far to the north that one can neither sail nor row there. But what do you want of Trouble and Care? Is this, perhaps, the princess who wanted to marry him?" asked the giantess. Yes, this was the princess, was the maid's reply. Then this giantess said in turn: "He must marry the great giantess in the golden forest, so you might just as well turn back home now as later!" But this the maidens did not want to do at all, and the maid asked whether, perhaps, she would not take them in for the night, and if it were only for the very darkest part of the night.

"Yes, I can take you in easily enough," said the giantess, "but when my husband comes home to-night he will tear off your heads and eat you up!" But there was nothing else to do; they could not travel on through the wood and wilderness, in the very darkest part of the night. Then the maid pulled out the yard of linen and made the giantess a present of it. "It can't be true! It can't be true!" cried she. "Here I have been married now for more than three hundred years, and have never yet had a bit of linen!" And she was so pleased that she invited the maidens in, and received them kindly, and let them want for nothing. "He is a ferocious fellow, is my husband, and he does away with every Christian soul that strays here," she said, when her guests had eaten. "But I will hide you in the anteroom. Perhaps he will not find you there." Then she carefully made up a soft bed for them, as fine as the finest in the world. But now the princess was weary and wretched and sleepy beyond all measure. She could no longer stand up at all, and finally had to lie down and sleep a little, and even though it were but a tiny little while. The maid was also so weary and wretched that she fell asleep standing, and fell over from time to time. Yet she still managed to keep her wits about her to the extent of seizing the princess, and holding her up, so that she did not bend her knees. Toward midnight it began to rumble and thunder so that the whole house shook, and it seemed as though the roof and walls would fall in. This was the great troll, who was coming home. When he thrust his first nose in at the door, he at once cried out in a manner so wild and harsh that the like had never been heard before: "Faugh! faugh! I smell Christian bodies!" and he fell into a white rage, so that sparks and flame flew from him. "Yes, a bird flew by, and let a bone from a Christian fall through the chimney. I threw it out as quickly as ever I could; but it may be that the smell still persists!" said the giantess, and tried to pacify her troll. And he was satisfied with her explanation. But when he awoke in the morning, she told him that the youngest princess and her maid had come in search of a prince named Trouble and Care, who lived in the golden forest. "O faugh! That is so far north that one can neither sail nor row there!" cried the great troll, just as the smaller trolls had. "But she will never get him as long as she lives, for to-morrow he must marry the great giantess. Where are they, these maidens? Hm, hm, hm, they will make tasty eating!" he cried, and danced around everywhere, and sniffed and snuffed with all his nine noses at once. "O no, you must not harm them!" cried the giantess. "They have given me a yard of linen, and here I have been married for more than three hundred years, and have never had a bit of linen yet. Therefore you must lend them your seven-mile waistcoat to the nearest neighbor." And when the super-troll heard that the maidens had been so kind, he was agreeable.

When they had strengthened themselves in the morning, he put his seven-mile waistcoat on them. "And now you must repeat: 'On, on! Over willow brush and pine tree, over hill and dale, to the nearest neighbor.' And when you reach your goal, you need only say: 'You must hang again to-night on the nail from which you were taken down this morning!'" said the great troll. They did as he had told them, and were carried farther and farther along, over hills and deep valleys.

At dusk they came to a large, large forest, where all the trees were black as coal. If one only so much as touched them, they made one look like a chimney-sweep. And in the middle of the forest was a clearing, and there stood a wretched hut, ready to fall apart; it was only held together by two beams, and looked more forlorn than the most wretched herdsman's hut. And in front of the door lay a rubbish heap of old shoes, dirty rags and other ugly stuff. Here the maid took off the seven-mile waistcoat, and said: "You must hang again to-night from the nail from which you were taken down this morning!" and the waistcoat wandered home all by itself.

"I will knock here!" said the maid. "O no, O no," wailed the princess, "please do not knock here, you can see how ugly everything is!" "If you do not do as I do, then it will be the worse for both of us!" said the maid; trampled through the rubbish-pile and knocked. An old, old troll-woman with a nose all of three yards long, looked out through the crack in the door. "If you girls want to come in, then come in, and if you do not want to, you can stay out!" said she, and made as though to close the door in their faces. "Yes, indeed, we want to come in," replied the maid, and drew the princess in with her. "If you girls want to come through the door, then come through, but if you do not want to, you can stay out," the woman said once more. "Yes, thanks, we want to come in," said the maid, and tramped over the threshold through the dirt and rags. "Alas, alas!" wailed the princess, and tramped after her. All was black and ugly inside, and as grimy and dirty as a corn-loft. After a while the giantess went out, and fetched them some milk to drink. "If you girls want to drink, why, drink, and if you do not, why, do without!" said she, and was about to carry it out again. "Yes, thanks, we want to drink," said the maid, and drank. "Alas, alas!" wailed the princess, when it came her turn, for the milk was in a pig-trough, and dirt and clots of hair were swimming in it. Then the giantess gave them something to eat. "If you girls want to eat, why, eat, and if you do not, why, do without," said the giantess. "Yes, indeed, we will be glad to," said the maid, before the ugly nosey could take the food away again. The bread was moldly, mice had been nibbling at the cheese, the meat was so old that one could smell it at a distance, and two dirty calves' tails were draped about the butter. "Alas, alas!" wailed the princess, and was ready to cry; but she had to do what her maid did, and taste the horrible dishes. Then they had to say they were much obliged. An old man, whom thus far they had not seen, lay on a bed covered with a few old odds and ends of fur and other rags. When they went up to him to thank him, he stood up, and when the princess gave him her hand he kissed it; and at that very moment he turned into a prince handsome beyond all measure, and the princess saw that he was Trouble and Care, for whom she had so greatly longed. "Now you have delivered me!" he said. "Woe to whoever has delivered you!" cried the giantess, and rushed out of the door; but on the doorstep she stood like a stone, for the forest was no longer black, and all the trees looked as though they had been gilded from root to crest, and glittered and sparkled more brightly than the sun at noon-day. The wretched, dirty hut had changed into a royal castle, immensely large and handsome. One might have thought that the roof and walls were made of the purest gold and silver, and so they were. "Now you may bend your knee again," said the prince, "and if you have hitherto known nothing but sorrow and care, you shall henceforth know all the more happiness."

The old giantess had brewed and baked, and prepared the whole wedding dinner. And when the next day dawned, the prince and the princess, and all the people in the castle, and in the whole country over which he was king, celebrated the wedding. And it lasted for four times fourteen days, so that the news spread through seven kingdoms, and reached the bride's father and her two sisters. And they would have celebrated it with them, had they not been so far away. I was invited to the feast myself, and the bridegroom made me chief cook, and I had to speak the toast for the bride and groom. But on the last day of the feast, I had to draw mead from a large, large cask that lay at the farthest end of the cellar. Before I sent off the filled jug, I took a taste myself, and the mead was so strong that it suddenly went to my head, and I flew through the air like a bird, and there I was, floating between heaven and earth for full nine years, and then I fell down here in the village, in front of the house up there on the hill. And out came Bertha Friendly, with a letter for me from the prince, who had become king in the meantime, and the letter said that he and the young queen were doing well, and that they sent me their greetings, and that I was to greet you for them, and that you and your sisters were invited to the castle Sunday after Michaelmas, and then you should see a pair of dear little princes, the golden forest, and the old stone giantess, who stands before the door with her nose three yards long.

OLA STORBAEKKJEN

Once upon a time there lived a man in the forest of Dovre whose name was Ola Storbaekkjen. He was of giant build, powerful and fearless. During the winter he did not work, but traveled from one fair to another, hunting up quarrels and brawls. From Christiansmarkt he went to Branaes and Konigsberg, and thence to Grundsaet, and wherever he came squabbles and brawls broke out, and in every brawl he was the victor. In the summer he dealt in cattle at Valders and the fjords, and fought with the fjord-folk and the hill people of Halling and Valders, and always had the best of it. But sometimes they scratched him a bit with the knife, did those folk.

Now once, at the time of the hay harvest, he was home at Baekkjen, and had lain down to take a little after-dinner nap under the penthouse. And he was taken into the hill, which happened in the following way: A man with a pair of gilded goat's horns came along and butted Ola, but Ola fell upon him so that the man had to duck back, again and again. But the stranger stood up once more, and began to butt again, and finally he took Ola under his arm like a glove, and then both of them flew straight off into the hill.

In the place to which they came all was adorned with silver plates and dishes, and with ornaments of silver, and Ola thought that the king himself had nothing finer. They offered him mead, which he drank; but eat he would not, for the food did not seem to him to be appetizing. Suddenly the man with the gilded goat's horns came in, and gave Ola a shove before he knew it; but Ola came back at him as before, and so they beat and pulled each other through all the rooms, and along all the walls. Ola was of the opinion that they had been at it all night long; but by that time the scuffle had lasted over four-teen days, and they had already tolled the church bells for him on three successive Thursday evenings. On the third Thursday evening he was in ill ease, for the people in the hill had in mind to thrust him forth. When the bells stopped ringing, he sat at a crack in the hill, with his head looking out. Had not a man come by and happened to spy him, and told the people to keep on ringing the church-bells, the hill would have closed over him again, and he would probably still be inside. But when he came out he had been so badly beaten, and was so miserable, that it passed all measure. The lumps on his head were each bigger than the other, his whole body was black and blue, and he was quite out of his mind. And from time to time he would leap up, run off and try to get back into the hill to take up his quarrel again, and fight for the gilded goat's horns. For those he wanted to break from the giant's forehead.

THE CAT WHO COULD EAT SO MUCH

Once upon a time there was a man who had a cat, and she ate so very much that he did not want to keep her any longer. So he decided to tie a stone around her neck, and throw her into the river; but before he did so she was to have something to eat just once more. The woman offered her a dish of mush and a little potful of fat. These she swallowed, and then jumped out of the window. There stood the man on the threshing-floor.

"Good-day, man in the house," said the cat.

"Good-day, cat," said the man. "Have you had anything to eat yet today?"

"O, only a little, but my fast has hardly been broken," said the cat. "I have had no more than a dish of mush and a little potful of fat, and I am thinking over whether I ought not to eat you as well," said she, and she seized the man and ate him up. Then she went into the stable. There sat the woman, milking.

"Good-day, woman in the stable," said the cat.

"Good-day, cat, is that you?" said the woman. "Have you eaten your food?" she asked.

"O, only a little today. My fast has hardly been broken," said the cat. "I have had no more than a dish of mush and a little potful of fat and the man in the house, and I'm thinking over whether I ought not to eat you as well," said she, and she seized the woman and ate her up.

"Good-day, cow at the manger," said the cat to the bell-cow.

"Good-day, cat," said the bell-cow. "Have you had anything to eat yet today?" "O, only a little. My fast has hardly been broken," said the cat. "I have had no more than a dish of mush and a little potful of fat and the man in the house and the woman in the stable, and I'm thinking over whether I ought not to eat you as well," said the cat, and seized the bell-cow and ate her up. Then she went up to the orchard, and there stood a man who was sweeping up leaves.

"Good-day, leaf-sweeper in the orchard," said the cat.

"Good-day, cat," said the man. "Have you had anything to eat yet today?"

"O, only a little. My fast has hardly been broken," said the cat. "I have had no more than a dish of mush and a little potful of fat and the man in the house and the woman in the stable and the bell-cow at the manger, and I'm thinking over whether I ought not to eat you up as well," said she, and seized the leaf-sweeper and ate him up.

Then she came to a stone-pile. There stood the weasel, looking about him.

"Good-day, weasel on the stone-pile," said the cat.

"Good-day, cat," said the weasel. "Have you had anything to eat yet today?"

"O, only a little. My fast has hardly been broken," said the cat. "I have had no more than a dish of mush and a little potful of fat and the man in the house and the woman in the stable and the bell-cow at the manger and the leaf-sweeper in the orchard, and I'm thinking over whether I ought not to eat you as well," said the cat, and seized the weasel and ate him up.

After she had gone a while, she came to a hazel-bush. There sat the squirrel, gathering nuts.

"Good-day, squirrel in the bush," said the cat.

"Good-day, cat! Have you already had anything to eat yet

today?" said the squirrel.

"O, only a little. My fast has hardly been broken," said the cat. "I have had no more than a dish of mush and a little potful of fat and the man in the house and the woman in the stable and the bell-cow at the manger and the leaf-sweeper in the orchard and the weasel on the stone-pile, and I'm thinking over whether I ought not to eat you up as well," said she, and seized the squirrel and ate him up.

After she had gone a little while longer, she met Reynard the fox, who was peeping out of the edge of the forest.

"Good-day, fox, you sly-boots," said the cat.

"Good-day, cat! Have you had anything to eat yet today?" said the fox.

"O, only a little. My fast has hardly been broken," said the cat. "I have had no more than a dish of mush and a little potful of fat and the man in the house and the woman in the stable and the bell-cow at the manger and the leaf-sweeper in the orchard and the weasel on the stone-pile and the squirrel in the hazel-bush, and I'm thinking over whether I ought not to eat you as well," said she, and seized the fox and ate him up too.

When she had gone a little further, she met a hare.

"Good-day, you hopping hare," said the cat.

"Good-day, cat! Have you had anything to eat yet today?" said the hare.

"O, only a little. My fast has hardly been broken," said the cat. "I have had no more than a dish of mush and a little potful of fat and the man in the house and the woman in the stable and the bell-cow at the manger and the leaf-sweeper in the orchard and the weasel on the stone-pile and the squirrel in the hazel-bush and the fox, the sly-boots, and I'm thinking over whether I ought not to eat you up as well," said she, and seized the hare and ate him up.

When she had gone a little further, she met a wolf.

"Good-day, you wild wolf," said the cat.

"Good-day, cat! Have you had anything to eat yet today?" said the wolf.

"O, only a little. My fast has hardly been broken," said the cat. "I have had no more than a dish of mush and a little potful of fat and the man in the house and the woman in the stable and the bell-cow at the manger and the leaf-sweeper in the orchard and the weasel on the stone-pile and the squirrel in the hazel-bush and the fox, the sly-boots, and the hopping hare, and I'm thinking over whether I ought not to eat you up as well," said she, and seized the wolf and ate him up, too.

Then she went into the wood, and when she had gone far and farther than far, over hill and dale, she met a young bear.

"Good-day, little bear brown-coat," said the cat.

"Good-day, cat! Have you had anything to eat yet today?" said the bear.

"O, only a little. My fast has hardly been broken," said the cat. "I have had no more than a dish of mush and a little pot of fat and the man in the house and the woman in the stable and the bell-cow at the manger and the leaf-sweeper in the orchard and the weasel on the stone-pile and the squirrel in the hazel-bush and the fox, the sly-boots, and the hopping hare and the wild wolf, and I'm thinking over whether I ought not to eat you up as well," said she, and seized the little bear and ate him up.

When the cat had gone a bit further, she met the mother bear, who was clawing at the tree-stems so that the bark flew, so angry was she to have lost her little one.

"Good-day, you biting mother bear," said the cat.

"Good-day, cat! Have you had anything to eat yet today?" said the mother bear.

"O, only a little. My fast has hardly been broken," said the cat. "I have had no more than a dish of mush and a little potful of fat and the man in the house and the woman in the stable and the bell-cow at the manger and the leaf-sweeper in the orchard and the weasel on the stone-pile and the squirrel in the hazel-bush and the fox, the sly-boots, and the hopping hare and the wild wolf and the little bear brown-coat, and I'm thinking over whether I ought not to eat you as well," said she, and seized the mother bear and ate her, too.

When the cat had gone on a little further, she met the bear himself.

"Good-day, Bruin Good-fellow," said she.

"Good-day, cat! Have you had anything to eat yet today?" asked the bear.

"O, only a little. My fast has hardly been broken," said the cat. "I have had no more than a dish of mush and a little potful of fat and the man in the house and the woman in the stable and the bell-cow at the manger and the leaf-sweeper in the orchard and the weasel in the stone-pile and the squirrel in the hazel-bush and the fox, the sly-boots, and the hopping hare and the wild wolf and the little bear brown-coat and the biting mother bear, and now I'm thinking over whether I ought not to eat you as well," said she, and she seized the bear and ate him up, too.

Then the cat went far and farther than far, until she came into the parish. And there she met a bridal party on the road.

"Good-day, bridal party on the road," said the cat.

"Good-day, cat! Have you had anything to eat yet today?"

"O, only a little. My fast is hardly broken," said the cat. "I have had no more than a dish of mush and a little potful of fat and the man in the house and the woman in the stable and the bell-cow at the manger and the leaf-sweeper in the orchard and the weasel on the stone-pile and the squirrel in the hazel-bush and the fox, the sly-boots, and the hopping hare and the wild wolf and the little bear brown-coat and the biting mother bear and bruin good-fellow and now I'm thinking whether I ought not to eat you up as well," said she, and she pounced on the whole bridal party, and ate it up, with the cook, the musicians, the horses and all.

When she had gone a bit farther, she came to the church. And there she met a funeral procession.

"Good-day, funeral procession at the church," said the cat.

"Good-day, cat! Have you had anything to eat yet today?" said the funeral procession.

"O, only a little. My fast has hardly been broken," said the cat. "I have had no more than a dish of mush and a little potful of fat and the man in the house and the woman in the stable and the bell-cow at the manger and the leaf-sweeper in the orchard and the weasel on the stone-pile and the squirrel in the hazel-bush and the fox, the sly-boots, and the hopping hare and the wild wolf and little bear brown-coat and the biting mother bear and bruin good-fellow and the bridal party on the road, and now I'm thinking over whether I ought not to eat you up as well," said she, and pounced on the funeral procession, and ate up corpse and procession.

When the cat had swallowed it all, she went straight on up to the sky, and when she had gone far and farther than far, she met the moon in a cloud.

"Good-day, moon in a cloud," said the cat.

"Good-day, cat! Have you had anything to eat yet today?" said the moon.

"O, only a little. My fast has hardly been broken," said the cat. "I have had no more than a dish of mush and a little potful of fat and the man in the house and the woman in the stable and the bell-cow at the manger and the leaf-sweeper in the orchard and the weasel on the stone-pile and the squirrel in the hazel-bush and the fox, the sly-boots, and the wild wolf and little bear brown-coat and the biting mother bear and bruin good-fellow and the bridal party on the road and the funeral procession at the church, and now I'm thinking over whether I ought not to eat you up as well," said she, and pounced on the moon and ate him up, half and full.

Then the cat went far and farther than far, and met the sun.

"Good morning, cat! Have you had anything to eat yet today?" said the sun.

"O, only a little," said the cat. "I have had no more than a dish of mush and a little potful of fat and the man in the house and the woman in the stable and the bell-cow at the manger and the leaf-sweeper in the orchard and the weasel on the stone-pile and the squirrel in the hazel-bush and the fox, the sly-boots, and the hopping hare and the wild wolf and little bear brown-coat and the biting mother bear and bruin good-fellow and the bridal party on the road and the funeral procession at the church and the moon in a cloud, and now I'm thinking over whether I ought not to eat you up as well," said she, and pounced on the sun in the sky and ate him up.

Then the cat went far and farther than far, until she came to a bridge, and there she met a large billy-goat.

"Good morning, billy-goat on the broad bridge," said the cat.

"Good morning, cat! Have you had anything to eat yet today?" said the goat.

"O, only a little. My fast has hardly been broken," said the cat. "I had no more than a dish of mush and a little potful of fat and the man in the house and the woman in the stable and the bell-cow at the manger and the leaf-sweeper in the orchard and the weasel on the stone-pile and the squirrel in the hazel-bush and the fox, the sly-boots, and the hopping hare and the wild wolf and little bear brown-coat and the biting mother bear and bruin good-fellow and the bridal party on the road and the funeral procession at the church and the moon in a cloud and the sun in the sky, and now I'm thinking over whether I ought not to eat you up as well," said she.

"We'll fight about that first of all," said the goat, and butted the cat with his horns so that she rolled off the bridge, and fell into the water, and there she burst.

Then they all crawled out, and each went to his own place, all whom the cat had eaten up, and were every one of them as lively as before, the man in the house and the woman in the stable and the bell-cow at the manger and the leaf-sweeper in the orchard and the weasel on the stone-pile and the squirrel in the hazel-bush and the fox, the sly-boots, and the hopping hare and the wild wolf and little bear brown-coat and the biting mother bear and bruin good-fellow and the bridal party on the road and the funeral procession at the church and the moon in a cloud and the sun in the sky.

EAST OF THE SUN AND WEST OF THE MOON

Once upon a time there was a poor tenant farmer who had a number of children whom he could feed but poorly, and had to clothe in the scantiest way. They were all handsome; but the most beautiful, after all, was the youngest daughter, for she was beautiful beyond all telling.

Now it happened that one Thursday evening late in the fall there was a terrible storm raging outside. It was pitch dark, and it rained and stormed so that the house shook in every joint. The whole family sat around the hearth, and each was busy with some work or other. Suddenly there were three loud knocks on the window-pane. The man went out to see who was there, and when he stepped outside, there stood a great white bear.

"Good evening," said the white bear.

"Good evening," returned the man.

"If you'll give me your youngest daughter, I will make you just as rich as now you are poor," said the bear.

The man was not ill-pleased that he was to become so rich; yet he did think that first he ought to speak to his daughter about it. So he went in again, and said that there was a white bear outside, who had promised to make him just as rich as he was poor now, if he could only have the youngest daughter for his bride. But the girl said no, and would not hear of it. Then the man went back to the bear again, and they both agreed that the white bear should return again the following Thursday and get his answer. In the meantime, however, the parents worked upon their daughter, and talked at length about all the riches they would gain, and how well she herself would fare. So at last she agreed, washed and mended the few poor clothes she had, adorned herself as well as she could, and made ready to travel. And what she was given to take along with her is not worth mentioning, either.

The following Thursday the white bear came to fetch his bride. The girl seated herself on his back with her bundle, and then he trotted off. After they had gone a good way, the white bear asked: "Are you afraid?"

"No, not at all," she answered.

"Just keep a tight hold on my fur, and then you will be in no danger," said the bear. So she rode on the bear's back, far, far away, until at last they came to a great rock. There the bear knocked, and at once a door opened through which they entered a great castle, with many brilliantly lighted rooms, where everything gleamed with gold and silver. Then they came into a great hall, and there stood a table completely covered with the most splendid dishes. Here the white bear gave the maiden a silver bell, and said that if there were anything she wanted, she need only ring the bell, and she should have it at once. And after the maiden had eaten, and evening came on, she felt like lying down and going to sleep. So she rang her bell; and at its very first peal she found herself transported to a room in which stood the most beautiful bed one might wish to have, with silken cushions and curtains with golden tassels; and all that was in the room was of gold and silver. Yet when she had lain down and put out the light, she saw a man come in and cast himself down in a corner. It was the white bear, who was allowed to throw off his fur at night; yet the maiden never actually saw him, for he never came until she had put out the light, and before dawn brightened he had disappeared again.

For a time all went well; but gradually the maiden grew sad and silent; for she had not a soul to keep her company the live-long day, and she felt very homesick for her parents and sisters. When the white bear asked her what troubled her, she told him she was always alone, and that she wanted so very much to see her parents and sisters again, and felt very sad because she could not do so. "O that can be managed," said the white bear. "But first you must promise me that you will never speak to your mother alone; but only when others are present. Very likely she will take you by the hand, and want to lead you into her room, so that she can speak to you alone. But this you must not allow, otherwise you will make us both unhappy."

And then, one Sunday, the white bear actually came and told her that now she might make the trip to her parents. So she seated herself on the bear's back, and the bear set out. After they had gone a very long distance, they at length came to a fine, large, white house, before which her brothers and sisters were running about and playing, and all was so rich and splendid that it was a real pleasure merely to look at it.

"This is where your parents live," said the white bear. "Only do not forget what I told you, or you will make us both unhappy." Heaven forbid that she should forget it, said the maiden; and when she had come to the house, she got down, and the bear turned back.

When the daughter entered her parents' home, they were more than happy; they told her that they could not thank her enough for what she had done, and that now all of them were doing splendidly. Then they asked her how she herself fared. The maiden answered that all was well with her, also, and that she had all that heart could desire. I do not know exactly all the other things she told them; but I do not believe she told them every last thing there was to tell. So in the afternoon, when the family had eaten dinner, it happened as the white bear had foretold; the mother wanted to talk to her daughter alone, in her room; but she thought of what the white bear had told her, and did not want to go with her mother, but said:

"All we have to say to each other can just as well be said here." Yet—she herself did not know exactly how it happened—her mother finally did persuade her, and then she had to tell just how things were. So she informed her that as soon as she put out the light at night, a man came and cast himself down in the corner of the room. She had never yet seen him, for he always went away before the dawn brightened. And this grieved her, for she did want to see him so very much, and she was alone through the day, and it was very dreary and lonely.

"Alas, perhaps he is a troll, after all," said the mother. "But I can give you some good advice as to how you can see him. Here is a candle-end, which you must hide under your wimple. When the troll is sleeping, light the light and look at him. But be careful not to let a drop of tallow fall on him."

The daughter took the candle-end and hid it in her wimple, and in the evening the white bear came to fetch her.

After they had gone a way the white bear asked whether everything had not happened just as he had said. Yes, such had been the case, and the maiden could not deny it.

"If you have listened to your mother's advice, then you will make us both unhappy, and all will be over between us," said the bear. "O, no, she had not done so," replied the maiden, indeed she had not.

When they reached home, and the maiden had gone to bed, all went as usual: a man came in and cast himself down in a corner of the room. But in the night, when she heard him sleeping soundly, she stood up and lighted the candle. She threw the light on him, and saw the handsomest prince one might wish to see. And she liked him so exceedingly well that she thought she would be unable to keep on living if she could not kiss him that very minute. She did so, but by mistake she let three hot drops of tallow fall on him, and he awoke.

"Alas, what have you done!" cried he. "Now you have made both of us unhappy. If you had only held out until the end of the year, I would have been delivered. I have a step-mother who has cast a spell on me, so that by day I am a bear, and at night a human being. But now all is over between us, and I must return to my step-mother. She lives in a castle that is east of the sun and west of the moon, where there is a princess with a nose three yards long, whom I must now marry."

The maiden wept and wailed; but to no avail, for the prince said he must journey away. Then she asked him whether she might not go with him. No, said he, that could not be.

"But can you not at least tell me the road, so that I can search for you. For surely that will be permitted me?"

"Yes, that you may do," said he. "But there is no road that leads there. The castle lies east of the sun and west of the moon, and neither now nor at any other time will you find the road to it!"

When the maiden awoke the next morning, the prince as well as the castle had disappeared. She lay in a green opening in the midst of a thick, dark wood, and beside her lay the bundle of poor belongings she had brought from home. And when she had rubbed the sleep out of her eyes, and had cried her fill, she set out and wandered many, many days, until at last she came to a great hill. And before the hill sat an old woman who was playing with a golden apple. The maiden asked the woman whether she did not know which road led to the prince who lived in the castle that was east of the sun and west of the moon, and who was to marry a princess with a nose three yards long.

"How do you come to know him?" asked the woman. "Are you, perhaps, the maiden he wanted to marry?"

"Yes, I am that maiden," she replied.

"So you are that girl," said the woman. "Well, my child, I am sorry to say that all I know of him is that he lives in the castle that is east of the sun and west of the moon, and that you will probably never get there. But I will loan you my horse, on which you may ride to my neighbor, and perhaps she can tell you. And when you get there just give the horse a blow back of his left ear, and order him to go home. And here, take this golden apple along!"

The maiden mounted the horse, and rode a long, long time. At length she again came to a hill, before which sat an old woman with a golden reel. The maiden asked whether she could not tell her the road which led to the castle that lay east of the sun and west of the moon. This woman said just what the other had, no, she knew no more of the castle than that it lay east of the sun and west of the moon. "And," said she, "you will probably never get there. But I will loan you my horse to ride to the nearest neighbor; perhaps she can tell you. And when you have reached her just give the horse a blow back of his left ear, and order him to go home again." And finally she gave the maiden the golden reel, for, said the old woman, it might be useful to her.

The maiden then mounted the horse, and again rode a long, long time. At length she once more came to a great hill, before which sat an old woman spinning at a golden spindle.

Then the maiden once more asked after the prince, and the castle that lay east of the sun and west of the moon. And everything happened exactly as on the two previous occasions.

"Do you happen to be the maiden the prince wanted to marry?" asked the old woman.

"Yes, I am that maiden," answered the maiden.

But this old woman knew no more about the road than the two others. "Yes, the castle lies east of the sun and west of the moon, that I know," said she. "And you will probably never get there. But I will loan you my horse, and you may ride on it to the East Wind and ask him. Perhaps he is acquainted there, and can blow you thither. And when you reach him, just give my horse a blow back of the left ear, and then he will return here of his own accord." Finally the old woman gave her her golden spindle. "Perhaps it may be useful to you," said she.

The maiden now rode for many days and weeks, and it took a long, long time before she came to the East Wind. But at last she did find him, and then she asked the East Wind whether he could show her the road that led to the prince who lived in the castle that was east of the sun and west of the moon.

O, yes, he had heard tell of the prince, and of the castle as well, said the East Wind, but he did not know the road that led to it, for he had never blown so far. "But if you wish, I will take you to my brother, the West Wind, and perhaps he can tell you, for he is much stronger than I am. Just sit down on my back, and I will carry you to him."

The maiden did as he told her, and then they moved swiftly away. When they came to the West Wind, the East Wind said that here he was bringing the maiden whom the prince who lived in the castle that lay east of the sun and west of the moon had wanted to marry, that she was journeying on her way to him, and looking for him everywhere, and that he had accompanied her in order to find out whether the West Wind knew where this castle might be.

"No," said the West Wind to the maiden, "I have never blown so far, but if you wish I will take you to the South Wind, who is much stronger than both of us, and has traveled far and wide, and perhaps he can tell you. Seat yourself on my back, and I will carry you to him."

The maiden did so, and then they flew quickly off to the South Wind. When they found him, the West Wind asked whether the South Wind could show them the road that led to the castle that lay east of the sun and west of the moon; and that this was the maiden who was to have the prince.

"Well, well, so this is the girl?" cried the South Wind. "Yes, it is true that I have gone about a good deal during my life," said he, "yet I have never blown so far. But if you wish, I will take you to my brother, the North Wind. He is the oldest and strongest of us all. If he does not know where the castle lies, then no one in the whole world can tell you. Seat yourself on my back, and I will carry you to him."

The maiden seated herself on the back of the South Wind, and he flew away with a roar and a rush. The journey did not take long.

When they had reached the dwelling of the North Wind, the latter was so wild and unmannerly that he blew a cold blast at them while they were still a good way off. "What do you want?" cried he, as soon as he caught sight of them, so that a cold shiver ran down their backs.

"You should not greet us so rudely," said the South Wind. "It is I, the South Wind. And this is the maiden who wanted to marry the prince who lives in the castle that lies east of the sun and west of the moon. She wishes to ask you whether you have ever been there, and if you can show her the road that leads to it; for she would like to find the prince again."

"O, yes, I know very well where the castle lies," said the North Wind. "I blew an aspen leaf there just once, and then I was so weary that I could not blow at all for many a long day. But if you want to get there above all things, and are not afraid of me, I will take you on my back, and see whether I can blow you there."

The maiden said that she must and would get to the castle, if it were by any means possible, and that she was not afraid, no matter how hard the journey might be. "Very well, then you must stay here over night," said the North Wind. "For if we are to get there to-morrow, we must have the whole day before us."

Early the next morning the North Wind awakened the maiden. Then he blew himself up, and made himself so large and thick that he was quite horrible to look at, and thereupon they rushed along through the air as though they meant to reach the end of the world at once. And everywhere beneath them raged such a storm that forests were pulled out by the roots, and houses torn down, and as they rushed across the sea, ships foundered by the hundreds. Further and further they went, so far that no one could even imagine it, and still they were flying across the sea; but gradually the North Wind grew weary, and became weaker and weaker. Finally he could hardly keep going, and sank lower and lower, and at last he flew so low that the waves washed his ankles.

"Are you afraid?" asked the North Wind.

"No, not at all," answered the maiden. By now they were

not far distant from the land, and the North Wind had just enough strength left to be able to set down the maiden on the strand, beneath the windows of the castle that lay east of the sun and west of the moon. And then he was so wearied and wretched that he had to rest many a long day before he could set out for home again.

The next morning the maiden seated herself beneath the windows of the castle and played with the golden apple, and the first person who showed herself was the monster with the nose, whom the prince was to marry.

"What do you want for your golden apple?" asked the princess with the nose, as she opened the window.

"I will not sell it at all, either for gold or for money," answered the maiden.

"Well, what do you want for it, if you will not sell it either for gold or for money?" asked the princess. "Ask what you will!"

"I only want to speak to-night to the prince who lives here, then I will give you the apple," said the maiden who had come with the North Wind.

The princess replied that this could be arranged, and then she received the golden apple. But when the maiden came into the prince's room in the evening, he was sleeping soundly. She called and shook him, wept and wailed; but she could not wake him, and in the morning, as soon as it dawned, the princess with the long nose came and drove her out.

That day the maiden again sat beneath the windows of the castle, and wound her golden reel. And all went as on the preceding day. The princess asked what she wanted for the reel, and the maiden answered that she would sell it neither for gold nor for money; but if she might speak that night to the prince, then she would give the reel to the princess. Yet when the maiden came to the prince, he was again fast asleep, and no matter how much she wept and wailed, and cried and shook, she could not wake him. But as soon as day dawned, and it grew bright, the princess with the long nose came and drove her out. And that day the maiden again seated herself beneath the windows of the castle, and spun with her golden spindle; and, of course, the princess with the long nose wanted to have that, too. She opened the window, and asked what she wanted for the golden spindle. The maiden replied, as she had twice before, that she would sell the spindle neither for gold nor money; but that the princess could have it if she might speak to the prince again that night. Yes, that she was welcome to do, said the princess, and took the golden spindle. Now it happened that some Christians, who were captives in the castle, and quartered in a room beside that of the prince, had heard a woman weeping and wailing pitifully in the prince's room for the past two nights. So they told the prince. And that evening when the princess came to him with his night-cap, the prince pretended to drink it; but instead poured it out behind his back, for he could well imagine that she had put a sleeping-powder into the cup. Then, when the maiden came in, the prince was awake, and she had to tell him just how she had found the castle.

"You have come just in the nick of time," said he, "for to-morrow I am to marry the princess; but I do not want the monster with the nose at all, and you are the only person who can save me. I will say that first I wish to see whether my bride is a capable housewife, and demand that she wash the three drops of tallow from my shirt. She will naturally agree to this, for she does not know that you made the spots, for only Christian hands can wash them out again, but not the hands of this pack of trolls. Then I will say I will marry none other than the maiden who can wash out the spots, and ask you to do so," said the prince. And then both rejoiced and were happy beyond measure.

But on the following day, when the wedding was to take place, the prince said: "First I would like to see what my bride can do!" Yes, that was no more than right, said his mother-in-law. "I have a very handsome shirt," continued the prince, "which I would like to wear at the wedding. But there are three tallow-spots on it, and they must first be washed out. And I have made a vow to marry none other than the woman who can do this. So if my bride cannot manage to do it, then she is worthless."

Well, that would not be much of a task, said the women, and agreed to the proposal. And the princess with the long nose at once began to wash. She washed with all her might and main, and took the greatest pains, but the longer she washed and rubbed, the larger grew the spots.

"O, you don't know how to wash!" said her mother, the old troll-wife. "Just give it to me!" But no sooner had she taken the shirt in her hand, than it began to look worse, and the more she washed and rubbed, the larger and blacker grew the spots. Then the other troll-women had to come and wash; but the longer they washed the shirt the uglier it grew, and finally it looked as though it had been hanging in the smokestack.

"Why, all of you are worthless!" said the prince. "Outside the window sits a beggar-girl. I'm sure she is a better washer-woman than all of you put together. You, girl, come in here!" he cried out of the window; and when the maiden came in he said: "Do you think you can wash this shirt clean for me?"

"I do not know," answered the maiden, "but I will try." And no more had she dipped the shirt in the water than it turned as white as newly fallen snow, yes, even whiter.

"Indeed, and you are the one I want!" said the prince.

Then the old troll-woman grew so angry that she burst in two, and the princess with the long nose and the rest of the troll-pack probably burst in two as well, for I never heard anything more of them. The prince and his bride then freed all the Christians who had been kept captive in the castle, and packed up as much gold and silver as they could possibly take with them, and went far away from the castle that lies East of the sun and West of the moon.

MURMUR GOOSE-EGG

Once upon a time there were five women who were standing in a field, mowing. Heaven had not given a single one of them a child, and each of them wanted to have one. And suddenly they saw a goose-egg of quite unheard-of size, well-nigh as large as a man's head. "I saw it first," said the one. "I saw it at the same time that you did," insisted another. "But I want it, for I saw it first of all," maintained a third. And thus they went on, and fought so about the egg that they nearly came to blows. Finally they agreed that it should belong to all five of them, and that all of them should sit on it, as a goose would do, and hatch out the little gosling. The first remained sitting on the egg for eight days, and hatched, and did not move or do a thing; and during this time the rest had to feed her and themselves as well. One of them grew angry because of this and scolded.

"You did not crawl out of the egg either before you could cry peep!" said the one who was sitting on the egg and hatching. "Yet I almost believe that a human child is going to slip out of the egg, for something is murmuring inside it without ever stopping: 'Herring and mush, porridge and milk,'" said she. "And now you can sit on it for eight days, while we bring you food."

When the fifth day of the eight had passed, it was plain to her that there was a child in the egg, which kept on calling: "Herring and mush, porridge and milk," and so she punched a hole in the egg, and instead of a gosling out came a child, and it was quite disgustingly homely, with a big head and a small body, and no sooner had it crawled out than it began to cry: "Herring and mush, porridge and milk!" So they named the child Murmur Goose-Egg.

In spite of the child's homeliness, the women at first took a great deal of pleasure in him; but before long he grew so greedy that he devoured everything they had. When they cooked a dish of mush or a potful of porridge that was to do for all six of them, the child swallowed it all by himself. So they did not want to keep him any longer. "I have not had a single full meal since the changling crawled out," said one of them; and when Murmur Goose-Egg heard that, and the rest agreed, he said that he would gladly go his own gait, for "if they had no need of him, then he had no need of them," and with that he went off. Finally he came to a farmstead that lay in a rocky section, and asked for work. Yes, they needed a workman, and the master told him to gather up the stones in the field. Then Murmur Goose-Egg gathered up the stones in the field; he picked up some that were so large that a number of horses could not have dragged them, and large and small, one and all, he put them in his pocket. Before long he had finished his work, and wanted to know what he was to do next.

"You have picked up the stones in the field?" said his master. "You cannot possibly have finished before you have really begun!"

But Murmur Goose-Egg emptied his pockets, and threw the stones on a pile. Then his master saw that he had finished his work, and that one would have to handle such a strong fellow with kid gloves. So he told him to come in and eat. That suited Murmur Goose-Egg, and he ate up everything that was to have supplied the master and his family, and the help, and then he was only half satisfied.

He was really a splendid worker; but a dangerous eater, like a bottomless cask, said the peasant. "Such a serving-man could eat up a poor peasant, house and ground, before he noticed it," said he. He had no more work for him, and the best thing to do would be to go to the king's castle.

So Murmur Goose-Egg went to the king, and was at once given a place, and there was enough to eat and drink in the castle. He was to be the errand-boy, and help the maids fetch wood and water, and do other odd jobs. So he asked what he was to do first.

For the time being he could chop fire-wood, said they. So Murmur Goose-Egg began to chop fire-wood, and hewed to the line in such fashion that the chips fairly flew. Before long he had chopped up all that there was, kindling wood and building wood, beams and boards, and when he was through with it, he came and asked what he was to do now.

"You can finish chopping the fire-wood," said they.

"There is none left," said Murmur Goose-Egg.

That could not be possible, said the superintendent, and looked into the wood-bin. Yes, indeed, Murmur Goose-Egg had chopped up everything, large and small, beams and boards. That was very bad, and therefore the superintendent said that Murmur Goose-Egg should have nothing to eat until he had chopped down just as much wood in the forest as he had just chopped up for fire-wood.

Then Murmur Goose-Egg went into the smithy, and had the smith make an iron ax of five hundred-weights. With that he went into the forest and began to chop. He chopped down big pine and fir trees, as thick as masts, and all that he found on the king's ground, as well as what he found on that of his neighbors. But he cut off neither the branches nor the tree-tops, so that all lay there as though felled by the storm. Then he loaded a sizable stack on the sled, and put to the horses.

But they could not move the load from the spot, and when he took them by the heads, in order to pull them forward, he tore off their heads. So he unharnessed them, and left them lying in the field, and put himself to the sled, and went off alone with the load. When he came to the king's castle, there stood the king with the master carpenter in the entrance, and they were ready to give him a warm reception, because of the destruction he had wrought in the forest. For the master carpenter had been there and seen the havoc he had made. But when Murmur Goose-Egg came along with half the forest, the king grew frightened as well as angry, and he thought that if Murmur was so strong, it would be best to handle him with care.

"Why, you are a splendid workman," said the king, "but tell me, how much do you really eat at once," he continued, "for I am sure you are hungry?"

If he were to have enough porridge, they would have to take twelve tons of meal to make it; but after he had eaten that, then he could wait a while, said Murmur Goose-Egg.

It took some time before so much porridge could be prepared, and in the meantime Murmur was to carry wood into the kitchen. So he piled the whole load of wood on a sled, but when he drove it through the door, he did not go to work about it very gently. The house nearly broke from its joints, and he well-nigh tore down the entire castle. When at last dinner was ready, they sent him out into the field, to call the help. He called so loudly that hill and vale reëchoed the sound. But still the people did not come quick enough to suit him. So he picked a quarrel with them, and killed twelve.

"You kill twelve of my people, and you eat for twelve times twelve of them, but how many men's work can you do?" asked the king.

"I do the work of twelve times twelve, too," said Murmur. When he had eaten, he was to go to the barn and thresh. So he pulled the beam out of the roof-tree, and made a flail out of it, and when the roof threatened to fall in, he took a pine-tree with all its boughs and branches, and set it up in place of the roof-beam. Then he threshed corn and hay and straw, all together, and it seemed as though a cloud hung over the royal castle.

When Murmur Goose-Egg had nearly finished threshing, the enemy broke into the land, and war began. Then the king told him to gather people about him, and go to meet the foe, and do battle with him, for he thought the enemy would probably kill him.

No, said Murmur Goose-Egg, he did not want to have the king's people killed, he would see that he dealt with the enemy himself.

All the better, thought the king, then I am sure to get rid of him. But he would need a proper club, said Murmur.

So they sent to the smith, and he forged a club of two hundred-weights. That would only do for a nut-cracker, said Murmur Goose-Egg. So he forged another that weighed six hundred-weights, and that would do to hammer shoes with, said Murmur Goose-Egg. But the smith told him that he and all his workmen together could not forge a larger one.

Then Murmur Goose-Egg went into the smithy himself, and forged himself a club of thirty hundred-weights, and it would have taken a hundred men just to turn it around on the anvil. This might do at a pinch, said Murmur. Then he wanted a knapsack with provisions. It was sewn together out of fifteen ox-skins, and stuffed full of provisions, and then Murmur wandered down the hill with the knapsack on his back, and the club over his shoulder.

When he came near enough for the soldiers to see him, they sent to ask whether he had a mind to attack them.

"Just wait until I have eaten," said Murmur, and sat him down behind his knapsack to eat. But the enemy would not wait, and began to fire at him. And it fairly rained and hailed musket-balls all around Murmur.

"I don't care a fig for these blueberries," said Murmur Goose-Egg, and feasted on quite at ease. Neither lead nor iron could wound him, and his knapsack stood before him, and caught the bullets like a wall.

Then the enemy began to throw bombs at him, and shoot at him with cannon. He hardly moved when he was struck. "O, that's of no account!" said he.

But then a bomb flew into his wind-pipe. "Faugh!" said he, and spat it out again, and then came a chain-bullet and fell into his butter-plate, and another tore away the bit of bread from between his fingers.

Then he grew angry, stood up, took his club, pounded the ground with it, and asked whether they wanted to take the food from his mouth with the blueberries they were blowing out at him from their clumsy blow-pipes. Then he struck a few more blows, so that the hills and valleys round about trembled, and all the enemy flew up into the air like chaff, and that was the end of the war.

When Murmur came back and asked for more work, the king was at a loss, for he had felt sure that now he was rid of him. So he knew of nothing better to do than to send him to the devil's place.

"Now you can go to the devil, and fetch the tribute from him," said the king. Murmur Goose-Egg went off with his knapsack on his back, and his club over his shoulder. He had soon reached the right spot; but when he got there the devil was away at a trial. There was no one home but his grand-mother, and she said she had never yet heard anything about a tribute, and that he was to come back some other time.

"Yes, indeed, come again to-morrow," said he. "I know that old excuse!" But since he was there, he would stay there, for he had to take home the tribute, and he had plenty of time to wait. But when he had eaten all his provisions, he grew wea-ry, and again demanded the tribute from the grandmother.

"You will get nothing from me, and that's as flat as the old fir-tree outside is fast," said the devil's grandmother. The fir-tree stood in front of the gate to the devil's place, and was so large that fifteen men could hardly girdle it with their arms. But Murmur climbed up into its top and bent and shook it to and fro as though it were a willow wand, and then asked the devil's grandmother once more whether she would now pay him the tribute.

So she did not dare to refuse any longer, and brought out as much money as he could possibly carry in his knapsack. Then he set out for home with the tribute, and now no sooner had he gone than the devil came home, and when he learned that Murmur had taken along a big bag of money, he first beat his grandmother, and then hurried after Murmur. And he soon caught up to him, for he ran over sticks and stones, and sometimes flew in between; while Murmur had to stick to the highway with his heavy knapsack. But with the devil at his heels, he began to run as fast as he could, and stretched out the club behind him, to keep the devil from coming to close quarters. And thus they ran along, one behind the other; while

Murmur held the shaft and the devil the end of the club, until they reached a deep valley. There Murmur jumped from one mountain-top to another, and the devil followed him so hotly that he ran into the club, fell down into the valley and broke his foot—and there he lay.

"There's your tribute!" said Murmur Goose-Egg, when he had reached the royal castle, and he flung down the knapsack full of money before the king, so that the whole castle tottered. The king thanked him kindly, and promised him a good reward, and a good character, if he wanted it; but Murmur only wanted more work to do.

"What shall I do now?" he asked. The king reflected for a while, and then he said Murmur should travel to the hill-troll, who had robbed him of the sword of his ancestors. He lived in a castle by the sea, where no one ventured to go.

Murmur was given a few cart-loads of provisions in his big knapsack, and once more set out. Long he wandered, though, over field and wood, over hills and deep valleys, till he came to a great mountain where the troll lived who had robbed the king of the sword.

But the troll was not out in the open, and the mountain was closed, so Murmur could not get it. So he joined a party of stone-breakers, who were working at a mountainside, and worked along with them. They had never had such a helper, for Murmur hewed away at the rocks till they burst, and stone bowlders as large as houses came rolling down. But when he was about to rest and eat up the first cart-load of his provisions, it had already been eaten up. "I have a good appetite myself," said Murmur, "but whoever got hold of it has an even better one, for he has eaten up the bones as well!"

Thus it went the first day, and the second was no better. On the third day he went to work again, and took along the third cart-load, lay down behind it, and pretended to be sleeping.

Then a troll with seven heads came out of the hill, began to smack his lips, and eat of his provisions.

"Now the table is set, so now I am going to eat," said he.

"First we'll see about that," said Murmur, and hewed away at the troll so that the heads flew from his body.

Then he went into the hill out of which the troll had come, and inside stood a horse eating out of a barrel of glowing ashes, while behind him stood a barrel filled with oats.

"Why don't you eat out of the barrel of oats?" asked Murmur Goose-Egg.

"Because I cannot turn around," said the horse.

"I will turn you around," said Murmur Goose-Egg.

"Tear my head off instead," pleaded the horse.

Murmur did so, and then the horse turned into a fine-looking man. He said that he had been enchanted, and turned into a horse by the troll. Then he helped Murmur look for the sword, which the troll had hidden under the bed. But in the bed lay the troll's grandmother, and she was snoring.

They went home by water, and just as they sailed off the old troll grandmother came after them; but she could not get at them, hence she commenced to drink, so that the water went down and grew lower. But at last she could not drink up the whole sea, and so she burst.

When they came ashore, Murmur sent to the king, and had him told to have the sword fetched; but though the king sent four horses, they could not move it from the spot. He sent eight, he sent twelve, but the sword remained where it was, and could not be moved from the spot by any means. Then

Murmur Goose-Egg took it up, and carried it alone.

The king could not believe his eyes when he saw Murmur once more; but he was very friendly and promised him gold and green forests. But when Murmur asked for more work, he told him to travel to his troll's castle, where no one dared go, and to remain there until he had built a bridge across the sound, so that people could cross. If he could do that, he would reward him well, yes, he would even give him his daughter, said the king. He would attend to it, said Murmur.

Yet no human being had ever returned thence alive; all who had gotten so far, lay on the ground dead, and crushed to a jelly, and the king thought, when sending him there, that he would never see him again.

But Murmur set out. He took with him his knapsack full of provisions, and a properly turned and twisted block of pine-wood, as well as an ax, a wedge and some wooden chips.

When he reached the sound, the river was full of drifting ice, and it roared like a waterfall. But he planted his legs firmly on the ground, and waded along until he got across. When he had warmed himself and satisfied his hunger, he wanted to sleep; but a tumult and rumbling started, as though the whole castle were to be turned upside down. The gate flew wide open, and Murmur saw nothing but a pair of yawning jaws that reached from the threshold to the top of the door.

"Let's see who you may be? Perhaps you are an old friend of mine," said Murmur. And sure enough, it was Master Devil. Then they played cards together. The devil would gladly have won back some of the tribute Murmur had forced from his grandmother for the king. Yet, no matter how he played, Murmur always won; for he made a cross on the cards. And after he had won all the devil had with him, the latter had to give him some of the gold and silver that was in the castle.

In the midst of their game the fire went out, so that they could no longer tell the cards apart.

"Now we must split wood," said Murmur. He hewed into the block of pine-wood with his ax, and drove in the wedge, but the tree-stump was tough, and would not split at once, though Murmur gave himself all manner of pains.

"You are supposed to be strong," he said to the devil. "Spit on your hands, slap in your claws here, and pull the block apart, so that I can see what you can do!"

The devil obediently thrust both hands into the split, and tore and clawed with all his might; but suddenly Murmur Goose-Egg knocked out the wedge, and there the devil was caught in a vice, while Murmur belabored his back with the ax. The devil wailed, and begged Murmur to let him go; but Murmur would hear nothing of it until he had promised never to come back and make a nuisance of himself again. Besides that, he had to promise to build a bridge over the sound, on which one could go back and forth at all seasons of the year. And the bridge was to be completed immediately after the breaking up of the ice-drift.

"Alas!" said the devil, but there was nothing for it but to promise if he wished to go free. Yet he made one condition, that he was to have the first soul that crossed the bridge as sound-toll.

He could have it, said Murmur. Then he let the devil out, and he ran straight home. But Murmur lay down and slept until far into the following day.

Then the king came to see whether Murmur Goose-Egg were lying crushed on the ground, or had merely been badly beaten. He had to wade through piles of money before he could reach the bed. The money was stacked up high along the walls in heaps and in bags, and Murmur lay in the bed and snored.

"May heaven help me and my daughter!" cried the king, when he saw that Murmur Goose-Egg was in the best of health. Yes, and no one could deny that everything had been well and thoroughly done, said the king; but there could be no talk of marriage as long as the bridge had not been built.

Then one day the bridge was finished; and on it stood the devil, ready to collect the toll promised him.

Murmur Goose-Egg wanted the king to be the first to try the bridge with him; but the king had no mind to do so, therefore Murmur himself mounted a horse, and swung up the fat dairy-maid from the castle before him on the saddle-bow—she looked almost like a gigantic block of wood—and dashed across the bridge with her so that the planks fairly thundered.

"Where is my sound-toll? Where is the soul?" cried the devil. "Sitting in this block of wood! If you want her, you must spit on your hands and catch hold of her," said Murmur Goose-Egg. "No, thank you! If she does not catch hold of me, then I'll certainly not catch hold of her," said the devil. "You caught me in a vice once, but you can't fool me a second time," said he, and flew straight home to his grandmother, and since then nothing more has been heard or seen of him.

But Murmur Goose-Egg hurried back to the castle and asked for the reward the king had promised him. And when the king hesitated and began to make all sorts of excuses, in order not to have to keep his promise, Murmur said it would be best to have a substantial knapsackful of provisions made ready, since now he, Murmur, was going to take his reward himself. This the king did, and when the knapsack was ready,

Murmur took the king along with him in front of the castle, and gave him a proper shove, so that he flew high up into the air. And he threw the knapsack up after him, so that he would not be left altogether without provisions; and if he has not come down yet, then he, together with the knapsack, is floating between heaven and earth to this very day.

THE TROLL-WIFE

Once upon a time, long, long years ago, there lived a well-to-do old couple on a homestead up in Hadeland. They had a son, who was a dragoon, a big, handsome fellow. They had a pasture in the hills, and the hut was not like most of the herdsmen's huts; but was well and solidly built, and even had a chimney, a roof and a window. And there they spent the summer; but when they came back home in the fall, the wood-cutters and huntsmen and fishermen, and whoever else had business in the woods at that time, noticed that the mountain folk had carried on its tricks with their herd. And among the mountain folk was a maiden who was so beautiful that her like had never been seen.

The son had often heard tell of her, and one fall, when his parents had already come home from the mountain pasture, he put on his full uniform, saddled his service horse, thrust his pistols in the holsters, and thus rode up into the hills. When he rode toward the pasture, such a fire burned in the herdsman's hut that it lit up every road, and then he knew that the mountain folk were inside. So he tied his horse to a pine-tree, took a pistol from its holster, crept up to the hut, and peeped through the window. And there sat an old man and a woman who were quite crooked and shriveled up with age, and so unspeakably ugly that he had never seen anything like it in his life; but with them was a maiden, and she was so surpassingly beautiful that he fell in love with her at once, and felt that he could not live without her. All had cow's tails, and the lovely maiden, too. And he could see that they had only just arrived, for everything was in disorder. The maiden was busy washing the ugly old man, and the woman was building a fire under the great cheese-kettle on the hearth.

At that moment the dragoon flung open the door, and shot off his pistol right above the maiden's head, so that she tottered and fell to the ground. And then she grew every bit as ugly as she had been beautiful before, and she had a nose as long as a pistol-case.

"Now you may take her, for now she belongs to you!" said the old man. But the dragoon stood as though rooted to the spot; stood where he stood, and could not take a single step, either forward or backward. Then the old man began to wash the girl; and she looked a little better; her nose was only half its original size, and her ugly cow's tail was tied back; but she was not as handsome, and any one who said so would not have been telling the truth.

"Now she is yours, my proud dragoon! Take her up before you on your horse, and ride into town and marry her. And you need only set the table for us in the little room in the bake-house; for we do not want to be with the other wedding-guests," said the old monster, her father, "but when the dishes make the round, you can stop in where we are."

He did not dare do anything else, and took her up before him on his horse, and made ready to marry her. But before she went to church, the bride begged one of the bridesmaids to stand close behind her, so that no one could see her tail fall off when the priest joined their hands.

So the wedding was celebrated, and when the dishes made the round, the bridegroom went out into the room where the table had been set for the old folk from the mountain. And at that time there was nothing to be seen there; but after the wedding-guests had gone, there was so much gold and silver, and such a pile of money lying there, as he had never seen together before.

For a long time all went well. Whenever guests came, his wife laid the table for the old folk in the bake-house, and on each occasion so much money was left lying there, that before long they did not know what to do with it all. But ugly she was, and ugly she remained, and he was heartily weary of her. So it was bound to happen that he sometimes flew into a rage, and threatened her with cuffs and blows. Once he wanted to go to town, and since it was fall, and the ground already frozen, the horse had first to be shod. So he went into the smithy—for he himself was a notable farrier—but, no matter what lie did, the horse-shoe was either too large or too small, and would not fit at all. He had no other horse at home, and he toiled away until noon and on into the afternoon. "Will you never make an end of your shoeing?" asked his wife. "You are not a very good husband; but you are a far worse farrier. I see there is nothing left for me but to go into the smithy myself and shoe the horse. This shoe is too large, you should have made it smaller, and that one is too small, you should have made it larger."

She went into the smithy, and the first thing she did was to take the horse-shoe in both hands and bend it straight.

"There, look at it," said she, "that is how you must do it." And with that she bent it together again as though it were made of lead. "Now hold up the horse's leg," said she, and the horse-shoe fitted to a hair, so that the best farrier could not have bettered it.

"You have a great deal of strength in your fingers," said her husband, and he looked at her.

"Do you think so?" was her reply. "What would have happened to me had you been as strong? But I love you far too dearly ever to use my strength against you," said she.

And from that day on he was the best of husbands.

THE KING'S HARES

Once upon a time there was a man who lived in the little back room. He had given up his estate to the heir; but in addition he had three sons, who were named Peter, Paul and Esben, who was the youngest. All three hung around at home and would not work, for they had it too easy, and they thought themselves too good for anything like work, and nothing was good enough for them. Finally Peter once heard that the king wanted a shepherd for his hares, and he told his father he would apply for the position, as it would just suit him, seeing that he wished to serve no one lower in rank than the king. His father, it is true, was of the opinion that there might be other work that would suit him better, for whoever was to herd hares would have to be quick and spry, and not a sleepy-head, and when the hares took to their heels in all directions, it was a dance of another kind than when one skipped about a room. But it was of no use. Peter insisted, and would have his own way, took his knapsack, and shambled down hill. After he had gone a while, he saw an old woman who had got her nose wedged in a tree-stump while chopping wood, and when Peter saw her jerking and pulling away, trying to get out, he burst into loud laughter.

"Don't stand there and laugh in such a stupid way," said the woman, "but come and help a poor, feeble old woman. I wanted to split up some fire-wood, and caught my nose here, and here I have been standing for more than a hundred years, pulling and jerking, without a bit of bread to chew in all that time," said she.

Then Peter had to laugh all the harder. He found it all very amusing, and said that if she had already been standing there a hundred years, then she could probably hold out for another hundred years or more.

When he came to court they at once took him on as a herdsman. The place was not bad, there was good food, and good wages, and the chance of winning the princess besides; yet if no more than a single one of the king's hares were to be lost, they would cut three red strips from his back, and throw him into the snake-pit.

As long as Peter was on the common or in the enclosure, he kept his hares together nicely, but later, when they reached the forest, they ran away from him across the hills. Peter ran after them with tremendous leaps, as long as he thought he could catch even a single hare, but when the very last one had vanished, his breath was gone, and he saw no more of them. Toward noon he went home, taking his time about it, and when he reached the enclosure, he looked around for them on all sides, but no hares came. And then, when he came to the castle, there stood the king with the knife in his hand. He cut three red strips from his back, and cast him into the snake-pit.

After a while Paul decided to go to the castle and herd the king's hares. His father told him what he had told Peter, and more besides; but he insisted on going, and would not listen, and he fared neither better nor worse than Peter had. The old woman stood and pulled and jerked at her nose in the tree-trunk, and he laughed, found it very amusing, and let her stand there and torment herself. He was at once taken into service, but the hares all ran away across the hills, though he pursued them, and worked away like a shepherd dog in the sun, and when he came back to the castle in the evening minus his hares, there stood the king with the knife in his hand, cut three broad strips from his back, rubbed in pepper and salt, and flung him into the snake-pit.

Then, after some time had passed, the youngest decided to set out to herd the king's hares, and told his father of his intention. He thought that would be just the work for him, to loaf about in forest and field, look for strawberry patches, herd a flock of hares, and lie down and sleep in the sun between times. His father thought that there was other work that would suit him better, and that even if he fared no worse than his brothers, it was quite certain that he would fare no better. Whoever herded the king's hares must not drag along as though he had lead in his soles, or like a fly on a limerod; and that when the hares took to their heels, it was a horse of another color from catching flees with gloved hands; whoever wanted to escape with a whole back, would have to be more than quick and nimble, and swifter than a bird. But there was nothing he could do. Esben merely kept on saying that he wanted to go to court and serve the king, for he would not take service with any lesser master, said he; and he would see to the hares, they could not be much worse than a herd of goats or of calves. And with that he took his knapsack and strolled comfortably down the hill.

After he had wandered a while, and began to feel a proper hunger, he came to the old woman who was wedged by the nose in the tree-trunk and who was pulling and jerking away, in order to get loose.

"Good day, mother," said Esben, "and why are you worrying yourself so with your nose, you poor thing?" "No one has called me mother for the last hundred years," said the old woman, "but come and help me out, and give me a bite to eat; for I have not had a bit to eat in all that time. And I will do something for your sake as well," said she.

Yes, no doubt she would need something to eat and drink badly, said Esben.

Then he hewed the tree-trunk apart, so that she got her nose out of the cleft, sat down to eat, and shared with her. The old woman had a good appetite, and she received a good half of his provisions.

When they were through she gave Esben a whistle which had the power that if he blew into one end, whatever he wished scattered was scattered to all the winds, and when he blew into the other, all came together again. And if the whistle passed from his possession, it would return as soon as he wished it back.

"That is a wonderful whistle!" thought Esben.

When he came to the castle, they at once took him on as a shepherd; the place was not bad, he was to have food and wages, and should he manage to herd the king's hares without losing one of them, he might possibly win the princess; but if he lost so much as a single hare, and no matter how small it might be, then they would cut three red strips from his back, and the king was so sure of his case that he went right off to whet his knife. It would be a simple matter to herd the hares, thought Esben; for when they went off they were as obedient as a herd of sheep, and so long as they were on the common, and in the enclosure, they even marched in rank and file. But when they reached the forest, and noon-time came, and the sun burned down on hill and dale, they all took to their heels and ran away across the hills.

"Hallo, there! So you want to run away!" called Esben, and blew into one end of his whistle, and then they scattered the more quickly to all the ends of the earth. But when he had reached an old charcoal-pit, he blew into the other end of his whistle, and before he knew it the hares were back again, and standing in rank and file so he could review them, just like a regiment of soldiers on the drill-ground.

"That is a splendid whistle!" thought Esben; lay down on a sunny hillock, and fell asleep. The hares were left to their own devices, and played until evening; then he once more whistled them together, and took them along to the castle like a herd of sheep.

The king and queen and the princess, too, stood in the hall-way, and wondered what sort of a fellow this was, who could herd hares without losing a single one. The king reckoned and added them up, and counted with his fingers, and then added them up again; but not even the teeny-weeniest hare was missing. "He is quite a chap, he is," said the princess.

The following day he again went to the forest, and herded his hares; but while he lay in all comfort beside a strawberry patch, they sent out the chamber-maid from the castle to him, and she was to find out how he managed to herd the king's hares.

He showed her his whistle, and blew into one end, and all the hares darted away across the hills in all directions, and then he blew into the other, and they came trotting up from all sides, and once more stood in rank and file. "That is a wonderful whistle," said the chamber-maid. She would gladly give him a hundred dollars, if he cared to sell it.

"Yes, it is a splendid whistle," said Esben, "and I will not sell it for money. But if you give me a hundred dollars, and a kiss with every dollar to boot, then I might let you have it."

Yes, indeed, that would suit her right down to the ground; she would gladly give him two kisses with every dollar, and feel grateful, besides.

So she got the whistle, but when she reached the castle, the whistle disappeared all of a sudden. Esben had wished it back again, and toward evening he came along, driving his hares like a herd of sheep. The king reckoned and counted and added, but all to no purpose, for not the least little hare was missing.

When Esben was herding his hares the third day, they sent the princess to him to get away his pipe from him. She was tickled to death, and finally offered him two hundred dollars if he would let her have the whistle, and would also tell her what she had to do in order to fetch it safely home with her.

"Yes, it is a very valuable whistle," said Esben, "and I will not sell it," but at last, as a favor to her, he said he would let her have it if she gave him two hundred dollars, and a kiss for every dollar to boot. But if she wanted to keep it, why, she must take good care of it, for that was her affair.

"That is a very high price for a hare-whistle," said the princess, and she really shrank from kissing him, "but since we are here in the middle of the forest, where no one can see or hear us, I'll let it pass, for I positively must have the whistle," said she. And when Esben had pocketed the price agreed upon, she received the whistle, and held it tightly clutched in her hand all the way home; yet when she reached the castle, and wanted to show it, it disappeared out of her hands. On the following day the queen herself set out, and she felt quite sure that she would succeed in coaxing the whistle away from him.

She was stingier, and only offered fifty dollars; but she had to raise her bid until she reached three hundred. Esben said it was a magnificent whistle, and that the price was a beggarly one; but seeing that she was the queen, he would let it pass. She was to pay him three hundred dollars, and for every dollar she was to give him a buss to boot, then she should have the whistle. And he was paid in full as agreed, since as regards the busses the queen was not so stingy.

When she had the whistle in her hands, she tied it fast, and hid it well, but she fared not a whit better than either of the others; when she wanted to show the whistle it was gone, and in the evening Esben came home, driving his hares as though they were a well-trained flock of sheep.

"You are stupid women!" said the king. "I suppose I will have to go to him myself if we really are to obtain this trumpery whistle. There seems to be nothing else left to do!" And the following day, when Esben was once more herding his hares, the king followed him, and found him at the same place where the women had bargained with him.

They soon became good friends, and Esben showed him the whistle, and blew into one end and the other, and the king thought the whistle very pretty, and finally insisted on buying it, even though it cost him a thousand dollars.

"Yes, it is a magnificent whistle," said Esben, "and I would not sell it for money. But do you see that white mare over yonder?" said he, and pointed into the forest.

"Yes, she belongs to me, that is my Snow Witch!" cried the king, for he knew her very well.

"Well, if you will give me a thousand dollars, and kiss the white mare that is grazing on the moor by the big pine, to boot, then you can have my whistle!" said Esben.

"Is that the only price at which you will sell?" asked the king.

"Yes," said Esben.

"But at least may I not put a silken handkerchief between?" asked the king.

This was conceded him, and thus he obtained the whistle. He put it in the purse in his pocket, and carefully buttoned up the pocket. Yet when he reached the castle, and wanted to take it out, he was in the same case as the women, for he no longer had the whistle. And in the evening Esben came home with his herd of hares, and not the least little hare was missing.

The king was angry, and furious because he had made a fool of them all, and had swindled the king's self out of the whistle into the bargain, and now he wanted to do away with Esben. The queen was of the same opinion, and said it was best to behead such a knave when he was caught in the act.

Esben thought this neither fair nor just; for he had only done what he had been asked to do, and had defended himself as best he knew how.

But the king said that this made no difference to him; yet if Esben could manage to fill the big brewing-cauldron till it ran over, he would spare his life.

The job would be neither long nor hard, said Esben, he thought he could warrant that, and he began to tell about the old woman with her nose in the tree-trunk, and in between he said, "I must make up plenty of stories, to fill the cauldron,"— and then he told of the whistle, and the chamber-maid who came to him and wanted to buy the whistle for a hundred dollars, and about all the kisses that she had had to give him to boot, up on the hillock by the forest; and then he told about the princess, how she had come and kissed him so sweetly for the whistle's sake, because no one could see or hear it in the forest—"I must make up plenty of stories, in order to fill the cauldron," said Esben. Then he told of the queen, and of how stingy she had been with her money, and how liberal with her busses—"for I must make up plenty of stories in order to fill the cauldron," said Esben.

"But I think it must be full now!" said the queen.

"O, not a sign of it!" said the king.

Then Esben began to tell how the king had come to him, and about the white mare who was grazing on the moor, "and since he insisted on having the whistle he had to—he had to—well, with all due respect, I have to make up plenty of stories in order to fill the cauldron," said Esben.

"Stop, stop! It is full, fellow!" cried the king. "Can't you see that it is running over?"

The king and the queen were of the opinion that it would be best for Esben to receive the princess and half the kingdom; there did not seem anything else to do.

"Yes, it was a magnificent whistle!" said Esben.

THE YOUNG FELLOW AND THE DEVIL

Once upon a time there was a young fellow, who was going along cracking nuts. He found a wormy one, and at the selfsame moment he met the devil. "Is it true," said the young fellow, "that the devil can make himself as small as he likes, and can slip through the eye of a needle, as the people say?" "Yes," answered the devil. "Well, I should certainly like to see you crawl into that nut!" said the young fellow. The devil did so. But when he had crawled through the hole, the young fellow stopped it up with a bit of wood. "Now I've got you!" said he, and put the nut in his pocket. After he had gone a while, he came to a smithy, and went in and asked the smith to break the nut for him. "Why, that is a mere trifle!" said the smith, took his smallest hammer, laid the nut on the anvil, and struck it; but the nut would not break. Then he took a somewhat larger hammer; but that was not heavy enough either. Then he took a still larger one, but could do nothing with it at all, and thereupon he grew angry, and took his heaviest hammer. "I'll break you yet!" said he, and struck it with all his might. And then the nut cracked, so that half the smithy roof was carried away, and there was a crash as though the whole hut were falling in. "I believe the devil was in that nut!" said the smith. "And so he was!" answered the young fellow.

FARTHER SOUTH THAN SOUTH, AND FARTHER NORTH THAN NORTH, AND IN THE GREAT HILL OF GOLD

Once upon a time there was a peasant who had a wheat-field, which was trampled down every Saturday night. Now the peasant had three sons, and he told each one of them to spend a Saturday night in the field, and to watch and see who trampled it down. The oldest was to make the first trial. So he lay down by the upper ridge of the field, and after he had lain there a while he fell asleep. The following morning the whole field had been trampled down, and the young fellow was unable to tell how it had happened.

Now the second son was to make the attempt; but he had the same experience. After he had lain a while he fell asleep, and in the morning he was unable to tell how the field had come to be trampled down.

Now it was the turn of John by the Ashes. He did not lie down by the upper ridge of the field; but lower down, and stayed awake. After he had lain there a while, three doves came flying along. They settled in the field, and that very moment shook off all their feathers, and turned into the most beautiful maidens one might wish to see. They danced with each other over the whole field; and while they did so, the young fellow gathered up all their feathers. Toward morning they wanted to put on their feathers again, but could not find them anywhere. Then they were frightened, and wept and searched and searched and wept. Finally, they discovered the young fellow, and begged him to give them back their feathers. "But why do you dance in our wheat-field?" said the young fellow. "Alas, it is not our fault," said the maidens. "The troll who has enchanted us sends us here every Saturday night to trample the field. But now give us our feathers, for morning is near." And they begged for them in the sweetest way. "I do not know about that," said the young fellow, "you have trampled down the field so very badly; perhaps—if I might choose and have one of you?" "That would please us," returned the maidens, "but it would not be possible; for three trolls guard us, one with three, one with six and one with nine heads, and they kill all who come to the mountain." But the young fellow said that one of them pleased him so very much that he would make the attempt, in spite of what they had told him. So he chose the middle one, for she seemed the most beautiful to him, and she gave him a ring and put it on his finger. And then the maidens at once put on their garments of dove feathers, and flew back across forest and hill.

When the young fellow returned home, he told what he had seen. "And now I must set out and try my luck," said he. "I do not know whether I will return, but I must make the venture." "O John, John by the Ashes!" said his brothers, and laughed at him. "Well, it makes no difference, even though I am worthless," said John by the Ashes. "I must try my luck." So the young fellow set out to wander to the place where the maidens lived. They had told him it was farther south than south, and farther north than north, in the great hill of gold. After he had gone a while, he met two poor lads who were quarreling with each other about a pair of old shoes and a bamboo cane, which their mother had left them. The young fellow said it was not worth quarreling about such things, and that he had better shoes and better canes at home. "You cannot say that," returned the brothers, "for whoever has these shoes on can cover a thousand miles in a single step, and whatever is touched with this cane must die at once." The young fellow went on to ask whether they would sell the things. They said that they ought to get a great deal for them. "But what you say of them is not true at all," the young fellow replied. "Yes, indeed, it is absolutely true," they answered. "Just let me see whether the boots will fit me," said the young fellow. So they let him try them on. But no sooner did the young fellow have the boots on his feet, and the cane in his hand, than he took a step and off he was, a thousand miles away.

A little later he met two young fellows who were quarreling over an old fiddle, which had been left them. "Now is that worth while doing?" said the young fellow. "I have a brand-new fiddle at home." "But I doubt if it has such a tone as ours," said one of the youths, "for if some one is dead, and you play this fiddle, he will come to life again." "That really is a good deal," said the young fellow. "May I draw the bow across the strings?" They told him he might, but no sooner did he have the fiddle in his hand than he took a step, and suddenly he was a thousand miles away.

A little later he met an old man, and him he asked whether he knew where the place might be that was "farther south than south, and farther north than north, and in the great hill of gold." The man said yes, he knew well enough, but it would not do the young fellow much good to get there, for the troll who lived there killed every one. "O, I have to make the attempt, whether it lead to life or death," said the young fellow, for he was fonder than fond of the middle one of the three maidens. So he learned the way from the old man, and finally reached the hill. There he had to pass through three rooms, before he came into the hall to the maidens. And there were locks on every door, and at each stood a watchman. "Where do you want to go?" asked the first watchman. "In to the maidens," said the young fellow. "In you may go, but you'll not get out again," said the watchman, "for now the troll will be along before long." But the young fellow said that, at any rate, he would make the attempt, and went on. So he came to the second watchman. "Where do you want to go?" asked the latter. "In to the maidens," said the young fellow. "In you may go, but you'll not get out again," said the watchman, "for the troll will be here any minute." "And yet I will make the attempt," said the young fellow, and the watchman let him pass. So he came to the third watchman. "Where do you want to go?" the latter asked him. "In to the maidens," said the young fellow. "In you may go, but you'll never get out again, for the troll will be here in three shakes of a lamb's tail," said the watchman. "And yet I will make the attempt," said the young fellow, and this watchman also let him pass. Then he reached the inner chamber where the maidens sat. They were so beautiful and distinguished, and the room was so full of gold and silver, that the young fellow never could have imagined anything like it. Then he showed the ring, and asked whether the maidens recognized it. Indeed they did recognize him and the ring. "But you poor unfortunate, this is the end of us and of you!" said they. "The troll with three heads will be along before long, and you had better hide behind the door!" "O, I'm so frightened, I'm so frightened!" wailed the maiden whom the young fellow had chosen. "Just you stop crying," said the young fellow. "I think fortune will favor us!"

The troll came that very moment and thrust his three heads into the door. "Uff, it smells like Christian blood here!"

said he. The young fellow struck at the heads with his bamboo cane, and the troll was dead in a minute. So they carried out the body and hid it. A little later the troll with six heads came home. "Uff, it smells like Christian blood here!" said he. "Some one must have crept into the place! But what has become of the other troll?" said he, when he did not see the troll with three heads. "He has not yet come home," said the maidens. "He must have come home," said the troll. "Perhaps he has gone to look for the fellow who crept in here." At that moment the young fellow struck all six of his heads with his bamboo cane, and the troll at once fell dead to the ground. Then they dragged out the corpse.

A while later came the troll with nine heads. "Uff, it smells like Christian blood here!" said he, and grew very angry. "But where are the two others?" said he. "They have not yet come home," said the maidens. "Indeed they have come," said the troll, "but they are probably looking for the Christian who has crept in here!" At that moment, the young fellow sprang from behind the door, and struck one head after another with his bamboo cane. But he had no more than reached the eighth than it seemed to him that the troll was getting the upper hand, and he ran out of the door. The troll was so furious that he came near bursting. He seized all the maidens and killed them, and then out he flew after the young fellow. The latter had hidden behind a big rock, and when the troll came darting up, showering sparks in his rage, he struck at his ninth head, too, and the troll fell on his back, dead. Then the young fellow ran in again, took his fiddle and played, and all the maidens came back to life. Now they wanted to go home; but did not know how to find the long road back. "I know what we must do," said the young fellow, "I will take you on my back, one by one, and then the journey will not be long for us." And this he did. He carried home all the gold and silver he found in the hill, and then celebrated his wedding with the middle one of the maidens, and if they have not died, they are living this very day.

LUCKY ANDREW

There was once a rich peasant who had two sons, named John Nicholas and Lucky Andrew. The oldest was one of those fellows of whom one never can quite make head or tail. He was a most unpleasant customer to deal with, and he was more grasping and greedy than the folk of the Northland are, as a rule, though it is only too rare to find them unblessed with these attractive qualities. The other, Lucky Andrew, was wild and high spirited, but always good natured, and no matter how badly off he might be, he would always insist that he had been born under a lucky star. When the eagle, in order to defend his nest, belabored his head and face till the blood ran, he would still maintain that he was born under a lucky star, if only he managed to bring home a single eaglet. Did his boat capsize, which occasionally happened, and did they discover him hanging to it, quite overcome with the water, cold and exertion, and asked him how he felt, he would reply: "O, quite well. I have been saved. I surely am in luck!"

When their father died, both of them were of age, and not long after they both had to go out to the sand-banks to fetch some fishing-nets, which had been left there since the summer fishing. It was late in the fall, after the time when most fishermen are busy with the summer fishing. Andrew had his gun along, which he carried with him wherever he went. John Nicholas did not say much while they were underway; but he thought all the harder. They were not ready to set out for home again until near evening.

"Hark, Lucky Andrew, do you know there will be a storm to-night?" said John Nicholas, and looked out across the sea. "I think it would be best if we stayed here until morning!"

"There'll be no storm," said Andrew. "The Seven Sisters have not put on their fog-caps, so you may be quite at rest."

But his brother complained of being weary, and at length they decided to remain there for the night. When Andrew awoke he found himself alone; and he saw neither brother nor boat, until he came to the highest point of the island. Then he discovered him far out, darting for land like a sea-gull. Andrew did not understand the whole affair. There were still provisions there, as well as a dish of curd, his gun and various other things. So Andrew wasted but little time in thought. "He will come back this evening," said he. "Only a fool loses heart so long as he can eat." But in the evening there was no brother to be seen, and Andrew waited day by day, and week by week; until at last, he realized that his brother had marooned him on this barren island in order to be able to keep their inheritance for himself, and not have to divide it. And such was the case, for when John Nicholas came in sight of land on his homeward trip, he had capsized the boat, and declared that Lucky Andrew had been drowned.

But the latter did not lose heart. He gathered drift-wood along the strand, shot sea-birds, and looked for mussels and roots. He built himself a raft of drift-timber, and fished with a pole that had also been left behind. One day, while he was at work, he happened to notice a depression or hollow in the sand, as though made by the keel of a large Northland schooner, and he could plainly trace the braidings of the hawsers from the strand up to the top of the island. Then he thought to himself that he was in no danger, for he saw there was truth in the report he had often heard, that the meer-folk made the island their abode, and did much business with their ships.

"God be praised for good company! That was just what

I needed. Yes, it is true, as I have always said, that I was born under a lucky star," thought Andrew to himself; perhaps he said so too, for occasionally he really had to talk a little. So he lived through the fall. Once he saw a boat, and hung a rag on a pole and waved with it; but that very moment the sail dropped, and the crew took to the oars and rowed away at top speed, for they thought the meer-trolls were making signs and waving.

On Christmas Eve Andrew heard fiddles and music far out at sea; and when he came out, he saw a glow of light that came from a great Northland schooner, which was gliding toward the land—yet such a ship he had never yet seen. It has a main-sail of uncommon size, which looked to him to be of silk, and the most delicate tackling, as thin as though woven of steel wire, and everything else was in proportion, as fine and handsome as any Northlander might wish to have. The whole schooner was filled with little people dressed in blue, but the girl who stood at the helm was adorned like a bride, and looked as splendid as a queen, for she wore a crown and costly garments. Yet any one could see that she was a human being, for she was tall, and handsomer than the meer-folk. In fact, Lucky Andrew thought that she was handsomer than any girl he ever had seen. The schooner headed for the land where Andrew stood; but with his usual presence of mind, he hurried to the fisherman's hut, pulled down his gun from the wall, and crept up into the large loft and hid himself, so that he could see all that passed in the hut. He soon noticed that the whole room was alive with people. They filled it completely and more, and still more of them came in. Then the walls began to crack, and the little hut spread out at all corners, and grew so splendid and magnificent that the wealthiest merchant could not have had its equal; it was almost like being in a royal castle. Tables were covered with the most exquisite silver and gold. When they had eaten they began to dance. Under cover of the noise, Andrew crept to the look-out at the side of the roof, and climbed down. Then he ran to the schooner, threw his flint-stone over it, and in order to make certain, cut a cross into it with his sharp-cutting knife. When he came back again, the dance was in full swing. The tables were dancing and the benches and chairs—everything else in the room was dancing, too. The only one who did not dance was the bride; she only sat there and looked on, and when the bridegroom came to fetch her, she sent him away. For the moment there was no thought of stopping. The fiddler knew neither rest nor repose, and did not pass his cap, but played merrily on with his left hand, and beat time with his foot, until he was dripping with sweat, and the fiddle was hidden by the dust and smoke. When Andrew noticed that his own feet began to twitch where he was standing, he thought to himself: "Now I had better shoot away, or else he will play me right off the ground!" So he turned his gun, thrust it through the window, and shot it off over the bride's head; but upside down, otherwise the bullet would have hit him. The moment the shot crashed, all the troll-folk tumbled out of the door together; but when they saw that the schooner was banned on the shore, they wailed and crept into a hole in the hill. But all the gold and silver dishes were left behind, and the bride, too, was still sitting there. She told Lucky Andrew that she had been carried into the hill when she was only a small child. Once, when her mother had gone to the pen to attend to the milking, she had taken her along; but when she had to go home for a moment, she left the child sitting under a juniper-bush, and told her that she might eat the berries if she only repeated three times:

> *"I eat juniper-berries blue,*
> *Wherein Jesu's cross I view.*
> *I eat whortle-berries red,*
> *Since 'twas for my sake He bled!"*

But after her mother had gone, she found so many berries that she forgot to say her verse, and so she was enchanted and taken into the hill. And there no harm had been done her, save that she had lost the top joint of the little finger of her left hand, and the goblins had been kind to her; yet it had always seemed to her as though something were not as it should be, she felt as though something weighed upon her, and she had suffered greatly from the advances of the dwarf who had been chosen for her husband. When Andrew learned who her mother and her people were, he saw that they were related to him, and they became very good friends. So Andrew could truly say he had been born under a lucky star. Then they sailed home, and took along the schooner, and all the gold and silver, and all the treasure which had been left in the hut, and then Andrew was far wealthier than his brother.

But the latter, who suspected where all this wealth had come from, did not wish to be any poorer than Andrew. He knew that trolls and goblins walk mainly on Christmas Eve, and for that reason he sailed out to the sand banks at that time. And on Christmas Eve he did see a light or fire, but it seemed to be like will-o'-the-wisps fluttering about. When he came nearer he heard splashes, horrible howls, and cold, piercing cries, and there was a smell of slime and sea-weed, as at ebb-tide. Terrified, he ran up into the hut, from whence he could see the trolls on the shore. They were short and thick like hay-ricks, completely covered with fur, with kirtles of skins, fishing boots, and enormous fist-gloves. In place of head and hair they had bundles of sea-weed. When they crawled up from the strand there was a gleam behind them like that of rotting wood, and when they shook themselves they showered sparks about them. When they drew nearer, John Nicholas crawled up into the loft as his brother had done. The goblins dragged a great stone into the hut, and began to beat their gloves dry against it, and meanwhile they screamed so that John Nicholas's blood turned to ice in his hiding-place. Then one of them sneezed into the ashes on the hearth in order to make the fire burn again; while the others carried in heather-grass and drift-wood, as coarse and heavy as lead. The smoke and the heat nearly killed the eavesdropper in the loft, and in order to catch his breath and get some fresh air, he tried to crawl out of the look-out in the roof; yet he was of much heavier build than his brother, stuck fast and could move neither in nor out. Then he grew frightened and began to scream; but the goblins screamed much louder, and roared and howled, and thumped and clamored inside and outside the hut. But when the cock crowed they disappeared, and John Nicholas freed himself, too. Yet when he returned home from his trip, he had lost his reason, and after that the same cold, sinister screams which are the mark of the troll in the Northland, might often be heard sounding from store-rooms and lofts where he happened to be. Before his death, however, his reason returned, and he was buried in consecrated ground, as they say. But after that time no human foot ever trod the sand-banks again. They sank, and the meer-folk, it is believed, went to the Lekang Islands. Andrew's luck held good; no ship made more successful trips than his own; but whenever he came to the Lekang Islands he lay becalmed—the goblins went aboard or ashore with their goods—but after a time he had fair winds, whether he happened to want to go to Bergen, or sail home. He had many children, and all of them were bright and vigorous, yet every one of them lacked the upper joint of the little finger of his left hand.

THE PASTOR AND
THE SEXTON

Once upon a time there was a pastor who was such a boor that when any one was driving toward him along the highway, he would shout to them, while still some distance off: "Get out of the way! Get out of the pastor's way!" One day, while he was doing this, along came the king. "Get out of the way! Get out of the way!" shouted the pastor. But the king drove as he had a mind to, and he drove so fast that this time it was the pastor who had to get out of the way, and when the king passed him, he called out: "See that you come to me at the castle to-morrow, and if you cannot answer three questions I put to you, then you will have to take off your pastor's gown as a punishment for your arrogance!"

This sounded different from what the pastor was used to hearing. Shout and bluster, and completely forget himself in his arrogance, that he knew how to do; but returning a plain answer to a plain question was not his strong point. So he went to the sexton, who was supposed to have more in his upper story than the pastor. He told him he did not venture to go to the castle, because "a fool can ask more than ten wise men can answer," said he, and he induced the sexton to go in his stead.

The sexton set forth, and came to the castle dressed in the pastor's gown and ruff. The king received him out in the entrance with crown and scepter, and was so splendidly dressed that he fairly gleamed and shone.

"Well, are you here?" Yes, indeed, there he was. "First tell me," said the king, "the distance from East to West." "It is one day's journey," said the sexton.

"And how is that?" asked the king. "Well, the sun rises in the East and goes down in the West, and manages to do so nicely in the course of a single day," said the sexton.

"Good," said the king, "but now tell me how much I am worth, just as I stand."

"Well, if our Lord Christ himself was valued at thirty pieces of silver, then I can hardly value you at more than twenty-nine," said the sexton.

"Well and good," said the king, "but since you are so wondrous wise, tell me what I am thinking now."

"Ah, my lord king, you are probably thinking that this is the pastor who is standing before you, but there you are greatly mistaken, for I am the sexton."

"Then drive straight home, and be the pastor, and the pastor shall be the sexton," said the king, and that is what happened, too.

THE SKIPPER AND
SIR URIAN

Once upon a time there was a master mariner who had the most unheard of good fortune in all that he undertook; none had such splendid cargoes, and none earned so much money as he did, for everything seemed to come to him. And it is quite certain that there were none who could risk taking the trips he did, for wherever he sailed he had fair winds, yes, it was even said that when he turned around his cap, the wind turned with it, to suit his wish.

Thus he sailed for many years with cargoes of lumber, and even went as far as China, and earned money like hay. But once he sailed the North Sea with all sails set, as though he had stolen ship and cargo. But the one who was after him sailed even more swiftly. And that was Sir Urian, the devil! With him the master mariner, as you may imagine, had made a bargain, and that very day and hour the contract expired, and the mariner had to be prepared, from moment to moment, to see him arrive to fetch him.

So he came up on deck, out of the cabin, and took a look at the weather. Then he called the ship's carpenter and several others, and told them to go down at once into the ship's hold, and bore two holes in the ship's bottom. Then they were to take the pumps from out their frames, and set them closely over the holes, so that the water would rise quite high in the pipes.

The men were surprised, and thought his orders passing strange, yet they did as he told them. They bored the holes, and set up the pumps closely over them, so that not even a drop of water could get at the cargo; yet the North Sea stood seven feet high in the pumps.

No more had they cast overboard their chips and litter than Sir Urian came along in a squall, and grabbed the master mariner by the collar. "Wait, old boy, the matter is not so terribly urgent!" said he, and began to defend himself, and pry loose the claws that held him with an awl. "Did you not bind yourself in your contract always to keep my ship tight and dry?" said the master mariner. "You are a nice article! Just take a look at the pumps! The water stands seven feet high in the pipes! Pump, devil, pump my ship dry, then you may take me to have and to hold as long as ever you wish!"

The devil was fool enough, and allowed himself to be hoaxed. He worked and sweat, and the perspiration ran down his cheeks in such streams that one might have run a mill with them, but he merely kept on pumping out of the North Sea into the North Sea. At last he had enough of it, and when he could pump no longer, he flew home to his grandmother to rest. He let the master mariner stay master mariner as long as he might choose, and if he has not died he is still sailing the seas at his own sweet will, and letting the wind blow according to how he turns his cap.

THE YOUTH WHO WAS TO SERVE THREE YEARS WITHOUT PAY

Once upon a time there was a poor man, who had only one son; but one who was so lazy and clumsy that he did not want to do a stroke of work. "If I am not to feed this bean-pole for the rest of my life, I'll have to send him far away, where not a soul knows him," thought the father. "Once he is knocking about in the world, he will not be so likely to come home again." So he took his son and led him about in the world, far and wide, and tried to get him taken on as a serving man; but no one would have him. Finally, after wandering a long time, they came to a rich man, of whom it was said that he turned every shilling around seven times before he could make up his mind to part with it. He was willing to take the youth for a servant, and he was to work three years without pay. But at the end of the three years, his master was to go into town, two days in succession, and buy the first thing he saw, and on the third morning the youth himself was to go to town and also buy the first thing he met. And all this he was to receive in lieu of his wage.

So the youth served out his three years, and did better than they had expected him to do. He was by no means a model serving-man; but then his master was none of the best, either, for he let him go all that time in the same clothes he had worn when he entered his service, until, finally, one patch elbowed the other.

Now when his master was to go to do his buying, he set out as early as possible in the morning. "Costly wares are only to be seen by day," said he, "they are not drifting about the street so early. It will probably cost me enough as it is, for what I find is a matter of purest chance." The first thing he saw on the street was an old woman, who was carrying a covered basket. "Good-day, granny," said the man. "And good day to you, daddy," said the old woman.

"What have you in your basket?" asked the man. "Would you like to know?" said the woman. "Yes," said the man, "for I have to buy the first thing that comes my way." "Well, if you want to know, buy it!" said the old woman. "What does it cost?" asked the man. She must have four shillings for it, declared the woman. This did not seem such a tremendous price to him, he would let it go at that, said he, and raised the cover. And there lay a pup in the basket. When the man got home from his journey to town, there stood the youth full of impatience and curiosity, wondering what his wage for the first year might be. "Are you back already, master?" asked the youth. "Yes, indeed," said his master. "And what have you bought?" asked the youth. "What I have bought is nothing so very rare," said the man. "I don't even know whether I ought to show it to you; but I bought the first thing to be had, and that was a pup," said he. "And I thank you most kindly for it," said the youth. "I have always been fond of dogs."

The following morning it was no better. The man set out as early as possible, and had not as yet reached town before he met the old woman with the basket. "Good-day, granny," said the man. "And good-day to you, daddy," said the old woman. "What have you in your basket today?" asked the man. "If you want to know, then buy it!" was again the answer. "What does it cost?" asked the man. She wanted four shillings for it, she had only the one price. The man said he would buy it, for he thought that this time he would make a better purchase. He raised the cover, and this time a kitten lay in the basket. When he reached home, there stood the youth, waiting to see what he was to get in lieu of his second year's wages. "Are you back again, master!" said he. "Yes, indeed," said the master. "What did you buy today?" asked the youth. "Alas, nothing better than I did yesterday," said the man, "but I did as we agreed, and bought the first thing I came across, and that was this kitten." "You could not have hit on anything better," said the youth, "for all my life long I have been fond of cats as well as of dogs." "I do not fare so badly this way," thought the man, "but when he sets out for himself, then the matter will probably turn out differently."

So the third morning the youth set out for himself, and when he entered town, he came across the same old woman with her basket on her arm. "Good morning, granny," said he. "And good morning to you, my boy," said the old woman. "What have you in your basket?" asked the youth. "If you want to know, then buy it!" answered the old woman. "Do you want to sell it?" asked the youth. Yes, indeed, and it would cost four shillings, said the old woman. That is a bargain, thought the youth, and wanted to take it, for he had to buy the first thing that came his way. "Well, you can take the whole blessed lot," said the old woman, "the basket and all that's in it. But do not look into it before you get home, do you hear!" No, indeed, he would be sure not to look in the basket, said he. But on the way, he kept wondering as to what might be in the basket, and willy-nilly—he could not keep from raising the cover a little, and looking through the crack. But that very minute a little lizard popped out of the crack, and ran across the road so quickly that it fairly hummed—and aside from the lizard there was nothing in the basket. "Stop, wait a minute, and don't run away! I just bought you," said the youth. "Stab me in the neck! Stab me in the neck!" cried the lizard. The youth did not have to be told twice. He ran after the lizard and stabbed it in the neck just as it was slipping into a hole in a wall. And that very moment it turned into a man, as handsome and splendid as the handsomest prince, and a prince he was, if truth be told.

"Now you have delivered me," said he, "for the old woman, with whom you and your master have been dealing, is a witch, and she turned me into a lizard, and my brother and sister into a dog and cat." The youth thought this a remarkable tale. "Yes, indeed," said the prince. "She was actually on the way to throw us into the sea and drown us; but if any one were to appear and want to buy us, she had to sell us for four shillings apiece, that had been agreed upon. And now you shall go home with me to my father, and be rewarded for your good deed." "Your home must be a good way off," said the youth. "O, it is not so far," declared the prince, "there it is!" And he pointed to a high hill in the distance.

They marched along as fast as they could, but still it was farther away than it seemed. So it was late at night before they reached their goal. The prince knocked. "Who is knocking at my door, and disturbing my sleep?" came a voice within the hill. And the voice was so powerful that the earth trembled. "Open, father, your son has come home!" cried the prince. Then the father was glad to open the door quickly. "I thought you were already lying at the bottom of the sea," said the old man. "But you are not alone?" "This is the chap who delivered me," said the prince, "and I asked him to come with me so that you could reward him." That he would attend to, said the old man. "Now you must come right in," said he, "for here you may rest in safety." They went in and sat down, and the old man laid an armful of wood and a couple of big logs on the fire, until every corner was as bright as day, and wherever they looked everything was indescribably splendid. The youth had never seen anything like it, and such fine things to eat and drink as the old man served up to him, he had never yet tasted. And the bowls and dishes, and goblets and plates, were all of pure silver and shining gold.

There was no need to urge the young folk. They ate and drank and enjoyed themselves, and then slept far into the next day. The youth was still asleep when the old man came and offered him a morning draft in a golden goblet. And when he had put on his rags and breakfasted, he was allowed to pick out what he wanted, as a reward for delivering the prince. There was much to see and still more to take, as you may believe. "Well, what do you want?" asked the king. "You may take what you will; for as you see there is enough from which to choose." The youth said he would have to think it over a bit, and speak to the prince. And that he was allowed to do. "Well, I suppose you have seen all sorts of beautiful things?" asked the prince. "That is a fact," said the youth. "But tell me, what ought I to choose among all these magnificent things? Your father said I might pick out whatever I wished." "You must choose none among all the things you have seen," answered the prince, "but my father wears a ring on his little finger, and you must ask him for that." This the youth did, and begged the king for the ring on his finger. "It is dearer to me than anything else I have," said the king, "but my son is just as dear to me, and therefore I will give you the ring. Do you know what powers it has?" No, that the youth did not know. "While you wear it on your finger, you can get everything that you want to have," said the king. The youth thanked him most kindly, and the king and the prince wished him all manner of luck on his journey, and charged him to take the best care of the ring.

He had not been long underway before it occurred to him to test what the ring could do. So he wished to be dressed in new clothes from head to toe, and no more had he uttered the wish than there he was in them. And he looked as handsome and bright as a new nickel. Then he thought to himself it would be pleasant to play a trick on his father. "He was none too friendly to me while I was still at home." And so the youth wished he were standing before his father's door, just as ragged as he had been before. And that very minute there he stood.

"Good-day, father, and many thanks for the last time!" said the youth. But when his father saw he had come home far more tattered and torn than when he had gone away, he grew angry and began to scold: "There is nothing to be made of you, if during all the long years of your service you have not even been able to earn a suit of clothes to your back."

"Now do not be so angry, father," said the youth. "You need not take for granted that a fellow is a vagabond because he goes about in rags. Now I want you to go to the king as my proxy, and ask his daughter's hand for me." "Come, come, why, that is utter folly and nonsense!" cried his father. But the youth insisted that it was gospel truth, and took a birch bough, and drove his father to the king's castle-gate. And the latter came stumbling right in to the king, and wept so that the tears just tumbled out.

"Well, what has happened to you, my dear fellow?" asked the king. "If a wrong has been done you, I will see that you get your rights." No, no wrong had been done him, said the man, but he had a son who gave him a great deal of trouble: it was

impossible to make a man of him, and now he had evident-
ly lost what few senses he did possess. "Because he has just
chased me to the castle-gate with a birch bough, and threatened me, if I do not get him the king's daughter for a bride,"
said the man. "Set your mind at rest, my good fellow," said the
king, "and send your son to me. Then we will see whether we
can come to an understanding."

The youth came rushing in to the king, so that his rags
fairly fluttered. "Do I get your daughter?" he cried. "Well, that
is just what we are going to discuss," said the king, "perhaps
she would not answer for you, and perhaps you would not answer for her," said he. That might be the case, said the youth.

Now a great ship from abroad had shortly before come
into port, and one could see it from the castle window. "Now
we'll see," said the king. "If you can build a ship that is the
exact counterpart of the one outside, and just as handsome,
in the space of an hour or two, then, perhaps, you may get my
daughter," said the king.

"If it be no more than that ..." said the youth. Then he
went down to the shore and sat on a sand-pile, and when he
had sat there long enough, he wished that a ship might lie out
in the fjord, completely equipped with masts and sails and
all that goes with them, and that it might resemble the ship
already lying there in every particular. And that very minute
there lay the ship, and when the king saw that there were two
ships at anchor instead of one, he came down to the shore
himself to look more closely into the matter. And then he saw
the youth. He was standing in a boat, with a broom in one
hand, as though he meant to give the ship a final cleaning; but
when he saw the king coming, he threw away the broom and
cried: "Now the ship is finished. Do I get your daughter now?"

"That is all very fine," said the king, "but you must stand yet another test. If you can build a castle that is just like mine in every particular within an hour or so, then we will go further into the matter."

"No more than that?" cried the youth. After he had strolled around for a long while, and the time set was nearly over, he wished that a castle might stand there that resembled the king's castle in every particular. And before long there it stood, as you may believe. And it did not take long, either, before the king, together with the queen and the princess, came to look at the new castle. The youth stood there with his broom again, and swept and cleaned. "Now the castle is in apple-pie order. Do I get her now?" he cried.

"That's all very fine," declared the king, "just come in and we'll talk it over," said he, for he had noticed that the youth knew a thing or two, and he was thinking over how he might get rid of him. The king went on ahead, and after him the queen, and then went the princess, just in advance of the youth. Then he at once wished to be the handsomest man in the world, and so he was, that very minute. When the princess saw what a splendid figure he suddenly cut, she nudged the queen, who in turn nudged the king, and after they had stared at him long enough, they at last realized that the youth was more than he had at first appeared to be, in his rags. So they decided that the princess was to treat him nicely, in order to find out how matters really stood, and the princess was as sweet and amiable as sugar-bread, and flattered the youth, and said that she could not do without him, night or day. And when it came toward the end of the first evening, she said: "Since you and I are to be married in any case, I am sure you will have no secrets from me, and you will not want to hide from me how you managed to do all these fine things."

"O, yes," said the youth. "You shall know about it, but first of all let us be married; before that nothing counts!"

The following evening the princess pretended to be quite unhappy. She was well aware, said she, that he did not attach much importance to her love, when he would not even tell her what she wanted so much to know. If he could not even oblige her in such a small matter, his love could not amount to a great deal. Then the youth fell into despair, and to make up with her again, he told her everything. She lost no time, and let the king and queen know all about it. Thereupon they agreed as to how they would go about getting the youth's ring away from him, and then, thought they, it would not really be hard to get rid of him.

In the evening the princess came with a sleeping potion, and said she wanted to give her lover a drink that would increase his love for her, since it was plain he did not love her enough. The youth suspected nothing, and drank, and at once fell so fast asleep that they could have pulled down the house over his head. Then the princess drew the ring from his finger, put it on herself, and wished the youth might be lying on the garbage-pile in the street, just as tattered and torn as he had come to them, and in his place she wanted the handsomest prince in the world. And that very minute everything happened just as she wished. After a time the youth woke up, out on the garbage-pile, and at first thought he was dreaming: but when he saw the ring was gone, he understood how it all had happened, and fell into such despair that he got up and wanted to jump right into the sea.

But then he met the cat his master had bought for him. "Where are you going?" she asked. "To throw myself into the sea and drown," was the youth's reply.

"Do not do so on any account," said the cat. "You will get your ring again."

"Yes, if that were so, then ..." said the youth.

The cat ran away. Suddenly a rat crossed her path. "Now I will pounce on you!" said the cat. "O do not do that," said the rat, "you shall have the ring again!"

"Well, if that is so, then ..." said the cat.

When the folk at the castle had gone to bed, the rat crept around, and sniffed and spied out the room of the prince and princess; and at last he found a little hole through which he crawled. Then he heard the prince and princess talking to each other, and saw that the prince was wearing the ring on his finger. Before she went, the princess said: "Good night. And see that you take good care of the ring, my dearest!"

"Pooh! no one will come in through the walls for the sake of a ring," said the prince, "but if you think it is not safe enough on my hand, why, I can put it in my mouth."

After a time he lay down on his back, and prepared to go to sleep. But just then the ring slipped down his throat, and he had to cough, so that the ring flew out and rolled along the ground. Swish!--the rat had caught it, and crept out with it to the cat, who was waiting at the rat-hole. But in the meantime the king had caught the youth, and had had him put in a great tower and condemned to death, because he had made a mock of his daughter—so the king said. And the youth was to sit in the tower until he was beheaded. But the cat kept prowling around the tower all the time, trying to sneak in with the ring. And then an eagle came along, caught her up in his claws and flew across the sea with her. And suddenly a hawk appeared, and flung himself on the eagle, and the eagle let the cat fall into the sea. When she felt the water, she grew afraid, let the ring fall, and swam to land. No sooner had she shaken the water from her fur than she met the dog whom the youth's master had bought for him.

"Well, what am I to do now?" said the cat, and wept and lamented. "The ring is gone, and they want to murder the youth." "That I do not know," said the dog, "but what I do know is that I have the very worst kind of an ache in my stomach," said he.

"There you have it. You have surely over-eaten," said the cat.

"I never eat more than I need," said the dog, "and just now I have eaten nothing at all, save a dead fish that was left here by the ebb-tide."

"Could the fish have swallowed the ring?" asked the cat. "And must you, also, lose your life, because you cannot digest gold?"

"That may well be the case," said the dog. "But then it would be best if I died at once, for then the youth might still be saved."

"O, that is not necessary!" said the rat—who was there, too—"I do not need a very large opening through which to crawl, and if the ring is really there, I am sure I can find it." So the rat slipped down into the dog, and before very long he came out again with the ring. And then the cat made her way to the tower, and clawed her way up till she found a hole through which she could thrust her paw, and thus brought back the ring to the youth.

No sooner was it on his finger than he wished that the tower might break down, and that very moment he was standing just before the tower-gate, and reviling the king and the queen and the king's daughter as though they were the lowest of the low. The king hastily called together his army, and told it to surround the tower, and take the youth prisoner, dead or alive. But the youth only wished the whole army might be sticking up to their necks in the big swamp in the hills, and there they had trouble enough getting out—those among them who did not stick fast. Then he went right on reviling where he had stopped, and finally, when he had told them all just what he thought of them, he wished that the king, the queen and the king's daughter might sit for the rest of their lives in the tower into which they had thrust him. And when they were sitting there, he took possession of the king's land and country on his own account. Then the dog changed into a prince, and the cat into a princess, and he made the latter his wife, and they were married and celebrated their wedding long and profusely.

THE YOUTH WHO WANTED TO WIN THE DAUGHTER OF THE MOTHER IN THE CORNER

Once upon a time there was a woman who had a son, and he was so lazy and slow that there was not a single blessed useful thing he would do. But he liked to sing and to dance, and that is what he did all day long, and far into the night as well. The longer this went on, the worse off his mother was. The youth was growing, and he wanted so much to eat that it was barely possible to find it, and more and more went for his clothes the older he grew, since his clothes did not last long, as you may imagine, because the youth skipped and dance about without stopping, through forest and field.

At length it was too much for his mother, so one day she told the young fellow that he ought at last to get to work, and really do something, or both of them would have to starve to death. But the youth had no mind to do so, he said, and would rather try to win the daughter of the mother in the corner, for if he got her, then he would live happily ever after, and could sing and dance, and would not have to plague himself with work.

When the mother heard that she thought it might not be such a bad idea after all, and she dressed up the youth as well as she could, so that he would make a good showing when he came to the mother in the corner, and then he set forth.

When he stepped out the sun was shining bright and warm; but it had rained during the night, and the ground was soft and full of water puddles. The youth took the short-est path to the mother in the corner, and sang and danced, as he always did. But suddenly, as he was hopping and skipping along, he came to a swamp, and there were only some logs laid down to cross it; and from the one log he had to jump over a puddle to a clump of grass, unless he wanted to dirty his shoes. And then he went kerflop! The very moment he set foot on the clump of grass, he went down and down until he was standing in a dark, ugly hole. At first he could see nothing at all, but when he had been there a little while, he saw that there was a rat, who was wiggling and waggling around, and had a bunch of keys hanging from her tail.

"Have you come, my boy?" said the rat. "I must thank you for coming to visit me: I have been expecting you for a long time. I am sure you have come to win me, and I can well imagine that you are in a great hurry. But you must have a little patience. I am to receive a large dower, and am not yet ready for the wedding; but I will do my best to see that we are married soon."

When she had said this, she produced a couple of egg-shells, with all sorts of eatables such as rats eat, and set them down before the youth, and said: "Now you must sit down and help yourself, for I am sure you are tired and hungry."

The youth had no great appetite for this food. "If I were only away and up above again," thought he, but he said nothing.

"Now I think you must surely want to get home again," said the rat. "I am well aware that you are waiting impatiently for the wedding, and I will hurry all I can. Take this linen thread along, and when you get up above, you must not turn around, but must go straight home, and as you go you must keep repeating: 'Short before and long behind!'" and with that she laid a linen thread in his hand.

"Heaven be praised!" said the youth when he was up above once more. "I'll not go down there again in a hurry." But he held the thread in his hand, and danced and sang as usual. And although he no longer had the rat-hole in mind, he began to hum:

> "*Short before and long behind!*
> *Short before and long behind!*"

When he stood before the door at home, he turned around; and there lay many, many hundred yards of the finest linen, finer than the most skillful weaver could have spun.

"Mother, come out, come out!" called and cried the youth. His mother came darting out, and asked what was the matter. And when she saw the linen, stretching as far as she could see, and then a bit, she could not believe her eyes, until the youth told her how it all happened. But when she had heard that, and had tested the linen between her fingers, she was so pleased that she, too, began to sing and dance.

Then she took the linen, cut it, and sewed shirts from it for her son and herself, and the remainder she took to town and sold for a good price. Then for a time they lived in all joy and comfort. But when that was over the woman had not a bite to eat in the house, and so she told her son that it was the highest time for him to take service, and really do something, or else both of them would have to starve to death.

But the youth preferred to go to the mother in the corner, and try to win her daughter. His mother did not think this such a bad idea, for now the youth was handsomely dressed, and made a good showing.

So she brushed him, and furbished him up as well as she

could, and he himself took a pair of new shoes, and polished them till they shone like a mirror, and when he had done so, off he went. Everything happened as before. When he stepped out, the sun was shining bright and warm; but it had rained during the night, and the road was soft and muddy, and every puddle was full of water. The youth took the shortest way to the mother in the corner, and sang and danced and danced and sang, as he always did. He followed another road, not the one he had taken before; but as he was hopping and skipping along, he suddenly came to the log across the swamp, and from the log he had to jump over a puddle to a clump of grass, unless he wanted to dirty his shoes. And then he went kerflop. And he sank down and could not stop, until he reached a horrible, dark, ugly hole. At first he could see nothing; but after he had stood there a while, he discovered a rat with a bunch of keys at the end of her tail, which she was wiggling and waggling in front of him.

"Have you come, my boy?" said the rat. "You are welcome among us! It was kind of you to come and visit me again so soon; no doubt you are very impatient, I can well imagine it. But you must really be patient a little while longer; for my trousseau is not quite complete, but by the time you come again all shall be ready." When she had said this she offered him egg-shells containing all sorts of food such as rats like. But it looked to the youth like food that had been eaten, and he said that he had no appetite. "If I were only safely away, and up above again," thought he, but he said nothing. After a time the rat said: "Now I think you must surely want to get up above again. I will hurry on the wedding as quickly as I can. And now take this woolen thread along, and when you get up above, you must not turn around, but go straight home, and underway you must keep on repeating: 'Short before and long behind!'" and with that she laid the woolen thread in his hand.

"Thank heaven, I have escaped!" said the youth to himself. "I am sure I'll never go there again," and then he sang and danced again as usual. He thought no more of the rat-hole, but fell to humming, and sang without stopping:

> *"Short before and long behind!*
> *Short before and long behind!"*

When he stood at the door of the house, he happened to look around; and there lay the finest woolen goods, many hundred yards of it, stretching for half a mile, and so fine that no city counselor wore a coat of finer cloth.

"Mother, mother, come out, come out!" cried the youth. His mother came to the door, clasped her hands together over her head, and nearly fainted with joy when she saw all the fine goods. And then the youth had to tell her how it had come to him, and all that had taken place, from beginning to end. This brought them a small fortune, as you may imagine. The youth had new clothes, and his mother went to town and sold the goods, yard by yard, and was handsomely paid for them. And then she decorated her room, and she herself, in her old days, went about in such style that she might have been taken for some lady of distinction. So they lived splendidly and happily, but finally this money, too, came to an end; and one day the woman had not a bite to eat left in the house, and told her son that now he had better look for work, and really do something, or both of them would starve to death.

But the youth thought it would be much better to go to the mother in the corner and try to win her daughter. This time his mother again agreed with him, and did not contradict the youth; for now he had fine new clothes, and looked so distinguished that it seemed out of the question to her that such a good-looking fellow would be refused. So she furbished him up and tricked him out in the handsomest way, and he himself took out his new shoes and polished them so brightly that you could see yourself in them, and when he had done so he set forth.

This time he did not choose the shortest road; but took a roundabout way, the longest he could find, for he did not want to go down to the rat again because he was sick of her eternal wiggling and waggling, and the talk about marriage. The weather and the road were exactly the same as when he had gone before. The sun shone, the swamp and the puddles gleamed, and the youth sang and danced as usual. And in the midst of his skipping and jumping, before he knew it, there he stood at the same crossing which led across the swamp. There he had to jump over a puddle to a clump of grass, unless he wanted to dirty his brightly polished shoes. "Kerflop!" and down he went, and did not stop until he stood once more in the same dark, ugly, dirty hole. At first he was pleased because he could see nothing. But after he had stood there a while, he once more discovered the ugly rat who was so repulsive to him, with the bunch of keys hanging from her tail.

"Good-day, my boy," said the rat. "You are welcome! I see that you can no longer live without me, and I thank you. And now everything is in readiness for our wedding, and we will go straight to church." Nothing will come of that, thought the youth, but he did not say a word. Then the rat whistled, and at once every corner was alive with swarms of mice and small rats, and six large rats came dragging along a frying-pan. Two mice sat up behind as grooms, and two sprang up in front to drive the coach. Several seated themselves within, and the rat with the bunch of keys took her place in their midst. To the youth she said: "The road is a little narrow here, so you will have to walk beside the coach, sweetheart, until the road is broader. And then you may sit beside me in the coach."

"How fine that will be!" thought the youth. "If I were only safely up above once more, I would run away from the whole pack of them," thought he, but he said nothing. He went along with the procession as well as he could; at times he had to crawl, at others he had to stoop, for the way was very narrow. But when it grew better, he walked in advance, and looked about to see how he might most easily steal away and make off. And then he suddenly heard a clear, beautiful voice behind him say: "Now the road is good! Come, sweetheart, and get into the coach!"

The youth turned around quickly, and was so astonished that his nose and ears nearly fell off. There stood a magnificent coach with six white horses, and in the coach sat a maiden as fair and beautiful as the sun, and about her were sitting others, as bright and kindly as the stars. It was a princess and her playmates, who had all been enchanted together. But now they were delivered, because he had come down to them, and had never contradicted.

"Come along now!" said the princess. Then the youth got into the coach, and drove to church with her. And when they drove away from the church, the princess said: "Now we will first drive to my home, and then we will send for your mother."

"That's all very fine," thought the youth—he said nothing, but he thought it would be better, after all, to drive to his home, instead of down into the hideous rat-hole. But suddenly they came to a beautiful castle, and there they turned in, for there it was they were to live. And at once a fine coach with six horses was sent for the youth's mother, and when she came the wedding festivities began. They celebrated for fourteen days, and perhaps they are celebrating yet. We must hurry, and perhaps we may still get there in time, and can drink the groom's health and dance with the bride!

THE CHRONICLE OF THE PANCAKE

Once upon a time there was a woman who had seven hungry children, and she was baking pancakes for them. There was dough made with new milk, and it lay in the pan, and was rising so plumply and comfortably, that it was a pleasure to watch it. The children stood around it, and their grandfather sat and looked on.

"Give me a little bit of pancake, mother, I'm so hungry!" said one of the children.

"Dear mother!" said the second.

"Dear, sweet mother!" said the third.

"Dear, sweet, good mother!" said the fourth.

"Dear, best, sweet, good mother!" said the fifth.

"Dear, best, sweet, good, dearest mother!" said the sixth.

"Dear, best, sweet, good, dearest, sweetest mother!" said the seventh, and so they all begged around the pancake, one more sweetly than the other, for they were all so hungry and so well-behaved.

"Yes, children, wait until it turns around," said she—until I have turned it around, she should have said—"then you shall all have a pancake, a lovely best-milk pancake. Just see how fat and comfortable it is lying there!"

When the pancake heard that it was frightened, turned itself around suddenly, and wanted to get out of the pan; but it only fell on its other side, and when this had baked a little, so that it took shape and grew firmer, it leaped out on the floor, and rolled off like a wheel, out of the door, and down the street.

Hey there! The woman was after it with the pan in one

hand, and the spoon in the other, as fast as she could, and after her came the children, and last of all, their grandfather came hobbling along.

"Will you wait! Halt! Catch it! Hold it!" they all cried together, and wanted to catch up with it and grab it on the run; but the pancake rolled and rolled, and sure enough, it got so far ahead of them that they could no longer see it, for it had nimbler legs than all of them. After it had rolled a while it met a man.

"Good-day, pancake," said the man.

"Good-day, Man Tan," said the pancake.

"Dear, good pancake, don't roll so fast; but wait a little and let me eat you!" said the man.

"Mother Gray and grandpa I've left behind, and the seven squallers, too, you'll find, so I think I can leave you as well, Man Tan!" said the pancake, and rolled and rolled until it met a hen.

"Good-day, pancake," said the hen.

"Good-day, Hen Glen," said the pancake.

"Dear, good pancake, don't roll so fast, wait a little and I will eat you up!" said the hen.

"Mother Gray and grandpa I've left behind, and the seven squallers, too, you'll find, and Man Tan, so I think I can leave you as well, Hen Glen!" said the pancake, and rolled along the road like a wheel. Then it met a rooster.

"Good-day, pancake," said the rooster.

"Good-day, Rooster Booster," said the pancake.

"Dear, good pancake, don't roll so fast. Wait a little and I will eat you up!" said the rooster.

"Mother Gray and grandpa I've left behind, and the seven squallers, too, you'll find, and Man Tan and Hen Glen, and so I think I can leave you as well, Rooster Booster," said the pancake, and rolled and rolled as fast as ever it could. And after it had rolled a long time it met a duck.

"Good-day, pancake," said the duck.

"Good-day, Duck Tuck," said the pancake.

"Dear, good pancake, don't roll so fast. Wait a little and I will eat you up!" said the duck.

"Mother Gray and grandpa I've left behind, and the seven squallers, too, you'll find, and Man Tan, and Hen Glen and Rooster Booster, so I think I can leave you as well," said the pancake, and rolled on as fast as ever it could. After it had rolled a long, long time, it met a goose.

"Good-day, pancake," said the goose.

"Good-day, Goose Loose," said the pancake.

"Dear, good pancake, don't roll so fast. Wait a little and I will eat you up!" said the goose.

"Mother Gray and grandpa I've left behind, and the seven squallers, too, you'll find, and Man Tan and Hen Glen and Rooster Booster and Duck Tuck, and I think I can leave you as well, Goose Loose," said the pancake, and rolled away.

After it had again rolled for a long, long time, it met a gander.

"Good-day, pancake," said the gander.

"Good-day, Gander Meander," said the pancake.

"Dear, good pancake, don't roll so fast. Wait a little and I will eat you up!" said the gander.

"Mother Gray and grandpa I've left behind, and the seven squallers, too, you'll find, and Man Tan and Hen Glen and Rooster Booster and Duck Tuck and Goose Loose, and I think I can leave you as well, Gander Meander," said the pancake, and began to roll as fast as ever it could.

After it had rolled a long, long time, it met a pig.

"Good-day, pancake," said the pig.

"Good-day, Pig Snig," said the pancake, and began to roll as fast as ever it could.

"Now wait a little," said the pig. "You need not hurry so, for we can keep each other company going through the forest and take our time, for it is said to be haunted." The pancake thought that such was quite apt to be the case, and so they started off; but after they had gone a while they came to a brook.

The pig swam across on his own bacon, which was easy enough; but the pancake could not get across.

"Sit down on my snout," said the pig, "and I will carry you over that way." The pancake did so.

"Uff, uff!" said the pig, and swallowed the pancake in one mouthful.

"And now, since the pancake no further goes,

This little chronicle comes to a close."

SORIA-MORIA CASTLE

Once upon a time there was a couple who had an only son named Halvor. While he was still but a little lad, he would do nothing at all; but was always sitting at the hearth, digging in the ashes. His parents apprenticed him here and apprenticed him there, to be taught something, but Halvor never stayed. When he had been anywhere for a few days, he ran away again, went back home, sat down at the hearth, and dug in the ashes. But once a master mariner came along and asked whether Halvor would not like to go with him, and sail the seas, and see foreign lands. Indeed, Halvor would like to do so very much, and it did not take him long to make up his mind.

How long they sailed the seas I do not know, but suddenly a powerful storm arose, and when it had passed, and all had grown quiet once more, they did not know where they were. They had been driven off their course to a foreign shore, which none among them recognized.

And then, since not a breeze was stirring, they lay there, and Halvor begged the master mariner for permission to go ashore, and look around, for he would rather do that than lie down and sleep. "Do you think you are fit to appear before people?" asked the master mariner. "The only clothes you have are the rags in which you stand and walk!" Yet Halvor insisted, and finally he was given permission. But he was to come back when the wind blew up. Halvor went, and it was a fair land. No matter where he came, there were great plains, with fields and pastures; but he saw no people at all. The wind blew up again, but Halvor decided that he had not yet seen enough, and wanted to go a little further, and see whether there were no people to be found at all. After a time he came to a great highway, which was so even one could have rolled an egg along it with ease. Halvor went on along this highway, and as evening drew near, he saw a great castle in the distance, that shone afar. Since he had been wandering all day long, without much in the way of food, he had a fine appetite; but the nearer he came to the castle, the more frightened he grew.

In the castle there was a fire on the hearth, and Halvor went into the kitchen, which was beautiful. The kitchenware was all of silver and gold; but there were no human beings to be seen. After Halvor had waited a while, and no one came out, he went and opened a door. There he saw a princess sitting and spinning. "Alas, no!" cried she. "Has a Christian soul really come here! But it would be best for you to go again, if you do not want the troll to swallow you; for a troll with three heads lives here."

"And though he had four, I should like to see him," said the youth. "And I am not going away, for I have done no wrong. But you must give me something to eat, for I am terribly hungry." When Halvor had eaten his fill, the princess told him to try and see whether he could swing the sword that hung on the wall. But he could not swing it, nor even raise it. "Well," said the princess, "you must take a swallow from the bottle that hangs beside it, for that is what the troll does when he wants to use the sword." Halvor took the swallow, and then could swing the sword at once as though it were nothing at all. Now, thought he, the troll could just come along any time. And sure enough, he did come along, roaring. Halvor placed himself behind the door. "Hu! it smells like Christian blood here!" said the troll, and poked his head in through the door. "Yes, you shall find out it is here and at once," cried Halvor, and hewed off all his heads. The princess was filled with joy at her deliverance, and danced and sang. But then she happened to think of her sisters, and said: "If only my sisters could also be delivered!" "Where are they?" asked Halvor. So she told him that one of them had been carried off by a troll to a castle six miles further away, and the other to a castle that lay nine miles away from the other.

"But now," said she, "you must first help me get this body out." Halvor was very strong, so he quickly cleared everything out, cleaned up, and put all in order. Then they ate, and the following morning he started off at dawn. He did not rest for a moment, but wandered all day long. When he spied the castle, he once more felt a little afraid; it was even handsomer than the other one; but here, too, there was not a human being to be seen. Then Halvor went into the kitchen, yet did not stop at all, but stepped right into the next room. "No, it cannot be possible that a Christian should venture here!" cried the princess. "I do not know how long I have been here; but during all that time I have not seen a single Christian soul. It would probably be best if you went away quickly; for a troll with six heads lives here." "No, I am not going," said Halvor, "not even if he had six heads more." "He will seize you and swallow you alive!" said the princess. But that made no difference, Halvor would not go, and he did not fear the troll. But he would have to eat and drink, for he was hungry and thirsty after his long tramp. He had as much as he wanted; and then the princess wanted to send him away again. "No," cried Halvor, "I am not going. I have done no wrong, and need not fear any one."

"That will not worry the troll," said the princess. "He will seize you without any questions asked. Yet, if you positively will not go, why, try and see whether you can swing the sword that the troll uses in war." He could not swing it; but then the princess told him to take a swallow from the bottle that hung beside it, and when he had done so he could swing the sword. Suddenly the troll came, and he was so large and so fat that he had to move sideways in order to get through the door. When he had thrust in his first head, he cried: "Huhu! I smell the blood of a Christian!" And that very moment Halvor hewed off his first head, and then all the rest. The princess was pleased beyond measure; but then she happened to think of her sisters, and she wished that they also might be delivered. Halvor thought this might be done, and wanted to start out at once. But first he had to help the princess get the dead troll out of the way and then, the following morning, he set out. It was a long way to the castle, and he hurried and ran in order to get there in good time. Toward evening he spied the castle, and it was much handsomer than both the others. This time he felt hardly any fear at all; but went through the kitchen and right on in. There sat a princess who was extraordinarily beautiful. Like the others, she said that no Christian soul had ever come to the castle since she had been there, and told him to go away again, as otherwise the troll would swallow him alive, for he had nine heads. "And though he had nine more, and nine on top of those, I will not go," said Halvor, and stood by the stove. The princess earnestly begged him to go, so that the troll would not devour him, but Halvor said: "Let him come whenever he wishes!" Then she gave him the troll sword, and told him to take a swallow from the bottle, so that he could swing it.

Suddenly the troll came roaring along. He was even larger and more powerful than both the others, and he also had to squeeze himself in at the door sideways. "Hu! I smell the blood of a Christian!" That very moment Halvor hewed off his first head, and then all of the others; but the last clung to life most toughly, and it cost Halvor a good deal of trouble to cut it off, though he found himself so very strong.

Now all the princesses met at the castle, and were happy as they never had been before, in all their lives, and they fell in love with Halvor and he with them, and he was to choose the one whom he loved best; but it was the youngest who loved him the most of all. Yet Halvor acted strangely, and grew quite silent and uncommunicative; so the princess asked him what he was longing for, and whether he did not enjoy being with them. Yes, he enjoyed it very much, for they had enough to live on, and he was well enough off, but yet he was homesick, for his parents were still living, and he would like to see them again. That could easily be arranged, said the princess. "You shall go and return without harm, if you will follow our advice." Indeed, and he would surely do nothing against their wishes, said Halvor. Then they dressed him up until he looked as handsome as a king's son, and put a ring on his finger that made it possible for the one wearing it to wish himself away, and back again. But he must not throw the ring away, and he must not mention their names, said the princesses, otherwise its power would be gone, all their joy would come to an end, and he would never see them again.

"I wish I might be back at the house at home!" said Halvor, and his wish was at once realized, and he was standing in front of his parents' house before he knew it. It was dusk, and when the old folk saw such a handsome, well-dressed stranger coming, it embarrassed them so that it seemed as though their bowing and scraping would never end. Halvor now asked them whether they could not give him a night's lodging. "No, they really could not do so, for they were quite unprepared for it," said they, "and we are lacking one thing, and another, which such a distinguished gentleman would wish to have. It would be best if the gentleman went up to the castle, whose chimney he can see from here, where the folk are well prepared." "No," said Halvor, "I'll not go there until to-morrow morning. And now let me stay here overnight. I will be content to sit by the hearth." The old folk could make no objection to this, and so Halvor sat down by the hearth, and began to dig in the ashes, as he used to when he was the lazybones at home. Then they chatted about all sorts of matters, and told Halvor about one thing and another, and finally he asked them whether they had no children. Yes, they had a son; but did not know whither he had wandered, or even whether he were still alive, or already dead.

"Could I not be this Halvor?" said Halvor.

"No, I am quite sure you could not," said the woman, starting up. "Halvor was so slow and lazy, and never wanted to do anything, and beside, he was so tattered that one rag got in the way of the other. He could never have turned into so fine a looking gentleman as yourself."

After a time the woman had to go to the hearth, and rake the fire, and as the firelight fell on Halvor, just as it used to when he dug in the ashes, she recognized him.

"No, can it really be you, Halvor?" she cried, and then the two old folk were happy beyond all power of words, and Halvor had to tell all that had happened to him, while his mother was so pleased with him, that she wanted to take him up to the castle at once, and show him to the girls who had always been so proud, and had turned up their noses at her son. So she went first and Halvor followed. When they came up, she told how Halvor had come back, and that they ought to see how fine he looked, just like a prince, said she. "We can imagine that," said the girls, and tossed their heads. "He is probably the same ragged fellow that he used to be." At that moment Halvor stepped in, and then the girls were so embarrassed that they ran out of the house without their caps. And when they came in again, they were so ashamed that they did not venture to look at Halvor, whom they had always treated with such scorn and contempt. "Well, you always acted as though you were so fine and handsome that no one on earth could compare with you. But you ought to see the oldest princess, whom I delivered," said Halvor. "Compared to her you look like dairy-maids, and the middle princess is still handsomer; while the youngest princess, who is my sweetheart, is more beautiful than the sun and moon. Would to God she were here, so that you might see her!" said Halvor.

No sooner had he finished speaking than there they stood; but then he was very much upset, for now he remembered what they had told him.

At the castle they gave a great feast in honor of the princesses, and made a great deal of them. But they would not stay. "We want to go to your parents," they said to Halvor, "and then we want to go out and look around." He went with them, and they came to a big sheet of water beyond the courtyard. Close beside it was a fair green hill, and there the princesses decided to sit and rest a while, "for it was so pleasant to look out over the water," said they. They sat down, and after they had rested a while, the youngest princess said: "Let me stroke your hair a little, Halvor!" Halvor laid his head in her lap, and she stroked his hair, and before very long Halvor fell asleep. Then she drew the ring from his finger, and gave him another in place of it, and said: "All hold on to me—I wish we were in Soria-Moria Castle!"

When Halvor woke up he saw very well that he had lost the princesses, and began to weep and wail, and was so beside himself with despair that no one could comfort him. And no matter how hard his parents begged him, he would not stay at home, but bade them farewell, and said that he would probably never see them again, for if he did not find his princesses, then it would not be worth his while to go on living.

He still had three hundred dollars, and these he put in his pocket and started out. After he had gone a while he met a man with a nice-looking horse. He decided to buy it, and began to talk with the man. "It is true I did not intend to sell the horse," said the man, "but perhaps we can come to an understanding." Halvor asked him what he wanted for it. "I did not pay much for it, nor is it worth very much: it is a good saddle horse, but as a draft horse it does not amount to much. Yet it could carry you and your knapsack without difficulty, if you were to walk a bit from time to time," said the man. At last they agreed on the price, and Halvor slung his knapsack across the horse, and from time to time he walked, and then he rode again. Toward evening he came to a green hill on which stood a large tree, beneath which he seated himself. He turned the horse loose, yet did not lie down to sleep, but took out his knapsack instead. When day came he wandered on again, for it seemed to him as though there were no place in which he could rest. He walked and rode all day long through a great forest, in which were many green clearings, that shimmered cheerfully among the trees. He did not know where he was, nor did he know whither he was going; but he allowed himself no more time to rest than his horse needed to feed in one of the green clearings, and himself to eat from his knapsack. He walked and rode, on and on, and thought the forest would never end.

But on the evening of the following day he saw something gleaming among the trees. "If the people there are still up, I could warm myself a little, and get something to eat!" thought Halvor. When he got there it was a wretched little hut, and through the window he saw an old couple sitting in it, as ancient and gray-headed as doves, and the woman had so long a nose that she used it at the hearth for a poker. "Good evening! Good evening!" said the old woman. "But what are you doing here? No Christian soul has come this way for the past hundred years." Halvor told her he was looking for Soria-Moria Castle, and asked whether she knew the way to it. "No," was the woman's answer, "I do not know, but here comes the moon, I will ask him. He ought to know, for he shines on everything." And then, when the moon rose bright and clear above the tree-tops, the woman went out. "You moon, you moon," she cried, "can you tell me the way to Soria-Moria Castle?" "No," said the moon, "I cannot do that, because when I was shining there, a cloud lay in my way."

"Just wait a little while," said the old woman to Halvor. "The West Wind will be right along, and he is sure to know, for he sweeps and blows about in every corner. Well, I declare, you have a horse, too!" said the old woman when she came in again. "Now don't let the poor beast stand by the door there and starve to death; but take it out to the pasture instead. Or would you like to change with me? We have a pair of old boots, that carry you twelve miles further with every step. I will give them to you in exchange for the horse, and then you will reach Soria-Moria Castle more quickly." Halvor at once agreed, and the old woman was so pleased with the horse, that she almost started dancing then and there. "For now I can ride to church, too," said she.

Halvor was very restless, and wanted to go right on again, but the woman said there was no need to hurry. "Lie down on the bench by the stove, and take a nap, for we have no bed for you," said she. "I will watch for the West Wind's coming."

All of a sudden the West Wind came rushing along so that the walls creaked. The woman ran out: "You West Wind! You West Wind! Can you tell me the way to Soria-Moria Castle? There is a fellow here who wants to know." "Yes, indeed," said the West Wind, "I have to go to that very place, and dry the wash for the wedding soon to be held. If he is quick afoot, he may come along with me." Halvor ran out. "You must hurry if you are going with me," said the West Wind; and at once he was up and off over hill and dale, land and sea, so that Halvor could hardly keep up with him. "Now I have no more time to keep you company," said the West Wind, "because I have first to tear down a stretch of pine forest, before I come to the bleaching-field and dry the wash. But if you keep going along the hills, you will meet some girls standing there and washing, and then you will not be far from Soria-Moria Castle."

After a time Halvor came to the girls who were washing, and they asked him whether he had seen anything of the West Wind, who was to come and dry the clothes for the wedding. "Yes," said Halvor. "He is only tearing down a stretch of pine forest, and will soon be here," and then he asked the way to Soria-Moria Castle. They showed it to him, and when he reached the castle it was fairly alive with men and horses. But Halvor was so tattered and torn because he had followed the West Wind over stick and stone, and through thick and thin, that he kept to one side, and could not come forward until the last day of the feast. Then all the folk, as was the custom, had to drink the health of the bride and groom, and the cupbearer had to pledge all of them in turn, knights and serving-men. So at length they came to Halvor. Halvor drank the health, and then let the ring which the princess had put on his finger when he lay by the water fall into the glass, and told the cupbearer to greet the bride, and bring her the ring. And the princess at once rose from the table. "Who do you think has first claim to the hand of one of us," she asked, "the man who delivered us, or the one who now sits here in the bridegroom's place?" There was only one opinion as to that, and when Halvor heard it, he did not delay, but cast off his rags and dressed himself as a bridegroom. "Yes, he is the right one!" cried the youngest princess when she caught sight of him, and she drove the other one away, and celebrated her wedding with Halvor.

KNÖS

Once upon a time there was a poor widow, who found an egg under a pile of brush as she was gathering kindlings in the forest. She took it and placed it under a goose, and when the goose had hatched it, a little boy slipped out of the shell. The widow had him baptized Knös, and such a lad was a rarity; for when no more than five years old he was grown, and taller than the tallest man. And he ate in proportion, for he would swallow a whole batch of bread at a single sitting, and at last the poor widow had to go to the commissioners for the relief of the poor in order to get food for him. But the town authorities said she must apprentice the boy at a trade, for he was big enough and strong enough to earn his own keep.

So Knös was apprenticed to a smith for three years. For his pay he asked a suit of clothes and a sword each year: a sword of five hundredweights the first year, one of ten hundredweights the second year, and one of fifteen hundredweights the third year. But after he had been in the smithy only a few days, the smith was glad to give him all three suits and all three swords at once; for he smashed all his iron and steel to bits.

Knös received his suits and swords, went to a knight's estate, and hired himself out as a serving-man. Once he was told to go to the forest to gather firewood with the rest of the men, but sat at the table eating long after the others had driven off and when he had at last satisfied his hunger and was ready to start, he saw the two young oxen he was to drive waiting for him. But he let them stand and went into the forest, seized the two largest trees growing there, tore them out by the roots, took one tree under each arm, and carried them back to the estate. And he got there long before the rest, for they had to chop down the trees, saw them up and load them on the carts.

On the following day Knös had to thresh. First he hunted up the largest stone he could find, and rolled it around on the grain, so that all the corn was loosened from the ears. Then he had to separate the grain from the chaff. So he made a hole in each side of the roof of the barn, and stood outside the barn and blew, and the chaff and straw flew out into the yard, and the corn remained lying in a heap on the floor. His master happened to come along, laid a ladder against the barn, climbed up and looked down into one of the holes. But Knös was still blowing, and the wind caught his master, and he fell down and was nearly killed on the stone pavement of the court.

"He's a dangerous fellow," thought his master. It would be a good thing to be rid of him, otherwise he might do away with all of them; and besides, he ate so that it was all one could do to keep him fed. So he called Knös in, and paid him his wages for the full year, on condition that he leave. Knös agreed, but said he must first be decently provisioned for his journey.

So he was allowed to go into the store-house himself, and there he hoisted a flitch of bacon on each shoulder, slid a batch of bread under each arm, and took leave. But his master loosed the vicious bull on him. Knös, however, grasped him by the horns, and flung him over his shoulder, and thus he went off. Then he came to a thicket where he slaughtered the bull, roasted him and ate him together with a batch of bread. And when he had done this he had about taken the edge off his hunger.

Then he came to the king's court, where great sorrow reigned because, once upon a time, when the king was sailing out at sea, a sea troll had called up a terrible tempest, so that the ship was about to sink. In order to escape with his life, the king had to promise the sea troll to give him whatever first came his way when he reached shore. The king thought his hunting dog would be the first to come running to meet him, as usual; but instead his three young daughters came rowing out to meet him in a boat. This filled the king with grief, and he vowed that whoever delivered his daughters should have one of them for a bride, whichever one he might choose. But the only man who seemed to want to earn the reward was a tailor, named Red Peter.

Knös was given a place at the king's court, and his duty was to help the cook. But he asked to be let off on the day the troll was to come and carry away the oldest princess, and they were glad to let him go; for when he had to rinse the dishes he broke the king's vessels of gold and silver; and when he was told to bring firewood, he brought in a whole wagon-load at once, so that the doors flew from their hinges.

The princess stood on the sea-shore and wept and wrung her hands; for she could see what she had to expect. Nor did she have much confidence in Red Peter, who sat on a willow-stump, with a rusty old sabre in his hand. Then Knös came and tried to comfort the princess as well as he knew how, and asked her whether she would comb his hair. Yes, he might lay his head in her lap, and she combed his hair. Suddenly there was a dreadful roaring out at sea. It was the troll who was coming along, and he had five heads. Red Peter was so frightened that he rolled off his willow-stump. "Knös, is that you?" cried the troll. "Yes," said Knös. "Haul me up on the shore!" said the troll. "Pay out the cable!" said Knös. Then he hauled the troll ashore; but he had his sword of five hundredweights at his side, and with it he chopped off all five of the troll's heads, and the princess was free. But when Knös had gone off, Red Peter put his sabre to the breast of the princess, and told her he would kill her unless she said he was her deliverer.

Then came the turn of the second princess. Once more Red Peter sat on the willow-stump with his rusty sabre, and Knös asking to be let off for the day, went to the sea-shore and begged the princess to comb his hair, which she did. Then along came the troll, and this time he had ten heads. "Knös, is that you?" asked the troll. "Yes," said Knös. "Haul me ashore!" said the troll. "Pay out the cable!" said Knös. And this time Knös had his sword of ten hundredweights at his side, and he cut off all ten of the troll's heads. And so the second princess was freed. But Red Peter held his sabre at the princess' breast, and forced her to say that he had delivered her.

Now it was the turn of the youngest princess. When it was time for the troll to come, Red Peter was sitting on his willow-stump, and Knös came and begged the princess to comb his hair, and she did so. This time the troll had fifteen heads.

"Knös, is that you?" asked the troll. "Yes," said Knös. "Haul me ashore!" said the troll. "Pay out the cable," said Knös. Knös had his sword of fifteen hundredweights at his side, and with it he cut off all the troll's heads. But the fifteen hundredweights were half-an-ounce short, and the heads grew on again, and the troll took the princess, and carried her off with him.

One day as Knös was going along, he met a man carrying a church on his back. "You are a strong man, you are!" said Knös. "No, I am not strong," said he, "but Knös at the king's court, he is strong; for he can take steel and iron, and weld them together with his hands as though they were clay." "Well, I'm the man of whom you are speaking," said Knös, "come, let us travel together." And so they wandered on.

Then they met a man who carried a mountain of stone on his back. "You are strong, you are!" said Knös. "No, I'm not strong," said the man with the mountain of stone, "but Knös at the king's court, he is strong; for he can weld together steel and iron with his hands as though they were clay."

"Well, I am that Knös, come let us travel together," said Knös. So all three of them traveled along together. Knös took them for a sea-trip; but I think they had to leave the church and the hill of stone ashore. While they were sailing they grew thirsty, and lay alongside an island, and there on the island stood a castle, to which they decided to go and ask for a drink. Now this was the very castle in which the troll lived.

First the man with the church went, and when he entered the castle, there sat the troll with the princess on his lap, and she was very sad. He asked for something to drink. "Help yourself, the goblet is on the table!" said the troll. But he got nothing to drink, for though he could move the goblet from its place, he could not raise it.

Then the man with the hill of stone went into the castle and asked for a drink. "Help yourself, the goblet is on the table!" said the troll. And he got nothing to drink either, for though he could move the goblet from its place, he could not raise it.

Then Knös himself went into the castle, and the princess was full of joy and leaped down from the troll's lap when she saw it was he. Knös asked for a drink. "Help yourself," said the troll, "the goblet is on the table!" And Knös took the goblet and emptied it at a single draught. Then he hit the troll across the head with the goblet, so that he rolled from the chair and died.

Knös took the princess back to the royal palace, and O, how happy every one was! The other princesses recognized Knös again, for they had woven silk ribbons into his hair when they had combed it; but he could only marry one of the princesses, whichever one he preferred, so he chose the youngest. And when the king died, Knös inherited the kingdom.

As for Red Peter, he had to go into the nail-barrel.

And now you know all that I know.

LASSE, MY THRALL!

Once upon a time there was a prince or a duke or whatever you choose to call him, but at any rate a noble tremendously high-born, who did not want to stay at home. And so he traveled about the world, and wherever he went he was well received, and hobnobbed with the very finest people; for he had an unheard of amount of money. He at once found friends and acquaintances, no matter where he came; for whoever has a full trough can always find pigs to thrust their snouts into it. But since he handled his money as he did, it grew less and less, and at last he was left high and dry, without a red cent. And there was an end to all his many friends; for they did just as the pigs do. When he had been well fleeced, they began to snivel and grunt, and soon scattered, each about his own business. And there he stood, after having been led about by the nose, abandoned by all. All had been glad to help him get rid of his money; but none were willing to help him regain it, so there was nothing left for him to do but to wander back home again like a journeyman apprentice, and beg his way as he went.

Late one evening he found himself in a big forest, without any idea as to where he might spend the night. And as he was looking around, his glance happened to fall on an old hut, peeping out from among the bushes. Of course an old hut was no lodging for such a fine gentleman; but when we cannot have what we want, we must take what we can get, and since there was no help for it, he went into the hut. There was not even a cat in it, not even a stool to sit on. But against one wall there was a great chest. What might there be in the chest? Suppose there were a few moldy crusts of bread in it? They would taste good to him, for he had not been given a single thing all day long, and he was so hungry that his inwards stuck to his ribs. He opened the chest. But within the chest was another chest, and in that chest still another chest, and so it went, one always smaller than the other, until they were nothing but little boxes. And the more there were of them the more trouble he took to open them; for whatever was hidden away so carefully must be something exceptionally beautiful, thought he.

At last he came to a tiny box, and in the tiny box was a slip of paper—and that was all he had for his pains! At first he was much depressed. But all at once, he saw that something was written on the piece of paper, and on closer examination he was even able to spell out the words, though they had a strange appearance. And he read:

"Lasse, my thrall!"

No sooner had he spoken these words than something answered, close to his ear:

"What does my master command?"

He looked around, but saw no one. That's strange, thought he, and once more read aloud:

"Lasse, my thrall!"

And just as before came the answer:

"What does my master command?"

"If there be some one about who hears what I say, he might be kind enough to get me a little something to eat," said he; and at that very moment a table, covered with all the good things to eat that one could imagine, was standing in the hut. He at once began to eat and drink and did well by himself. I have never had a better meal in my life, thought he. And when his hunger was completely satisfied, he grew sleepy and took up his scrap of paper again.

"Lasse, my thrall!"

"What does my master command?"

"Now that you have brought me food and drink, you must also bring me a bed in which to sleep. But it must be a very fine bed," said he; for as you may well imagine, his ideas were more top-lofty now that he had eaten well. His command was at once obeyed; and a bed so fine and handsome stood in the hut, that a king might have been glad to have found such sleeping accommodations. Now this was all very well and good; but the good can always be bettered, and when he had lain down, he decided that, after all, the hut was far too wretched for such a fine bed. He took up the scrap of paper:

"Lasse, my thrall!"

"What does my master command?"

"If you can produce such a meal, and such a bed here in the wild wood, you must surely be able to give me a better room; for you know I am one of those who are used to sleeping in a castle, with golden mirrors and rugs of gold brocade and luxuries and conveniences of every kind," said he. And no sooner had he spoken the words, than he was lying in the most magnificent room he had ever seen.

Now matters were arranged to suit him, and he was quite content as he turned his face to the wall and closed his eyes.

But the room he had slept in was not the end of his magnificence. When he woke the following morning and looked around, he saw that he had been sleeping in a great castle. There was one room after another, and wherever he went walls and ceilings were covered with ornaments and decorations of every kind, all glittering so splendidly when the rays of the sun fell on them that he had to put his hand to his eyes; for wherever he looked everything sparkled with gold and silver. Then he glanced out of the window and first began to realize how really beautiful everything was. Gone were the fir-trees and juniper bushes, and in their place showed the love-liest garden one might wish to see, filled with beautiful trees and roses of every variety, in bush and tree form. But there was not a human being in sight, not even a cat. Yet he found it quite natural that everything should be so fine, and that he should once more have become a great lord.

He took up the scrap of paper:

"Lasse, my thrall!"

"What does my master command?"

"Now that you have provided me with food and a castle in which to dwell, I am going to stay here, because it suits me," said he, "but I cannot live here all alone in this fashion. I must have serving-men and serving-maids, at my command." And so it was. Servants and lackeys and maids and serving-women of every description arrived, and some of them bowed and others courtseyed, and now the duke really began to feel content.

Now it happened that another great castle lay on the opposite side of the forest, in which dwelt a king who owned the forest, and many broad acres of field and meadow round about. And when the king came and happened to look out of his window, he saw the new castle, on whose roof the gold-en weathercocks were swinging to and fro, from time to time, shining in his eyes.

"This is very strange," thought he, and sent for his court-iers. They came without delay, bowing and scraping.

"Do you see the castle yonder?" said the king.

Their eyes grew as large as saucers and they looked.

Yes, indeed, they saw the castle.

"Who has dared to build such a castle on my ground?"

The courtiers bowed and scraped, but did not know. So the king sent for his soldiers. They came tramping in and presented arms.

"Send out all my soldiers and horsemen," said the king, "tear down the castle instantly, hang whoever built it, and see to this at once."

The soldiers assembled in the greatest haste and set forth. The drummers beat their drums and the trumpeters blew their trumpets, and the other musicians practiced their art, each in his own way; so that the duke heard them long before they came in sight. But this was not the first time he had heard music of this sort, and he knew what it meant, so once more he took up the scrap of paper:

"Lasse, my thrall!"

"What does my master command?"

"There are soldiers coming," said he, "and now you must provide me with soldiers and horsemen until I have twice as many as the folk on the other side of the forest. And sabers and pistols and muskets and cannon, and all that goes with them—but you must be quick about it!"

Quick it was, and when the duke looked out there was a countless host of soldiers drawn up around the castle.

When the king's people arrived, they stopped and did not dare advance. But the duke was by no means shy. He went at once to the king's captain and asked him what he wanted.

The captain repeated his instructions.

"They will not gain you anything," said the duke. "You can see how many soldiers I have, and if the king chooses to listen to me, we can agree to become friends, I will aid him against all his enemies, and what we undertake will succeed."

The captain was pleased with this proposal, so the duke invited him to the castle, together with all his officers, and his soldiers were given a swallow or two of something wet and plenty to eat along with it. But while the duke and the officers were eating and drinking, there was more or less talk, and the duke learned that the king had a daughter, as yet unmarried and so lovely that her like had never been seen. And the more they brought the king's officers to eat, the stronger they inclined to the opinion that the king's daughter would make a good wife for the duke. And as they talked about it, the duke himself began to think it over. The worst of it was, said the officers, that she was very haughty, and never even deigned to look at a man. But the duke only laughed. "If it be no worse than that," he said, "it is a trouble that may be cured."

When at last the soldiers had stowed away as much as they could hold, they shouted hurrah until they woke the echoes in the hills, and marched away. One may imagine what a fine parade march it was, for some of them had grown a little loose-jointed in the knees. The duke charged them to carry his greetings to the king, and say that he would soon pay him a visit.

When the duke was alone once more, he began to think of the princess again, and whether she were really as beautiful as the soldiers had said. He decided he would like to find out for himself. Since so many strange things had happened that day, it was quite possible, thought he.

"Lasse, my thrall!"

"What does my master command?"

"Only that you bring the king's daughter here, as soon as she has fallen asleep," said he. "But mind that she does not wake up, either on her way here, or on her way back." And before long there lay the princess on the bed. She was sleeping soundly, and looked charming as she lay there asleep. One had to admit that she was as sweet as sugar. The duke walked all around her; but she appeared just as beautiful from one side as from the other, and the more the duke looked at her, the better she pleased him.

"Lasse, my thrall!"

"What does my master command?"

"Now you must take the princess home again," said he, "because now I know what she looks like and to-morrow I shall sue for her hand."

The following morning the king stepped to the window. "Now I shall not have to see that castle across the way," he thought to himself. But the evil one must have had a hand in the matter—there stood the castle just as before, and the sun was shining brightly on its roof, and the weather-vanes were sending beams into his eyes.

The king once more fell into a rage, and shouted for all his people, who hurried to him with more than usual rapidity. The courtiers bowed and scraped and the soldiers marched in parade step and presented arms.

"Do you see that castle there?" roared the king.

They stretched their necks, their eyes grew large as saucers and they looked.

Yes, indeed, they saw it.

"Did I not order you to tear down that castle and hang its builder?" he said.

This they could not deny; but now the captain himself stepped forward and told what had occurred, and what an alarming number of soldiers the duke had, and how magnificent his castle was.

Then he also repeated what the duke had said, and that he had sent his greetings to the king.

All this made the king somewhat dizzy, and he had to set his crown on the table and scratch his head. It was beyond his comprehension—for all that he was a king; since he could have sworn that it had all come to pass in the course of a single night, and if the duke were not the devil himself, he was at least a magician.

And as he sat there and thought, the princess came in.

"God greet you, father," she said, "I had a most strange and lovely dream last night."

"And what did you dream, my girl?" said the king.

"O, I dreamt that I was in the new castle over yonder, and there was a duke, handsome and so splendid beyond anything I could have imagined, and now I want a husband."

"What, you want a husband, and you have never even deigned to look at a man; that is very strange!" said the king.

"Be that as it may," said the princess, "but that is how I feel now; and I want a husband, and the duke is the husband I want," she concluded.

The king simply could not get over the astonishment the duke had caused him.

Suddenly he heard an extraordinary beating of drums, and sounding of trumpets and other instruments of every kind. And a message came that the duke had arrived with a great retinue, all so magnificently attired that every seam of their dresses was sparkling with gold and silver. The king, in his crown and finest robe of state, stood looking down the stairway, and the princess was all the more in favor of carrying out her idea as quickly as possible.

The duke greeted the king pleasantly, and the king returned his greeting in the same way, and discussing their affairs together they became good friends. There was a great banquet, and the duke sat beside the princess at the table. What they said to each other I do not know, but the duke knew so well how to talk that, no matter what he said, the princess could not say no, and so he went to the king and begged for her hand. The king could not exactly refuse it, for the duke was the kind of a man whom it was better to have for a friend than for an enemy; but he could not give his answer out of hand, either. First he wished to see the duke's castle, and know how matters stood with regard to this, that and the other—which was natural.

So it was agreed that they should pay the duke a visit and bring the princess with them, in order that she might examine his possessions, and with that they parted.

When the duke reached home, Lasse had a lively time of it, for he was given any number of commissions. But he rushed about, carrying them out, and everything was arranged so satisfactorily that when the king arrived with his daughter, a thousand pens could not have described it. They went through all the rooms and looked around, and everything was as it should be, and even better thought the king, who was very happy. Then the wedding was celebrated and when it was over, and the duke returned home with his young wife, he, too, gave a splendid banquet, and that is how it went.

After some time had passed, the duke one evening heard the words:

"Is my master content now?" It was Lasse, though the duke could not see him.

"I am well content," answered the duke, "for you have brought me all that I have."

"But what did I get for it?" said Lasse.

"Nothing," replied the duke, "but, heaven above, what was I to give you, who are not flesh and blood, and whom I cannot even see," said he. "Yet if there be anything I can do for you, why let me know what it is, and I will do it."

"I would very much like to have the little scrap of paper that you keep in the box," said Lasse.

"If that is all you want, and if such a trifle is of any service to you, your wish shall be granted, for I believe I know the words by heart now," said the duke.

Lasse thanked him, and said all the duke need do, would be to lay the paper on the chair beside his bed, when he went to sleep, and that he would fetch it during the night.

This the duke did, and then he went to bed and fell asleep.

But toward morning the duke woke up, freezing so that his teeth chattered, and when he had fully opened his eyes, he saw that he had been stripped of everything, and had scarcely a shirt to his name. And instead of lying in the handsome bed in the handsome bed-room in the magnificent castle, he lay on the big chest in the old hut. He at once called out:

"Lasse, my thrall!" But there was no answer.

Then he cried again:

"Lasse, my thrall!" Again there was no answer. So he called out as loudly as he could:

"Lasse, my thrall!" But this third call was also in vain.

Now he began to realize what had happened, and that Lasse, when he obtained the scrap of paper, no longer had to serve him, and that he himself had made this possible. But now things were as they were, and there stood the duke in the old hut, with scarcely a shirt to his name. The princess herself was not much better off, though she had kept her clothes; for they had been given her by her father, and Lasse had no power over them.

Now the duke had to explain everything to the princess, and beg her to leave him, since it would be best if he tried to get along as well as he could himself, said he. But this the princess would not do. She had a better memory for what the pastor had said when he married them, she told him, and that she was never, never to leave him.

At length the king awoke in his castle, and when he looked out of the window, he saw not a single stone of the other castle in which his son-in-law and his daughter lived. He grew uneasy and sent for his courtiers.

They came in, bowing and scraping.

"Do you see the castle there, on the other side of the forest?" he asked. They stretched their necks and opened their eyes. But they could see nothing.

"What has become of it?" said the king. But this question they were unable to answer.

In a short time the king and his entire court set out, passed through the forest, and when they came to the place where the castle, with its great gardens, should have been standing, they saw nothing but juniper-bushes and scrub-pines. And then they happened to see the little hut amid the brush. He went in and—O the poor king!--what did he see?

There stood his son-in-law, with scarcely a shirt to his name, and his daughter, and she had none too much to wear, and was crying and sniveling at a fearful rate. "For heaven's sake, what is the trouble here?" said the king. But he received no answer; for the duke would rather have died than have told him the whole story.

The king urged and pressed him, first amiably, then in

anger; but the duke remained obstinate and would have nothing to say. Then the king fell into a rage, which is not very surprising, for now he realized that this fine duke was not what he purported to be, and he therefore ordered him to be hung, and hung on the spot. It is true that the princess pleaded earnestly for him, but tears and prayers were useless now, for he was a rascal and should die a rascal's death—thus spake the king.

And so it was. The king's people set up a gallows and put a rope around the duke's neck. But as they were leading him to the gallows, the princess got hold of the hangman and gave him a gratuity, for which they were to arrange matters in such wise that the duke need not die. And toward evening they were to cut him down, and he and the princess would disappear. So the bargain was made. In the meantime they strung him up and then the king, together with his court and all the people, went away.

Now the duke was at the end of his rope. Yet he had time enough to reflect about his mistake in not contenting himself with an inch instead of reaching out at once for an ell; and that he had so foolishly given back the scrap of paper to Lasse annoyed him most of all. If I only had it again, I would show every one that adversity has made me wise, he thought to himself. But when the horse is stolen we close the stable door. And that is the way of the world.

And then he dangled his legs, since for the time being there was nothing else for him to do.

It had been a long, hard day for him, and he was not sorry when he saw the sun sinking behind the forest. But just as the sun was setting he suddenly heard a most tremendous Yo ho! and when he looked down there were seven carts of worn-out shoes coming along the road, and a-top the last cart was a little old man in gray, with a night-cap on his head. He had the face of some horrible specter, and was not much better to look at in other respects.

He drove straight up to the gallows, and stopped when he was directly beneath them, looked up at the duke and laughed—the horrible old creature!

"And is this the measure of your stupidity?" he said, "but then what is a fellow of your sort to do with his stupidity, if he does not put it to some use?"—and then he laughed again. "Yes, there you hang, and here I am carting off all the shoes I wore out going about on your silly errands. I wonder, some-times, whether you can actually read what is written on that scrap of paper, and whether you recognize it," said he, laugh-ing again, indulging in all sorts of horse-play, and waving the scrap of paper under the duke's nose.

But all who are hanging on the gallows are not dead, and this time Lasse was the greater fool of the two.

The duke snatched—and tore the scrap of paper from his hand!

"Lasse, my thrall!"

"What does my master command?"

"Cut me down from the gallows at once, and restore the castle and everything else just as it was before, then when it is dark, bring the princess back to it."

Everything was attended to with alarming rapidity, and soon all was exactly as it had been before Lasse had decamped.

When the king awoke the following morning, he looked out of the window as usual, and there the castle was standing as before, with its weathercocks gleaming handsomely in the sunlight. He sent for his courtiers, and they came in bowing and scraping.

"Do you see the castle over yonder?" asked the king.

They stretched their necks, and gazed and stared. Yes, indeed, they could see the castle.

Then the king sent for the princess; but she was not there. Thereupon the king set off to see whether his son-in-law was hanging in the appointed spot; but no, there was not a sign of either son-in-law or gallows.

Then he had to take off his crown and scratch his head. Yet that did not change matters, and he could not for the life of him understand why things should be as they were. Finally he set out with his entire court, and when they reached the spot where the castle should have been standing, there it stood.

The gardens and the roses were just as they had been, and the duke's servitors were to be seen in swarms beneath the trees. His son-in-law in person, together with his daughter, dressed in the finest clothes, came down the stairs to meet him.

The devil has a hand in it, thought the king; and so strange did all seem to him that he did not trust the evidence of his own eyes.

"God greet you and welcome, father!" said the duke. The king could only stare at him. "Are you, are you my son-in-law?" he asked.

"Why, of course," said the duke, "who else am I supposed to be?"

"Did I not have you strung up yesterday as a thief and a vagabond?" inquired the king.

"I really believe father has gone out of his mind on the way over to us," said the duke and laughed.

"Does father think that I would allow myself to be hanged

SCANDINAVIAN TALES

so easily? Or is there any one present who dare suppose such a thing?" he said, and looked them straight in the eye, so that they knew he was looking at them. They bent their backs and bowed and scraped.

"And who can imagine any such thing? How could it be possible? Or should there be any one present who dare say that the king wishes me ill, let him speak out," said the duke, and gazed at them with even greater keenness than before. All bent their backs and bowed and scraped.

How should any of them come to any such conclusion? No, none of them were foolish to such a degree, they said.

Now the king was really at a loss to know what to think. When he looked at the duke he felt sure that he could never have wished to harm him, and yet—he was not quite sure.

"Was I not here yesterday, and was not the whole castle gone, and had not an old hut taken its place, and did I not enter the hut and see you standing there with scarcely a shirt to your name?" he asked.

"How father talks," said the duke. "I am afraid, very much afraid, that trolls have blinded you, and led you astray in the forest. What do you think?" he said and turned to the courtiers.

They at once bowed and cringed fifty times in succession, and took the duke's side, as stands to reason.

The king rubbed his eyes and looked around.

"It must be as you say," he told the duke, "and I believe that I have recovered my reason, and have found my eyes again. And it would have been a sin and shame had I had you hung," said he. Then he grew joyful and no one gave the matter further thought.

But adversity teaches one to be wise, so people say, and

the duke now began to attend to most things himself, and to see to it that Lasse did not have to wear out so many pairs of shoes. The king at once bestowed half the kingdom upon him, which gave him plenty to do, and people said that one would have to look far in order to find a better ruler.

Then Lasse came to the duke one day, and though he did not look much better than before, he was more civil and did not venture to grin and carry on.

"You no longer need my help," said he, "for though formerly I used to wear out all my shoes, I now cannot even wear out a single pair, and I almost believe my legs are moss-grown. Will you not discharge me?"

The duke thought he could. "I have taken great pains to spare you, and I really believe that I can get along without you," he replied. "But the castle here and all the other things I could not well dispense with, since I never again could find an architect like yourself, and you may take for granted that I have no wish to ornament the gallows-tree a second time. Therefore I will not, of my own free will, give you back the scrap of paper," said he.

"While it is in your possession I have nothing to fear," answered Lasse.

"But should the paper fall into other hands, then I should have to begin to run and work all over again and that, just that, is what I would like to prevent. When a fellow has been working a thousand years, as I have, he is bound to grow weary at last."

So they came to the conclusion that the duke should put the scrap of paper in its little box and bury it seven ells underground, beneath a stone that had grown there and would remain there as well. Then they thanked each other for pleasant comradeship and separated. The duke did as he had agreed to do, and no one saw him hide the box. He lived happily with his princess, and was blessed with sons and daughters. When the king died, he inherited the whole kingdom and, as you may imagine, he was none the worse off thereby, and no doubt he is still living and ruling there, unless he has died.

As to the little box containing the scrap of paper, many are still digging and searching for it.

FINN, THE GIANT, AND THE MINSTER OF LUND

There stands in the university town of Schonen, the town of Lund, the seat of the first archbishopric in all Scandinavia, a stately Romanic minster, with a large, handsome crypt beneath the choir. The opinion is universal that the minster will never be altogether finished, but that something will always be lacking about the structure. The reason is said to be as follows:

When St. Lawrence came to Lund to preach the Gospel, he wanted to build a church; but did not know how he was to obtain the means to do so.

While he was cudgelling his brains about it, a giant came to him and offered to build the church on condition that St. Lawrence tell him his name before the church was completed. But should St. Lawrence be unable to do so, the giant was to receive either the sun, the moon or St. Lawrence's eyes. The saint agreed to his proposal.

The building of the church made rapid progress, and ere long it was nearly finished. St. Lawrence thought ruefully about his prospects, for he did not know the giant's name; yet at the same time he did not relish losing his eyes. And it happened that while he was walking without the town, much concerned about the outcome of the affair, he grew weary, and sat down on a hill to rest. As he sat there he heard a child crying within the hill, and a woman's voice began to sing:

> *"Sleep, sleep, my baby dear,*
> *To-morrow your father, Finn, will be here;*
> *Then sun and moon you shall have from the skies*

To play with, or else St. Lawrence's eyes."

When St. Lawrence heard that he was happy; for now he knew the giant's name. He ran back quickly to town, and went to the church. There sat the giant on the roof, just about to set the last stone in place, when at that very moment the saint called out:

> *"Finn, Finn,*
> *Take care how you put the stone in!"*

Then the giant flung the stone from him, full of rage, said that the church should never be finished, and with that he disappeared. Since then something has always been missing from the church.

Others say that the giant and his wife rushed down into the crypt in their rage, and each seizing a column were about to tear down the church, when they were turned into stone, and may be seen to this day standing beside the columns they had grasped.

THE SKALUNDA GIANT

In the Skalunda mountain, near the church, there once lived a giant in the early days, who no longer felt comfortable after the church had been built there. At length he decided that he could no longer stand the ringing of the church bells; so he emigrated and settled down on an island far out in the North Sea. Once upon a time a ship was wrecked on this island, and among those saved were several people from Skalunda.

"Whence do you hail?" asked the giant, who by now had grown old and blind, and sat warming himself before a log fire.

"We are from Skalunda, if you wish to know," said one of the men saved.

"Give me your hand, so that I may feel whether there is still warm blood to be found in the Swedish land," said the giant.

The man, who feared to shake hands with the giant, drew a red-hot bar of iron from the fire and handed it to him. He seized it firmly, and pressed it so hard that the molten iron ran down between his fingers.

"Yes, there is still warm blood to be found in Sweden," said he. "And tell me," he continued, "is Skalunda mountain still standing?"

"No, the hens have scratched it away," the man answered.

"How could it last?" said the giant. "My wife and daughter piled it up in the course of a single Sunday morning. But surely the Hallenberg and the Hunneberg are still standing, for those I built myself."

When the man had confirmed this, the giant wanted to know whether Karin was still living in Stommen. And when they told him that she was, he gave them a girdle, and with it the message that Karin was to wear it in remembrance of him.

The men took the girdle and gave it to Karin upon their return home; but before Karin put it on, she clasped it around the oak-tree that grew in the court. No sooner had she done so than the oak tore itself out of the ground, and flew to the North, borne away by the storm-wind. In the place where it had stood was a deep pit, and the roots of the tree were so enormous that one of the best springs in Stommen flows from one of the root-holes to this very day.

YULETIDE SPECTERS

Once upon a time there lived two peasants on a homestead called Vaderas, just as there are two peasants living on it now. In those days the roads were good, and the women were in the habit of riding when they wanted to go to church.

One Christmas the two women agreed that they would ride to Christmas night mass, and whichever one of them woke up at the right time was to call the other, for in those days there was no such thing as a watch. It was about midnight when one of the women thought she heard a voice from the window, calling: "I am going to set out now." She got up hurriedly and dressed herself, so that she might be able to ride with the other woman; but since there was no time to eat, she took a piece of bread from the table along with her. In those times it was customary to bake the bread in the shape of a cross. It was a piece of this kind that the woman took and put in her pocket, in order to eat it underway. She rode as fast as she could, to catch up with her friend, but could not overtake her. The way led over a little stream which flows into Vidostern Lake, and across the stream was a bridge, known as the Earth Bridge, and on the bridge stood two witch trolls, busy washing. As the woman came riding across the bridge, one of the witch trolls called out to the other, "Hurry, and tear her head from her shoulders!"

"That I cannot do" returned the other, "because she has a bit of bread in the form of a cross in her pocket."

The woman, who had been unable to catch up with her neighbor, reached the church at Hanger alone.

The church was full of lights, as was always the case when the Christmas mass was said. As quickly as ever she could the woman tied up her horse, and hurriedly entered the church. It seemed to her that the church was crowded with people; but all of them were headless, and at the altar stood the priest, in full canonicals but without a head. In her haste she did not at once see how things were; but sat down in her accustomed place. As she sat down it seemed to her that some one said: "If I had not stood godfather to you when you were christened, I would do away with you as you sit there, and now hurry and make yourself scarce, or it will be the worse for you!" Then she realized that things were not as they should be, and ran out hastily.

When she came into the church-yard, it seemed to her as though she were surrounded by a great crowd of people. In those days people wore broad mantles of unbleached wool, woven at home, and white in color. She was wearing one of these mantles and the specters seized it. But she flung it away from her and managed to escape from the church-yard, and run to the poor-house and wake the people there. It is said it was then one o'clock at night.

So she sat and waited for the early mass at four o'clock in the morning. And when day finally dawned, they found a little piece of her mantle on every grave in the church-yard.

A similar experience befell a man and his wife who lived in a hut known as Ingas, below Mosled.

They were no more than an hour ahead of time; but when they reached the church at Hanger, they thought the service had already begun, and wanted to enter at once; but the church was barred and bolted, and the phantom service of the dead was nearing its end. And when the actual mass began, there was found lying at every place some of the earth from the graves of those who shortly before had been worshiping. The man and his wife thereupon fell grievously ill, because they had disturbed the dead.

SILVERWHITE AND LILLWACKER

Once upon a time there was a king, who had a queen whom he loved with a great love. But after a time the queen died, and all he had left was an only daughter. And now that the king was a widower, his whole heart went out to the little princess, whom he cherished as the apple of his eye. And the king's young daughter grew up into the most lovely maiden ever known.

When the princess had seen the snows of fifteen winters, it happened that a great war broke out, and that her father had to march against the foe.

But there was no one to whom the king could entrust his daughter while he was away at war; so he had a great tower built out in the forest, provided it with a plenteous store of supplies, and in it shut up his daughter and a maid. And he had it proclaimed that every man, no matter who he might be, was forbidden to approach the tower in which he had placed his daughter and the maid, under pain of death.

Now the king thought he had taken every precaution to protect his daughter, and went off to war. In the meantime the princess and her maid sat in the tower. But in the city there were a number of brave young sons of kings, as well as other young men, who would have liked to have talked to the beautiful maiden. And when they found that this was forbidden them, they conceived a great hatred for the king. At length they took counsel with an old woman who was wiser than most folk, and told her to arrange matters in such wise that the king's daughter and her maid might come into disrepute, without their having anything to do with it. The old hag promised to help them, enchanted some apples, laid them in a basket, and went to the lonely tower in which the maidens lived.

When the king's daughter and her maid saw the old woman, who was sitting beneath the window, they felt a great longing to try the beautiful apples.

So they called out and asked how much she wanted for her precious apples; but the old woman said they were not for sale. Yet as the girls kept on pleading with her, the old woman said she would make each of them a present of an apple; they only need let down a little basket from the tower. The princess and her maid, in all innocence, did as the troll-woman told them, and each received an apple. But the enchanted fruit had a strange effect, for in due course of time heaven sent them each a child. The king's daughter called her son Silverwhite, and the son of her maid received the name of Lillwacker.

The two boys grew up larger and stronger than other children, and were very handsome as well. They looked as much alike as one cherry-pit does to another, and one could easily see that they were related.

Seven years had passed, and the king was expected home from the war. Then both girls were terrified, and they took counsel together as to how they might hide their children. When at length they could find no other way out of the difficulty, they very sorrowfully bade their children farewell, and let them down from the tower at night, to seek their fortune in the wide, wide world. At parting the king's daughter gave Silverwhite a costly knife; but the maid had nothing to give her son.

The two foster-brethren now wandered out into the world. After they had gone a while, they came to a dark forest. And in this forest they met a man, strange-looking and very tall. He wore two swords at his side, and was accompanied by six great dogs. He gave them a friendly greeting:

"Good-day, little fellows, whence do you come and whither do you go?" The boys told him they came from a high tower, and were going out into the world to seek their fortune. The man replied:

"If such be the case, I know more about your origin than any one else. And that you may have something by which to remember your father, I will give each of you a sword and three dogs. But you must promise me one thing, that you will never part from your dogs; but take them with you wherever you go." The boys thanked the man for his kind gifts, and promised to do as he had told them. Then they bade him farewell and went their way.

When they had traveled for some time they reached a cross-road. Then Silverwhite said:

"It seems to me that it would be the best for us to try our luck singly, so let us part." Lillwacker answered: "Your advice is good; but how am I to know whether or not you are doing well out in the world?"

"I will give you a token by which you may tell," said Silverwhite, "so long as the water runs clear in this spring you will know that I am alive; but if it turns red and roiled, it will mean that I am dead." Silverwhite then drew runes in the water of the spring, said farewell to his brother, and each of them went on alone. Lillwacker soon came to a king's court, and took service there; but every morning he would go to the spring to see how his brother fared.

Silverwhite continued to wander over hill and dale, until he reached a great city. But the whole city was in mourning, the houses were hung in black, and all the inhabitants went about full of grief and care, as though some great misfortune had occurred.

Silverwhite went though the city and inquired as to the cause of all the unhappiness he saw. They answered: "You must have come from far away, since you do not know that the king and queen were in danger of being drowned at sea, and he had to promise to give up their three daughters in order to escape. To-morrow morning the sea-troll is coming to carry off the oldest princess." This news pleased Silverwhite; for he saw a fine opportunity to wealth and fame, should fortune favor him.

The next morning Silverwhite hung his sword at his side, called his dogs to him, and wandered down to the sea-shore alone. And as he sat on the strand he saw the king's daughter led out of the city, and with her went a courtier, who had promised to rescue her. But the princess was very sad and cried bitterly. Then Silverwhite stepped up to her with a polite greeting. When the king's daughter and her escort saw the fearless youth, they were much frightened, because they thought he was the sea-troll. The courtier was so alarmed that he ran away and took refuge in a tree. When Silverwhite saw how frightened the princess was, he said: "Lovely maiden, do not fear me, for I will do you no harm." The king's daughter answered:

"Are you the troll who is coming to carry me away?" "No," said Silverwhite, "I have come to rescue you." Then the princess was glad to think that such a brave hero was going to defend her, and they had a long, friendly talk. At the same time Silverwhite begged the king's daughter to comb his hair. She complied with his request, and Silverwhite laid his head in her lap; but when he did so the princess drew a golden ring from her finger and, unbeknown to him, wound it into his locks.

Suddenly the sea-troll rose from the deeps, setting the waves whirling and foaming far and near. When the troll saw Silverwhite, he grew angry and said: "Why do you sit there beside my princess?" The youth replied: "It seems to me that she is my princess, not yours." The sea-troll answered: "Time enough to see which of us is right; but first our dogs shall fight." Silverwhite was nothing loath, and set his dogs at the dogs of the troll, and there was a fierce struggle. But at last the youth's dogs got the upper hand and bit the dogs of the sea-troll to death. Then Silverwhite drew his sword with a great sweep, rushed upon the sea-troll, and gave him such a tremendous blow that the monster's head rolled on the sand. The troll gave a fearsome cry, and flung himself back into the sea, so that the water spurted to the very skies. Thereupon the youth drew out his silver-mounted knife, cut out the troll's eyes and put them in his pocket. Then he saluted the lovely princess and went away.

Now when the battle was over and the youth had disappeared, the courtier crawled down from his tree, and threatened to kill the princess if she did not say before all the people that he, and none other, had rescued her. The king's daughter did not dare refuse, since she feared for her life. So she returned to her father's castle with the courtier, where they were received with great distinction.

And joy reigned throughout the land when the news spread that the oldest princess had been rescued from the troll.

On the following day everything repeated itself. Silverwhite went down to the strand and met the second princess, just as she was to be delivered to the troll.

And when the king's daughter and her escort saw him,

they were very much frightened, thinking he was the sea-troll. And the courtier climbed a tree, just as he had before; but the princess granted the youth's petition, combed his hair as her sister had done, and also wound her gold ring into his long curls.

After a time there was a great tumult out at sea, and a sea-troll rose from the waves. He had three heads and three dogs. But Silverwhite's dogs overcame those of the troll, and the youth killed the troll himself with his sword. Thereupon he took out his silver-mounted knife, cut out the troll's eyes, and went his way. But the courtier lost no time. He climbed down from his tree and forced the princess to promise to say that he, and none other, had rescued her. Then they returned to the castle, where the courtier was acclaimed as the greatest of heroes.

On the third day Silverwhite hung his sword at his side, called his three dogs to him, and again wandered down to the sea-shore. As he was sitting by the strand, he saw the youngest princess led out of the city, and with her the daring courtier who claimed to have rescued her sisters. But the princess was very sad and cried bitterly. Then Silverwhite stepped up and greeted the lovely maiden politely. Now when the king's daughter and her escort saw the handsome youth, they were very much frightened, for they believed him to be the sea-troll, and the courtier ran away and hid in a high tree that grew near the strand. When Silverwhite noticed the maiden's terror, he said:

"Lovely maiden, do not fear me, for I will do you no harm." The king's daughter answered: "Are you the troll who is coming to carry me away?" "No," said Silverwhite, "I have come to rescue you." Then the princess was very glad to have such a brave hero fight for her, and they had a long, friendly talk with each other. At the same time Silverwhite begged the lovely maiden to do him a favor and comb his hair. This the king's daughter was most willing to do, and Silverwhite laid his head in her lap. But when the princess saw the gold rings her sisters had wound in his locks, she was much surprised, and added her own to the others.

Suddenly the sea-troll came shooting up out of the deep with a terrific noise, so that waves and foam spurted to the very skies. This time the monster had six heads and nine dogs. When the troll saw Silverwhite sitting with the king's daughter, he fell into a rage and cried: "What are you doing with my princess?" The youth answered: "It seems to me that she is my princess rather than yours." Thereupon the troll said: "Time enough to see which of us is right; but first our dogs shall fight each other." Silverwhite did not delay, but set his dogs at the sea-dogs, and they had a battle royal. But in the end the youth's dogs got the upper hand and bit all nine of the sea-dogs to death. Finally Silverwhite drew out his bare sword, flung himself upon the sea-troll, and stretched all six of his heads on the sand with a single blow. The monster uttered a terrible cry, and rushed back into the sea so that the water spurted to the heavens. Then the youth drew his silver-mounted knife, cut out all twelve of the troll's eyes, saluted the king's young daughter, and hastily went away.

Now that the battle was over, and the youth had disappeared, the courtier climbed down from his tree, drew his sword and threatened to kill the princess unless she promised to say that he had rescued her from the troll, as he had her sisters.

The king's daughter did not dare refuse, since she feared

for her life. So they went back to the castle together, and when the king saw that they had returned in safety, without so much as a scratch, he and the whole court were full of joy, and they were accorded great honors. And at court the courtier was quite another fellow from the one who had hid away in the tree. The king had a splendid banquet prepared, with amusements and games, and the sound of string music and dancing, and bestowed the hand of his youngest daughter on the courtier in reward for his bravey.

In the midst of the wedding festivities, when the king and his whole court were seated at table, the door opened, and in came Silverwhite with his dogs.

The youth stepped boldly into the hall of state and greeted the king. And when the three princesses saw who it was, they were full of joy, leaped up from their places, and ran over to him, much to the king's surprise, who asked what it all meant. Then the youngest princess told him all that had happened, from beginning to end, and that Silverwhite had rescued them, while the courtier sat in a tree. To prove it beyond any chance of doubt, each of the king's daughters showed her father the ring she had wound in Silverwhite's locks. But the king still did not know quite what to think of it all, until Silverwhite said: "My lord king! In order that you need not doubt what your daughters have told you, I will show you the eyes of the sea-trolls whom I slew." Then the king and all the rest saw that the princesses had told the truth. The traitorous courtier received his just punishment; but Silverwhite was paid every honor, and was given the youngest daughter and half of the kingdom with her.

After the wedding Silverwhite established himself with his young bride in a large castle belonging to the king, and there they lived quietly and happily.

One night, when all were sleeping, it chanced that he heard a knocking at the window, and a voice which said: "Come, Silverwhite, I have to talk to you!" The king, who did not want to wake his young wife, rose hastily, girded on his sword, called his dogs and went out. When he reached the open air, there stood a huge and savage-looking troll. The troll said: "Silverwhite, you have slain my three brothers, and I have come to bid you go down to the sea-shore with me, that we may fight with one another." This proposal suited the youth, and he followed the troll without protest. When they reached the sea-shore, there lay three great dogs belonging to the troll. Silverwhite at once set his dogs at the troll-dogs, and after a hard struggle the latter had to give in. The young king drew his sword, bravely attacked the troll and dealt him many a mighty blow. It was a tremendous battle. But when the troll noticed he was getting the worst of it, he grew frightened, quickly ran to a high tree, and clambered into it. Silverwhite and the dogs ran after him, the dogs barking as loudly as they could. Then the troll begged for his life and said: "Dear Silverwhite, I will take wergild for my brothers, only bid your dogs be still, so that we may talk." The king bade his dogs be still, but in vain, they only barked the more loudly. Then the troll tore three hairs from his head, handed them to Silverwhite and said: "Lay a hair on each of the dogs, and then they will be as quiet as can be." The king did so and at once the dogs fell silent, and lay motionless as though they had grown fast to the ground. Now Silverwhite realized that he had been deceived; but it was too late. The troll was already descending from the tree, and he drew his sword and again began to fight. But they had exchanged no more than a few blows, before Silverwhite received a mortal wound, and lay on the earth in a pool of blood.

But now we must tell about Lillwacker. The next morning he went to the spring by the cross-road and found it red with blood. Then he knew that Silverwhite was dead. He called his dogs, hung his sword at his side, and went on until he came to a great city. And the city was in festal array, the streets were crowded with people, and the houses were hung with scarlet cloths and splendid rugs. Lillwacker asked why everybody was so happy, and they said: "You must hail from distant parts, since you do not know that a famous hero has come here by the name of Silverwhite, who has rescued our three princesses, and is now the king's son-in-law." Lillwacker then inquired how it had all come about, and then went his way, reaching the royal castle in which Silverwhite dwelt with his beautiful queen in the evening.

When Lillwacker entered the castle gate, all greeted him as though he had been the king. For he resembled his foster-brother so closely that none could tell one from the other. When the youth came to the queen's room, she also took him for Silverwhite. She went up to him and said: "My lord king, where have you been so long? I have been awaiting you with great anxiety." Lillwacker said little, and was very taciturn. Then he lay down on a couch in a corner of the queen's room.

The young woman did not know what to think of his actions; for her husband did not act queerly at other times. But she thought: "One should not try to discover the secrets of others," and said nothing.

In the night, when all were sleeping, there was a knocking at the window, and a voice cried: "Come, Lillwacker, I have to talk to you!" The youth rose hastily, took his good sword, called his dogs and went. When he reached the open air, there stood the same troll who had slain Silverwhite. He said: "Come with me, Lillwacker, and then you shall see your foster-brother!" To this Lillwacker at once agreed, and the troll led the way. When they came to the sea-shore, there lay the three great dogs whom the troll had brought with him. Somewhat further away, where they had fought, lay Silverwhite in a pool of blood, and beside him his dogs were stretched out on the ground as though they had taken root in it. Then Lillwacker saw how everything had happened, and thought that he would gladly venture his life, if he might in some way call his brother back from the dead. He at once set his dogs at the troll-dogs, and they had a hard struggle, in which Lillwacker's dogs won the victory. Then the youth drew his sword, and attacked the troll with mighty blows. But when the troll saw that he was getting the worst of it, he took refuge in a lofty tree. Lillwacker and his dogs ran after him and the dogs barked loudly.

Then the troll humbly begged for his life, and said: "Dear Lillwacker, I will give you wergild for your brother, only bid your dogs be still, so that we may talk." At the same time the troll handed him three hairs from his head and added: "Lay one of these hairs on each of your dogs, and then they will soon be quiet." But Lillwacker saw through his cunning scheme, took the three hairs and laid them on the troll-dogs, which at once fell on the ground and lay like dead.

When the troll saw that his attempt had failed, he was much alarmed and said: "Dearest Lillwacker, I will give you wergild for your brother, if you will only leave me alone." But the youth answered:

"What is there you can give me that will compensate for my brother's life?" The troll replied: "Here are two flasks. In one is a liquid which, if you anoint a dead man with it, it will restore him to life; but as to the liquid in the other flask, if you moisten anything with it, and some one touches the place you have moistened, he will be unable to move from the spot. I think it would be hard to find anything more precious than the liquid in these flasks." Lillwacker said: "Your proposal suits me, and I will accept it. But there is something else you must promise to do: that you will release my brother's dogs." The troll agreed, climbed down from the tree, breathed on the dogs and thus freed them. Then Lillwacker took the two flasks and went away from the sea-shore with the troll. After they had gone a while they came to a great flat stone, lying near the highway. Lillwacker hastened on in advance and moistened it with liquid from the second flask. Then, as he was going by, Lillwacker suddenly set all six of his dogs at the troll, who stepped back and touched the stone. There he stuck, and could move neither forward nor backward. After a time the sun rose and shone on the stone. And when the troll saw the sun he burst—and was as dead as a doornail!

Lillwacker now ran back to his brother and sprinkled him with the liquid in the other flask, so that he came to life again, and they were both very happy, as may well be imagined. The two foster-brothers then returned to the castle, recounting the story of their experiences and adventures on the way. Lillwacker told how he had been taken for his brother. He even mentioned that he had lain down on a couch in a corner of the queen's room, and that she had never suspected that he was not her rightful husband. But when Silverwhite heard that, he thought that Lillwacker had offended against the queen's dignity, and he grew angry and fell into such a rage that he drew his sword, and thrust it into his brother's breast. Lillwacker fell to earth dead, and Silverwhite went home to the castle alone. But Lillwacker's dogs would not leave their master, and lay around him, whining and licking his wound.

In the evening, when the young king and his wife retired, the queen asked him why he had been so taciturn and serious the evening before. Then the queen said: "I am very curious to know what has befallen you during the last few days, but what I would like to know most of all, is why you lay down on a couch in a corner of my room the other night?" Now it was clear to Silverwhite that the brother he had slain was innocent of all offense, and he felt bitter regret at having repaid his faithfulness so badly. So King Silverwhite at once rose and went to the place where his brother was lying. He poured the water of life from his flask and anointed his brother's wound, and in a moment Lillwacker was alive again, and the two brother's went joyfully back to the castle.

When they got there, Silverwhite told his queen how Lillwacker had rescued him from death, and all the rest of their adventures, and all were happy at the royal court, and they paid the youth the greatest honors and compliments. After he had stayed there a time he sued for the hand of the second princess and obtained it. Thereupon the wedding was celebrated with great pomp, and Silverwhite divided his half of the kingdom with his foster-brother. The two brothers continued to live together in peace and unity, and if they have not died, they are living still.

FAITHFUL AND UNFAITHFUL

Once upon a time there was a couple of humble cottagers who had no children until, at last, the man's wife was blessed with a boy, which made both of them very happy. They named him Faithful and when he was christened a *huldra* came to the hut, seated herself beside the child's cradle, and foretold that he would meet with good fortune. "What is more," she said, "when he is fifteen years of age, I will make him a present of a horse with many rare qualities, a horse that has the gift of speech!" And with that the *huldra* turned and went away.

The boy grew up and became strong and powerful. And when he had passed his fifteenth year, a strange old man came up to their hut one day, knocked, and said that the horse he was leading had been sent by his queen, and that henceforward it was to belong to Faithful, as she had promised. Then the ancient man departed; but the beautiful horse was admired by all, and Faithful learned to love it more with every passing day.

At length he grew weary of home. "I must away and try my fortune in the world," said he, and his parents did not like to object; for there was not much to wish for at home. So he led his dear horse from the stable, swung himself into the saddle, and rode hurriedly into the wood. He rode on and on, and had already covered a good bit of ground, when he saw two lions engaged in a struggle with a tiger, and they were well-nigh overcome. "Make haste to take your bow," said the horse, "shoot the tiger and deliver the two lions!" "Yes, that's what I will do," said the youth, fitted an arrow to the bow-string, and in a moment the tiger lay prone on the ground. The two lions drew nearer, nuzzled their preserver in a friendly and grateful manner, and then hastened back to their cave.

Faithful now rode along for a long time among the great trees until he suddenly spied two terrified white doves fleeing from a hawk who was on the point of catching them. "Make haste to take your bow," said the horse, "shoot the hawk and save the two doves!" "Yes, that's what I'll do," said the youth. He fitted an arrow to the bow-string, and in a moment the hawk lay prone on the ground. But the two doves flew nearer, fluttered about their deliverer in a tame and grateful manner, and then hurried back to their nest.

The youth pressed on through the wood and by now was far, far from home. But his horse did not tire easily, and ran on with him until they came to a great lake. There he saw a gull rise up from the water, holding a pike in its claws. "Make haste to take your bow," said the horse, "shoot the gull and save the pike!" "Yes, that's what I'll do," answered the youth, fitted an arrow to his bow-string, and in a moment the gull was threshing the ground with its wings, mortally wounded. But the pike who had been saved swam nearer, gave his deliverer a friendly, grateful glance, and then dove down to join his fellows beneath the waves.

Faithful rode on again, and before evening came to a great castle. He at once had himself announced to the king, and begged that the latter would take him into his service. "What kind of a place do you want?" asked the king, who was inclined to look with favor on the bold horseman.

"I should like to be a groom," was Faithful's answer, "but first of all I must have stable-room and fodder for my horse." "That you shall have," said the king, and the youth was taken on as a groom, and served so long and so well, that every one in the castle liked him, and the king in particular praised him highly.

But among the other servitors was one named Unfaithful who was jealous of Faithful, and did what he could to harm him; for he thought to himself:

"Then I would be rid of him, and need not see him continue to rise in my lord's favor." Now it happened that the king was very sad, for he had lost his queen, whom a troll had stolen from the castle. It is true that the queen had not taken pleasure in the king's society, and that she did not love him. Still the king longed for her greatly, and often spoke of it to Unfaithful his servant. So one day Unfaithful said: "My lord need distress himself no longer, for Faithful has been boasting to me that he could rescue your beautiful queen from the hands of the troll." "If he has done so," replied the king, "then he must keep his word."

He straightway ordered Faithful to be brought before him, and threatened him with death if he did not at once hurry into the hill and bring back the wife of whom he had been robbed. If he were successful great honor should be his reward. In vain Faithful denied what Unfaithful had said of him, the king stuck to his demand, and the youth withdrew, convinced that he had not long to live. Then he went to the stable to bid farewell to his beautiful horse, and stood beside him and wept. "What grieves you so?" asked the horse. Then the youth told him of all that had happened, and said that this was probably the last time he would be able to visit him. "If it be no more than that," said the horse, "there is a way to help you. Up in the garret of the castle there is an old fiddle, take it with you and play it when you come to the place where the queen is kept. And fashion for yourself armor of steel wire, and set knives into it everywhere, and then, when you see the troll open his jaws, descend into his maw, and thus slay him. But you must have no fear, and must trust me to show you the way." These words filled the youth with fresh courage, he went to the king and received permission to leave, secretly fashioned his steel armor, took the old fiddle from the garret of the castle, led his dear horse out of the stable, and without delay set forth for the troll's hill.

Before long he saw it, and rode directly to the troll's abode. When he came near, he saw the troll, who had crept out of his castle, lying stretched out at the entrance to his cave, fast asleep, and snoring so powerfully that the whole hill shook. But his mouth was wide open, and his maw was so tremendous that it was easy for the youth to crawl into it. He did so, for he was not afraid, and made his way into the troll's inwards where he was so active that the troll was soon killed. Then Faithful crept out again, laid aside his armor, and entered the troll's castle. Within the great golden hall sat the captive queen, fettered with seven strong chains of gold. Faithful could not break the strong chains; but he took up his fiddle and played such tender music on it, that the golden chains were moved, and one after another, fell from the queen, until she was able to rise and was free once more. She looked at the courageous youth with joy and gratitude, and felt very kindly toward him, because he was so handsome and courteous. And the queen was perfectly willing to return with him to the king's castle.

The return of the queen gave rise to great joy, and Faithful received the promised reward from the king. But now the queen treated her husband with even less consideration than before. She would not exchange a word with him, she did not laugh, and locked herself up in her room with her gloomy thoughts. This greatly vexed the king, and one day he asked the queen why she was so sad: "Well," said she, "I cannot be happy unless I have the beautiful golden hall which I had in the hill at the troll's; for a hall like that is to be found nowhere else."

"It will be no easy matter to obtain it for you," said the king, "and I cannot promise you that anyone will be able to do it." But when he complained of his difficulty to his servant Unfaithful, the latter answered: "The chances of success are not so bad, for Faithful said he could easily bring the troll's golden hall to the castle." Faithful was at once sent for, and the king commanded him, as he loved his life, to make good his word and bring the golden hall from the troll's hill. It was in vain that Faithful denied Unfaithful's assertions: go he must, and bring back the golden hall.

Inconsolable, he went to his beautiful horse, wept and wanted to say farewell to him forever. "What troubles you?" asked the horse. And the youth replied: "Unfaithful has again been telling lies about me, and if I do not bring the troll's golden hall to the queen, my life will be forfeited." "Is it nothing more serious than that?" said the horse. "See that you obtain a great ship, take your fiddle with you and play the golden hall out of the hill, then hitch the troll's horses before it, and you will be able to bring the glistening hall here without trouble."

Then Faithful felt somewhat better, did as the horse had told him, and was successful in reaching the great hill. And as he stood there playing the fiddle, the golden hall heard him, and was drawn to the sounding music, and it moved slowly, slowly, until it stood outside the hill. It was built of virgin gold, like a house by itself, and under it were many wheels. Then the youth took the troll's horses, put them to the golden hall, and thus brought it aboard his ship. Soon he had crossed the lake, and brought it along safely so that it reached the castle without damage, to the great joy of the queen. Yet despite the fact, she was as weary of everything as she had been before, never spoke to her husband, the king, and no one ever saw her laugh.

Now the king grew even more vexed than he had been, and again asked her why she seemed so sad. "Ah, how can I be happy unless I have the two colts that used to belong to me, when I stayed at the troll's! Such handsome steeds are to be seen nowhere else!" "It will be anything but easy to obtain for you what you want," declared the king, "for they were untamed, and long ago must have run far away into the wildwood." Then he left her, sadly, and did not know what to do. But Unfaithful said: "Let my lord give himself no concern, for Faithful has declared he could easily secure both of the troll's colts." Faithful was at once sent for, and the king threatened him with death, if he did not show his powers in the matter of the colts. But should he succeed in catching them, then he would be rewarded.

Now Faithful knew quite well that he could not hope to catch the troll's wild colts, and he once more turned to the stable in order to bid farewell to the *huldra's* gift. "Why do you weep over such a trifle?" said the horse. "Hurry to the wood, play your fiddle, and all will be well!" Faithful did as he was told, and after a while the two lions whom he had rescued came leaping toward him, listened to his playing and asked him whether he was in distress. "Yes, indeed," said Faithful, and told them what he had to do. They at once ran back into the wood, one to one side and the other to the other, and returned quickly, driving the two colts before them. Then Faithful played his fiddle and the colts followed him, so that he soon reached the king's castle in safety, and could deliver the steeds to the queen.

The king now expected that his wife would be gay and happy. But she did not change, never addressed a word to him, and only seemed a little less sad when she happened to speak to the daring youth.

Then the king asked her to tell him what she lacked, and why she was so discontented. She answered: "I have secured the colts of the troll, and I often sit in the glittering hall of gold; but I can open none of the handsome chests that are filled to the brim with my valuables, because I have no keys. And if I do not get the keys again, how can I be happy?" "And where may the keys be?" asked the king. "In the lake by the troll's hill," said the queen, "for that is where I threw them when Faithful brought me here." "This is a ticklish affair, this business of those keys you want!" said the king. "And I can scarcely promise that you will ever see them again." In spite of this, however, he was willing to make an attempt, and talked it over with his servant Unfaithful. "Why, that is easily done," said the latter, "for Faithful boasted to me that he could get the queen's keys without any difficulty if he wished." "Then I shall compel him to keep his word," said the king. And he at once ordered Faithful, on pain of death, to get the queen's keys out of the lake by the troll's hill without delay.

This time the youth was not so depressed, for he thought to himself: "My wise horse will be able to help me." And so he was, for he advised him to go along playing his fiddle, and to wait for what might happen. After the youth had played for a while, the pike he had saved thrust his head out of the water, recognized him, and asked whether he could be of any service to him. "Yes, indeed!" said the youth, and told him what it was he wanted. The pike at once dived, quickly rose to the surface of the water with the golden keys in his mouth, and gave them to his deliverer. The latter hastened back with them, and now the queen could open the great chests in the golden hall to her heart's content.

Notwithstanding, the king's wife was as sorrowful as ever, and when the king complained about it to Unfaithful, the latter said: "No doubt it is because she loves Faithful. I would therefore advise that my lord have him beheaded. Then there will be a change." This advice suited the king well, and he determined to carry it out shortly. But one day Faithful's horse said to him: "The king is going to have your head chopped off. So hurry to the wood, play your fiddle, and beg the two doves to bring you a bottle of the water of life. Then go to the queen and ask her to set your head on your body and to sprinkle you with the water when you have been beheaded." Faithful did so. He went to the wood that very day with his fiddle, and before long the two doves were fluttering around him, and shortly after brought back the bottle filled with the water of life. He took it back home with him and gave it to the queen, so that she might sprinkle him with it after he had been beheaded. She did so, and at once Faithful rose again, as full of life as ever; but far better looking. The king was astonished at what he had seen, and told the queen to cut off his own head and then sprinkle him with the water. She at once seized the sword, and in a moment the king's head rolled to the ground. But she sprinkled none of the water of life upon it, and the king's body was quickly carried out and buried. Then the queen and Faithful celebrated their wedding with great pomp; but Unfaithful was banished from the land and went away in disgrace. The wise horse dwelt contentedly in a wonderful chamber, and the king and queen kept the magic fiddle, the golden hall, and the troll's other valuables, and lived in peace and happiness day after day.

STARKAD AND BALE

Starkad, the hero of the legends, the bravest warrior in the army of the North, had fallen into disgrace with the king because of a certain princess, so he wandered up into Norland, and settled down at Rude in Tuna, where he was known as the Thrall of the Alders or the Red Fellow.

In Balbo, nine miles from Rude, dwelt another hero, Bale, a good friend and companion-at-arms of Starkad.

One morning Starkad climbed the Klefberg in Tuna, and called over to Bale: "Bale in Balbo, are you awake?"

"Red Fellow!" answered Bale, nine miles away, "the sun and I wake together! But how goes it with you?"

"None too well. I eat salmon morning, noon and night. Come over with a bit of meat!"

"I'll come!" Bale called back, and in a few hours time he was down in Tuna with an elk under each arm.

The following morning Bale in Balbo stood on a hill in Borgsjo and called: "Red Fellow! Are you awake?"

"The sun and I wake together!" answered Starkad. "And how goes it with you?"

"Alas, I have nothing to eat but meat! Elk in the morning, elk at noon and elk at night. Come over and bring a fish-tail along with you!"

"I'm coming!" called out Starkad, and in a short time he had joined his friend with a barrel of salmon under each arm.

In this fashion the two friends provided themselves with all the game to be found in the woods and in the water, and spread terror and destruction throughout the countryside. But one evening, when they were just returning to the sea from an excursion, a black cloud came up, and a tempest broke. They hurried along as fast as they could; but got no further than Vattjom, where a flash of lightning struck Starkad and flung him to the ground. His friend and companion-at-arms buried him beneath a stone cairn, about which he set five rocks: two at his feet, two at his shoulders, and one at his head; and that grave, measuring twenty ells in length, may still be seen near the river.

THE WEREWOLF

Once upon a time there was a king, who reigned over a great kingdom. He had a queen, but only a single daughter, a girl. In consequence the little girl was the apple of her parents' eyes; they loved her above everything else in the world, and their dearest thought was the pleasure they would take in her when she was older. But the unexpected often happens; for before the king's daughter began to grow up, the queen her mother fell ill and died. It is not hard to imagine the grief that reigned, not alone in the royal castle, but throughout the land; for the queen had been beloved of all. The king grieved so that he would not marry again, and his one joy was the little princess.

A long time passed, and with each succeeding day the king's daughter grew taller and more beautiful, and her father granted her every wish. Now there were a number of women who had nothing to do but wait on the princess and carry out her commands. Among them was a woman who had formerly married and had two daughters. She had an engaging appearance, a smooth tongue and a winning way of talking, and she was as soft and pliable as silk; but at heart she was full of machinations and falseness. Now when the queen died, she at once began to plan how she might marry the king, so that her daughters might be kept like royal princesses. With this end in view, she drew the young princess to her, paid her the most fulsome compliments on everything she said and did, and was forever bringing the conversation around to how happy she would be were the king to take another wife. There was much said on this head, early and late, and before very long the princess came to believe that the woman knew all there was to know about everything. So she asked her what sort of a woman the king ought to choose for a wife. The woman answered as sweet as honey: "It is not my affair to give advice in this matter; yet he should choose for queen some one who is kind to the little princess. For one thing I know, and that is, were I fortunate enough to be chosen, my one thought would be to do all I could for the little princess, and if she wished to wash her hands, one of my daughters would have to hold the wash-bowl and the other hand her the towel." This and much more she told the king's daughter, and the princess believed it, as children will.

From that day forward the princess gave her father no peace, and begged him again and again to marry the good court lady. Yet he did not want to marry her. But the king's daughter gave him no rest; but urged him again and again, as the false court lady had persuaded her to do. Finally, one day, when she again brought up the matter, the king cried: "I can see you will end by having your own way about this, even though it be entirely against my will. But I will do so only on one condition." "What is the condition?" asked the princess. "If I marry again," said the king, "it is only because of your ceaseless pleading. Therefore you must promise that, if in the future you are not satisfied with your step-mother or your step-sisters, not a single lament or complaint on your part reaches my ears." This she promised the king, and it was agreed that he should marry the court lady and make her queen of the whole country.

As time passed on, the king's daughter had grown to be the most beautiful maiden to be found far and wide; the queen's daughters, on the other hand, were homely, evil of disposition, and no one knew any good of them. Hence it was not surprising that many youths came from East and West to sue for the princess's hand; but that none of them took any interest in the queen's daughters. This made the step-mother very angry; but she concealed her rage, and was as sweet and friendly as ever. Among the wooers was a king's son from another country. He was young and brave, and since he loved the princess dearly, she accepted his proposal and they plighted their troth. The queen observed this with an angry eye, for it would have pleased her had the prince chosen one of her own daughters. She therefor made up her mind that the young pair should never be happy together, and from that time on thought only of how she might part them from each other.

An opportunity soon offered itself. News came that the enemy had entered the land, and the king was compelled to go to war. Now the princess began to find out the kind of step-mother she had. For no sooner had the king departed than the queen showed her true nature, and was just as harsh and unkind as she formerly had pretended to be friendly and obliging. Not a day went by without her scolding and threatening the princess; and the queen's daughters were every bit as malicious as their mother. But the king's son, the lover of the princess, found himself in even worse position. He had gone hunting one day, had lost his way, and could not find his people. Then the queen used her black arts and turned him into a werewolf, to wander through the forest for the remainder of his life in that shape. When evening came and there was no sign of the prince, his people returned home, and one can imagine what sorrow they caused when the princess learned how the hunt had ended. She grieved, wept day and night, and was not to be consoled. But the queen laughed at her grief, and her heart was filled with joy to think that all had turned out exactly as she wished.

Now it chanced one day, as the king's daughter was sitting alone in her room, that she thought she would go herself into the forest where the prince had disappeared. She went to her step-mother and begged permission to go out into the forest, in order to forget her surpassing grief. The queen did not want to grant her request, for she always preferred saying no to yes. But the princess begged her so winningly that at last she was unable to say no, and she ordered one of her daughters to go along with her and watch her. That caused a great deal of discussion, for neither of the step-daughters wanted to go with her; each made all sorts of excuses, and asked what pleasures were there in going with the king's daughter, who did nothing but cry. But the queen had the last word in the end, and ordered that one of her daughters must accompany the princess, even though it be against her will. So the girls wandered out of the castle into the forest. The king's daughter walked among the trees, and listened to the song of the birds, and thought of her lover, for whom she longed, and who was now no longer there. And the queen's daughter followed her, vexed, in her malice, with the king's daughter and her sorrow.

After they had walked a while, they came to a little hut, lying deep in the dark forest. By then the king's daughter was very thirsty, and wanted to go into the little hut with her step-sister, in order to get a drink of water. But the queen's daughter was much annoyed and said: "Is it not enough for me to be running around here in the wilderness with you? Now you even want me, who am a princess, to enter that wretched little hut. No, I will not step a foot over the threshold! If you want to go in, why go in alone!" The king's daughter lost no time; but did as her step-sister advised, and stepped into the little hut. When she entered she saw an old woman sitting there on a bench, so enfeebled by age that her head shook. The princess spoke to her in her usual friendly way: "Good evening, motherkin. May I ask you for a drink of water?" "You are heartily welcome to it," said the old woman. "Who may you be, that step beneath my lowly roof and greet me in so winning a way?" The king's daughter told her who she was, and that she had gone out to relieve her heart, in order to forget her great grief. "And what may your great grief be?" asked the old woman. "No doubt it is my fate to grieve," said the princess, "and I can never be happy again. I have lost my only love, and God alone knows whether I shall ever see him again." And she also told her why it was, and the tears ran down her cheeks in streams, so that any one would have felt sorry for her. When she had ended the old woman said: "You did well in confiding your sorrow to me. I have lived long and may be able to give you a bit of good advice. When you leave here you will see a lily growing from the ground. This lily is not like other lilies, however, but has many strange virtues. Run quickly over to it, and pick it. If you can do that then you need not worry, for then one will appear who will tell you what to do." Then they parted and the king's daughter thanked her and went her way; while the old woman sat on the bench and wagged her head. But the queen's daughter had been standing without the hut the entire time, vexing herself, and grumbling because the king's daughter had taken so long.

So when the latter stepped out, she had to listen to all sorts of abuse from her step-sister, as was to be expected. Yet she paid no attention to her, and thought only of how she might find the flower of which the old woman had spoken. They went through the forest, and suddenly she saw a beautiful white lily growing in their very path. She was much pleased and ran up at once to pick it; but that very moment it disappeared and reappeared somewhat further away.

The king's daughter was now filled with eagerness, no longer listened to her step-sister's calls, and kept right on running; yet each time when she stooped to pick the lily, it suddenly disappeared and reappeared somewhat further away. Thus it went for some time, and the princess was drawn further and further into the deep forest. But the lily continued to stand, and disappear and move further away, and each time the flower seemed larger and more beautiful than before. At length the princess came to a high hill, and as she looked toward its summit, there stood the lily high on the naked rock, glittering as white and radiant as the brightest star. The king's daughter now began to climb the hill, and in her eagerness she paid no attention to stones nor steepness. And when at last she reached the summit of the hill, lo and behold! the lily no longer evaded her grasp; but remained where it was, and the princess stooped and picked it and hid it in her bosom, and so heartfelt was her happiness that she forgot her step-sisters and everything else in the world.

For a long time she did not tire of looking at the beautiful flower. Then she suddenly began to wonder what her step-mother would say when she came home after having remained out so long. And she looked around, in order to find the way back to the castle. But as she looked around, behold, the sun had set and no more than a little strip of daylight rested on the summit of the hill. Below her lay the forest, so dark and shadowed that she had no faith in her ability to find the homeward path. And now she grew very sad, for she could think of nothing better to do than to spend the night on the hill-top. She seated herself on the rock, put her hand to her cheek, cried, and thought of her unkind step-mother and step-sisters, and of all the harsh words she would have to endure when she returned. And she thought of her father, the king, who was away at war, and of the love of her heart, whom she would never see again; and she grieved so bitterly that she did not even know she wept. Night came and darkness, and the stars rose, and still the princess sat in the same spot and wept. And while she sat there, lost in her thoughts, she heard a voice say: "Good evening, lovely maiden! Why do you sit here so sad and lonely?" She stood up hastily, and felt much embarrassed, which was not surprising. When she looked around there was nothing to be seen but a tiny old man, who nodded to her and seemed to be very humble. She answered: "Yes, it is no doubt my fate to grieve, and never be happy again. I have lost my dearest love, and now I have lost my way in the forest, and am afraid of being devoured by wild beasts." "As to that," said the old man, "you need have no fear. If you will do exactly as I say, I will help you." This made the princess happy; for she felt that all the rest of the world had abandoned her. Then the old man drew out flint and steel and said: "Lovely maiden, you must first build a fire." She did as he told her, gathered moss, brush and dry sticks, struck sparks and lit such a fire on the hill-top that the flame blazed up to the skies. That done the old man said: "Go on a bit and you will find a kettle of tar, and bring the kettle to me." This the king's daughter did. The old man continued: "Now put the kettle on the fire." And the princess did that as well. When the tar began to boil, the old man said: "Now throw your white lily into the kettle." The princess thought this a harsh command, and earnestly begged to be allowed to keep the lily. But the old man said: "Did you not promise to obey my every command? Do as I tell you or you will regret it." The king's daughter turned away her eyes, and threw the lily into the boiling tar; but it was altogether against her will, so fond had she grown of the beautiful flower.

The moment she did so a hollow roar, like that of some wild beast, sounded from the forest. It came nearer, and turned into such a terrible howling that all the surrounding hills reëchoed it. Finally there was a cracking and breaking among the trees, the bushes were thrust aside, and the princess saw a great grey wolf come running out of the forest and straight up the hill. She was much frightened and would gladly have run away, had she been able. But the old man said: "Make haste, run to the edge of the hill and the moment the wolf comes along, upset the kettle on him!" The princess was terrified, and hardly knew what she was about; yet she did as the old man said, took the kettle, ran to the edge of the hill, and poured its contents over the wolf just as he was about to run up. And then a strange thing happened: no sooner had she done so, than the wolf was transformed, cast off his thick grey pelt, and in place of the horrible wild beast, there stood a handsome young man, looking up to the hill. And when the king's daughter collected herself and looked at him, she saw that it was really and truly her lover, who had been turned into a werewolf.

It is easy to imagine how the princess felt. She opened her arms, and could neither ask questions nor reply to them, so moved and delighted was she. But the prince ran hastily up the hill, embraced her tenderly, and thanked her for delivering him. Nor did he forget the little old man, but thanked him with many civil expressions for his powerful aid. Then they sat down together on the hill-top, and had a pleasant talk. The prince told how he had been turned into a wolf, and of all he had suffered while running about in the forest; and the princess told of her grief, and the many tears she had shed while he had been gone. So they sat the whole night through, and never noticed it until the stars grew pale and it was light enough to see. When the sun rose, they saw that a broad path led from the hill-top straight to the royal castle; for they had a view of the whole surrounding country from the hill-top. Then the old man said: "Lovely maiden, turn around! Do you see anything out yonder?" "Yes," said the princess, "I see a horseman on a foaming horse, riding as fast as he can." Then the old man said: "He is a messenger sent on ahead by the king your father. And your father with all his army is follow-ing him." That pleased the princess above all things, and she wanted to descend the hill at once to meet her father. But the old man detained her and said: "Wait a while, it is too early yet. Let us wait and see how everything turns out."

Time passed and the sun was shining brightly, and its rays fell straight on the royal castle down below. Then the old man said: "Lovely maiden, turn around! Do you see anything down below?" "Yes," replied the princess, "I see a number of people coming out of my father's castle, and some are going along the road, and others into the forest." The old man said: "Those are your step-mother's servants. She has sent some to meet the king and welcome him; but she has sent others to the forest to look for you." At these words the princess grew uneasy, and wished to go down to the queen's servants. But the old man withheld her and said: "Wait a while, and let us first see how everything turns out."

More time passed, and the king's daughter was still look-ing down the road from which the king would appear, when the old man said: "Lovely maiden, turn around! Do you see anything down below?" "Yes," answered the princess, "there is a great commotion in my father's castle, and they are hanging it with black." The old man said: "That is your step-mother and her people. They will assure your father that you are dead." Then the king's daughter felt bitter anguish, and she implored from the depths of her heart: "Let me go, let me go, so that I may spare my father this anguish!" But the old man detained her and said: "No, wait, it is still too early. Let us first see how everything turns out."

Again time passed, the sun lay high above the fields, and the warm air blew over meadow and forest. The royal maid and youth still sat on the hill-top with the old man, where we had left them. Then they saw a little cloud rise against the horizon, far away in the distance, and the little cloud grew larger and larger, and came nearer and nearer along the road, and as it moved one could see it was agleam with weapons, and nodding helmets, and waving flags, one could hear the rattle of swords, and the neighing of horses, and finally recognize the banner of the king. It is not hard to imagine how pleased the king's daughter was, and how she insisted on going down and greeting her father. But the old man held her back and said: "Lovely maiden, turn around! Do you see anything happening at the castle?" "Yes," answered the princess, "I can see my step-mother and step-sisters coming out, dressed in mourning, holding white kerchiefs to their faces, and weeping bitterly." The old man answered: "Now they are pretending to weep because of your death. Wait just a little while longer. We have not yet seen how everything will turn out."

After a time the old man said again: "Lovely maiden, turn around! Do you see anything down below?" "Yes," said the princess, "I see people bringing a black coffin—now my father is having it opened. Look, the queen and her daughters are down on their knees, and my father is threatening them with his sword!" Then the old man said: "Your father wished to see your body, and so your evil step-mother had to confess the truth." When the princess heard that she said earnestly: "Let me go, let me go, so that I may comfort my father in his great sorrow!" But the old man held her back and said: "Take my advice and stay here a little while longer. We have not yet seen how everything will turn out."

Again time went by, and the king's daughter and the prince and the old man were still sitting on the hill-top. Then the old man said: "Lovely maiden, turn around! Do you see anything down below?" "Yes," answered the princess, "I see my father and my step-sisters and my step-mother with all their following moving this way." The old man said: "Now they have started out to look for you. Go down and bring up the wolf's pelt in the gorge." The king's daughter did as he told her. The old man continued: "Now stand at the edge of the hill." And the princess did that, too. Now one could see the queen and her daughters coming along the way, and stopping just below the hill. Then the old man said: "Now throw down the wolf's pelt!" The princess obeyed him, and threw down the wolf's pelt according to his command. It fell directly on the evil queen and her daughters. And then a most wonderful thing happened: no sooner had the pelt touched the three evil women than they immediately changed shape, and turning into three horrible werewolves, they ran away as fast as they could into the forest, howling dreadfully.

No more had this happened than the king himself arrived at the foot of the hill with his whole retinue. When he looked up and recognized the princess, he could not at first believe his eyes; but stood motionless, thinking her a vision. Then the old man cried: "Lovely maiden, now hasten, run down and make your father happy!" There was no need to tell the princess twice. She took her lover by the hand and they ran down the hill. When they came to the king, the princess ran on ahead, fell on her father's neck, and wept with joy. And the young prince wept as well, and the king himself wept; and their meeting was a pleasant sight for every one. There was great joy and many embraces, and the princess told of her evil step-mother and step-sisters and of her lover, and all that she had suffered, and of the old man who had helped them in such a wonderful way. But when the king turned around to thank the old man he had completely vanished, and from that day on no one could say who he had been or what had become of him.

The king and his whole retinue now returned to the castle, where the king had a splendid banquet prepared, to which he invited all the able and distinguished people throughout the kingdom, and bestowed his daughter on the young prince. And the wedding was celebrated with gladness and music and amusements of every kind for many days. I was there, too, and when I rode through the forest I met a wolf with two young wolves, and they showed me their teeth and seemed very angry. And I was told they were none other than the evil step-mother and her two daughters.

THE LAME DOG

Once upon a time there lived a king, like many others. He had three daughters, who were young and beautiful to such a degree that it would have been difficult to have found handsomer maidens. Yet there was a great difference among them; for the two older sisters were haughty in their thoughts and manners; while the youngest was sweet and friendly, and everyone liked her. Besides, she was fair as the day and delicate as the snow, and far more beautiful than either of her sisters.

One day the king's daughters were sitting together in their room, and their talk happened to turn on their husbands-to-be. The oldest said: "If I ever marry, my husband must have golden hair and a golden beard!" And the second exclaimed: "And mine must have silver hair and a silver beard!" But the youngest princess held her tongue and said nothing. Then her sisters asked her whether she did not want to wish for a husband. "No," she answered, "but if fate should give me a husband, I will be content to take him as he is, and were he no more than a lame dog." Then the two other princesses laughed and joked about it, and told her the day might easily come when she would change her mind.

But many speak truth and do not know it! Thus it chanced with the king's daughters; since before the year had come to an end, each had the suitor for whom she had wished. A man with golden hair and golden beard sued for the oldest princess and won her consent to his suit. And a man with silver hair and a silver beard sued for the second and she became his bride; but the youngest princess had no other suitor than a lame dog. Then she recalled her talk with her sisters in their room, and thought to herself: "May God aid me in the marriage into which I must enter!" Yet she would not break the word she had once passed; but followed her sisters' example and accepted the dog. The wedding lasted a number of days and was celebrated with great pomp and splendor. But while the guests danced and amused themselves, the youngest princess sat apart and wept, and when the others were laughing, her tears flowed till it made one sad to see them.

After the wedding the newly married pairs were each to drive off to their castle. And the two older princesses each drove off in a splendidly decorated coach, with a large retinue, and all sorts of honors. But the youngest had to go afoot, since her husband, the dog, had neither coach nor driver. When they had wandered long and far, they came to a great forest, so great that it seemed endless; but the dog limped along in advance, and the king's daughter followed after, weeping. And as they went along she suddenly saw a magnificent castle lying before them, and round about it were beautiful meadows and green woods, all of them most enjoyable to see. The princess stopped and asked to whom the great mansion might belong. "That," said the dog, "is our home. We will live here, and you shall rule it as you see fit." Then the maiden laughed amid her tears, and could not overcome her surprise at all she saw. The dog added: "I have but a single request to make to you, and that you must not refuse to grant." "What is your request?" asked the princess. "You must promise me," said the dog, "that you will never look at me while I am asleep: otherwise you are free to do whatever you wish." The princess gladly promised to grant his request, and so they went to the great castle. And if the castle was magnificent from without, it was still more magnificent within. It was so full of gold and silver that the precious metals gleamed from every corner; and there was such abundance of supplies of every kind, and of so many other things, that everything in the world one might have wished to have was already there. The princess spent the live-long day running from one room to another, and each was handsomer than the one she had just entered. But when evening came and she went to bed, the dog crept into his own, and then she noticed that he was not a dog; but a human being. Yet she said not a word, because she remembered her promise, and did not wish to cross her husband's will.

Thus some time passed. The princess dwelt in the beautiful castle, and had everything her heart might desire. But every day the dog ran off, and did not reappear until it was evening and the sun had set. Then he returned home, and was always so kind and friendly that it would have been a fine thing had other men done half as well. The princess now began to feel a great affection for him, and quite forgot he was only a lame dog; for the proverb says: "Love is blind." Yet time passed slowly because she was so much alone, and she often thought of visiting her sisters and seeing how they were. She spoke of it to her husband, and begged his permission to make the journey. No sooner had the dog heard her wish than he at once granted it, and even accompanied her some distance, in order to show her the way out of the wood.

When the king's daughters were once reunited, they were naturally very happy, and there were a great many questions asked about matters old and new. And marriage was also discussed. The oldest princess said: "It was silly of me to wish for a husband with golden hair and golden beard; for mine is worse than the veriest troll, and I have not known a happy day since we married." And the second went on: "Yes, and I am no better off; for although I have a husband with silver hair and a silver beard, he dislikes me so heartily that he begrudges me a single hour of happiness." Then her sisters turned to the youngest princess and asked how she fared. "Well," was her answer, "I really cannot complain; for though I only got a lame dog, he is such a dear good fellow and so kind to me that it would be hard to find a better husband." The other princesses were much surprised to hear this, and did not stop prying and questioning, and their sister answered all their questions faithfully. When they heard how splendidly she lived in the great castle, they grew jealous because she was so much better off than they were. And they insisted on knowing whether there was not some one little thing of which she could complain. "No," said the king's daughter, "I can only praise my husband for his kindness and amiability, and there is but one thing lacking to make me perfectly happy." "What is it?" "What is it?" cried both sisters with a single voice. "Every night, when he comes home," said the princess, "he turns into a human being, and I am sorry that I can never see what he really looks like." Then both sisters again with one voice, began to scold the dog loudly; because he had a secret which he kept from his wife. And since her sisters now continually spoke about it, her own curiosity awoke once more, she forgot her husband's command, and asked how she might manage to see him without his knowing it. "O," said the oldest princess, "nothing easier! Here is a little lamp, which you must hide carefully. Then you need only get up at night when he is asleep, and light the lamp in order to see him in his true shape." This advice seemed good to the king's daughter; she took the lamp, hid it in her breast, and promised to do all that her sisters had counseled.

When the time came for them to part, the youngest princess went back to her beautiful castle. The day passed like every other day. When evening came at last and the dog had gone to bed, the princess was so driven by curiosity that she could hardly wait until he had fallen asleep. Then she rose, softly, lit her lamp, and drew near the bed to look at him while he slept. But no one can describe her astonishment when throwing the light on the bed, she saw no lame dog lying there; but the handsomest youth her eyes had ever beheld. She could not stop looking at him; but sat up all night bending over his pillow, and the more she looked at him the handsomer he seemed to grow, until she forgot everything else in the world. At last the morning came. And as the first star began to pale in the dawn, the youth began to grow restless and awaken. The princess much frightened, blew out her lamp and lay down in her bed. The youth thought she was sleeping and did not wish to wake her, so he rose quietly, assumed his other shape, went away and did not appear again all day long.

And when evening came and it grew late, everything happened as before. The dog came home from the forest and was very tired. But no sooner had he fallen asleep than the princess rose carefully, lit her lamp and came over to look at him. And when she cast the light on his bed it seemed to her as though the youth had grown even handsomer than the day before, and the longer she looked the more handsome he became; until she had to laugh and weep from sheer love and longing. She could not take her eyes from him, and sat all night long bent over his pillow, forgetful of her promise and all else, only to be able to look at him. With the first ray of dawn the youth began to stir and awake. Then the princess was again frightened, quickly blew out her lamp and lay down in her bed. The youth thought she was sleeping, and not wishing to waken her, rose softly, assumed his other shape, went away and was gone for the entire day.

At length it grew late again, evening came and the dog returned home from the forest as usual. But again the princess could not control her curiosity; no sooner was her husband sleeping than she rose quietly, lit her lamp, and drew near carefully in order to look at him while he slept. And when the light fell on the youth, he appeared to be handsomer than ever before, and the longer she looked the more handsome he grew, until her heart burned in her breast, and she forgot all else in the world looking at him. She could not take her eyes from him, and sat up all night bending over his pillow. And when morning came and the sun rose, the youth began to move and awaken. Then the princess was much frightened, because she had paid no heed to the passing of time, and she tried to put out her lamp quickly. But her hand trembled, and a warm drop of oil fell on the youth and he awoke. When he saw what she had done, he leaped up, terrified, instantly turned into a lame dog, and limped out into the forest. But the princess felt so remorseful that she nearly lost her senses, and she ran after him, wringing her hands and weeping bitterly, and begging him to return. But he did not come back.

The king's daughter now wandered over hill and dale, along many a road new to her, in order to find her husband, and her tears flowed the while till it would have moved a stone. But the dog was gone and stayed gone, though she looked for him North and South. When she saw that she could not find him, she thought she would return to her handsome castle. But there she was just as unfortunate. The castle was nowhere to be seen, and wherever she went she was surrounded by a forest black as coal. Then she came to the conclusion that the whole world had abandoned her, sat down on a stone, wept bitterly, and thought how much rather she would die than live without her husband. At that a little toad hopped out from under the stone, and said: "Lovely maiden, why do you sit here and weep?" And the princess answered: "It is my hard fate to weep and never be happy again. First of all I have lost the love of my heart, and now I can no longer find my way back to the castle. So I must perish of hunger here, or else be devoured by wild beasts." "O," said the toad, "if that is all that troubles you, I can help you! If you will promise to be my dearest friend, I will show you the way." But that the princess did not want to do. She replied: "Ask of me what you will, save that alone. I have never loved any one more than my lame dog, and so long as I live will never love any one else better." With that she rose, wept bitterly, and continued her way. But the toad looked after her in a friendly manner, laughed to himself, and once more crept under his stone.

After the king's daughter had wandered on for a long, long way, and still saw nothing but forest and wilderness, she grew very tired. She once more sat down on a stone, rested her chin on her hand, and prayed for death, since it was no longer possible for her to live with her husband. Suddenly there was a rustling in the bushes, and she saw a big gray wolf coming directly toward her. She was much frightened, since her one thought was that the wolf intended to devour her. But the wolf stopped, wagged his tail, and said: "Proud maiden, why do you sit here and weep so bitterly?" The princess answered: "It is my hard fate to weep and never be happy again. First of all I have lost my heart's dearest, and now I cannot find my way back to the castle and must perish of hunger, or be devoured by wild beasts." "O," said the wolf, "if that is all that troubles you, I can help you! Let me be your best friend and I will show you the way." But that did not suit the princess, and she replied: "Ask of me what you will, save that alone. I have never loved any one more than my lame dog, and so long as I live I will never love any one else better." With that she rose, weeping bitterly, and continued on her way. But the wolf looked after her in a friendly manner, laughed to himself and ran off hastily.

After the princess had once more wandered for a long time in the wilderness, she was again so wearied and exhausted that she could not go on. She sat down on a stone, wrung her hands, and wished for death, since she could no longer live with her husband. At that moment she heard a hollow roaring that made the earth tremble, and a monstrous big lion appeared and came directly toward her. Now she was much frightened; for what else could she think but that the lion would tear her to pieces? But the beast was so weighed down with heavy iron chains that he could scarcely drag himself along, and the chains clashed at either side when he moved. When the lion finally reached the princess he stopped, wagged his tail, and asked: "Beautiful maiden, why do you sit here and weep so bitterly?" The princess answered: "It is my hard fate to weep and never be happy again. First of all I have lost my heart's dearest, and now I cannot find my way to the castle, and must perish of hunger, or be devoured by wild beasts." "O," said the lion, "if that is all that troubles you, I can help you! If you will loose my chains and make me your best friend, I will show you the way." But the princess was so terrified that she could not answer the lion, far less venture to draw near him. Then she heard a clear voice sounding from the forest: it was a little nightingale, who sat among the branches and sang:

"Maiden, maiden, loose his chains!"

Then she felt sorry for the lion, grew braver, went up to him, unloosed his chains and said: "Your chains I can loose for you; but I can never be your best friend. For I have never loved any one more than my lame dog and will never love any one else better." And then a wondrous thing took place: at the very moment the last chain fell from him, the lion turned into a handsome young prince, and when the princess looked at him more closely, it was none other than her heart's dearest, who before had been a dog. She sank to the ground, clasped his knees, and begged him not to leave her again. But the prince raised her with deep affection, took her in his arms and said: "No, now we shall never more be parted, for I am released from my enchantment, and have proved your faith toward me in every way."

Then there was joy indescribable. And the prince took his young wife home to the beautiful castle, and there he became king and she was his queen. And if they have not died they are living there to this very day.

THE MOUNT OF THE GOLDEN QUEEN

Once upon a time a lad who tended the cattle in the wood was eating his noon-tide meal in a clearing in the forest. As he was sitting there he saw a rat run into a juniper-bush. His curiosity led him to look for it; but as he bent over, down he went, head over heels, and fell asleep. And he dreamed that he was going to find the princess on the Mount of the Golden Queen; but that he did not know the way.

The following day he once more pastured his cattle in the wood, when he came to the same clearing, and again ate his dinner there. And again he saw the rat and went to look for it, and again when he bent down he went head over heels, and fell fast asleep. And again he dreamed of the princess on the Mount of the Golden Queen, and that in order to get her he would need seventy pounds of iron and a pair of iron shoes. He awoke and it was all a dream; but by now he had made up his mind to find the Mount of the Golden Queen, and he went home with his herd. On the third day, when he led out his cattle, he could not reach the clearing of his happy dream too soon. Again the rat showed itself and when he went to look for it, he fell asleep as he had done each preceding day. And again he dreamed of the princess on the Mount of the Golden Queen, and that she came to him, and laid a letter and a band of gold in his pocket. Then he awoke and to his indescribable surprise, he found in his pocket both of the things of which he had dreamed, the letter and the band. Now he had no time to attend to the cattle any longer, but drove them straight home. Then he went into the stable, led out a horse, sold it, and bought seventy pounds of iron and a pair of iron shoes with the money. He made the thole-pins out of the iron, put on his iron shoes, and set forth. For a time he traveled by land; but at last he came to the lake which he had to cross. He saw naught but water before and behind him, and rowing so long and steadily that he wore out one thole-pin after another, he at length reached land, and a green meadow, where no trees grew. He walked all around the meadow, and at last found a mound of earth from which smoke was rising. When he looked more closely, out came a woman who was nine yards long. He asked her to tell him the way to the Mount of the Golden Queen. But she replied: "That I do not know. Go ask my sister, who is nine yards taller than I am, and who lives in an earth-mound which you can find without any trouble." So he left her and came to a mound of earth that looked just like the first, and from which smoke was also rising. A woman at once came out who was tremendously tall, and of her he asked the way to the Mount of the Golden Queen. "That I do not know," said she. "Go ask my brother, who is nine yards taller than I am, and who lives in a hill a little further away." So he came to the hill, from which smoke was also rising, and knocked. A man at once came out who was a veritable giant, for he was twenty-seven yards in length, and of him he asked the way to the Mount of the Golden Queen. Then the giant took a whistle and whistled in every direction, to call together all the animals to be found on the earth. And all the animals came from the woods, foremost among them a bear. The giant asked him about the Mount of the Golden Queen, but he knew nothing of it. Again the giant blew his whistle in every direction to call together all the fishes to be found in the waters. They came at once, and he asked them about the Mount of the Golden Queen; but they knew nothing of it. Once more the giant blew his whistle in every direction, and called together all the birds of the air. They came, and he asked the eagle about the Mount of the Golden Queen, and whether he knew where it might be. The eagle said: "Yes!" "Well then, take this lad there," said the giant "but do not treat him unkindly!" This the eagle promised, allowed the youth to seat himself on his back, and then off they were through the air, over fields and forests, hill and dale, and before long they were above the ocean, and could see nothing but sky and water. Then the eagle dipped the youth in the ocean up to his ankles and asked: "Are you afraid?" "No," said the youth. Then the eagle flew on a while, and again dipped the youth into the water, up to his knees and said: "Are you afraid?" "Yes," answered the youth, "but the giant said you were not to treat me unkindly." "Are you really afraid?" asked the eagle once more. "Yes," answered the youth. Then the eagle said: "The fear you now feel is the very same fear I felt when the princess thrust the letter and the golden band into your pocket." And with that they had reached a large, high mountain in one side of which was a great iron door. They knocked, and a serving-maid appeared to open the door and admit them. The youth remained and was well received; but the eagle said farewell and flew back to his native land. The youth asked for a drink, and he was at once handed a beaker containing a refreshing draught. When he had emptied it and returned the beaker, he let the golden band drop into it. And when the maid brought back the beaker to her mistress—who was the princess of the Mount of the Golden Queen—the latter looked into the beaker, and behold, there lay a golden band which she recognized as her own. So she asked: "Is there some one here?" and when the maid answered in the affirmative, the princess said: "Bid him come in!" And as soon as the youth entered she asked him if he chanced to have a letter. The youth drew out the letter he had received in so strange a manner, and gave it to the princess. And when she had read it she cried, full of joy: "Now I am delivered!" And at that very moment the mountain turned into a most handsome castle, with all sorts of precious things, servants, and every sort of convenience, each for its own purpose. (Whether the princess and the youth married the story does not say; yet we must take for granted that a wedding is the proper end for the fairy-tale).

OLD HOPGIANT

Once upon a time there were two neighbors: one of them rich and the other poor. They owned a great meadow in common, which they were supposed to mow together and then divide the hay.

But the rich neighbor wanted the meadow for himself alone, and told the poor one that he would drive him out of house and home if he did not come to an agreement with him that whichever one of them mowed the largest stretch of the meadowland in a single day, should receive the entire meadow.

Now the rich neighbor got together as many mowers as ever he could; but the poor one could not hire a single man. At last he despaired altogether and wept, because he did not know how he could manage to get so much as a bit of hay for the cow.

Then it was that a large man stepped up to him and said: "Do not grieve so. I can tell you what you ought to do. When the mowing begins, just call out 'Old Hopgiant!' three times in succession, and you'll not be at a loss, as you shall see for yourself." And with that he disappeared.

Then the poor man's heart grew less heavy, and he gave over worrying. So one fine day his rich neighbor came along with no fewer than twenty farmhands, and they mowed down one swath after another. But the poor neighbor did not even take the trouble to begin when he saw how the others took hold, and that he himself would not be able to do anything alone.

Then the big man occurred to him, and he called out: "Old Hopgiant!" But no one came, and the mowers all laughed at him and mocked him, thinking he had gone out of his mind. Then he called again: "Old Hopgiant!" And, just as before, there was no hopgiant to be seen. And the mowers could scarcely swing their scythes; for they were laughing fit to split.

And then he cried for the third time: "Old Hopgiant!" And there appeared a fellow of truly horrible size, with a scythe as large as a ship's mast.

And now the merriment of the rich peasant's mowers came to an end. For when the giant began to mow and fling about his scythe, they were frightened at the strength he put into his work. And before they knew it he had mown half the meadow.

Then the rich neighbor fell into a rage, rushed up and gave the giant a good kick. But that did not help him, for his foot stuck to the giant, while the latter no more felt the kick than if it had been a flea-bite, and kept right on working.

Then the rich neighbor thought of a scheme to get free, and gave the giant a kick with his other foot; but this foot also stuck fast, and there he hung like a tick. Old Hopgiant mowed the whole meadow, and then flew up into the air, and the rich man had to go along hanging to him like a hawser. And thus the poor neighbor was left sole master of the place.

THE PRINCESS AND THE GLASS MOUNTAIN

Once upon a time there was a king who took such a joy in the chase, that he knew no greater pleasure than hunting wild beasts. Early and late he camped in the forest with hawk and hound, and good fortune always followed his hunting. But it chanced one day that he could rouse no game, although he had tried in every direction since morning. And then, when evening was coming on, and he was about to ride home, he saw a dwarf or wild man running through the forest before him. The king at once spurred on his horse, rode after the dwarf, seized him and he was surprised at his strange appearance; for he was small and ugly, like a troll, and his hair was as stiff as bean-straw. But no matter what the king said to him, he would return no answer, nor say a single word one way or another. This angered the king, who was already out of sorts because of his ill-success at the hunt, and he ordered his people to seize the wild man and guard him carefully lest he escape. Then the king rode home.

Now his people said to him: "You should keep the wild man a captive here at your court, in order that the whole country may talk of what a mighty huntsman you are. Only you should guard him so that he does not escape; because he is of a sly and treacherous disposition." When the king had listened to them he said nothing for a long time. Then he replied: "I will do as you say, and if the wild man escape, it shall be no fault of mine. But I vow that whoever lets him go shall die without mercy, and though he were my own son!"

The following morning, as soon as the king awoke, he remembered his vow.

He at once sent for wood and beams, and had a small house or cage built quite close to the castle. The small house was built of great timbers, and protected by strong locks and bolts, so that none could break in; and a peephole was left in the middle of the wall through which food might be thrust.

When everything was completed the king had the wild man led up, placed in the small house, and he himself took and kept the key. There the dwarf had to sit a prisoner, day and night, and the people came afoot and a-horseback to gaze at him. Yet no one ever heard him complain, or so much as utter a single word.

Thus matters went for some time. Then a war broke out in the land, and the king had to take the field. At parting he said to the queen: "You must rule the kingdom now in my stead, and I leave land and people in your care. But there is one thing you must promise me you will do: that you will guard the wild man securely so that he does not escape while I am away." The queen promised to do her best in all respects, and the king gave her the key to the cage. Thereupon he had his long galleys, his "sea-wolves," push out from the shore, hoisted sail, and took his course far, far away to the other country.

The king and queen had only one child, a prince who was still small; yet great in promise. Now when the king had gone, it chanced one day that the little fellow was wandering about the royal courtyard, and came to the wild man's cage. And he began to play with an apple of gold he had. And while he was playing with it, it happened that suddenly the apple fell through the window in the wall of the cage. The wild man at once appeared and threw back the apple. This seemed a merry game to the little fellow: he threw the apple in again, and the wild man threw it out again, and thus they played for a long time. Yet for all the game had been so pleasant, it turned to sorrow in the end: for the wild man kept the apple of gold, and would not give it back again. And when all was of no avail, neither threats nor prayers, the little fellow at last began to weep. Then the wild man said: "Your father did ill to capture me, and you will never get your apple of gold again, unless you let me out." The little fellow answered: "And how can I let you out? Just you give me back my apple again, my apple of gold!" Then the wild man said: "You must do what I now tell you. Go up to your mother, the queen, and beg her to comb your hair. Then see to it that you take the key from her girdle, and come down and unlock the door. After that you can return the key in the same way, without any one knowing anything about it."

After the wild man had talked to the boy in this way, he finally did as he said, went up to his mother, begged her to comb his hair, and took the key from her girdle. Then he ran down to the cage and opened the door. And when they parted, the dwarf said: "Here is your apple of gold, that I promised to give back to you, and I thank you for setting me free. And another time when you have need of me, I will help you in turn." And with that he ran off on his own way. But the prince went back to his mother, and returned the key in the same way he had taken it.

When they learned at the king's court that the wild man had broken out, there was great commotion, and the queen sent people over hill and dale to look for him. But he was gone and he stayed gone. Thus matters went for a while and the queen grew more and more unhappy; for she expected her husband to return every day. And when he did reach shore his first question was whether the wild man had been well guarded. Then the queen had to confess how matters stood, and told him how everything had happened. But the king was enraged beyond measure, and said he would punish the malefactor, no matter who he might be. And he ordered a great investigation at his court, and every human being in it had to testify. But no one knew anything. At last the little prince also had to come forward. And as he stood before the king he said: "I know that I have deserved my father's anger; yet I cannot hide the truth; for I let out the wild man." Then the queen turned white, and the others as well, for there was not one who was not fond of the prince. At last the king spoke: "Never shall it be said of me that I was false to my vow, even for the sake of my own flesh and blood! No, you must die the death you have deserved." And with that he gave the order to take the prince to the forest and kill him. And they were to bring back the boy's heart as a sign that his command had been obeyed.

Now sorrow unheard of reigned among the people, and all pleaded for the little prince. But the king's word could not be recalled. His serving-men did not dare disobey, took the boy in their midst, and set forth. And when they had gone a long way into the forest, they saw a swine-herd tending his pigs. Then one said to another: "It does not seem right to me to lay hand on the king's son; let us buy a pig instead and take its heart, then all will believe it is the heart of the prince." The other serving-men thought that he spoke wisely, so they bought a pig from the swine-herd, led it into the wood, butchered it and took its heart. Then they told the prince to go his way and never return. They themselves went back to the king's castle, and it is easy to imagine what grief they caused when they told of the prince's death.

The king's son did what the serving-men had told him. He kept on wandering as far as he could, and never had any other food than the nuts and wild berries that grow in the forest. And when he had wandered far and long, he came to a mountain upon whose very top stood a fir-tree. Said he to himself: "After all, I might as well climb the fir-tree and see whether I can find a path anywhere." No sooner said than done: he climbed the tree. And as he sat in the very top of its crown, and looked about on every side, he saw a large and splendid royal castle rising in the distance, and gleaming in the sun. Then he grew very happy and at once set forth in that direction. On the way he met a farm-hand who was plough-ing, and begged him to change clothes with him, which he did. Thus fitted out he at last reached the king's castle, went in, asked for a place, and was taken on as a herdsman, to tend the king's cattle. Now he went to the forest early and late, and in the course of time forgot his grief, grew up, and became so tall and brave that his equal could not be found.

And now our story turns to the king who was reigning at the splendid castle. He had been married, and he had an only daughter. She was lovelier by far than other maidens, and had so kind and cheerful a disposition that whoever could some day take her to his home might well consider himself fortunate. Now when the princess had completed her fifteenth year, a quite unheard of swarm of suitors made their appear-ance, as may well be imagined; and for all that she said no to all of them, they only increased in number. At last the princess said: "None other shall win me save he who can ride up the high Glass Mountain in full armor!" The king thought this a good suggestion. He approved of his daughter's wish, and had proclaimed throughout the kingdom that none other should have the princess save he who could ride up the Glass Moun-tain.

And when the day set by the king had arrived, the princess was led up the Glass Mountain. There she sat on its highest peak, with a golden crown on her head, and a golden apple in her hand, and she looked so immeasurably lovely that there was no one who would not have liked to risk his life for her. Just below the foot of the hill all the suitors assembled with splendid horses and glittering armor, that shone like fire in the sun, and from round about the people flocked together in great crowds to watch their tilting. And when everything was ready, the signal was given by horns and trumpets, and then the suitors, one after another, raced up the mountain with all their might. But the mountain was high, as slippery as ice, and besides it was steep beyond all measure. Not one of the suitors rode up more than a little way, before he tumbled down again, head over heels, and it might well happen that arms and legs were broken in the process. This made so great a noise, together with the neighing of the horses, the shouting of the people, and the clash of arms, that the tumult and the shouting could be heard far away.

And while all this was going on, the king's son was rambling about with his oxen, deep in the wood. But when he heard the tumult and the clashing of arms, he sat down on a stone, leaned his cheek on his hand, and became lost in thought. For it had occurred to him how gladly he would have fared forth with the rest. Suddenly he heard footsteps and when he looked up, the wild man was standing before him. "Thank you for the last time!" said he, "and why do you sit here so lonely and full of sorrow?" "Well," said the prince, "I have no choice but to be sad and joyless. Because of you I am a fugitive from the land of my father, and now I have not even a horse and armor to ride up the Glass Mountain and fight for the princess." "Ah," said the wild man, "if that be all you want, then I can help you! You helped me once before and now I will help you in turn." Then he took the prince by the hand, led him deep down into the earth into his cave, and behold, there hung a suit of armor forged out of the hardest steel, and so bright that a blue gleam played all around it. Right beside it stood a splendid steed, saddled and bridled, pawing the earth with his steel hoofs, and champing his bit till the white foam dropped to the ground. The wild man said: "Now get quickly into your armor, ride out and try your luck! In the meantime I will tend your oxen." The prince did not wait to be told a second time; but put on helmet and armor, buckled on his spurs, hung his sword at his side, and felt as light in his steel armor as a bird in the air. Then he leaped into the saddle so that every clasp and buckle rang, laid his reins on the neck of his steed, and rode hastily toward the mountain.

The princess's suitors were about to give up the contest, for none of them had won the prize, though each had done his best. And while they stood there thinking it over, and saying that perhaps fortune would favor them another time, they suddenly saw a youth ride out of the wood straight toward the mountain. He was clad in steel from head to foot, with helmet on head, sword in belt and shield on arm, and he sat his horse with such knightly grace that it was a pleasure to look at him. At once all eyes were turned to the strange knight, and all asked who he might be; for none had ever seen him before. Yet they had had but little time to talk and question, for no sooner had he cleared the wood, than he rose in his stirrups, gave his horse the spurs, and shot forward like an arrow straight up the Glass Mountain. Yet he did not ride up all the way; but when he had reached the middle of the steep ascent, he suddenly flung around his steed and rode down again, so that the sparks flew from his horse's hoofs. Then he disappeared in the wood like a bird in flight. One may imagine the excitement which now seized upon all the people, and there was not one who did not admire the strange knight. All agreed they had never seen a braver knight.

Time passed, and the princess's suitors decided to try their luck a second time. The king's daughter was once more led up the Glass Mountain, with great pomp and richly gowned, and was seated on its topmost peak, with the golden crown on her head, and a golden apple in her hand. At the foot of the hill gathered all the suitors with handsome horses and splendid armor, and round about stood all the people to watch the contest. When all was ready the signal was given by horns and trumpets, and at the same moment the suitors, one after another, darted up the mountain with all their might. But all took place as at the first time. The mountain was high, and as slippery as ice, and besides, it was steep beyond all measure; not one rode up more than a little way before tumbling down again head over heels. Meanwhile there was much noise, and the horses neighed, and the people shouted, and the armor clashed, so that the tumult and the shouting sounded far into the deep wood.

And while all this was going on, the young prince was tending his oxen, which was his duty. But when he heard the tumult and the clashing of arms, he sat down on a stone, leaned his cheek on his hand, and wept; for he thought of the king's beautiful daughter, and it occurred to him how much he would like to take part and ride with the rest. That very moment he heard footsteps and when he looked up, the wild man was standing before him. "Good-day!" said the wild man, "and why do you sit here so lonely and full of sorrow?" Thereupon the prince replied: "I have no choice but to be sad and joyless. Because of you I am a fugitive from the land of my father, and now I have not even a horse and armor to ride up the mountain and fight for the princess!" "Ah," said the wild man, "if that be all you want, then I can help you! You helped me once before, and now I will help you in turn." Then he took the prince by the hand, led him deep down in the earth into his cave, and there on the wall hung a suit of armor altogether forged of the clearest silver, and so bright that it shone afar. Right beside it stood a snow-white steed, saddled and bridled, pawing the earth with his silver hoofs, and champing his bit till the foam dropped to the ground. The wild man said: "Now get quickly into your armor, ride out and try your luck! In the meantime I will tend your oxen." The prince did not wait to be told a second time; but put on his helmet and armor in all haste, securely buckled on his spurs, hung his sword at his side, and felt as light in his silver armor as a bird in the air. Then he leaped into the saddle so that every clasp and buckle rang, laid his reins on the neck of his steed, and rode hastily toward the Glass Mountain.

The princess's suitors were about to give over the contest, for none of them had won the prize, though each had played a man's part. And while they stood there thinking it over, and saying that perhaps fortune would favor them the next time, they suddenly saw a youth ride out of the wood, straight toward the mountain. He was clad in silver from head to foot, with helmet on head, shield on arm, and sword at side, and he sat his horse with such knightly grace that a braver-looking youth had probably never been seen. At once all eyes were turned toward him, and the people noticed that he was the same knight who had appeared before. But the prince did not leave them much time for wonderment; for no sooner had he reached the plain, than he rose in his stirrups, spurred on his horse, and rode like fire straight up the steep mountain. Yet he did not ride quite up to the top; but when he had come to its crest, he greeted the princess with great courtesy, flung about his steed, and rode down the mountain again till the sparks flew about his horse's hoofs. Then he disappeared into the wood as the storm flies. As one may imagine, the people's excitement was even greater than the first time, and there was not one who did not admire the strange knight. And all were agreed that a more splendid steed or a handsomer youth were nowhere to be found.

Time passed, and the king set a day when his daughter's suitors were to make a third trial. The princess was now once more led to the Glass Mountain, and seated herself on its highest peak, with the golden crown and the golden apple, as she had before. At the foot of the mountain gathered the whole swarm of suitors, with splendid horses and polished armor, handsome beyond anything seen thus far, and round about the people flocked together to watch the contest. When all was ready the suitors, one after another, darted up the mountain with all their might. The mountain was as smooth as ice, and besides, it was steep beyond all measure; so that not one rode up more than a little way, before tumbling down again, head over heels. This made a great noise, the horses neighed, the people shouted, and the armor clashed, till the tumult and the shouting echoed far into the wood.

While this was all taking place the king's son was busy tending his oxen as usual. And when he once more heard the noise and the clash of arms, he sat down on a stone, leaned his cheek on his hand, and wept bitterly. Then he thought of the lovely princess, and would gladly have ventured his life to win her. That very moment the wild man was standing before him: "Good-day!" said the wild man, "And why do you sit here so lonely and full of sorrow?" "I have no choice but to be sad and joyless," said the prince. "Because of you I am a fugitive from the land of my father, and now I have not even a sword and armor to ride up the mountain and fight for the princess!" "Ah," said the wild man, "if that be all that troubles you I can help you! You helped me once before, and now I will help you in turn." With that he took the prince by the hand, led him into his cave deep down under the earth, and showed him a suit of armor all forged of the purest gold, and gleaming so brightly that its golden glow shone far and wide. Beside it stood a magnificent steed, saddled and bridled, pawing the earth with its golden hoofs, and champing its bit until the foam fell to the ground. The wild man said: "Now get quickly into your armor, ride out and try your luck! In the meantime I will tend your oxen." And to tell the truth, the prince was not lazy; but put on his helmet and armor, buckled on his golden spurs, hung his sword at his side, and felt as light in his golden armor as a bird in the air. Then he leaped into the saddle, so that every clasp and buckle rang, laid his reins on the neck of his steed, and rode hastily toward the mountain.

The princess's suitors were about to give up the contest; for none of them had won the prize, though each had done his best. And while they stood there thinking over what was to be done, they suddenly saw a youth come riding out of the wood, straight toward the mountain. He was clad in gold from head to foot, with the golden helmet on his head, the golden shield on his arm, and the golden sword at his side, and so knightly was his bearing that a bolder warrior could not have been met with in all the wide world. At once all eyes were turned toward him, and one could see that he was the same youth who had already appeared at different times. But the prince gave them but little time to question and wonder; for no sooner had he reached the plain than he gave his horse the spurs, and shot up the steep mountain like a flash of lightning. When he had reached its highest peak, he greeted the beautiful princess with great courtesy, kneeled before her, and received the golden apple from her hand. Then he flung about his steed, and rode down the Glass Mountain again, so that the sparks flew about the golden hoofs of his horse, and a long ribbon of golden light gleamed behind him. At last he disappeared in the wood like a star. What a commotion now reigned about the mountain! The people broke forth into cheers that could be heard far away, horns sounded, trumpets called, horses neighed, arms clashed, and the king had proclaimed far and near that the unknown golden knight had won the prize.

Now all that was wanting was some information about the golden knight; for no one knew him; and all the people expected that he would at once make his appearance at the castle. But he did not come. This caused great surprise, and the princess grew pale and ill. But the king was put out, and the suitors murmured and found fault day by day. And at length, when they were all at their wits' end, the king had a great meeting announced at his castle, which every man, high and low, was to attend; so that the princess might choose among them herself. There was no one who was not glad to go for the princess's sake, and also because it was a royal command, and a countless number of people gathered together. And when they had all assembled, the princess came out of the castle with great pomp, and followed by her maids, passed through the entire multitude. But no matter how much she looked about her on every side, she did not find the one for whom she was looking. When she reached the last row she saw a man who stood quite hidden by the crowd. He had a flat cap and a wide gray mantle such as shepherds wear; but its hood was drawn up so that his face could not be seen. At once the princess ran up to him, drew down his hood, fell upon his neck and cried: "Here he is! Here he is!" Then all the people laughed; for they saw that it was the king's herdsman, and the king himself called out: "May God console me for the son-in-law who is to be my portion!" The man, however, was not at all abashed, but replied: "O, you need not worry about that at all! I am just as much a king's son as you are a king!"

With that he flung aside his wide mantle. And there were none left to laugh; for instead of the grey herdsman, there stood a handsome prince, clad in gold from head to foot, and holding the princess's golden apple in his hand. And all could see that it was the same youth who had ridden up the Glass Mountain.

Then they prepared a feast whose like had never before been seen, and the prince received the king's daughter, and with her half of the kingdom. Thenceforward they lived happily in their kingdom, and if they have not died they are living there still. But nothing more was ever heard of the wild man. And that is the end.

For the full listing of our titles visit
www.sophenebooks.com

All of our titles are available on amazon.com, amazon.co.uk,
amazon.de, amazon.fr, amazon.es, and amazon.it

SOPHENE

Printed in Great Britain
by Amazon

56756902R00244